MASTERS OF SPACE

Humbolt had betrayed him. The plot to fake the murder and turn the Lorr on his trail reeked of his political manipulations.

"We have reached a unanimous decision," the agent-general said. "Normal crimes are punishable by local imprisonment. This is no ordinary crime." The Lorr shivered delicately.

"Barton Kinsolving, you are hereby sentenced to life imprisonment on the world with no name. Exile to this world is permanent. Starships land prisoners. No one ever leaves.

"Ever."

Masters of Space

Robert E. Vardeman

NEW ENGLISH LIBRARY
Hodder and Stoughton

*The characters and situations in
this book are entirely imaginary
and bear no relation to any real
person or actual happenings.*

First published in the United
States of America as three
separate volumes:

MASTERS OF SPACE: THE
STELLAR DEATH PLAN ©
1987 by Robert E. Vardeman
Published by Avon Books

MASTERS OF SPACE 2: THE
ALIEN WEB © 1987 by Robert
E. Vardeman
Published by Avon Books

MASTERS OF SPACE 3: A
PLAGUE IN PARADISE © 1987
by Robert E. Vardeman
Published by Avon Books

First published as an omnibus
edition in Great Britain in 1990
by New English Library
paperbacks

*A New English Library
paperback original*

British Library C.I.P.

Vardeman, Robert E.
   Masters of space
   I. Title
   823'.914 [F]
   ISBN 0-450-52092-7

Printed and bound in Great Britain
for Hodder and Stoughton
paperbacks, a division of Hodder
and Stoughton Ltd., Mill Road,
Dunton Green, Sevenoaks, Kent
TN13 2YA (Editorial Office: 47
Bedford Square, London WC18
3DP) by Richard Clay Ltd,
Bungay, Suffolk.

THE STELLAR DEATH PLAN

For Mike Montgomery

CHAPTER ONE

THE BLARE of the siren brought Barton Kinsolving out of a deep sleep. He had partially dressed before he came fully awake and had reached the door to his small house before he even realized he responded to the undulating warning.

Thick, work-hardened fingers pressed shut the last fastener on his shirt as he dashed outside and into the compound. Already, harsh carbon-arc lights had come on all around.

"What's happened?" he yelled over the siren. A curly-haired woman shook her head. She appeared to be in a daze. Kinsolving cursed under his breath. This was the fourth time in as many weeks that the alarms had gone off. And each disaster deep within the bowels of the planet had been worse than the time before. Kinsolving hoped that this was only a short circuit, a false alarm, a mistake on a new recruit's part that would give him something to rail against, then peacefully return to his bed and sleep without nightmares.

His dark eyes focused on the rising plumes of bone-white smoke from the mouth of the distant mine shaft. The turbulent dust, sprinkled with flecks of mica that turned into artificial lightning bugs when the spotlight hit them, told the story. Kinsolving ran a hand through his hair and tried to calm himself. At this time of night it wasn't likely that many humans would be deep within the rare earth mines.

But what of the robot miners? Kinsolving cursed so loudly at the thought of losing another shift of the machines that several of his gathering co-workers edged away from him. He ignored them and ran to the control center.

"Ala!" he cried. He stopped just inside the door and looked at the lovely woman seated behind the console. Some of the anger at his sorry fate faded. When Ala Markken was near, things always went better for Kinsolving. He knew that wasn't strictly true, but it seemed that way and that was all that counted.

"Glad you got here, Bart," she said. Even mixed with the wail of the warning siren, her voice was level, low, sultry and exciting. "Stoop twenty-three went this time. Got a damp warning, then a gas release and..." She shrugged her shoulders. Kinsolving forced himself to concentrate on the read-outs rather than the brief flash of bare shoulder she gave him.

He bent forward, frowning. A few minutes' work on the computer gave him numbers that weren't as bad as he'd expected—but were still far from pleasing.

"The robominer in the stoop failed to detect moisture and drilled through into an artesian spring. That's the only way it could have happened." He sighed. This shouldn't have happened. The robot sensory equipment was better than that—yet it *had* occurred.

"What about the gas indication?" the brunette asked him. "I got a strong positive reading for methane."

Kinsolving shook his head and straightened. "I think the sensors shorted out when the water hit them. We're going to have to drop a hose from number seventeen and pump out the water before we reopen."

"If we're lucky, you mean. There's no way to tell if the robot hit an underground river or just a trapped pocket of fossil water."

"There's a way. Send down the fiber optic probe. Check the rate of water flowing through the stoop, use visuals, use IR if necessary to find the robominer and see if we can't repair it by remotes, get it back online. You know the drill."

Ala turned and looked him squarely in the eye. "Bart," she said softly, "the foptic probe equipment is gone. It was on twenty. Water's already risen to nineteen." She tapped the readout on the control console for emphasis. "We're going to have to close three entire levels. Might even take more than that by the time we're finished."

"Level nineteen!" Kinsolving yelled. He spun and thrust aside an empty chair to get to another computer console. A cold lump formed in the pit of his stomach when he saw that the storage bins had been lost. The lanthanite and gadolinite holding areas were gone. The rare earth oxide ores were separated on level nineteen, then transported to the surface once a week when the heavy-lifter robots were brought over from the other mine shaft.

He had lost more than five days worth of output from the mine. Kinsolving reached over and pulled the chair toward him. He sank into it, the soft pneumatic wheezing of the chair adjusting to his burly frame equalling his own heavy sigh.

"I'm going to find myself in a dole line back on Earth for this one," he said. "Four years of good record, now this. Four major setbacks in as many weeks. I'm going to be fired and buried as deep as—as that robominer." Kinsolving pointed toward the steady red light glaring at him from the console indicating a malfunctioning miner unit.

"We're almost three months behind production quota," Ala told him. "The yields on the gandolinite and monazite haven't been up to assay."

The woman's fingers ran lightly over the panel until most of the red lights went out, replaced by blinking amber caution signals. This was all anyone could do until the mine was pumped and cleaned. She rose lithely and came to him, arms circling his neck. She held him close, her head resting next to his. Ala kissed his shoulder and turned her face slightly so that she looked around at him.

"It's not your fault," she said. "The powers that be at IM know that. You're a good engineer, Bart. A damned good one. They won't fire you over this. It's not your fault. The readouts will prove it."

"Mining is a dangerous profession," Kinsolving said, resting his hand on Ala's soft cheek. "But Humbolt made it clear that high production and no glitches were what he expected—or he'd replace me."

"Humbolt's a fool. What does he know about field-work? He sits at a desk all day and makes pointless decisions."

"He might be a fool," Kinsolving said, "but he's still our boss." Kinsolving swung around and let Ala sit on his lap. Her nearness usually pushed back the darkness he often felt, but this time his depression had plunged to too great a depth in his soul. Interstellar Materials held a ten-year lease to mine the rare earth oxides on this alien-held planet only through great diplomatic skill and immense fees paid on the precious 57–71 atomic number metals lifted from the surface. Barton Kinsolving had been drawn to IM because of the high salary—payable at the end of his contract—and the chance to leave Earth.

To leave Earth. He almost snorted in disgust. Earthmen had heaved themselves out to the stars a century earlier only to find a dozen alien races already populating the nearby star systems. Humans were less than an oddity—they were an annoyance to the older, better established races. Worst of all for a culture that had exhausted most of the resources of its planet, the juiciest plums had already been picked.

Deepdig was one such plum. The humanoid Lorr had established colonies on the planet fifty years before the first primitive starships had warped the four point three light years from Earth orbit to Alphacent. In the council of stargoing races, this century and a half of habitation gave the Lorr full rights to the planet's exploitation. Kinsolving had no idea what IM had promised the Lorr in exchange for the rare earth oxides, but he knew it had to be significant.

Earth needed the gadolinium and cerium for optical glasses and the lanthanum for fiber optics. Most of all it needed the pink and green samarium salts for use in the stardrives. Without it, the starspanning engines wouldn't function reliably. And without a dependable stardrive, Earth would again be isolated and choking in its own debris.

Kinsolving held Ala close, her warmth driving away some of the tenseness in his body and her scent making him feel things would work out.

"I've got to go down into the mine," he said at length. Reluctantly, he pushed her away.

"You take this too personally, Bart," she said. "Accidents happen."

He started to ask why she hadn't picked up the robot's sensor signal indicating water and turned off the unit, but he held back. Ala Markken was more than his lover, she was the best technician on his crew. Too many of the others had rotated through, going on to other jobs with Interstellar Materials.

Ala had stayed for the full four years he had been
here.

Only her presence had saved his sanity. The Lorr
inspectors were openly hostile, existing only to find
minute violations of their intricate safety and lifting agreements. Humbolt came to Deepdig once a
planetary year for on-site inspections. Ala placated
him and acted as a buffer between corporate director and mine supervisor. For this alone, Kinsolving
loved her.

He stared at her soft brunette hair, her deep, pen-
etrating eyes, the face that rivalled any tri-dee
star's. Ala Markken had been a minor functionary
at IM's headquarters on Gamma Tertius 4 before
coming to Deepdig. He had always wondered why
she had left the heart of corporate power and had
asked her once, getting no real answer. Ala could
have progressed far up the IM corporate structure
by now if she'd remained at headquarters. But she
had chosen to do fieldwork.

Kinsolving was glad that she had. The four years
at this mine would have been intolerable without
her. And the past few months would have driven
him to suicide.

Robot miner breakdowns, lower grade ore than
expected, now this major disaster.

"All units are gone, Bart," she said. "Why not
order over the heavy-lifters from the other mine
and work back down? The ore bins on level nineteen
might be intact."

He shook his head. Kinsolving knew better than
to hope for a miracle of this scale. "If the robot dug
into a river, the surge would have scattered the ore
and put the separated dust into collodial suspen-
sion. Who knows where it has washed to by now?"

"No way to siphon off the water and distill it?"

He didn't laugh at her. Kinsolving knew that
Ala's knowledge of computers was without limit but

her instincts about mining operations left something to be desired.

"No way," he said.

"It's not your fault. Not even Humbolt can blame you for the shoddy equipment they send out. It's been malfunctioning for months and months. It's a wonder that you've been able to hold it together."

"I know," Kinsolving said. He frowned. When he had come to work on Deepdig only the finest robot equipment had been shipped to him. Why send broken-down units forty-nine light years from Gamma Tertius 4? Especially when the rare earths were so desperately needed by Earth? Kinsolving wondered if Humbolt—or someone at operations and supply on GT 4—wasn't siphoning off funds for the top of the line equipment and sending the cheapest robominers available.

"What now?" Ala asked.

"We follow the logged procedures. Call the Lorr representative, get him out to investigate. I'll send a message packet to Humbolt. He'll probably want to drag his fat ass out here to personally fire me."

"Bart," Ala chided gently.

"All right, all right, no more self-pity. Get on the com-line and arrange for the Lorr agent. I'll see if anything can be done down in the mine."

"Be careful," Ala said. She bent and gave him a quick kiss.

"For more of that, I'll be *damned* careful," he said, smiling a little.

Ala Markken turned back to begin the report that would summon the Lorr. Kinsolving left the control center and shouted orders to his human workers as he walked to the mouth of the mine shaft. Seldom did humans enter the underground world of the rare earth mine. At the periphery of the hole stood a wide variety of computerized equipment, all the inputs funneled to Ala Markken in the control center.

It didn't surprise Kinsolving to find that no humans had been on duty at the shaft. As long as no trouble developed, Ala was capable of running the entire operation.

"Who was scheduled to be on-site?" he asked. Kinsolving looked around the small circle of technicians. No one volunteered the information. "Garibaldi, check it out for me. Get the roster up and on a screen where I can see it."

The man tapped in the request. Kinsolving peered over his shoulder as the data emerged from the control computer. Kinsolving frowned and ran a hand through his sweat-lank hair at the answer.

"Keep checking," he said. "I don't believe no one was scheduled to be out here."

"No one was, Mr. Kinsolving," spoke up the curly-haired woman he had seen back in the compound. Nina Porchek pushed through the crowd. "I told Ala she'd missed posting anyone to oversee operations tonight but she said I didn't know what I was talking about. If someone had been present, the robominer might have been shut down in time when its automatic cutoff failed."

Kinsolving frowned even more. Nina Porchek was a replacement for a transfered computer operator. Her interests lay more with promotion to a management post than mine output. She had seen Kinsolving's attachment to Ala and had instantly resented the brunette. Kinsolving had little time for such politics.

But he saw that Porchek was right. If an operator had been present at the mine shaft controls, this would have given another chance to shut down before such extensive damage occurred.

"We've had too much equipment failure in the past few months," Kinsolving said. "I want a full maintenance check of all circuits, plus a visual of all mechanicals."

Groans of protest rose.

"Get to it now," Kinsolving said, voice cold. "Section chiefs, I want detailed reports by dawn. The Lorr representative will accept no less. I'm not going to be the one to lose IM's lease on Deepdig. Get to work. Now!" Kinsolving took no pleasure seeing the twenty hasten to their chores. He was left alone with his thoughts to stare down into the dark mouth of the shaft.

The rising dust had settled. Straining, Kinsolving heard the deep, dangerous rumble of water eighteen hundred meters below. Level twenty-three, another forty meters deeper, would be impassable except by sophisticated rescue equipment—which he didn't have.

Kinsolving made a cursory examination of the monitoring equipment, then started down into the mine. Nina Porchek called out to him, "Mr. Kinsolving! You're not supposed to go down alone! That's against the rules!"

"Give me your com-link. And get back to work."

"But the safety regs say—"

"Back to work," he snapped. He was in no mood to argue over such trivial matters with a power-hungry underling. Kinsolving took her com-link and switched it to central control frequency. He flipped the Attention toggle until Ala Markken answered.

"Ala, this is Bart. I'm going to look around a bit down in the mine shaft."

"No, wait, Bart, wait!"

"I'll be fine," he said, angry that she would duplicate Porchek's objection. "Kinsolving, out." He savagely thumbed off the unit. The flashing red indicator showed that Ala tried to reach him. He kept the sound off. Let it record and nothing more,

he decided. The com-link's optical and audio sensors
would pick up much that he missed with a visual
inspection.

Swinging down the steps two at a time brought
him to level one. Kinsolving took the time to put on
a heavy respirator. In spite of his feeling that only
water had invaded the lowest levels of the mine,
Ala had gotten a transient indication of gas. The
com-link would warn him of unsafe air, but Kinsolving preferred to avoid the chance of a microburst of methane rendering him unconscious for
even a few seconds. Such might prove deadly in a
mine inoperative due to disaster.

He found a hand flash and shone the brilliant
light along the equipment shaft. Kinsolving saw
nothing amiss; he descended to the next level. He
wished that he dared use the elevator but as long as
the water boiled at level nineteen, it was more pru-
dent to leave off any electrical power to avoid further equipment damage.

He smiled ruefully. He worried about equipment
damage more than electrocution. Being supervisor
for four years had given him a skewed picture of
safety, at least for himself. Better to risk himself
than either other human personnel or the increasingly precious robot mining equipment.

Kinsolving found the emergency ladder at the
side of the shaft. He turned the flash down into
the depths of the stygian cavern and shuddered.
The light failed to pick out the raging torrent of
water far below—but he heard its hellish din. Only
luck would keep him from losing another level to
the rising underground river.

Carefully descending, Kinsolving checked the
readouts at every level, both on the permanently
mounted equipment and on his com-link. Temperature rose, atmosphere remained breathable although he kept his respirator on, the automated

mining equipment worked independently and well. Kinsolving shook his head. It was always this way, it seemed. The levels with the lowest grade ores had the least problems. As he continued on his way down past the fifth level, Kinsolving felt a shivering in the ladder's plastic rungs.

The power came back on, the emergency lights momentarily blinding him. Ala had determined that no further damage would be done. Kinsolving heaved a sigh of relief as he swung into level six. His shoulders had begun to ache from the descent. He was glad he wouldn't have to climb back; his muscles would be sore for a week. For all the complaining he did about desk jockeys and petty bureaucrats, Kinsolving knew he was hardly better. What did he need muscle for when tireless robo-miners pulled out a kilogram of ore every minute of every twenty-hour day? The full automation of the rare earth mine allowed production unheard of, even back on Earth.

Kinsolving started to check in with Ala, then saw that the flashing light on the com-link still told of the woman's insistence to warn him back. Obstinately, Kinsolving ignored it and pressed the elevator call button. It came rumbling down from above; he swung in and found the control panel. Careful scrutiny showed danger warnings for every level below eighteen.

Kinsolving descended to seventeen.

As he stepped out, spray from ten meters below came up the shaft and soaked his clothing. He wiped clear the eye lenses of his respirator and peered down, shining the hand flash onto the churning surface of the water. The lowest levels of this mine might be closed permanently, he realized. For all his experience, he had never seen such complete destruction from water.

Kinsolving started to stand, then caught sight of

something that seemed out of place. His sharp cone of light came to rest on severed cables. Kinsolving pointed the com-link sensors at the cut while his mind raced. He knew the wiring diagrams for the mine by heart, but it took several seconds before he recognized this as a secondary control circuit. The robominer cut directly into the rock, following programmed instructions. This far underground, simple radio broadcast proved impossible and foptic or laser links too expensive or impractical. A hard wire came from the unit to a transmitter.

Kinsolving looked at the junction box for the robot miner's safety sensors.

Someone had cut the wire so that the robominer was unable to warn the operator when it encountered the underground river.

"Sabotage?" Kinsolving asked himself. His voice echoed strangely inside the respirator and he almost took it off. A quick, instinctive check of the com-link showed that the air was no longer breathable here. He needed the heavy mask to stay alive.

"It might have been cut by flying debris," he said. "That's it. Debris." Kinsolving wormed around on his belly, leaning far over the edge of the level eighteen elevator platform. The transmitter and the cut wire were still several meters lower; with the churning, frothy water in the shaft he wasn't sure what he saw.

Kinsolving pulled himself back onto the elevator platform when he found telltale gouges on the sides of the shaft that could have been made only by a heavy-lifter robot. An unauthorized use of such equipment constituted not only immediate dismissal by IM but also violated IM's agreement with the Lorr. They monitored every lifting of ore from the mine; their representative levied taxes on the spot. If a heavy-lifter had been used, that meant the Lorr had been cheated—and possibly that no ore had remained on level nineteen when the flooding occurred.

"Sabotage to cover the theft of rare earth ores," Kinsolving muttered. "But why?"

That proved impossible to answer. Interstellar Materials and the Lorr controlled all off-planet flight. How could anyone expect to sneak down, load such a massive quantity of ore—even reduced ore —and get away with it? And why? Any single lifting from the mine wouldn't be profitable enough for such piracy.

The words began to echo in Kinsolving's skull: Any single lifting.

What if the ore theft had been going on for some time? Months? Years? The value of such rare earths would be immense over a span of years.

That still didn't answer the question of who. And how. Starflight was too well controlled for a modern-day Captain Kidd aboard an interstellar pirate ship.

Kinsolving shook off such fanciful notions. He might never have noticed the heavy-lifter rock scars before. Coming down into the mine was an occasional trek for him. And the cut sensor circuit might have happened after the flooding. He began tinkering with control boxes powered by emergency fuel cells. Within ten minutes the powerful auxiliary pumps had begun their slow work. Another twenty minutes saw level eighteen pumped out, and Kinsolving watched as the churning water dropped lower and lower. He made a few quick estimates and decided that two more levels would be drained by morning.

He settled bone-tired onto the floor of the elevator and crossed his long legs. Wincing at the pain in his muscles, he reached up and pressed the ground level button.

The elevator shuddered and began the almost two kilometer climb to the surface.

It had gone only five hundred meters when the power failed. Aches forgotten, Kinsolving surged to his feet and slammed his fist hard against the emergency brake activator button.

He screamed inside his respirator when the braking failed. His stomach rose into his throat as the elevator plummeted back into the mine—back into the dark depths toward the flooded lower levels.

CHAPTER TWO

THE ROCKY, barren planet swung around a sun emitting far too much ultraviolet for comfortable human habitation, but humans did populate Gamma Tertius 4. From the stellar-radiation-cracked plains rose a magnificent spire that shone the purest jade green from multifaceted sides. Within this gleaming structure the board of directors for Interstellar Materials met.

At the head of the polished Earth-ebony table sat a small, wizened man hardly able to hold up his head. Every time Hamilton H. Fremont slumped tiredly to one side an attentive nurse gently shook his shoulder. The man motioned the nurse away with a weak gesture of a hand so pale and translucent that it might have been made of beige plastic. Only when seven others entered the room and took their places behind pneumatic chairs did the chairman of the corporation nod slightly. The nurse took a small packet from her uniform pocket and emptied the contents into a glass of water. The mixture sizzled and hissed and turned the distilled water a pale blue. She helped Fremont drink the stimulant. The seven waited with barely concealed impatience until the drug took control and transformed their chairman into a more dynamic person.

"Be seated," Fremont ordered in a voice surprisingly strong and deep for one in such debilitated condition. Shaky hands rested on the black wood

15

table in front of him, Fremont leaned forward slightly. "There is a problem on Deepdig. Report, Mr. Humbolt."

Kenneth Humbolt cleared his throat and tried to hide his nervousness. Nothing escaped Fremont's sharp gaze. Not for the first time, Humbolt wished he knew the secret of the potion given Fremont by his nurse. If such a drug turned a doddering, senile old man into an executive capable of running a star-spanning financial empire, what would it do to a man a quarter as old and twice as ambitious?

"Mr. Chairman, members of the board," Humbolt began.

"You may skip the preamble. I am old and have no time left for such time-wasting maneuvers. Get on with your report. Deepdig. The rare earth mines. The troubles we are having there. You *do* remember, don't you, Humbolt?"

"Yes, sir," Humbolt said, damning the old man, while trying to retain his composure. He was a member of the board of one of the most powerful conglomerates in human-controlled space. He had earned the position. He had *earned* it! He wouldn't let Fremont intimidate him.

But the old man's presence did cause Humbolt real discomfort.

"The Lorr representative has expressed extreme displeasure with our operations in Deepdig number two," Humbolt said. He had no need to refer to his notes. The report burned brightly, deep in his mind. With responsibility for ten different mining operations on four planets, Humbolt could stay abreast of only the general matters, but Deepdig presented distinct problems of importance to more than just the IM profit margins.

"Will we be forced to negotiate once more?" asked Vladimir Metchnikoff from Humbolt's right.

"No. The Lorr consider us as only bungling inferiors. There is no hint that they know of the Plan or how the liftings from Deepdig number two enter into it."

"It'd be your head if they had even an inkling," snapped Fremont. "What of production? What of the flooding?"

"Mine supervisor Kinsolving had regained control of the situation much quicker than anticipated and had begun pumping three flooded levels, leaving only the lowest three closed. The rare earths storage area has been cleared."

"He knows?" asked Metchnikoff.

"There is no way he couldn't have discovered the sabotage and pilfering of the oxides," Humbolt said, angry that Metchnikoff forced such a confession. Humbolt felt his power slipping and Metchnikoff's star rising. The flux of influence on the board was always thus. Humbolt would have to salvage what he could and continue, perhaps undermining Metchnikoff's transport division in some fashion.

His brief inattention brought a stern reprimand from Fremont.

"Sorry, sir," Humbolt said, feeling like a small child caught stealing his parent's credit access. "Kinsolving is too efficient in his cleanup procedures. My office had estimated at least six months' work to pump down to the storage area, by which time we would have been able to justify total loss of the ores."

"The Lorr have put in an inquiry?"

"No, sir. Not yet, but I am sure that they will. We were lifting six thousand kilos of high-grade ore a week, of which fully half was not being counted and taxed by the Lorr agent. The intentional flooding of the mine would have hidden another twenty thousand kilograms of output from the Lorr."

"But not now," prodded Fremont.

"No, sir, not now." The words burned like acid on

Humbolt's tongue. "We have done what we can to correct this."

"Is this Kinsolving so efficient that he should be promoted?" asked Fremont. The old man's eyes fixed dagger-hard on Humbolt.

"It was necessary to sacrifice him in another 'accident,'" said Humbolt.

"Another accident?" Fremont coughed. His nurse handed him a small handkerchief to wipe his lips. "Unfortunate. This Kinsolving seems the sort we need to carry out the Plan."

"His profile did not indicate that, sir," said Humbolt. "He was stubborn and—"

"A quality we need. What did he feel about the damned Bizarres running the universe and holding us back?"

"There's some evidence to show that Kinsolving felt that the Bizzies, such as the Lorr, were acting within acceptable limits," Humbolt said carefully.

"You mean he was a goddamn traitor, that he sympathized with aliens over his own kind?" Fremont's anger caused a flush to come to his pale, wrinkled face.

"Yes, sir, that seems true."

"He's better off dead. How did you arrange it? Never mind. That's merely a detail."

"Our agent is very efficient, sir. I recommend promotion to headquarters."

"Promotion first to mine supervisor. We need those rare earths, dammit. We can't build the Bizzie brain-burners without them. And new starships can't be built without samarium. You know that, Humbolt. After we've milked what we can out of the Bizarres on Deepdig, then you will promote. Understood, Mr. Humbolt?"

"As you wish, sir."

Humbolt sat down, his legs shaking in reaction. Nothing had gone right with his scheme to increase the lift from the Deepdig oxide mines. The carefully orchestrated accident had attracted Lorr attention. If they checked the records with their usual dedication, they would find exactly how many kilos of the precious rare earths had been stolen. With this information shared with other Bizzie species, they might stumble onto a small portion of the Plan.

Humbolt shuddered, then tried to cover the involuntary reaction by rearranging the papers in front of him. His life would be forfeit if Fremont thought any part of the Plan had been revealed, even one as insignificant as the five-times-larger-than-declared Earth starship fleet. The Bizzies allowed only so much commerce with their worlds; they controlled too much. Humbolt's anger began to mount against the unfairness of the alien strictures.

One day that would change. And he would live to see it. He would live to preside over it. He would enjoy distributing the brain-burners, too. That was small enough retribution for the Bizarres holding back the human race!

Humbolt jerked around and came out of his reverie to hear Vladimir Metchnikoff complete a favorable report on IM's fleet growth, both declared and clandestine. The woman to Metchnikoff's right stood. Humbolt watched her with some lust and a great deal of fear. Maria Villalobos had risen quickly in IM ranks and was the youngest at the table. Humbolt wasn't sure that she wasn't also the most diabolical—and, from corporate spy reports on her personal habits, the most depraved.

Metchnikoff was an annoyance to Humbolt. Villalobos would be a major stumbling block unless he found a way of using her against Fremont, cancelling the influence and power of both the chairman of IM and an able opponent.

"Mr. Chairman," the small, dark, intense woman began. "As Director of Security I have identified several problems within the corporate head-quarters. Two employees have been...terminated." The feral gleam in her eyes told Humbolt that the pretty woman enjoyed this "termination." He wondered where the bodies had been hidden, if Villalobos left behind such crass evidence of her handiwork.

"Were they Bizzie agents?"

"The Plan and our part in it has not been compromised," Villalobos assured Fremont. "I have taken steps to tighten security procedures and have hired an enforcement officer of unparalleled reputation to expedite matters off-planet."

"Who is this?" asked Metchnikoff.

"I am sure you have heard of Cameron," Villalobos said with obvious gusto.

Vladimir Metchnikoff paled. Humbolt looked around the table at the other directors. None spoke up to protest the hiring of such a bloody-handed assassin.

"Cameron?" asked Fremont. "The one who did the work for us last year on Loki 2?"

"Yes, sir. The man is a noted expert on robotic tracking and has a reputation for tenacity and... remorselessness."

"That's one word for it," Humbolt said. Villalobos' dark eyes flared like rocket blasts in the night. He quickly said, "I put a motion before the board to not only approve of Cameron's hiring but also to commend Director Villalobos for such a brilliant use of personnel."

This quieted Villalobos and forced the others on the board to approve Cameron. To openly challenge Villalobos now, they would also have to take on Humbolt. While he might not be in as high standing with Chairman Fremont as before the Deepdig debacle, Humbolt still wielded considerable influence at Interstellar Materials.

Humbolt smiled slightly and nodded in Villalobos' direction. The woman and he were not considered allies by the others—especially Metchnikoff, from the cold stare he received from the man. Humbolt smiled a little more. Was that betrayal flickering across Metchnikoff's face? Were the rumors about him and Villalobos being lovers true? What would Villalobos' passion be like? Humbolt would have to delve further into that to see if a more powerful wedge might be driven between the pair.

"Finance. Give me a finance report, Mr. Liu."

Humbolt leaned back and half listened to the march of numbers given by IM's financial genius. The corporation was in sound condition but if any alien auditor demanded their books as a condition of trade on a Bizarre-held world, the Bizzies would find only a tottering giant made of paper and hot air and borrowed funds.

One day that would change. Humbolt and the others worked for it. Interstellar Materials' part in the Plan might be small compared to others', but all humans and their talents would be needed. Even ones like Villalobos and her pet killer, Cameron.

CHAPTER THREE

THE IMPACT of the elevator platform against the surface of the water knocked Barton Kinsolving flat. He fell heavily and rolled to one corner of the elevator. Dirty water sloshed up. Dazed, he struggled to sit up. The world spun in crazy circles around him; a large knot at the back of his head oozed sticky blood. Just touching the spot sent laser cuts of pain into his head.

Kinsolving tried to stand. He fell back, too weak to accomplish even this simple task. Hip deep in water he sat, trying to regain his senses. Slowly, everything fit into a broader pattern. The power to the elevator had failed; he had plunged downward. The emergency brakes had caught but had scant time to slow the descent. Hesitantly, Kinsolving reached out to touch the brake assembly. He jerked back when the blistering hot metal burned his fingertips.

Cursing, he fought to his feet. The level of water rose to his thighs now. The elevator platform sank inexorably into the murky, watery bowels of the mine. Kinsolving tried to set the brakes more securely and failed. He used his hand flash to examine the area around. He had fallen just past level nineteen.

Struggling to open the elevator's restraining door, he found some slight support to climb up to nineteen. Panting, he lay on the rocky floor until he regained his strength.

Kinsolving shook himself as dry as he could, then got to his feet. The sharp light from the flash showed the extensive damage done by the flood waters, but even more revealing were the empty storage bins. The waters hadn't rushed past long enough to erase the mark left by the recent passage of a heavy-lifter. All the rare earth oxides had been taken before the flooding.

Of this Kinsolving had no doubt.

He rummaged around in the level nineteen storage area but found no clue to the thief—and saboteur.

Kinsolving checked his com-link and found it still functional. He moved its sensor around to record what he could, but he had no illusions about finding the thief—or thieves. Finishing, he slung the device at his hip and returned to the elevator shaft. The platform had continued to sink and was now half-submerged. The pumps worked noisily to remove the water from the lower stoops, but the elevator was lost to him.

Even if he had been able to restart the elevator, Kinsolving didn't like the notion of rising a dozen levels only to have it repeat the power loss. A second time would completely destroy the brakes—and undoubtedly kill him.

Kinsolving looked up into the darkness. A tiny spot of light showed at the mouth of the shaft. Kinsolving wondered if this meant sunrise or the carbon-arc spotlight. He hadn't worn his watch and had the feeling of considerable time passing. Sighing, he reached down to his belt and pulled free the com-link and plugged it into the respirator's circuitry. He toggled the call button.

"Are you there, Ala? Come in, Ala. I'm trapped on level nineteen. Elevator's not operational." Even as

the words came from his lips, fat blue sparks
jumped up from below as the final elevator circuits
shorted out.

"Ala, come in. I don't want to climb almost two
kilometers to the surface. Can you send help?
Over."

The com-link's indicator lights shone but otherwise gave no evidence of the device working. Kinsolving toggled the button a few more times and got
a soft hiss indicating that the unit still functioned.
But he got no response from above.

Cursing, he slung the com-link once more at his
belt and reached up to grab the plastic rungs of the
escape ladder leading to the surface. His shoulders
protested the strain and by the time he had gone up
four levels Kinsolving felt faint and nauseated. He
rested on level fourteen and once more tried to raise
Ala Markken.

When he failed, he again began to climb. This
time Kinsolving got two levels before tiring. He
curled up in the middle of the stoop and, shivering
and cold and aching, dropped off into a heavy sleep
that was more a coma.

The rumble of equipment coming down the shaft
woke Kinsolving. The rush of hot air past his face
and the concussion from an explosion far below him
knocked him back a dozen paces. He sat down heavily and simply stared, dazed and unable to move.

The gases and heavy dust filled level twelve and
obliterated what vision he had through his respirator lenses. Kinsolving worked on them a few minutes and succeeded in activating the infrared sensor
in the left eyepiece. One-eyed, he moved through
the dense fog until he came to the shaft. Shining his
hand flash downward availed him nothing, but the
IR eyepiece gave a chilling picture of destruction—
and what would have been his death if he'd remained on any of the lower levels.

The heavy-lifter had fallen from level one and crashed into the top of the elevator cage, totally destroying its locked brakes and plunging it to the lowest level—under water. The collision between the falling heavy-lifter and the stalled, disabled elevator had produced a minor explosion and enough heat to dispel the bone-chilling cold, even seven hundred meters up-shaft.

Kinsolving sucked in a deep breath, took off the respirator long enough to wipe away the sweat damming up against his bushy eyebrows, then put the heavy mask back on. The stale air coming through the filter bothered his sinuses and made his nose clog and begin dripping, but he knew it was better than not breathing at all. One glance at the air quality indicator mounted at the edge of the shaft told him how deadly Deepdig number two had become.

Looking up the shaft, Kinsolving saw a steady bright light. Definitely daylight, he decided. Once more he pulled out the com-link and, holding it out into the shaft to prevent signal damping by the heavy rock, he called, "Ala, come in, Ala. This is Bart. Are you there? Is anyone there?"

The mocking hiss gave no indication that any human lived above. Kinsolving wondered if there'd be any alive in the shaft much longer. His arms and legs had turned to lead and the brief rest hadn't given him back lost strength.

"Up we go," he said. As he climbed, he worried over the theft of the rare earths, Ala Markken, their last vacation together on the seacoast, the number of days left until his contract was completed, anything to keep from thinking about the pain gathering in joints and muscles.

Level ten came and went. Barton Kinsolving rested. And once more he tried the com-link.

No good, he finally decided. The receive mode

might work—the hiss told him that much. But somewhere in his travails he had damaged the transmitter circuit. His luck had been like that lately. The one item to fail was always the vital one.

Two more levels. Rest. Weakness flooded him just as the water did the mine tunnels below. Darkness. The sun setting? Or had he fallen into unconsciousness? Kinsolving couldn't decide.

More climbing. One level. Rest. Two. Two more. Voices echoing from above. The sound of heavy-duty cycle pumps laboring to remove water from the flooded levels.

Kinsolving had no idea what level he had reached. Four? Two? He swung in from the shaft and the interminable plastic rungs and fell to the floor at the feet of a dozen technicians.

He didn't even remember them carrying him back to his quarters.

Sunlight fell across his face, warm and soothing. Kinsolving moaned slightly as he rolled over in bed, this small motion enough to activate every pain center in his body.

"Don't move, Bart," came Ala's worried voice. "The doctor did the best he could, but he said there really wasn't much wrong with you. Just exhaustion. He gave you a light sedative."

"Not much wrong?" Kinsolving fought to sit up. Weakness surged and threatened to rob him of bodily control. He pushed it back, refusing to give in. "He ought to be inside my skin. Bet a kilo of cerium he wouldn't say that then."

"What happened?" the woman asked. She sat on the edge of his bed and took his plasti-skin bandaged hand in hers. "You went down in the shaft, then we lost contact."

"I took along a com-link. Thought that would let me stay in touch. I must have hit it. Transmitter went out."

"Nina found it hooked onto your belt. It was her unit."

"Have you done a dump on its memory? I want a full—"

"Calm down, Bart." The expression on Ala's lovely face made Kinsolving wary.

"What happened to the unit?"

"I checked it out. The circuitry was entirely destroyed. Nothing recorded from the minute you took it from Nina."

"Nothing?"

Ala looked away, then her dark eyes came back and fixed squarely on his. "Nothing," she said.

"There's more. What's happened?"

"You...the heavy-lifter. It fell down the shaft. I don't know how it happened. Weak stanchion, I just don't know."

"It missed me. I was resting just inside the shaft on level twelve."

Ala nodded slowly. Kinsolving didn't like that look on her face at all.

"Who ordered it into the mine? It wasn't due for another three days."

"I'm sorry, Bart," she said. "I'm responsible. I thought we might lower the heavy-lifter and salvage some equipment."

"What caused it to fall?"

"We're checking into that. A new recruit might have missed a few of the security dogs. Or maybe the bolts weren't fastened tightly enough. We don't know yet. But we will. I promise!"

"What more's gone wrong at the bottom?" Kinsolving asked, changing the subject. "I started the auxiliary pumps and had two levels drained. I remember hearing the primary pumps before I passed out."

"The levels are flooded again, Bart. All the way up to fifteen. I've put in a request to headquarters for complete rescue equipment. We're lucky it wasn't worse."

Kinsolving said nothing. When he had started the auxiliaries, the water had gone down swiftly. With all pumps functioning, level twenty-three should have been dry once more.

"Who was in charge? While I was below?"

The question took Ala by surprise. "I was," she said. "I didn't know you'd gone down, though. You should have told me. Taken a command com-link instead of Nina's. Something!"

Kinsolving sensed a mixture of emotions fighting inside the woman. He reached out a bandaged hand and lightly brushed her cheek. A tear had formed and had begun a slow track down.

"Don't cry," he said. He bent forward gingerly and kissed her.

"I'll be in central control. You rest, Bart. The Lorr agent-general will be out tomorrow to investigate. You'll have to deal with him. You know how they are about humans."

Kinsolving knew. The Lorr dealt only with those in charge and refused to acknowledge the presence of any human underling. He had never decided if they ran their own society in this way or if it merely showed contempt for those they considered inferiors. Kinsolving didn't like the Lorr agent-general personally but he had some sympathy for their position. Allowing another race to exploit valuable resources might seem ridiculous, but Kinsolving had found that the Lorr lacked the mining equipment and technology, and pride kept them from buying it from humans.

Kinsolving settled back on the bed, sunlight warming his aching body. He closed his eyes and listened intently. For a long minute, Ala Markken stayed beside his bed. Then she left quickly. The click of the door sliding shut told him she had gone.

Kinsolving opened his eyes cautiously and looked around the room. All seemed intact, nothing disturbed, nothing added.

The uneasiness mounted within him, however. Something *was* amiss. It took careful study to find the answer. His desk com-link had been turned around so that it faced a blank wall. His first thought was that Ala had stood beside the desk to use it, but that wasn't physically possible. She would have had to bend over the top of the com-link. Better to turn it around or leave it where it had been.

Hating himself for being so paranoid, Kinsolving carefully rose from the bed, moving slowly and making no sound. On bare feet he went to his desk and studied the side of the com-link facing his bed. The small scratches on the side plate showed how it had been tampered with.

What had been placed inside? Kinsolving guessed that it was a sensitive audio pickup since the opaque casing of the com-link didn't provide for visual spectrum optics. He looked closer to be sure no fiber optic cable poked out; it didn't. This wasn't a good job of spying, done hurriedly and with whatever material was at hand.

Who had done it?

Kinsolving didn't want to face the answer to that question.

Moving carefully, he pulled on clothing and slipped into the sanitary chamber. Kinsolving finished dressing, wincing at the leftover agony arrowing into his body from the ordeal in the mine. Climbing through the small window and dropping to the ground outside, he made his way to the records computer behind central control.

As he silently passed the opened door of the control room he saw Ala Markken hunched over the com-panel. He couldn't hear her words but judging from her expression she was speaking with someone she'd rather avoid.

Kinsolving entered the empty records room and went directly to the storage computer. He settled in a chair and tried to make himself comfortable.

"Couldn't afford a pneumatic chair," he grumbled, regretting the earlier economy on his part. Kinsolving reached out and called up production records, set up correlations, comparisons, ran charts, did a complete workup of mine output.

. Two intense hours later, he sat back in the chair. His body still hurt, but a deeper agony now possessed him. The theft of the high grade rare earth oxides from the mine had been more extensive than he'd thought. The lifting masses failed to match the reduced ore masses by a factor of two. Fully half of everything mined at Deepdig number two had been stolen.

Seeing the evidence of the heavy-lifter and the empty ore storage bins on level nineteen had alerted him to this possibility. What hurt the most was his analysis of the person most likely to have done it.

He had suspected any of a half dozen people. All had opportunity, even if he couldn't understand what they would do with such massive amounts of stolen ore.

Any of six could have been responsible, and might be implicated. But Kinsolving had pinpointed the one person definitely a thief.

Ala Markken.

Barton Kinsolving felt sick to his stomach as he stood and went to confront her with the evidence.

CHAPTER FOUR

BARTON KINSOLVING'S LEGS wobbled under him as he made his way into the control center. Ala Markken hunched over the computer console and worked feverishly, then vented a deep sigh and leaned back. The light from the terminal caught her face and turned it soft, giving a vulnerability that Kinsolving now wondered about. He loved her, but his work seemed without mistake.

She had stolen a considerable amount of rare earth ore from Interstellar Materials—and had tried to kill him, not once but twice. Kinsolving stared at her, the light brown halo of hair floating about her and turning her into something more than mortal.

Ala stiffened slightly, sensing his presence. She turned and saw him standing beside the doorway.

"Bart, you shouldn't be up yet. You're not well."

"You thought the drugs would keep me out for another week, didn't you?" His tone carried a steel edge that made Ala stiffen even more.

"What are you saying? Of course the drugs would put you to sleep. You need it after all you've been through."

"After all you've put me through."

Her eyes narrowed. To her credit Ala Markken didn't try to argue, to profess ignorance. She turned back to the computer console and tapped in an ac-

31

cess code. The parade of data told her the complete story of Kinsolving's probing.

"You'd never understand, Bart," she said softly. "I argued with them at first, but they won me over. I thought you might come around to our way of thinking, but it's not in you. I see that now."

"Why, Ala? You're well paid. Back on Earth eighty percent of everyone is jobless, on some form of dole. Most are merely existing."

"Subsistence living, they call it," Ala said bitterly. "We deserve more."

"You *have* more!" Kinsolving cried. He sank down to a chair. His legs had turned rubbery and he didn't know if he could continue much longer.

"Me? Oh, yes, I have more than most of those on Earth. I have a job and a good one."

"Why did you steal the ore, then?" Kinsolving blinked at her expression.

Ala covered it quickly. She said, "There's always need for more money. The rare earths are better than any currency. I can retire in another few months."

"You could have retired after stealing one storage bin of ore," he said. "A hundred kilograms of ore would reduce to enough to keep us all in luxury for the rest of our lives. It's more, Ala, it's got to be more. Why?"

"How much do you think I've stolen?"

"You've been doing it for years. I couldn't tell for sure but it looked as if you had started immediately after arriving. Four years of theft." Kinsolving shook his head. His tongue felt fuzzy and thick. His head pounded like the ground under a rocket exhaust and the aches in his body returned to slowly drain him of stamina.

"I have expensive tastes. You know that, Bart."

He sat, trying to keep from fainting. The only thing that allowed Kinsolving to keep some semblance of rationality was his driving need to find a way out for Ala. Condoning theft from IM wasn't really possible, he knew, and she would have to confess to the crime, but there had to be mitigating circumstances, some way to keep her from prison— or worse.

Kinsolving had heard that off-planet justice often entailed the death penalty. He tried to remember the covenants of business that IM worked under on Deepdig. Were such crimes the responsibility of the company or the Lorr?

"The Lorr," he said, all strength draining from his body. He slumped forward. "I'd forgotten about them. Stealing the ore means IM hasn't been paying severance taxes due the Lorr."

"They have strict penalties, Bart," Ala Markken said softly. "They might execute me."

"No, no, that won't happen. We...we'll tell Humbolt."

"He'll see that I'm punished," she said, almost seeming to enjoy taunting him.

"You'll have to stand trial somewhere. I'd prefer it in IM court with Earth laws rather than letting the Lorr try you."

"The Bizarres," she mused. "They seem to be the problem, don't they? Who was hurt? Not IM. Only the Bizzies aren't getting their blood money. Is that so bad, Bart?"

"Yes," he said with returning fire. "IM signed an agreement with them. We have to honor it."

"They're only aliens. And they only want to hold Earth back, keep us in grinding poverty. If it hadn't been for them, we'd be masters of the stars now, not second-raters begging for crumbs."

"That's not true and you know it. We caused our own problems on Earth, and we can work through them."

"If the Bizzies would let us."

"They couldn't care less about us. We're almost beneath their contempt."

"Exactly!"

"Ala, please. You broke the law and you must pay for it." Kinsolving wiped cold sweat from his forehead and closed his eyes for a second to try to still the violent hammering in his temples. The ache had turned to pain.

"You love me. I love you, Bart. Let's see if we can't hide this. What does it matter to the Lorr? I'll see that you get a cut. You'll be rich!"

Anger flooded Kinsolving and burned away aches, pain and weakness. "If you think that's all I want, you're wrong, Ala. Completely wrong."

"What have you done?" she asked suspiciously, seeing his new resolve.

"I've alerted Humbolt. Sent a message packet to GT 4."

"No." The single word barely came from her mouth.

"I don't like him, but—"

"You fool! The Lorr intercept every message packet and read the contents."

"I coded it."

"They know all our codes. All of them!"

Ala Markken fell back heavily in the chair and just stared at Kinsolving. He tried to read the emotion of that look and failed. It wasn't love or hate; it was inscrutable and all the more disquieting for that.

The Lorr investigators arrived at the mine less than an hour later.

"Is this a formal hearing?" asked Kenneth Humbolt. "If so, I feel that Interstellar Materials should be given the courtesy of adequate legal counsel."

The Lorr agent peered at Humbolt, face unreadable. Barton Kinsolving had tried for four years to find some trace of emotion in the aliens and had always failed. Their gray faces appeared to be chiseled from some strange, living granite, and he had never seen one that did not have squinting amber, pupilless eyes. The agent-general for Deepdig sat quietly behind a huge, cut stone table, fingers folding and unfolding in front of him in boneless ways not shared by humans. Other than this—a nervous gesture?—Kinsolving got no hint of the seriousness of the matter. He'd have to let Humbolt handle it, even though Humbolt had been less than responsive in the past six days since arriving.

Kinsolving frowned as he considered this. He'd sent the message packet directly to company headquarters on GT 4, almost fifty light years distant. Even with the supershift acceleration used by the message encapsulation, it couldn't have been received in less than three days. Humbolt had to have been en route and could never have read the contents of the packet, even though he claimed to have come in response.

Kinsolving wondered if Humbolt lied to keep an innocent facade in front of the Lorr. He had noticed Ala's attitude toward the aliens hardening more than it had been; if her feeling toward the Lorr was hard, Humbolt's was vicious and paranoid.

"This is a formal hearing to determine guilt," said the Lorr agent-general. The long fingers rippled, as if they were reflections in a pond rather than real digits. When the Lorr spoke, his thin lips pulled back in an expression similar to a human grimace, but no human's dark, pebbly tongue thrust from between lips to produce such a startling effect. And no human's teeth shone in a solid white dental plate. "There will be penalties assessed as a result of the findings this day."

"We demand counsel," said Humbolt in a voice too

loud for the small room. The gathered Lorr trained their pupilless eyes on him and remained silent.

"Mr. Humbolt," Kinsolving said softly. "Can we get the hearing postponed?"

"I tried," Humbolt said. "The Bizzies wouldn't do it. They want to convict us all right now."

"They were thorough going over the mine's shipment records," Kinsolving said. "It might be wise to admit guilt and take whatever punishment they have."

"Are you crazy?" Humbolt's eyes widened in shock.

"They're not stupid, Mr. Humbolt. We don't want to lose the rare earth mines for IM, do we? The Lorr might revoke our mining permit unless we do confess guilt." Kinsolving looked over at Ala Markken, who sat straight in a chair, eyes focused on a blank wall. Kinsolving had tried several times to talk to her and she had refused.

"The Bizzies won't go that far," Humbolt said, but no confidence rang in his voice on this point.

"What did she do with all the ore?" mused Kinsolving.

"What? Markken, you mean? Don't let it trouble you, Kinsolving. You're doing a fine job."

"I missed the pilfering. As mine supervisor, it was my duty to check everything, and I missed it." Kinsolving could barely bring himself to call the loss of over one hundred thousand kilograms of rare earth oxides "pilfering." He wasn't sure he had a word encompassing such a scale of theft, though.

"Primary among the charges against your company," spoke up the agent-general, "is fraud in not paying severance taxes." The Lorr twisted forward at an angle showing too few bones in his ribcage as he read the amounts. Kinsolving recoiled as a disagreeable odor rose. The Lorr's expression never changed but Kinsolving felt the extreme tension—

the alien's stench seemed to be an indication of loathing or fear of the humans. "Your supervisor and my auditors have agreed that taxes are delinquent on two hundred thousand kilos."

Humbolt held Kinsolving down at the inflated number. "Interstellar Materials agrees to pay these sums," Humbolt said, face pinched. "But we request graduated payments. The recent disaster at the mine has left us in precarious financial condition."

"No."

"But—"

"No," said the Lorr, voice flat and brooking no argument. "Further, we will in the future monitor on-site all liftings from the mine. No more can we allow your numbers to stand."

"This isn't part of our agreement," protested Humbolt.

"The amount of ore reaching your cargo ships is now in question," said the agent-general. He raised the curiously boned hand and the fingers rippled like tentacles. "We are investigating all avenues of exit from this planet to discover how the stolen ores were removed."

Kinsolving found himself nodding. This had bothered him, too. It appeared that Ala was guilty—and the other five he had suspected. But how had she removed the ore from Deepdig? That required the use of heavy equipment to move, to load, to get into orbit and onto a starship. And where did the stolen ore go? The amounts of pure samarium and the other rare earths might reach the tens of kilos by this time. Who could use such quantities without accounting for its source? Kinsolving knew that Earth authorities were meticulous in checking for contraband brought onto their home planet.

Still, a few kilos over four years could be missed by even the most careful of searches.

That did not answer the questions of who and

what did they do with material of such specific technological use.

"No fewer than five agent-captains will be stationed at each of your mines," the Lorr went on. "Their job will be to detect illicit activity detrimental to Lorr security and revenues. Any argument with them will constitute grounds for permanent revocation of Interstellar Materials' license."

"I protest. On the behalf of IM, I demand a hearing with legal counsel." Humbolt looked as if he'd been trapped and fought desperately to escape.

"Refused," the Lorr said. Kinsolving detected the first trace of emotion on the alien's part: triumph.

"We can live with it," Kinsolving said to Humbolt. The man spun and glared at him.

"We *can't* live with it, dammit," flared Humbolt.

"We retain the mining agreement," Kinsolving pointed out. Humbolt's expression told him that he was missing a key element in this. The ore was important to IM, but there was more. What? Kinsolving felt as if he'd been cast adrift and had lost sight of all land. And no one in the lifeboat would tell him where to paddle.

"How do we appeal this ruling?" called out Humbolt.

The Lorr bobbed his narrow head, amber eyes fixed on Humbolt. "This is the court of final rulings. You have lost in all lesser courts. My decision is final."

"But this is only the preliminary hearing!" Kinsolving blurted.

"You don't understand," said Humbolt. "They don't want us to win. They can make up whatever rules they want as they go along. This one puts their guards in the mines. Dammit!"

"This matter is closed," said the Lorr agent-general. "The next case is of lesser importance and has been decided." The Lorr pointed and Ala

Markken and the other five Kinsolving had decided were implicated in the ore theft were seized by the guards. "Take these to our prison to begin their sentences."

"Wait, you can't do this, you damned Bizzie!" shouted Humbolt.

The Lorr faced Kinsolving and said, "The agent-general and the Grand Council of Lorr thank Barton Kinsolving for his service in bringing these felons to justice."

"But I didn't do anything!" Kinsolving protested. He turned to Ala. Her eyes had widened in shock. Now fury burned in them—and it was directed at him.

"I didn't tell them anything. Ala, believe me. I didn't!"

The woman wasn't allowed to speak. The Lorr guards hurried her and the others from the room.

"Mr. Humbolt, I swear it. I never gave any evidence to the agent-general. He's lying!"

"His evidence came from somewhere," said Humbolt. The man heaved a sigh and sagged back in his chair. "I'm sorry, Kinsolving. I know you wouldn't betray any of your kind to a Bizarre."

"I don't have your...distaste for the Lorr," Kinsolving said, "but they're not my friends, either. I'd never willingly turn Ala over to them."

"You believe all that space gas put out about the Bizzies? Did you swallow it all without question?"

"What are you talking about?"

"Back on Earth. The appeasement faction in power now."

"I don't understand," said Kinsolving.

"They spew out all that shit about how we can live with the Bizzies, how they'll accept us if we're sweet and smile at our betters. They want to exist under the Bizzies' heel as slaves rather than as free men. That's the only way they think they can stay in power."

Humbolt's words came like a lecture—or a sermon. Kinsolving said, "I've got nothing against aliens. These—the agent-general—seems to carry a grudge against us. It might be directed at IM instead of at Ala and the others. He just sees a way to get even."

"We must keep them away from the mines," said Humbolt. He closed his case and stood. "Return to Deepdig number two and see if you can't get those lower levels opened. And if you happen to accidentally lose a few of the Bizzies, fine."

With that Kenneth Humbolt left the room.

Kinsolving watched and found himself beginning to despair. Ala Markken had been taken to prison, the impression given that he had been responsible. And Humbolt's attitude struck Kinsolving as totally wrong. Payment of the fine had galled the man, but having Lorr agents present at the mine site sent him into a real panic.

Why? Kinsolving felt that a world once logical and sane had turned upside down around him.

Worst of all, he wondered what new and terrible fate lay in store for him. He felt it coming, inexorably, and had no way of dodging.

CHAPTER FIVE

KENNETH HUMBOLT settled down in a chair and tried to relax. The man kept worrying over the problems posed by the Lorr agent-general — and the limitless trouble this would create with the board of directors. Humbolt had seen the chairman of the board angry before. Fremont usually downed his strength potion and rose, gnarled knuckles on the table, and then bellowed.

He bellowed and ranted and spat and the one on the receiving end of the tirade would try to sink into the floor. No one was strong enough, emotionally or politically, to endure the chairman's full wrath for longer than a few seconds.

Humbolt doubted such dismissal on Fremont's part was all that occurred. Not once had Humbolt ever heard of anyone after they had been removed from the board of Interstellar Materials. They vanished completely. Never did they appear on another company's board nor did they assume lesser roles in IM.

They disappeared without trace.

Humbolt rubbed his forehead nervously, hand coming away with sweat in spite of the air-conditioning working valiantly to keep the room at GT 4's lower mean temperature.

He finally realized that it wasn't the air conditioner that was failing. And this made Humbolt even more nervous. He leaned back in his chair and folded his arms tightly around himself, eyes closed to help him concentrate.

Things had glitched beyond his control. The flooding of the mine had gone according to schedule. It should have been enough to keep the Lorr agent-general and his auditors from ever determining the true output from the mine. No matter what the Lorr claimed, IM could make the counter that even more rare earth ore had been lost.

"Damn Kinsolving," he said aloud. He had appointed the man in spite of distinct reservations. He had nothing against Kinsolving's engineering ability. The man's ratings had been the highest. But he had been too steeped in the drivel poisoning the schools on Earth.

Give in to the aliens. Don't make them mad. Fit into a tiny niche and pick up their crumbs. Soon enough mankind would be allowed to join in. Soon. Very soon.

Humbolt snorted and rubbed his nose. He didn't accept such a passive philosophy for an instant. Not after he'd heard the Plan.

Humbolt opened his eyes and rocked slightly to one side. He idly punched up Kinsolving's file. He shook his head. Along with the ability to squeeze more ore from Deepdig number two than any other engineer employed by IM went a certainty that bordered on monomania. The man's stubbornness once he thought he was right was without limit.

His nose twitched again. Humbolt rubbed it, then jumped out of his chair when a soft, oily voice said, "There are drugs that might alter his opinions."

"What?" Humbolt's hand sank into the folds of his jacket to touch the handle of a stun rod. His eyes narrowed when he saw the overdressed man who had managed to enter the room, circle behind him and watch unobserved for—how long?

The man smiled disarmingly and held out his

hands to silently proclaim himself harmless. Humbolt almost accepted that. The man's clothing bordered on the absurd. Soft pinks and mint greens melted in formless swirls on a silk doublet with frilled white lace cuffs. The collar hung open to reveal a dozen platinum- and diamond-studded necklaces, any of which would have looked better around a woman's neck. Tight black stretch breeches with a codpiece and calf-high leather boots turned a parody of fashion into an outright joke

But Humbolt didn't laugh. Something about the man's eyes warned him this would be dangerous. And his unannounced visitor had entered without tripping any of the alarms Humbolt had planted for security.

"The alarms, good sir?" the man said in his unctuous voice. "Is that the point worrying you so?"

"Those were the best IM has. They didn't malfunction."

"But of course not." The man smiled, showing perfect white teeth rimmed in gold with occasional diamond, ruby and emerald embeddings. "I must caution those on the board of directors about this model." From nowhere the man produced one of the alarms. He tossed it casually onto the table.

"Who are you? You're not with the company."

An even wider smile almost dazzled Humbolt. For the first time, true fear stabbed at his heart. His knuckles turned white as he tensed on the handle of the stun rod.

"Of course I am."

"I'm a director. I know all the company personnel on Deepdig."

"Yes, you are a director, good sir." The man moved with fluid grace and settled daintily into a chair in front of Humbolt's desk. Foppishly crossing his legs and smoothing nonexistent wrinkles in his black breeches, the man asked, "Do you think this codpiece is too, well, too much? I was torn between its more daring fashion statement and modesty. I chose the former, of course. Never hesitate to be yourself, eh? But your opinion is of some importance, Mr. Humbolt."

Humbolt sank back into his chair and tapped the indent-key on the computer console. The screen blinked instantly, signalling a null match.

"Company records show you're not an employee, but no one except Interstellar Materials' personnel is allowed on planet. That's part of our agreement with the Lorr."

"You're asking how I came to this rather out-of-the-way spot?" The man fluffed his collar ruffles and smiled. This time the expression chilled Humbolt completely.

He wasn't sure even his weapon would be enough against this dandy. And he didn't know why he felt that. Becoming director of IM hadn't been easy. He had killed along the way—and worse.

Kenneth Humbolt wasn't sure even his quick reflexes would be enough. And he didn't know why. Uncertainty always worried him. Sweat began beading on his forehead.

"Is it too warm for you? Oh, pardon me. I am so rude at times. You are just in from GT 4. A chilly place, that, and not one I care for. Warmer climes are better suited for living though the cooler ones afford greater opportunity for displaying a well-developed ...wardrobe."

The man gestured and Humbolt almost froze. The simple pass of a hand had caused the thermostat to drop to its lowest setting.

"How'd you get here?" Humbolt asked again.

"How do you get the ore off Deepdig?" the man riposted. "We need not concern ourselves with trivial matters. My time is valuable, and I am ever so sure yours is, also. Am I correct in this, Mr. Humbolt?"

Humbolt's shoulders rippled as he jerked out the stun rod, finger pressing the firing stud before the weapon had even cleared its holster. The back of the chair where the man had been exploded, splinters flying everywhere.

The man stood beside Humbolt, thumb and forefinger lightly touching Humbolt's wrist.

"Drop the stun rod, Mr. Humbolt," he said, the hint of true amusement dancing on his too-handsome features. Dark-painted eyes gleamed with a feral cruelty. Humbolt twitched, then screamed. The thumb and forefinger grip tightened with steely intensity.

"Stop it!" Humbolt shrieked. "You're breaking my wrist!"

"Oh, sorry, Mr. Humbolt. It wouldn't do to damage you, would it? Your services are of considerable importance to IM." As if brushing off an insect, the man pushed Humbolt's wrist away.

"You're Villalobos', aren't you?" Humbolt demanded. "You're Cameron."

"I do confess to the latter, Mr. Humbolt." Cameron made a broad, mocking bow as if he paid obeisance to some Earthly king of a dozen centuries earlier. "But to state that I somehow belong to Dr. Villalobos is wrong. I work tirelessly for IM, as you do. Maria happens to be my immediate superior, that's all."

"Maria?" Humbolt had never heard anyone use Villalobos' first name so casually. The small, dark director was more commonly referred to as "that bitch."

Cameron's laugh carried true scorn in it. Humbolt couldn't decide whether it was scorn for Villalobos or himself.

"The good lady's relationship is special to me in

ways other than that of employer–employee, but
then yours is special with her, also, is it not?"

Humbolt would gladly break her spine and leave
her paralyzed for the rest of her natural life if he
could.

"Yes, we share a special rapport," Humbolt said.
He straightened in the chair and forced himself to
keep from rubbing his still-hurting wrist. "Why are
you on Deepdig? IM business, of course, but what? I
was not informed."

Cameron made a dismissing gesture with his
hand. "An oversight, I am sure. The bureaucratic
nightmare on GT 4 will drown us all in trivia and
misplaced orders one day."

"You are here under my command?"

A slight sneer rippled along Cameron's lips. "But
of course! How can it be any other way? You, after
all, are a director and I am only a lowly paid employee."

"How did you circumvent the alarm system?"

"My knowledge is extensive when it comes to
robot devices. The alarm system can be thought of
as disembodied sensors for a robot. I merely approached it in that fashion and, not wanting to disturb you while you were so hard at work, entered
and waited to be noticed."

Humbolt reached out tentatively for the stun rod.
Cameron made no move to prevent it. Humbolt almost jerked it back across the desk. Cameron paid
no attention to the furtive movement. Humbolt felt
as if the assassin had dismissed him completely as a
threat; primping and smoothing his costume ranked
higher.

"Why are you here?"

Cameron looked up, long eyelashes almost flut-
tering. The glint of sunlight coming through a skylight caught an emerald mounted in a front tooth
and reflected away, almost blinding Humbolt.

"You must learn to be more diplomatic in your queries," Cameron chided. "It seldom pays to rush forward without knowing the exact nature of the terrain."

"I have work to do. Why did Villalobos send you to Deepdig?"

"Dr. Villalobos is my immediate superior," Cameron said, "but she did not send me. Chairman Fremont did."

Humbolt forced himself to stay silent. Anything he said now would be wrong. He couldn't show weakness, indecision, any hint of vacillation. If Fremont distrusted him and sent a watchdog to report the slightest mistake, it might be necessary to arrange an accident for the spy. How he would do that conveniently escaped Humbolt at the moment. Cameron's reputation hardly seemed credible, but Humbolt faced him and sensed more than the fop in him.

Without realizing he did so, Humbolt rubbed his injured wrist.

"Come along, Mr. Humbolt. I have a small demonstration prepared just for your benefit." The way Cameron spoke turned the request into a knife-edged order.

"I have work to do. Kinsolving is a problem that must be—"

"Supervisor Kinsolving is *my* problem now, Mr. Humbolt. Chairman Fremont has decided that the psychological profile on the man indicates that we lavish attention on him exceeding that of which you are capable."

Humbolt felt the storm clouds of anger mounting.

"It has been deemed best that you not dirty your hands with such minor matters. Allow me to do my task, then leave. Keeping the Lorr pacified and Deepdig open to IM exploitation is paramount. The Plan must be served."

"The Plan *will* be served," Humbolt said bitterly.

Cameron stood and walked on silent feet to the door. Humbolt didn't see how the man did it but the door slid back without Cameron touching the opener. Humbolt tucked the stun rod into its holster and hurried after Cameron. The assassin walked with a deceptively easy step, his long legs covering more ground than Humbolt could comfortably match without almost doubling his own stride.

"Where are we going?" Humbolt still had a mental picture of Fremont raging against Humbolt and how the Lorr had taken control of the situation— and Fremont ordering the elimination of those he considered responsible.

"Not far. There. See the Bizzie?"

Humbolt nodded.

"Don't worry. The agent-general won't miss this one. It is a...derelict."

The alien hunkered down, glaring at them with those haunting, pupilless eyes. Fingers like tentacles wove intricate patterns Humbolt interpreted as obscene gestures.

Cameron barked something in the Lorr tongue that made the Bizarre jump to his feet and run like the wind.

"The study of Bizzie languages has been a minor hobby for some time," Cameron explained. "It is always proper to study your enemy, to learn all you can of him before destroying him."

"What are you going to do?"

"Robots," Cameron went on, paying no attention to Humbolt. "Robots are not a hobby with me. They are my life. They can achieve perfection in their limited universe. It is that perfection which draws me the most strongly. For instance, the Bizzie has been promised his life if he can escape."

"You can't kill him!" protested Humbolt. "If the agent-general learns about this—"

"The Lorr will never find this one. See how he dodges and runs." Cameron's voice became cold and tinted with a hatred that made Humbolt take an involuntary step away. "Those boneless legs will soon cease their rush away. No human could match the Bizzie's speed or endurance. But my friend is not human."

A soft hum filled the air. Humbolt spun and saw a small robot floating on a repulsor field a meter to his left. Small ceramic plates turned on mobile bases and a whip antenna fluttered behind the tubular body like a dog's tail.

"Surface acoustic wave sensors," said Cameron. "Those plates. They pick up the Bizzie's scent a thousand times better than the keenest bloodhound. Even without the other sensing devices—mostly of my own design—the SAWS could follow a single Bizzie—or human—through the most crowded city on the most crowded planet."

"And?" prompted Humbolt, fascinated in spite of himself. Cameron silently handed over a pair of goggles. Humbolt donned them and blinked at the unexpected view. Focusing at the end of his nose gave the countryside as seen by the robot. Focusing farther gave him normal vision. A sudden rush staggered him.

"It requires practice," Cameron said, mocking him. "Watch carefully."

Humbolt brought his eyes in close and saw everything that the robot hunter did. In less than a minute it had weaved in and out of rocks and scrubby trees and gone across a stream to find the alien. The Lorr died horribly within five seconds of the robotic attack.

Cameron removed the goggles from Humbolt's head and tucked them away in the voluminous folds of his blouse. "Remarkable, isn't it?"

"What's the purpose of showing me this?"

Surprise crossed Cameron's face. "Why, I thought you would enjoy seeing a Bizzie destroyed. One less for the Plan."

"That's all?"

Cameron laughed. "That's all. Now I must attend to business. Chairman Fremont has requested my immediate presence back on GT 4—bringing back the sad news that Supervisor Kinsolving has died an accidental death."

Cameron said nothing more. He left in a haze of pastel silks and flashing black-clad legs. Humbolt watched until the killer vanished in the serene countryside. Humbolt pitied Barton Kinsolving. The man was a good engineer and might have been an asset for IM if his profile had only shown a greater acceptance for the divine destiny of mankind.

The Plan would be served. No matter who died, the Plan would be served.

CHAPTER SIX

EVERYWHERE HE TURNED Barton Kinsolving ran into a Lorr agent-captain. They insisted on prying into every nook and cranny of the mine until no work was being done. Kinsolving resigned himself to letting the aliens do their job. He didn't like it, but he knew that the sooner they satisfied themselves, the sooner they would leave.

Kinsolving went into his office and sank into the wheezing pneumatic chair. He moved around uncomfortably, aware that the chair failed to match his contours in several places. Like everything else, the chair refused to do its job properly. He sighed and tried to get it all straight in his mind.

Kinsolving wasn't sure that he did a good job. Since the disaster with the robominer and the flooding of the lower levels, nothing had gone as it should.

Ala Markken. Kinsolving went numb inside thinking of her. How he loved her. How he *had* loved her. Kinsolving worried over the confusion he felt. Just because he had found that she'd stolen a considerable amount of ore from Interstellar Materials didn't make him love her any less, but she had tried to kill him. The man found that almost impossible to believe, yet the facts were obvious.

Ala had been in charge when the robot miner had lasered into the underground river. This Kinsolving pushed aside. It might have been an accident or Ala might have done it deliberately to hide the massive ore thefts. With waters raging almost two kilometers under the surface, anything seemed believable. Kinsolving smiled wanly. The Lorr agent-general might have even believed that a considerable amount of ore had been lost.

Kinsolving's smile tightened. The ore on level nineteen had been lifted. And the same heavy-lifter had been dropped down the elevator shaft in an attempt to crush him.

Ala Markken. She had done it. His lover had tried to kill him.

"You. Human one. Where are the assay reports?" came a harsh demand.

Kinsolving looked up, eyes misted with the impact of Ala's deliberate actions. "What?"

"It is required that we obtain assay reports for each level, for each vein of ore. They are not in your files."

Kinsolving stared at the Lorr, then heaved himself to his feet. He went to a slave-station computer the alien could use and banged in the access code. The information flashed on the screen. "This is it. We put it in the same database as the personnel records. Much the same format, saves space and time and—"

"Your alibis are of no importance to me." The Lorr swiveled on his crazy-hinged knees and stalked out.

Kinsolving's anger mounted, then faded. Officious, rude bureaucrats were the least of his worries. In his graduate school's required xeno culture and psychology class he had been taught that the aliens resented mankind's venturing to the stars, but that this attitude could be overcome. Not easily, not quickly, but their confidence and cooperation could be won. Sometimes he wondered.

"To hell with them," he said. Why should the Lorr be different from human auditors? He had the same problems when IM sent out their fleet of nameless, gnomelike accountants.

Kinsolving frowned. IM audited the mine records once every planetary year. Ala had been on-planet for four years. How had she hidden the discrepancy between lifting from the mine and lifting from the planet's surface? Kinsolving pulled the master console closer to his desk and began examining the records to find some clue. Several times he found a block on the records; the Lorr shut him off.

But the evidence of how Ala had stolen so much ore—and where she had sent it—remained a mystery.

Idly, Kinsolving punched up the woman's personnel record. Her lovely oval face stared at him from the screen. Almost savagely, he punched the Cancel button. Without knowing it, Kinsolving requested his own files and found his own likeness staring out at him.

As mine supervisor, Kinsolving had access to all personnel records but he had never taken the time to examine his own. He did his job, he got good raises and promotions and that was enough for him. He took pride in his work and what difference did it make what had been entered on his company files?

He examined them now. And he was not certain he agreed with the IM psychologist's appraisal. Then Kinsolving chuckled.

"Stubborn to a fault, recalcitrant, complete self-assurance, that's me," he decided. He frowned when he found a special flag at the end of the record. Working for a few minutes to access the corresponding tag file resulted in repeated Entry Denied warnings flashing on the screen. Kinsolving hunched forward and worked in earnest to break into this area of the database.

He was the supervisor. He should be able to see all the records. An hour of futile effort hadn't diminished his curiosity or determination, but Kinsolving slowly came to the realization that the tag had been put on his file back on Gamma Tertius 4 and no corresponding entry existed in the mine's database.

None of the other personnel records carried a similar flag, and this made Kinsolving all the more determined to find what IM thought of him—and wanted kept from prying eyes.

He glanced up when one of his few remaining workers poked his head inside the office door.

"Mr. Kinsolving?"

"What is it, Mac?"

"Don't know for sure. Getting odd readings from deep in the mine. Level nineteen. I ran a foptic probe and didn't find anything."

Kinsolving knew the limits of the fiber optic probes mounted on robotic surveyors. Not every frequency of visible light was transmitted since their primary use was detecting underground hot spots and areas of cold where water might run—rivers such as the one Ala Markken had ordered the robo-miner to drill into.

"How odd?" Kinsolving asked. "Anything to endanger the equipment?"

"Could be," the man said. Kinsolving knew he'd have to pry every bit of information from McClanahan. He was the most junior of those remaining and felt inadequate for the job he assumed.

Kinsolving didn't want to tell the man that he *was* inadequate, that his training and temperament were not suited to direct an entire shift. But Deep-dig number two ran shorthanded because of Ala and the others. Even if valuable automated equipment hadn't been lost, Kinsolving would have been hard-pressed to keep the mine operating at nominal capacity.

"Gas indications? More damp readings?" Kinsolving asked.

"Weirder than that. I know those indicators. You want to take a look at the board?"

Kinsolving rose silently and followed McClanahan to the control center. They passed two Lorr on the way. Each group pointedly ignored the other. Kinsolving swung into the command chair and scanned the console. Most of the indicators showed normal readings, but one flashed a slow, deliberate purple.

"You're right. This isn't usual." Ala Markken might have recognized the signal, but Kinsolving didn't. He punched up a Help on the screen and read it twice. "Never seen this before," he told McClanahan. "I'm going down. This shows that we hit a pocket of radon gas, but that's not possible. Not in this ore structure. And all we have mounted on the robominers are Geiger counters. I don't see any way we could get this indication."

"You mean it's showing radon gas but we don't have any equipment to detect it?"

"That's it. I'm afraid this might be a malfunction in the detector circuitry."

"But I checked that, first thing," the man protested. "All came out normal within limits."

Kinsolving shrugged. When working almost two kilometers underground, only one level above a flooded network, anything was possible. One piece of equipment failing in this manner might indicate bigger problems brewing in the bowels of the mine.

More problems were the last thing Kinsolving needed.

"We don't have time to pull it from the stoop and get it back up the shaft to examine. Keep the robot working. I'll assume manual control at the shaft, turn it off and then check it out."

"Manual overrides my controls, right?" McClanahan didn't sound happy about this.

"Safety measure. You know that. Where's the tool kit? Good, there it is." Kinsolving picked up the pack containing spare block circuits and other control components. With luck he could be down in the mine, fix the problem and return before the end of the shift.

"I can do that, if you want, Mr. Kinsolving," the man offered.

Kinsolving considered this offer seriously. He had no lingering traces of claustrophobia in spite of being trapped at the bottom of the mine. He felt *comfortable* in mine shafts. But more than this, he didn't want McClanahan shutting down the robominer. The only job the young man did worse than running the control console was repair work.

"Thanks, but I'll see to it. I'll take a com-link. Keep in touch. If anything more goes wrong, let me know right away."

"Yes, sir."

Kinsolving hefted the pack containing the repair parts and went to the head of the shaft. He stood and stared at the open cage for a moment, then entered. A deep breath, a slightly shaking hand touching the level eighteen button and he plummeted into the bowels of the planet.

"You there, Mac?" he asked, toggling his com-link.

"Here, sir. No problems. No more problems, I should say. Atmosphere levels normal, no damp, nothing but the robominer's radon indication."

"I'll wear a respirator," Kinsolving told him. "That won't pose much of a problem communicating."

"Muffles your voice, that's all," McClanahan said.

Kinsolving fitted the bulky head gear onto his face, hung the com-link at his belt and stepped out on level eighteen. The throb of pumps working on the lowest levels came to him as vibrations through his boot soles. Almost half of all his robot equipment strove to clean out the bottom four levels. He couldn't afford to have even one robominer on the upper levels out of commission.

Setting his hand flash, Kinsolving walked briskly along the stoop, the walls brushing either shoulder and occasional ceiling protrusions causing him to duck. By the time he reached the end of the stoop where the robominer's laser sizzled and popped and worked on the ore vein, Kinsolving scooted along on hands and knees.

He used the com-link controls to deactivate the robominer. Using his flash, he examined the immediate area. It appeared no different from any other vein found in the mine. He knew trapped pockets of any gas wouldn't be visible, but he saw no reason to expect the chemically inert radioactive gas in this strata. The 57–71s weren't usually found in sands containing thorium or pitchblende or even coal. He had studied the geologist's report and no radium had been found.

The detector on the robot had to be faulty. There was no other explanation.

The rock where the laser had been directed cooled enough to allow Kinsolving to slide forward. He touched the back of the robominer's metallic carapace. No heat. That meant the internal equipment probably functioned properly. Kinsolving opened the repair hatch and shone his light inside. All internal readouts were normal.

"Mac, you there?" he called, toggling the com-link.

"Yes, sir. Find something?"

"When was this unit in the repair shop last?"

"Routine maintenance over three months ago, sir. The lasing chamber had developed a leak and we had to replace the tube. Nothing else detected then."

"Someone's been inside. Bright scratches on the inner casing where a board has been replaced recently." Kinsolving knew that the robominer's normal operation would have oxidized those scratches in less than a week. Someone had tampered with the warning circuits—within the past day or two.

He pulled the suspect board, leaving new scratches on the robot's casing. Kinsolving plugged it into a portable tester and watched the readings. One after another blinked green until he came to one of a dozen circuits that weren't operational in this model robominer.

"Someone's added a false warning," he told McClanahan. He got no immediate response. "Mac? You still there? Mac!"

"Sir, get the hell out of there. I'm getting bad readings all over level eighteen. Vibration. The strain gauges show the roof is collapsing!"

Kinsolving didn't need the remote warning. The walls trembled and dust began to fall, obscuring vision for more than a few meters. Kinsolving started to crawl back to the larger part of the stoop, then stopped. His flash beam hit the wall of billowing dust and cut him off from seeing more than an arm's length now. The rumbles told the real story, however.

Kinsolving flopped over onto his back, got to the robominer and activated it. Red lights flared inside, indicating that he hadn't reinstalled the warning circuits. He didn't care. The robot would work without those boards. He manually programmed it to reverse the direction of its cutting laser, then started it to work.

The coherent beam snapped into existence just centimeters above his head. Kinsolving pressed close to the metallic side of the robominer and worked around it as the machine began to trace its way back toward the elevator shaft. The laser drilled a hole through dust and debris and afforded a better view than he could have hoped for without it.

Less than ten meters from the shaft and the elevator that would get him to the surface, the roof collapsed. Kinsolving choked, as the shockwave of dust and stony fragments momentarily forced away all the air from the mouth of his respirator filter.

He shone his flash against the solid wall. To dig through it with his bare hands would be impossible. Kinsolving started the robominer cutting. He hoped it would break through before another tremor brought down all those tons of rock on his head.

He sat and watched and waited, unable to do anything more except worry.

CHAPTER SEVEN

BARTON KINSOLVING longed to reach over to the working robominer and turn up the cutting laser's power. He held back. The trapped air in the stoop had turned stale quickly. To increase the robominer's cutting speed would reduce the oxygen in the air even more. Kinsolving sat and wheezed and wondered what had gone wrong this time.

After all, Ala Markken was in the Lorr prison. She couldn't be responsible for a second attempt on his life.

Kinsolving came to the gloomy conclusion that mining, in spite of the almost total automation, was still a dangerous business.

"Sir?" The com-link crackled with static. "You there, Mr. Kinsolving?"

"Still here, Mac," he said, not wanting to use any more oxygen than necessary. "What happened?"

"Lost you for a minute. Getting a spotty signal."

Kinsolving didn't answer. McClanahan would get to the point in his own time. Kinsolving hoped he'd be around to hear it.

"You there, Mr. Kinsolving? I got readings of severe vibration. The computer analysis is that some damn fool was blasting in a stoop running parallel to the one you're in. Too much explosive and weakened supports from the flooding caused the roof collapse." A long pause with almost deafening static, then, "You there, Mr. Kinsolving?"

60

"I'm here," Kinsolving said. He sat with his arms locked around his knees, thinking hard. Another attempt on his life. Blasting on this level hadn't been approved for almost eight months. The laser cutters worked faster and better once the first tunnel had been opened. Why weaken the stoops with dangerous explosives when the robominer's operation cut through the heart of the ore vein and left a fused tunnel stronger than the uncut rock?

If it wasn't Ala who tried to kill him this time, who could it be?

The only answer possible made Kinsolving furious. When he got out, he'd find Kenneth Humbolt and snap his neck.

Kinsolving looked up to see the robominer's readouts showing a decreasing power level. He started to take the chance and increase cutting power when he noticed the reason for the slowing. Sonic probes measured the distance to the far side of the rock fall. The robot was within centimeters of breakthrough.

"This can't be right," Kinsolving said aloud. His breath momentarily fogged the inner lenses of the respirator. He waited for a clearing, then checked the robominer. It had bored through only six meters of rock. By his estimate another four meters remained.

A sudden rush of air caused dust to swirl around him. He squinted as he looked into a powerful hand flash.

"You all right, Kinsolving?" came a voice he knew too well.

"I'm fine," he answered. Kinsolving turned off the robominer and gingerly picked his way over the still-hot, lasered rock. He tumbled out to find himself sitting at Humbolt's feet. The man helped Kinsolving to his feet and started brushing him off.

"That's all right, Humbolt," he said brusquely. "I'll get cleaned up after we're out of the mine."

"I thought we'd lost you," said Humbolt, slapping Kinsolving on the back. "Glad to see you're still alive."

"Why are you here?"

Humbolt tipped his head and peered at Kinsolving. "You sound suspicious. Hell, Barton, I just *rescued* you. Oh, you'd have cut your way out in a while, but you're out in less than half the time it'd have taken your unit."

"Thanks. But what are you doing here?" Kinsolving refused to be mollified.

"I returned to the compound just as the quake hit. I heard your McClanahan and figured you needed help. Been a long time since I've been in a mine. I got my start in the field and, well, I decided to give you a hand."

"You ran a robominer from this side?"

"They haven't changed much," Humbolt said with some pride.

"It wasn't a quake," said Kinsolving.

Kinsolving watched Humbolt's expression. If he hadn't been studying the IM director carefully he would have missed the quickly passing cloud of anger. Humbolt knew it wasn't a natural quake; he knew this was no accident. But if Humbolt had orchestrated the new disaster, why bother rescuing the victim?

"You saved me another hour trapped back there," said Kinsolving. "Again, thank you." He didn't offer his hand, nor did Humbolt seem to expect the gratitude to extend that far.

"Let's get back to the surface. Your Mr. McClanahan can keep these robots busy from the control center. How long before they can be producing ore again?"

"Cleanup for this level will be minimal," said

Kinsolving, the engineer in him rising to the surface and hiding the suspicious, paranoid part of his nature. "If we keep at it—no letup on the night shifts—the stoop will be producing again within a day or two. Might need to shore up the roof. One robominer is adequate for that. The other can burrow back and find the vein."

"A day?" said Humbolt. "Good. I'll expect a report at the end of the week."

The elevator came to a smooth halt at the surface. Kinsolving ran from the cage and fell to the ground in appreciation for being free of a mine shaft that had for a second time almost been his grave. He sheepishly looked at Humbolt, embarrassed at this display of relief. But the director had already left the compound, walking briskly to a waiting vehicle. Even before Kinsolving could call out, the repulsor field of the vehicle hummed to life and it surged into the distance.

Kenneth Humbolt was in a hurry to get somewhere.

But where? Kinsolving wanted to know this as much as he wanted to know who had been responsible for the explosion in the mine. If it had been Humbolt, he saw no reason for the director to abruptly change his mind and rescue his victim.

"Mac, what's the status below?" he asked as he entered the control center. The young man bent over the console, working furiously.

"Got things programmed. Might be able to get ore production to nominal by this time tomorrow. Not much damage to the shaft or stoops." McClanahan's expression turned grim. "It was almost as if the explosion was meant to trap only you, Mr. Kinsolving."

He didn't bother telling McClanahan about the circuit board that had been tampered with. The spurious reading had been a lure. When he had descended the explosives had been detonated.

"Can you handle it, Mac? I've got to find Humbolt."

"Haven't seen him. You might try in town at the agent-general's office. Think I heard someone say he was there this afternoon for another hearing. But you'd know that, wouldn't you?"

"Right, Mac. I'd know all about that."

With grim determination, Barton Kinsolving went to his quarters, washed and changed his clothing, then went hunting for Humbolt. If the director had been scheduled to meet with the Lorr agent-general, what had brought him to the mine so unexpectedly—and at such an opportune time to save Kinsolving?

By the time he reached the suite of rooms he'd taken as an office while on Deepdig, Kenneth Humbolt was in a rage. He stormed into the room and bellowed to a robutler, "Get me Cameron! Get him now!"

"There's no need to be so upset, Director Humbolt," came the silky smooth voice from across the room. Humbolt spun and faced Cameron. The assassin sat in a chair, one lavender-colored linen-encased leg dangling indolently over the low arm. He smoothed back a vagrant strand of his sandy hair and patted it into place. All Humbolt saw were the heavy gold rings on the hand.

"Do you like this?" Cameron asked. "I had thought the Lorr lacking in even the basics of fashion, but I found this interesting cloth and had a rather good tailor make it into this for me." He held out his arms and displayed a forest green shirt with gold and silver highlights glinting in it. Large silver buttons with an eagle stamped in the metal paraded up the front to add contrast to the shirt.

"Why did you try to kill Kinsolving?" demanded Humbolt. "I don't care about your damned clothing. Why did you try to kill my mine supervisor?"

"I thought the matter had been settled, Director." Cameron swung his leg off the chair arm and lounged back, strong fingers tented just under his chin. "Do you think I would look more dashing with a beard? Nothing ostentatious, mind you. Just a small goatee?"

"Damn your facial hair!" shrieked Humbolt. Fists clenched, Humbolt forced control on himself. Only when he had regained control did he continue. "Answer me. Why did you try to kill Kinsolving?"

"Director, you had been told that Fremont instructed me to handle matters as I saw fit. It was obvious that Kinsolving's removal facilitated much." Cameron's expression changed from mocking amusement to something harder. "Why did I *try* to kill him?"

"You failed. He's still alive," Humbolt said, revelling in the assassin's surprise and chagrin. "You failed. Villalobos' pet killer failed. How will that look to Fremont?"

"What happened? I had planned this carefully. The computer results showed a ninety-five percent confidence level of success." Cameron eyed Humbolt coldly. "You intervened. You did something to thwart my plan to carry out Chairman Fremont's wishes."

"I arrived just as your explosives went off." Humbolt heaved a deep breath. "It's been quite a few years since I've been down in a mine, but I haven't forgotten how to run a robominer."

"You dug him out."

"He would have been free within another hour, even without my aid. If I had never appeared, Kinsolving would still be alive."

"Impossible. The explosive would have collapsed the entire stoop."

"It didn't. And he had repaired the robominer in the stoop and aimed it at the rock fall."

"The air. It wouldn't have been sufficient."

"It was. Kinsolving is used to the conditions in a mine. He had a respirator with him. What else would you expect of a man going to investigate on anomalous radon leak?"

"The respirator shouldn't have been enough. It doesn't *supply* oxygen, does it?" Cameron rubbed a forefinger along the line of his jaw as he worried over the problem. "He can be removed in other ways that appear to be accidental."

"You are not listening, Cameron. Kinsolving will *not* be removed under any circumstance. When I arrived and heard of his...misfortune...I retrieved him."

Cameron eyed the director coldly.

"You work for Interstellar Materials," Humbolt said, now in control. "I need Kinsolving alive. I order you *not* to harm him. If you don't like it, take my orders to the chairman."

"Chairman Fremont has given me orders contrary to yours," Cameron said lightly. "Are you recommending that I ignore him?"

"I'm recommending that you allow me to do my job. A clumsy attempt to remove Kinsolving almost ruined my plans for him. The chairman won't have any complaints when I am finished on Deepdig. No one loyal to IM and adhering to the Plan will be dissatisfied."

"What is it you want from me, Director Humbolt?"

Humbolt felt a rush of excitement. Cameron would never be his pawn, not with players the caliber of Maria Villalobos in the game, but it would be possible to use Cameron to his benefit.

This time.

Humbolt smiled and went to his desk. Sitting down, he lounged back and stared up at the skylight, considering how best to phrase his orders. "Your talents will be required in less than a day, I am sure. It would be nice if you had a few of your tracking robots ready. I foresee extreme problems brewing at Deepdig number two." Humbolt smiled even more. "It might even be a new disaster for us."

"Supervisor Kinsolving dies?"

"Not at all. The Bizzies might have the wrong people jailed for tax evasion and the other tedious crimes against Lorr law. Wouldn't that be a shame?"

"Chairman Fremont, shall we say, *requested* that Barton Kinsolving be removed permanently. Our chairman feels that the man is a danger to the Plan."

"The Plan will prevail. And Barton Kinsolving will be in no position to harm either IM or the Plan. In fact, he will aid the Plan."

"What more can we ask, eh?" said Cameron.

"Nothing more. Prepare your equipment, Mr. Cameron. When everything comes together—soon—it will be needed in a hurry."

"It will be a true pleasure, Director, to demonstrate my expertise once again for the good of IM and the Plan."

Humbolt said nothing, his eyes flashing from the assassin to the door, giving Cameron a silent dismissal. He watched as the particolored fop strode across the room and vanished. Humbolt kept from laughing in relief, the nervous strain removed.

When he succeeded on Deepdig, perhaps he could find a way of using Cameron against Villalobos to permanently remove her as a director. Perhaps,

perhaps. Humbolt turned to finish last-minute preparations. Kinsolving was due at the prison soon, or so said the computer projections based on the man's personality. Kenneth Humbolt wanted everything to be ready when the mine supervisor arrived.

CHAPTER EIGHT

BARTON KINSOLVING needed to know. Nothing of the past few weeks made any sense to him. Life had been easy—good—before the mine accident, before Ala Markken had tried to kill him, before everything had fallen into ruin.

Kinsolving's anger rose and faded as he guided the car across the countryside. Being out of control wouldn't help. He had to keep his emotions in check and learn. *Learn,* he thought with some bitterness. He knew enough now to be upset and hurt. Finding out all the details might hurt even more. But not to know the truth would haunt him the rest of his life.

Ala loved him. He was sure of that. And he still loved her. It hadn't been easy for him to fall in love initially, and he now refused to stop in spite of all that had happened.

"Must be an explanation. Must be," he muttered over and over. With automatic skill, he drove until he saw the small city looming from the grassy prairie. The Lorr presence on Deepdig had never been great, and the size of the city proved this. Hardly more than ten thousand lived here, their duties primarily that of an overseer.

What else they did on Deepdig Kinsolving couldn't say. He had never been curious enough to ask before. Ten thousand aliens weren't needed to enforce mining regulations and tariffs. The rest must do something. Support? What support did the

69

Lorr require? A small shuttle field stood seven kilometers off to the east, but the repair facilities there were minimal. IM's workers outnumbered the Lorr two to one.

Kinsolving had driven past the prison building many times in his tenure on Deepdig but had never been inside. Now he idled the car and went up the steep steps not made for human legs. Kinsolving puffed and panted before he finished scaling them.

To the guard just inside the door he said, "I want to talk to a prisoner. Ala Markken."

"No visitors, human," the guard snapped.

Kinsolving had spent a lifetime dealing with petty functionaries. Alien or human didn't matter. They all thought in the same patterns, had the same concerns. Protecting their private power domains ranked highest in their universe and anyone challenging their authority was not only suspect but was the enemy.

"I need to speak with her. Can you help me with the proper procedure?" This got him noticed. Any appeal to superior ability—allowing the bureaucrat to function—got noticed.

"Down the corridor, to the left, to the left again. See the watch commander."

"Thank you, Lieutenant," Kinsolving said. He had no idea what the Lorr's rank might be, but he knew that an officer wouldn't be standing guard duty. The inflated rank inflated the guard's ego. He gruffly motioned Kinsolving into the depths of the prison.

Smiling slightly at this minor victory, Kinsolving knew it would be only a matter of waiting, patience and humoring the Lorr before he got to see Ala. Not for the first time Kinsolving silently thanked his professor in xeno relations for the tough semesters and the needed experience gained in dealing with aliens.

"Watch Commander?" Kinsolving asked.

The Lorr seated behind a desk that seemed more a single plank set on two sawhorses glared at him. Kinsolving repeated all he'd said before, offered to fill out the paperwork, complimented the alien repeatedly—and an hour later was shown into a small, bare cell where Ala Markken sat cross-legged on the floor.

"Ala!" he exclaimed. He bit back his outrage at the conditions until the watch commander had left. To complain would only worsen the woman's stay. "This is awful!"

She had been stripped to the waist and a solid steel chain fastened firmly about her middle. The end of the chain had been bolted into the wall. Ala could stand and move almost a meter before coming to the end of her bonds. Of sanitary facilities, Kinsolving saw none.

"First time to visit a Bizzie holding pen?" she asked. The anger and bitterness he'd expected were seriously absent.

"I'll try to get you some furniture—and free from the chain. God! They can't do this to you."

"It gets cold in here at night, being naked like this," she said, folding her arms over her breasts. "But there's nothing sexual about it. Not with the Lorr. They treat all their prisoners the same. That's what our treaty with them says."

"What about sanitary facilities. They must..."

"They let us use the facilities down the hall twice a day. I have to plan." She smiled weakly. "But then, what else do I have to do?"

"I'll do something. Get you out. There has to be bail. Why hasn't Humbolt bailed you out?"

"There's no bail in the Lorr legal system. Anyone arrested is assumed guilty, so why let loose preconvicted felons? Besides, darling Bart, I *have* been tried and convicted. You remember the trial?"

"There must be an appeal."

"We're dealing with Bizarres," she said. "We don't share the same criminal systems."

"You don't need to be insulting to them. This is all—it's a mistake. I'll take care of it."

"Why?" she asked, cocking her head to one side. Once-lustrous hair fell in grimy ropes and her face needed a good washing, but her eyes were still sharp and clear—and accusing. "You're talking to the woman who tried to kill you. I stole all that ore. I'm a desperate criminal, not your lover."

Kinsolving went to her, dropped to his knees and threw his arms around her. For an instant, she resisted, then relaxed and flowed against him as she always had before. Her body shook and salty tears dampened his shoulder. But when she pulled away, she had herself under control once more.

"Why are you here, Bart?"

"I love you. I don't know why you stole the ore. I don't even care."

"And trying to kill you?"

"Why, Ala? You must have had a reason. Explain it to me. Make me understand. I want to try."

She pushed entirely free of his arms and sat with her bare back pressed into the cold stone corner of the cell. Her dark eyes fixed on his and she said in an even voice, "You have so many endearing qualities. I *do* love you, Bart, but you can't understand. You just can't. It's not in you."

"Please."

She heaved a deep breath and her eyes dropped. "All right. You wondered what I did with the thousands of kilos of ore I pirated. It went off-planet on IM's regularly scheduled ships. I was ordered by IM to steal the rare earths."

"To avoid paying the Lorr their duties and severance taxes? But that's a minor expense compared with the benefit of the metals."

"I didn't expect you to understand." She heaved another deep sigh. "IM doesn't want the Bizzies to know how much we are really lifting. If they did, they'd close down the mines to prevent us from building more starships."

"What do the Lorr care?"

"Not just the Lorr. All the Bizarres. They want to hold Earth back. They want to keep us humans a second-rate race. But we won't let them. The extra samarium is going into stardrive engines they know nothing about. We'll expand and beat them at their own game!"

Ala's passion couldn't be denied. A flush tinted her cheeks, and her eyes now blazed with the fanaticism of a religious convert. One of the strongest influences on Kinsolving and his view of the universe came from Professor Delgado's xeno culture course. Everything he held to be an indisputable fact he heard Ala Markken denying.

"They're not evil." He looked at the way Ala was chained. "They just don't do things the way we do. Different histories, different ideas."

He paused when she didn't answer. "Why did you try to kill me?"

"Orders."

"From Humbolt?"

Ala nodded. Licking her lips and pulling her knees in close to her body, she said, "I didn't want to, Bart. You'll never know how hard it was for me to do it. Maybe that's why you're still alive. I . . . I unconsciously didn't do my best. I made mistakes that allowed you to live." She smiled a little and added, "I'm glad for that. If only you'd see it our way."

"So Humbolt shares your twisted view of the Lorr?"

"Of all aliens!" she flared. "You fool! They want to see us eradicated like vermin. I'm not going to let them. Oh, no, I won't let them! No one who believes in the Plan will!"

"The Plan?" he asked.

"Leave me alone. Go drain the mine. Do what you do best, Bart. Just don't come to see me again."

"What's this Plan?"

Ala Markken pulled her knees even tighter to her chest and rested her forehead on her knees. Kinsolving saw that she'd not speak to him again. He stood, heart threatening to explode in his chest. Calling for the watch commander and being let out of the cell, he left on putty-weak legs. Once, as he went down the corridor toward the alien's office, Kinsolving had to reach out and support himself. The watch commander swiveled on his strangely hinged knees and simply stared. Kinsolving failed to read any expression.

"Why do you keep her like that? Chained like an animal?"

"She is."

Kinsolving tried to hit the Lorr, but the alien's reflexes were far too fast. Kinsolving's fist missed by centimeters. The Lorr grabbed Kinsolving's wrist and jerked hard enough to send the human sprawling.

"Leave. Now. What the prisoner told you—believe it. Do not return here."

"You were listening!"

The Lorr pointed toward the door leading back the way Kinsolving had entered. Kinsolving got to his feet, even shakier than before, and obeyed the silent order. He ought to have realized that the Lorr would listen to any conversation. Ala was a prisoner and therefore denied all rights, even to common decency.

Kinsolving shook himself when he got outside. He couldn't judge the aliens by Earth standards. Most stargoing cultures treated criminals with more brutality than the Lorr. But in spite of Ala's order to never see her again, Kinsolving knew he wouldn't stop trying to free her. She had tried to kill him, she had robbed the Lorr of taxes—and he still loved her. He knew that a few weeks away from Humbolt and IM and Deepdig with him would work miracles. Ala Markken had been duped into this theft, possibly by Kenneth Humbolt.

And if not by Humbolt, then by others high up in IM's power structure. Kinsolving believed her when she said that the pilfered ore left Deepdig on IM freighters. The Lorr's surveillance satellite network around the planet would prevent any regular boosting of the rare earth oxides to pirate freighters.

Kinsolving refused to get back into his vehicle. Instead he walked the city streets aimlessly, trying to think, failing at it. Nothing came together properly in his mind. Kinsolving prided himself on logical, orderly thought processes. None of this seemed logical. Facts were missing. And Ala remained in prison.

Somehow Kinsolving's path took him to the solitary building where Kenneth Humbolt had established his office. He couldn't trust the IM director—not after Ala's revelation of the man's complicity and guilt—but he needed Humbolt's cooperation to free Ala. There was no other way.

Starting up the steps, Kinsolving paused and studied the street running perpendicular to the one he'd approached on. A large official Lorr vehicle was parked there. Two armed guards lounged against the fender, trading off-color jokes. Kinsolving shook his head. They might appear more birdlike than humans and have those bizarre amber, pupilless eyes but they were so similar in behavior.

Was he the only human who saw the similarities rather than the differences? What lies had Professor Delgado burned into his brain?

Kinsolving knew they weren't lies. Delgado had taught the truth, the only way that Earth might cfassume its place among the older, better established alien races.

Loud voices made Kinsolving hurry up the steps and slip inside the partially opened door, seeking the first refuge he could find. Just inside a sitting room he listened to the argument going on farther down the hall in the room Humbolt used for an office.

"It's proof, Agent-General. Look at it. Those six are innocent. They were nothing more than dupes."

"Following orders?" the Lorr demanded.

"They were ignorant. You have convicted the wrong ones. Examine the documents."

Kinsolving peered about and saw no one. On light feet he went to the opened office door and hazarded a quick glance inside. The Lorr agent-general stood swivelling to and fro on his universal joint knees, fingers rubbing along the side of the folder Humbolt had thrust across the desk.

"Why do you do this?"

"Interstellar Materials does not wish to see innocent employees punished. We have nothing but contempt for anyone stealing from you—and our company."

The agent-general nodded. Kinsolving saw that his final touch to the argument convinced the alien. Humans would steal from the Lorr, but they wanted revenge when humans stole from other humans. The logic appealed even to Kinsolving.

"We will examine these documents. If they reveal the data you claim, your six employees will be released and compensation delivered in accordance with our established procedures for such inequities."

"I am certain that IM will wish to contribute any such money to the Lorr to defray the loss caused by our thieving employee."

"That is another matter." The agent-general almost caught Kinsolving by surprise. Without a word of leave-taking, he swung about and started for the door. Not wanting to be caught spying, Kinsolving ducked down behind a table and pressed his sweaty back into the wall, trying to vanish. He succeeded enough that the Lorr stalked by him without even glancing down.

When the Lorr exited, Kinsolving heaved himself to his feet and went into Humbolt's office. He had never cared for the man, but if the director had evidence to free Ala Markken and the others, Kinsolving wanted to thank him.

Humbolt glanced up as Kinsolving entered, an expression mingling surprise and fear on his features.

"Supervisor," Humbolt said, almost stuttering, "I didn't expect you so soon."

"So soon?"

"I left a message for you with—what's his name? McClanahan. Yes, that's it. I told him to have you report here as soon as possible. But I just transmitted a code message. He's hardly had time to decipher, much less contact you."

"Code message? Did it have something to do with the evidence clearing Ala and the others?"

"Well, yes. Sit down, Kinsolving—Bart. This isn't easy for me, but please believe me when I say that IM has your best interests at stake in this sorry matter."

Kinsolving frowned. "What information could you give the Lorr to exonerate Ala?" She had confessed to Kinsolving. He knew she had committed the crimes.

"We decided to trade six employees for one. Wait!" Humbolt cried, holding up his hand when Kinsolving rocketed from the chair. "It's not like that at all. The documents I gave the Bizzie incriminate you.

That's true. As mine supervisor, you had the opportunity and means."

"You sold me out?"

"It means freeing Ala," Humbolt said, shrewdness in his every word.

"And letting me rot in their prison in her place!"

"Wait!" Humbolt's command froze Kinsolving. "Sit down and keep quiet. Time is important."

Kinsolving sat down, seething inside at the injustice.

"The Lorr needed someone to pin the blame on. They'd never allow Markken and the others to go free without finding a guilty party. The documents I handed over are fakes, but good ones. Ala Markken will be released; you will be the sole criminal in Lorr eyes."

"And?" asked Kinsolving, not knowing what to expect.

"And you will be long gone from Deepdig and far beyond Lorr justice. We're transferring you back to GT 4 immediately. There are other worlds requiring your special talents."

"How do you intend getting me there? The Lorr control access to Deepdig. Even more tightly now that this ore piracy has become known."

"We have a ship waiting at the spaceport right now for you. Go directly there and we'll boost you to a waiting speedster—it's mine."

"You'll tell the Lorr I stole it?"

"A nice touch." Humbolt tapped out a notation on his console. "That'll give even more credence to the story. You'll be back on GT 4, and Ala will join you soon."

"I don't like being made the scapegoat for all that's happened here. I know you ordered her to steal the oxides."

Humbolt's face hardened. "There is no other way

to free her. Or would you rather allow her to die in
the Bizzie jail? She drew a forty-year sentence."

Kinsolving sat speechless. He'd never heard the
sentence, just the guilty verdict. He couldn't allow
Ala to spend forty years in such conditions.

"She tried to kill me," he said in a voice almost
too low for Humbolt to hear.

"An unfortunate business, that," said Humbolt.
"But you really have no other choice but to go directly to the spaceport. My scheme has been set into
motion. The agent-general is not likely to believe
me if I tell him the documents he has are all for-
geries, not when it means a jail term for me. Forg-
ery and lying to a Lorr senior field officer are both
felonies."

"She'll be along soon?"

"Within a month or so," Humbolt assured him.

"I don't like this. I don't like my name being
smeared."

"You'll like prison even less if you don't hurry. Go,
Bart, go! Now!"

"Who do I contact?" Kinsolving asked.

"A man named Cameron. He's waiting for you,"
said Humbolt. The director rose and thrust out his
hand. Hesitantly, Kinsolving shook it.

"Go. Hurry," urged Humbolt.

"Cameron?" asked Kinsolving, still unsure.

"Ask for no one else."

Kinsolving left at a run. It all made sense. Humbolt covered his part in the ore theft by pinning the
blame on Kinsolving. But to IM it made no difference since if Ala was to be believed, the company
ended up with all the rare earths. Kinsolving might
even be greeted as a hero. The Lorr would have
been thwarted and all IM personnel freed from their
stinking jails.

But Barton Kinsolving still worried. He felt he
was missing something.

CHAPTER NINE

BARTON KINSOLVING drove too fast, taking
turns in the road with reckless abandon, but the
pressure of time weighed heavily on him. He had
misjudged Humbolt; the director actually cared
about his employees. All his employees. Although
Kinsolving didn't like being the one to carry the
guilt for the thefts at the mine, he thought over
Humbolt's scheme and decided it was workable.

The Lorr would never release Ala and the others
without a bigger criminal in custody.

Kinsolving had to be that criminal.

He tensed as the vehicle skidded and ran over the
edge of the roadway. For an instant the repulsor
field faded when it failed to find the flat surface it
expected. Auxiliary power cut in and held the vehicle up until Kinsolving wrestled it back onto the
roadway. When the familiar hum returned and the
whine vanished, he accelerated once more. He could
have put it on automatic but the safety limiting circuits wouldn't have allowed such a breakneck pace.

Kinsolving trembled at the need to get away from
Deepdig. The spaceport came up suddenly as he
topped a low rise. The complex spread out for kilometers toward the east and north, most of it belonging to Interstellar Materials. Several of the stubby
dark gray carbon-composite-hulled shuttles stood at
the near side of the field, their blue and gold

trident-and-star insignia gleaming in the pale sunlight.

Slowing slightly, Kinsolving guided the vehicle to
a spot where the Lorr guards at the field wouldn't
notice his approach. A dozen or more roads led into
the field, most of them normally filled with heavy
ore transports from the two rare earth mines. Those
the Lorr guards checked for exit permits and tax
stamps. Individual vehicles mattered little to them.

For that Kinsolving thanked his lucky stars.

He pulled up next to a corrugated shed and idled
the vehicle. He wouldn't need it again. Kinsolving
closed his eyes and mentally pictured the shuttle
launch, the heavy pulsed laser beamed against the
shuttle's underside splash plate, the entire vessel
surging higher and higher until it reached orbit.
From there it would be a matter of an hour or less
to rendezvous with the speedster that had brought
Humbolt from GT 4.

"Hey, you can't park there," came a querulous
voice. "Move it or I'll dismantle the damn thing."

Kinsolving jerked, torn from his reverie. The mechanic approaching carried a small electronic circuitry work kit in one hand and a large torsion
wrench in the other.

"You deaf?"

"I don't recognize you," Kinsolving said. "I'm supervisor at mine number two."

"Kinsolving?" the man asked, his attitude changing. "Sorry. I'm new here. Just got in a few days
ago. Name's Cameron."

"You're the man I'm looking for," Kinsolving said,
relief flooding through him. "Humbolt sent me."

"He did, eh?" Cameron smiled, his mouth flaring
in the sunlight. Gold rimmed teeth and embedded
reflecting gems made Kinsolving squint. Something
about the mechanic made Kinsolving wary. His
mouth alone carried more wealth than the vast ma-

jority of people on weary, worn Earth saw in a lifetime. But the manner more than the riches so os-
tentatiously displayed put Kinsolving on his guard.

"Do you know what's been happening at the
mine?" he asked.

The mechanic smiled even broader and shook his
head. "Don't care. I take my orders from the big
boss. Whatever Mr. Humbolt says is law, far as I'm
concerned." .

This bothered Kinsolving even more. Cameron's
tone mocked, as if he knew something that no one
else did.

"Where's the shuttle? It's supposed to be ready for
immediate takeoff."

"That one. See it? The one with the white steering
fin?"

"I see it," Kinsolving said, "but it looks deserted.
There's no activity in the firing pit." Before shuttle
launch the heavy lasers required massive amounts
of liquid nitrogen coolant. The plumes of condensa-
tion were vented to either side of the shuttle. During launch the plumes became so thick it appeared
that the shuttle had developed a rocket thrust kick-
ing up dust. Only when the vessel reached an altitude of a few hundred meters did the illusion
vanish.

"Told to keep everything quiet. You running from
something?" Cameron cocked his head to one side,
as if listening for more than Kinsolving's reply.

"Just follow Mr. Humbolt's orders."

"Will do. Start hiking. By the time you get there,
the pilot'll be anxious to push the launch button."
Cameron pointed with the end of the wrench. Kinsolving started walking, only looking back when
he'd gone a few paces.

Cameron had vanished into the building. On impulse, Kinsolving reversed his path, stopping just

outside the door. From inside he heard Cameron's voice plainly.

"Is it wrong to obey the law, Agent-Captain?"

"No," came a Lorr's deep voice. "But why do you insist on obeying *our* law? This fugitive might have escaped. Are you a traitor to your own kind?"

Cameron laughed. "No sir, nothing like that." Kinsolving winced at the viciousness carried in those words. "But Director Humbolt ordered us all to obey your law to the letter. Said we've had enough trouble, and he wants to smooth out relations between the company and you...people."

"Shuttle twenty-three is the fugitive's destination?"

"That's right. You can pick him up easily enough. He took off walking. Be a good ten minutes to get to the shuttle."

"When is your shuttle due to launch?"

Cameron laughed louder. "Not for a week or more. Got a busted steering vane and a fused control circuit that looks like glass. Couldn't lift if it had to."

Kinsolving looked around frantically. Cameron had betrayed him. Or had it been Humbolt? His mind raced, tiny pieces that had troubled him falling into a more coherent picture. Other than Humbolt's arrival weeks ago, there hadn't been any new IM personnel grounding on Deepdig. Cameron couldn't have just come in, as he claimed. And Kinsolving knew most of the ground crew by name and the rest by sight from his many trips here to ferry the ore into orbit.

It had to be Humbolt who betrayed him. He'd ordered him to seek out Cameron.

Kinsolving ran to the vehicle and powered it up. If shuttle twenty-three wasn't the one for him, another would do. Get off Deepdig, get into orbit, hijack Humbolt's speedster and get away. Back on GT

4 things would look different. Humbolt might try to throw him to the Lorr in exchange for Ala Markken and the others, but Kinsolving thought he might be able to follow the spurious plan—and still come out a free man.

The vehicle powered up, Kinsolving shoved the throttle forward to the maximum position. Acceleration slammed him into the cushions and caused a cloud of dust to rise from the tarmac. He rotated about the vehicle's vertical axis as he changed direction and headed for the far side of the launch field. The telltale plumes of nitrogen liquid turning to vapor came from beneath shuttle seventeen.

But Kinsolving's heart turned into ice when he saw that the shuttle didn't prepare for liftoff. Technicians worked on the launch laser, testing its cooling system.

"Hey, McKenna!" Kinsolving called to the head technician. "Are any of the shuttles ready to go up?"

The woman peered up from her work. "Hi, Bart. Can't say any are. Humbolt's been riding us hard about routine maintenance ever since he grounded. Won't be a launch for another week. You needing to get into orbit?"

"Right now," he said. The woman brushed back dark hair shot with strands of gray and shook her head.

"No time soon. We do have a small shuttle to reach Humbolt's speedster if he needs it. But it'll take about six hours to launch."

"Not good enough," he said.

"What's the hurry?"

"Too many problems," he said. "Say, do you know anything about the new mechanic? Cameron's his name."

"Cameron? Never heard of him. Or do you mean Carmen? She's over in shipping." The woman smiled. "She's still got it bad for you. She'd like nothing better than to console you about Ala."

"Can't a man have any secrets in this place?" he said with mock anger. The sound of sirens turned him cold inside. "Got to run."

"Bart, wait. Are they coming after you? We can hide you in the laser pit."

"Can't stay. If they ask after me, tell them everything." Kinsolving slammed the throttle forward again. He didn't want to get McKenna or any of her crew in trouble with the Lorr. That the aliens were racing across the tarmac with sirens blaring showed that they were on his trail.

"Not much of a trail," he muttered to himself as he weaved in and out of buildings and idled shuttles. Kinsolving worked at the wheel with grim concentration, but the Lorr inexorably narrowed the distance between vehicles. The fleeing human found himself circling about and returning to the same building where he'd met Cameron.

A new determination filled Kinsolving. He'd never be able to elude the Lorr. Out on this prairie they could see him for kilometers and kilometers. But he might have a few minutes before they caught him.

Those few minutes might be well spent beating the truth out of Cameron. The pleasure of breaking those gold-rimmed teeth appealed to Kinsolving in a savage way. It might not gain him anything—except needed emotional release—but he'd see.

He killed the repulsor field and let the vehicle slide along the ground on its underside. Fat blue sparks leaped into space as metal tore off and the car crashed into the side of the building. Kinsolving exploded from the interior in time to get his feet. Cameron came from inside, a curious expression on his face.

Kinsolving swung and connected with the man's

belly. Cameron doubled up, but the impact sent pain lancing all the way to Kinsolving's shoulder. It felt as if he'd struck a solid steel plate.

"Wh-what's wrong?" gasped Cameron.

"You turned me over to the Lorr."

"No, no! You've got it wrong! I was only doing as Mr. Humbolt wanted. Part of the escape. Send the Bizzies in the other direction so you can escape."

Kinsolving noticed that Cameron used the derogatory term for the aliens that Humbolt and Ala Markken had. He said, "Not a single shuttle is ready to launch. I talked with the technicians."

"They aren't in on this. Shuttle twenty-three's ready! Did you check it?" Cameron straightened. Kinsolving saw nothing in the man's face except for the glittering teeth and the cold, cold eyes.

"No," he admitted reluctantly.

"Then—damn! The Lorr! There they come. Quick. Hide inside. I'll try to decoy them away. Do it!"

Kinsolving obeyed the sharp command. He ducked inside and pressed himself against the inner wall, listening to what Cameron said to the alien police.

"Kinsolving. Where is he?" demanded the Lorr agent-captain. Kinsolving heard the shuffle of alien feet as four others joined Cameron. For a moment there was only silence, then a loud shriek of pain echoed across the still launch site.

Kinsolving hazarded a quick glance around the door. The agent-captain clutched his midsection, inhumanly bright crimson blood spurting around his snakelike fingers. His mouth worked to form another scream but death came first. He fell face forward onto the ground.

"There he is!" cried Cameron, pointing. "He shot your captain!"

Kinsolving got a quick glimpse of Cameron slipping a small tube into his coveralls. Then the doorway filled with angry Lorr out to avenge the death of their leader.

Kinsolving struck out, fist hitting the first Lorr directly in the mouth. The alien stumbled back, momentarily blocking the entrance. Kinsolving reeled away, unsteady on his feet. He recovered enough to dive through a window, plastic cutting at his body as he went through. He landed heavily. For an instant Kinsolving wondered why he had trouble standing. The ground seemed unnaturally slippery.

He saw a small puddle of blood from his own cuts had formed under his feet. He rolled to the side and got up. Behind him the Lorr shouted for him to halt.

The world changed around Kinsolving. Time dragged. He turned to see Cameron standing to one side, an evil smile on his lips. Lorr comically tumbled from the building. The dead agent-captain lay on the ground, muscle contractions shaking him.

Kinsolving felt as if he pushed through water to get to the Lorr vehicle. He dropped into the uncomfortable seat and slapped the throttle forward. The Lorr scattered as the car rocketed past them.

Without a vehicle to pursue him, the Lorr were temporarily stranded. But Barton Kinsolving realized the reprieve would be brief.

He had nowhere to go, no one to turn to.

CHAPTER TEN

BARTON KINSOLVING found it more difficult to
control the Lorr vehicle than he'd thought. The controls didn't respond properly and the seat was uncomfortable; it hadn't been designed for a bulky
human. Weaving and wobbling from side to side,
Kinsolving decided that he had to abandon the vehicle. The Lorr might have a tracing device inside.
He had no idea how the Lorr police might think.
Did it ever occur to them that someone might steal
their vehicle?

He doubted it.

Pulling to the side of the road, Kinsolving got out
and stretched his cramped limbs. He looked around
and knew that it would be minutes before they
found him. But he wouldn't surrender easily. He
couldn't. Cameron had murdered the agent-captain
and placed the blame all too firmly on Kinsolving.
If Ala Markken received forty years in a primitive
cell for ore theft and tax evasion. Kinsolving didn't
want to think what the punishment would be for
slaying a Lorr officer.

Forty years of torture? Kinsolving shuddered at
the idea. Earth might have problems competing
with the stargoing cultures and seem barbaric in
comparison, but criminals were treated humanely.

Humanly, Kinsolving mentally corrected. The Lorr
had their own ideas of punishment, and they didn't
seem to include rehabilitation. Did they execute

those convicted of capital offenses? He had no idea, nor did he want to find out.

Barton Kinsolving started hiking. On foot he had little chance against flyers and the repulsor-powered ground vehicles, but he might get lucky. How he had no idea.

But he had to try.

"This is a sorry chapter in human–Lorr history, Agent-General. I assure you that Interstellar Materials is not responsible, that we will do all within our power to capture this dangerous renegade." Kenneth Humbolt studied the Lorr officer to see if his lie had been accepted. It had.

"We do not understand how such a heinous crime could be committed," the Lorr said. "We do not slay each other. From all evidence, including the witness of your mechanic, this Kinsolving took a small explosive pellet weapon and fired it into the belly of the agent-captain."

Cameron nodded slowly, as if remembering a painful event in his life. "It was a silver tube, not twenty centimeters long. I heard a sound behind me, saw Supervisor Kinsolving in the doorway with it in his hand—and then he fired! There was only a small noise, then your officer doubled over holding his stomach." Cameron smirked in spite of the sour look that Humbolt shot him.

"What can we do to aid your search for him?" Humbolt asked.

"You need do nothing. My surveillance teams hunt him now. They will find him."

Humbolt shifted nervously from one foot to the other. "Uh, Agent-General, it's been several hours since you found the vehicle Kinsolving stole. Is there any progress in *capturing* him?"

"We are not used to conducting such hunts. None in my command can remember one; I contacted my superior. She cannot remember such a search, either."

"I again offer the full Interstellar Materials equipment and personnel for your official use, Agent-General. My mechanic is skilled in many areas. Perhaps he could construct a robot able to find Kinsolving's trail."

"Yes," cut in Cameron, suddenly eager for the hunt. "I know of certain ways that ordinary robot maintenance machines can be converted to efficient hunters."

"How is this possible?" the Lorr asked, face contorting in thought.

"Certain devices. Infrared scanners to follow heat imprints, footprints on the ground."

"This Kinsolving is hours gone."

"My sensors are capable of detecting a trail hours old." Cameron almost lost his temper. Humbolt motioned him to silence. The assassin paid him no heed. "There are other devices. Scent detectors. The slightest pheromone profile is traceable, after days or even weeks. I've found men in the midst of huge cities."

"For what reason?" asked the Agent-General. "Are you a policeman for Interstellar Materials?"

"Uh, no, nothing of that sort. This is . . . a hobby."

"I do not understand the word." The Lorr turned to an assistant, who worked feverishly at a translation computer. He showed the screen to his superior, who shook his head like a bird pecking at a worm. "There is no analog in our language for this 'hobby.'"

"That's not important," Humbolt cut in. "Please let us try to find Kinsolving for you."

"You do not seek this one of your own kind to aid in off-planet escape?" The Lorr seemed perplexed at this turn.

"Agent-General, my most fervent hope is that he

is brought to justice." Humbolt waited until the alien bobbed his head once more in agreement.

"Do what you will, but two of my officers will accompany your Cameron on the search."

"We wouldn't have it any other way," said Humbolt. For the first time, relief flooded throughout his body and allowed him to relax. When the alien left, Humbolt spun and faced Cameron.

"You fool! Don't be so damned eager. And try not to give away technology to them. They don't seem to have the IR detectors or SAWS for their robots."

"I know that part of the Plan," Cameron said. "There is no need to lecture me, Director."

"The Plan," mused Humbolt. "The damned Plan. You know that Markken spoke of it to Kinsolving?"

Cameron's eyebrows rose. "I had no idea. I would have burned him instead of the Bizzie if I'd known."

"She had no reason for mentioning it. He made her angry and it slipped out. She will have to be disciplined for that, but it won't be anything severe. Markken and the others will be rotated back to GT 4 when this matter with Kinsolving is settled."

"Could I be the one to discipline her?" asked Cameron. "She..."

"No!" Humbolt snapped. "She will play a larger role in the future. Markken has done well here. She's kept the Bizzies from bleeding us to death with their severance taxes, and the samarium from her thefts insures us of millions of brain-burners." Humbolt smiled crookedly. "She thinks the rare earths will be used only for a full fleet of starships otherwise denied us. She may yet learn the true use for the rare earths. Markken will do well for IM and the Plan in the future."

"And perhaps an ambitious director of Interstellar Materials has personal plans for her?" Cameron suggested.

"That is none of your concern. Get your robots out

and find that son of a bitch before the Bizzies do. I don't want him telling them anything he might have guessed about the Plan."

Cameron waved off the suggestion of ruin. "He is discredited in their amber eyes. Nothing your former supervisor has to say will be believed." Cameron's laugh echoed throughout the building.

"I hope so—for your sake." With that, Kenneth Humbolt stalked out. Cameron's mocking laugh followed him as he left.

Kinsolving couldn't believe his luck. He had hardly abandoned the Lorr vehicle when a heavily laden truck came along the road. As the repulsor field under the truck strained to hold the vehicle upright and propel its mass up the steep hill, Kinsolving raced out from his cover by the road and jumped onto the back. He almost lost his grip when the truck topped the hill and sped downward.

A quick twist and Kinsolving got into the back. The stench made him want to vomit, but he held down his rising gorge. He'd stowed away on a garbage truck from the city. Trying to decide where it was headed, Kinsolving rested and collected his wits. Events had moved too swiftly to do anything but react.

It was now time to reflect.

"Humbolt and IM want me dead—or in Lorr prison," he said. "Why? To cover up Ala's thefts?" He couldn't believe that. Kinsolving didn't delude himself for an instant. For the huge corporation his skills were more valuable than Ala's or any of the others'.

Or were they? The woman had mentioned a mysterious plan. The Plan, she had said. Kinsolving had heard the capital letters as she spoke. Interstellar Materials had to be involved; Kenneth Humbolt knew the details. They cheated the Lorr out of taxes, and Ala had mentioned that IM was responsible. Did IM have a secret construction project to build starships that the aliens knew nothing about?

"A war fleet?" Kinsolving mused. The idea of interstellar war had been one hotly debated when he'd been in college. The logistics presented problems no race could overcome. The distances were too great, the physics of the stardrive too cumbersome to move enough troops and materiel—and why lay waste to an entire planet? Wars were not simply killing your enemy. Something had to be gained.

Could Ala and Humbolt and the others at IM be so hostile toward all aliens that they'd consider planetary bombardment and genocide? Kinsolving found that difficult to believe. Stargoing races weren't clustered on single planets. To destroy all aliens would require resources far exceeding anything Earth could hope to muster.

Kinsolving snorted in disgust. Earth barely fed its own people. Jobs were scarce and many scholars pointed to this century as a new Dark Ages. This wasn't the time to raise the banner for a new crusade against aliens.

Or was it?

He rose and peered out the rear of the truck when it began to slow. Kinsolving didn't hesitate. He jumped and rolled to the side of the road rather than wait for eventual discovery. Rising up, he looked around. The truck had come to the Lorr sanitary torch where debris was fed into a plasma jet. The resulting increase in heat helped power the unit, making it partially self-sustaining.

"Garbage. I almost ended up as garbage."

He made his way across the gently rolling hills, taking a few minutes' break every hour to rest. Kinsolving had no idea where he went. Just getting away from the Lorr topped the list of priorities.

After he had found a secure hideout, he could worry about IM and Humbolt and the rest of the puzzle.

Standing atop a low hill, he looked toward the sunset. Dust had risen earlier in the day as a brisk wind came up, making the sunset gorgeous. He remembered the days he and Ala had watched the sunsets. A lump rose in his throat.

Those days were gone.

Kinsolving had no hint that anyone was closer than a hundred kilometers to him when a slight scraping sound caused him to turn. He then heard the hum from the robot as its repulsor field drove it up the hillside and bowled him over. He fought but the robot body had been electrified. The lightest touch made him wince. The robot powered down atop him. The shock he received stunned him.

Through a haze he saw Cameron and two Lorr standing over him. Cameron laughed and laughed and laughed.

Barton Kinsolving passed out.

"There is no honor in this sentence," the agent-general intoned. "Usual court procedure is for three officers to sit in final judgment." Kinsolving noted that seven were on the court. That made the matter even more serious.

He looked around the small room. Ala Markken sat with her hands folded in her lap, eyes straight ahead. He tried to catch her gaze and failed. On either side of her sat Cameron and Kenneth Humbolt. Both men looked satisfied with themselves.

Kinsolving wished he could free himself of the bonds holding him to the floor long enough to strangle both men. His mind turned over different ways of killing them, of which to kill first. He couldn't decide who would die first. Humbolt had betrayed him. The plot to fake the murder and turn the Lorr on his trail reeked of Humbolt's political manipulations. But Cameron had actually slain the Lorr officer. The expression of sheer delight on the man's face had told Kinsolving that Cameron was a psychopathic killer, the likes of which he had only heard of roaming about in the worst sections of Earth cities.

"We have reached a unanimous decision," the agent-general said. "Normal crimes are punishable by local imprisonment. This is no ordinary crime." The Lorr shivered delicately. "You are sentenced to life imprisonment on the world with no name."

Kinsolving frowned. He had no idea what this meant. Looking over his shoulder, he saw that Humbolt rose from his seat to protest. Cameron reached across and tugged on the director's sleeve and whispered for several seconds.

Kinsolving had no idea what they discussed, but it had to be the severity of his sentence. Humbolt had wanted the death penalty to remove all problems posed by Kinsolving's existence. But Cameron had convinced him that this sentence was as good.

Kinsolving shuddered at the idea of imprisonment worse than that the Lorr used on Ala Markken and the others.

"Agent-General," he spoke up. "What is the world with no name?"

The Lorr made a hand-whipping gesture. When he spoke it was to Humbolt and not to Kinsolving. "The world with no name is a planet used by many starfaring races. Only a select few know its location. Exile to this world is permanent. Starships land prisoners. No one ever leaves the world. Ever."

Kinsolving had never heard of such a planet. He tried to protest but Lorr guards unfastened the chains binding him to the floor and dragged him out of the room. For a brief instant, his eyes locked with Ala's.

Tears welled and ran down her cheeks. Other than this, she betrayed no emotion.

In shock, Kinsolving allowed his captors to shove him into a vehicle. In twenty minutes he was on a Lorr shuttle lifting for orbit. In forty, the starship shifted for the world with no name.

CHAPTER ELEVEN

BARTON KINSOLVING allowed the Lorr to do
with him as they desired. The shock he felt at the
repeated betrayals robbed him of all will until the
alien starship shifted into orbit around the planet
they refused to name.

Kinsolving experienced the gut-wrenching hyperspace transition and struggled to keep from vomit-
ing. With his hands securely chained and another
loop of chain around his waist fastened to a deck
plate he wasn't able to move easily.

"Please," he called weakly from between chapped
lips. The Lorr hadn't fed him or given him a drop of
water since the sentence had been passed on Deepdig. Kinsolving tried to guess how long ago that had
been and could only estimate four days. "Where are
we?"

"Your home," snapped his guard. The alien sat in
a comfortable couch and stared suspiciously at him,
as if he'd get up and run away. Even if he could
manage such a feat, as weak and battered emotionally as he was, Kinsolving had nowhere to go.

Interstellar Materials was no longer his employer. Kenneth Humbolt had betrayed him. His
lover Ala Markken had forsaken him. The mysterious, murderous Cameron had made it seem that
he'd committed a crime that had resulted in his
exile. Kinsolving had nowhere to turn.

"What is it? Where is it?"

"The planet with no name," the guard said. "Only a few know its location. We use it for our...debris."

Kinsolving started to protest his innocence, then stopped. It would do no good. Even if the guard believed him—and there was no reason that he would—Kinsolving gained nothing. Every beat of his heart took a little more strength. He slumped back to the cold metal deck plate and curled up in the fetal position he had assumed throughout the four-day trip.

Four days. The alien starships were more efficient than those built on Earth. Somehow they escaped what, for Earth scientists, were "speed limits" in hyperspace, much as the speed of light limited travel in four-space. Kinsolving tried to decide if they'd come a hundred light years or a thousand from Deepdig.

In the end he came to the sorry conclusion that it no longer mattered. He believed the guard when he said that the location of the prison planet was a secret. And who would want to rescue Barton Kinsolving? Everything was tied up in such a neat, presentable package with him rotting on some forsaken planet tucked away at the edge of the universe.

Interstellar Materials maintained its rare earth mines on Deepdig. Ala and the others were cleared of the felony charges. And the Lorr believed they had brought the guilty party to justice, not only for killing an agent-captain but also for the heinous crime of tax evasion and stealing oxide ores.

And it was all part of what Ala Markken had called the Plan. Like the prison planet below the orbiting starship, this, too, was a secret, a mystery, something Kinsolving would never discover before he died.

"Out," came the guard's rough command. Tentaclelike fingers circled Kinsolving's wrists and pulled him erect. Try as he might, Kinsolving couldn't get his muscles to obey. He sank back to the deck. Resolve not to show weakness in the face of such adversity made him stand on shaking legs. This time he did not collapse. The guard shoved him roughly through a passageway to a shuttle. When Kinsolving could no longer walk, the guard grabbed the chains and dragged him.

By the time the shuttle touched down on the planet's surface, Kinsolving was more dead than alive.

"Your new home. May you live long and suffer horribly." The guard heaved Kinsolving out the small hatchway and slammed it behind immediately. The man pulled himself up to a sitting position. The world swung in crazy circles around him. He heard fuel pumps working to feed the ignition chambers in the tiny shuttle.

It came to him through the thick mist of confusion and abuse that he would be fried unless he avoided the shuttle's rocket blast. No laser powered this ship into orbit. There wasn't even a formal landing field. Some grass had been scorched off a patch of dirt in the prairie. This appeared to be the only hint that anyone existed—or had ever existed—on the face of the planet.

Kinsolving struggled to drag himself away from the shuttle. The hot exhaust gases scorched his back and set tiny fires burning in his clothing when the shuttle launched. Rolling over and over put out the fires and left Kinsolving staring up at a heavily overcast sky. The leaden clouds billowed and gathered directly above. The rains, when they came, brought Kinsolving much needed water and the surcease of unconsciousness.

* * *

"You're looking better," came the voice speaking in a guttural mangling of Interspace, the lingua franca used by a score of spacefaring races. Kinsolving tried to blink and experienced a surge of panic. "Calm, now, calm. You're not blind. Here." A rag was taken from Kinsolving's eyes. He squinted at the tiny fire blazing merrily. He reached up to rub his temples. For a moment, he worried that something was wrong.

"My chains. They're gone!" Kinsolving repeated it in Interspace, when his first words produced no response.

"Of course they are. There's no need of your going around with them, now is there? Unless you want them back? But that's not possible. Sold them. Metal's scarce."

"You sold them?" Although weak, Kinsolving felt better than he had since leaving Deepdig. He sat up and turned to face his benefactor. Kinsolving almost yelped in surprise. The creature sitting across the fire from him could hardly be described as human or even humanoid.

"Got a fair price. Wanted to split it with you, we did, but you owed, so we took your part. Only fair, only fair."

Kinsolving rubbed his wrists and reveled in the freedom he'd thought he would never again experience. And the hollowness in his belly seemed filled.

"You fed me?"

"That we did," the toadlike creature said. Long, powerful hind legs moved it around and tiny hands more human than those of the Lorr worked at a dish and spoon carved from wood. The food in the bowl vanished into a huge mouth lined with dual rows of sharp, wicked teeth. The forward-looking eyes and those needlelike teeth told Kinsolving that his rescuer was a predator and a carnivore by evolution.

"Thanks."

"Nothing on this world's free," the creature said. The sharp eyes fixed on Kinsolving and bored into his soul. "You don't think a few links of chain are enough repayment, do you?"

"Perhaps, perhaps not. I need to know something."

"Information's costly. Know things and you can do things."

"You can't eat information," said Kinsolving. "When they put me here—"

"Who is this 'they'?" asked the creature. It bobbed up and down on its strong hind legs. Kinsolving tried not to think of frog legs. His stomach rumbled at the thought of Earth food.

"The Lorr. Aren't they the ones who sent you here, too?"

"Don't know any Lorr. Might have heard of them but forgot. Too many damn races out there with their fancy laws and ways. The Rua'Kinth convicted me and sent me here. May their legs turn weak!"

"I'm Barton Kinsolving."

"Never heard of that race, either," the creature said. Kinsolving explained that this was his name, a concept the creature had obviously encountered before but hadn't successfully mastered.

"Can't understand why individual names are needed," the creature said. "We come from Sussonssa. Great hunting, good people. No rules like out there." A tiny hand pointed upward.

"Is it always overcast?" asked Kinsolving, trying to find a wink of starlight and failing.

"Always. Never seen clear skies once in more

than a year on-planet. No one else has, either. One
reason they chose it, maybe."

"What are we supposed to do? Report to a jailer?"

The creature laughed heartily at this—at least
Kinsolving hoped the strange croaking noises were
laughter.

"We go and come as we please. Eat, live, not eat,
die. It matters nothing to them. We are free to roam
the planet for the rest of our lives."

Kinsolving turned cold inside. He had harbored
some faint hope of reprieve, of bribing a guard, of
escape. Now it evaporated like mist in a sun he
would never see. The Lorr and the other alien races
simply dropped their prisoners onto this planet and
let them survive or not. If only a handful of naviga-
tors knew the location of the world, rescue attempts
would be impossible.

There were too many stars to search simply to
find one planet. And Kinsolving knew of no one interested in finding him. He was written off, a null, a
closed chapter in IM history.

"Then there aren't any laws?" asked Kinsolving.

"Only what we make. Criminals are not good at
enforcing laws. If you do not like the local laws,
move. The planet is wide and big. Travel is by foot,
but you have plenty of time. All the time left in
your life!" Again the creature laughed.

"You seem cheerful about it. Why?"

"You laugh or you cry. We laugh."

Kinsolving glanced around. As far as he could
tell, they were alone. "Why do you refer to yourself
in the plural?"

"Sussonssans are telepathic. Hard to be alone.
Only fourteen of us on this world, but from time to
time we join physically in harmony and community."

"Is there any chance you could communicate and

when the next ship lands bringing—" The creature's harsh laughter cut off Kinsolving's words.

"Not possible. Not. Always they scan the ground with sensors before landing. And the landings might happen one-two-three soon or be years apart. And they land in different places. And—"

"I get the picture," said Kinsolving, feeling glum. "How do you live?"

"Poorly, but we live."

"What do you do? Farm?"

"Hunter gatherer is all we can do. No metal, no hope of making more. Light metal planet, this one is. Your chains are valuable for what they can be made into. Why develop city? Most of us are thieves and we would only steal from each other." This struck the creature as hilarious. Tiny hands held bulging mottled gray sides as it laughed.

For the first time, Kinsolving had the sense of true desolation fall like a cloak around him. What crime had his benefactor committed? Murder? Worse? What would be worthy of lifelong exile? Tax evasion? Kinsolving didn't think that was likely.

"So we just survive as long as we can, then we die?" he asked.

"Is that not the definition of life?"

"I expect more."

"What a strange race yours is. You resemble several we have seen, but you are much uglier and stupider."

"The feeling's mutual."

The creature made a choking noise, then hopped around to hunker down beside Kinsolving by the fire. "We can do well as a team, you and we. My brains and your height will go far on this world."

"How?"

"The beast to whom we sold the chains. He has many links garnered over the years. He sharpens them and mounts them as spear heads. Some knives. We can steal these from him."

"Is this the only way to live?" asked Kinsolving.

"Why live any other? To scrabble for roots in this desolate place is difficult. The grains growing wild are poor fodder. What is not dusty and flat on this world is rocky and mountainous."

"Oceans?"

"Who knows or cares?" Before the creature could utter another word, the sound of movement brought them both around.

Kinsolving shrieked and rolled onto his back, feet going out. He caught a humanoid creature in the belly. A hand with a knife slashed for his throat; Kinsolving snared the wrist and pulled, using the humanoid's momentum to pull it on over and land it in the fire.

The creature screeched and tried to escape the flames. The Sussonssan's tiny hands pinned it where it lay until its clothing caught fire. Only then did Kinsolving's benefactor allow the creature to escape. It fled into the night, a living torch lighting a small dirt path.

"We were careless, but your reflexes are good. Now, about the one with the metal."

"Wait," said Kinsolving, confused. "Who was that? *What* was it?"

"That?" The Sussonssan waved its tiny hands about in a gesture of dismissal. "A predator. But we are all predators here. It thought to find an easy meal, a new cloak, a weapon."

"A weapon!" The Sussonssan pounced on the ground near the fire and rooted through the dirt until it found the knife. Tiny fingers circling the hilt, it held up the weapon. "A knife! And a fine one. I will take this as payment for the blood debt you owe me."

"Done," said Kinsolving, not wanting any more to do with the ugly creature.

"Oh, we will make such a fine pair, you and we. Your ignorance will fade soon under our excellent tutelage. You will have nothing to fear and will prosper on this poor world. Wait to see if we do not speak the truth!"

Barton Kinsolving worried that the Sussonssan might be right. He couldn't simply give up and die. But what manner of life could he lead, preying on the other convicts, having them prey on him? That wasn't a fit life.

It wasn't a fit life, but it was one he'd have to lead. Kinsolving settled down to listen to his mentor expound on how they would approach this new crime and the rewards to be reaped.

CHAPTER TWELVE

BARTON KINSOLVING did not fit into the ways of
the prison planet. Life proved a cheap commodity
when no one had anything more to look forward to
than a lifetime of wandering the barren planet's
face. But Kinsolving refused to kill for sport, unlike
his Sussonssan companion. The toadlike being
thrilled to murder, whether it was dropping a heavy
rock on another's head or running him down and
using those powerful hind legs to pummel him to
death.

"You lack the proper attitude, Kinsolving," the
toad creature told him one day after they had been
together for almost two planetary months. Kinsolving had learned what he could do and wouldn't do,
and had managed to survive. But as much as the
Sussonssan called them a team, Kinsolving knew
that it wasn't true.

If the toad being needed something Kinsolving
had and the human refused to hand it over, those
powerful hind legs would kick out and the sharp
talons on the toes would slice open Kinsolving's
belly. And the Sussonssan would feel not one whit of
remorse.

Kinsolving knew why the creatures had been
placed on this world even though he had never
asked. Without any hint of conscience, the being
would prove too much a menace for any civilized
society. The only question that burned inside Kin-

solving, and the one he didn't dare ask, concerned the other aliens. If this Sussonssan maintained telepathic contact, were the others also as lacking in conscience? And what of their entire race?

The prisoners Kinsolving encountered in his wanderings tended to be of similar bent. It almost brought him to tears thinking that the Lorr considered him a worthy addition to this planet's prison population.

"There are ways of getting what you want without killing," Kinsolving told the toad creature. "I'm not above thievery to get what we need. I may not like it, but I'll do it."

He snorted and shivered a little in the cold. Theft had kept him alive for the first month. He had desperately needed clothing against the frigid nights. Without money or anything to trade, theft had been his only recourse. Occasional lean-tos constituted cities on this planet, and no one trusted another enough to "hire" help. Mostly, the prisoners lived nomadic existences, drifting from one place to another, any spot the equal of the last—or the next.

"But we kill for pleasure. Do you not get a thrill feeling your enemy dying on your talons?" The Sussonssan canted its head to one side and peered at Kinsolving. "Your talons *are* feeble weapons. Perhaps this explains your lack of enjoyment."

"On my planet argument takes the place of killing."

"How dull."

"Not really," said Kinsolving. "If you beat an opponent in an argument, you're likely to be able to do it again. We can win repeatedly. You can only kill an opponent once."

"True," mused the toad creature. "But your kind tends to confuse quantity and quality. It must be a wan reward to duel with words. A thousand victories cannot equal one rimmed with blood."

"Are all your people like you?"

"All on this planet," the Sussonssan answered without hesitation.

Kinsolving let the matter drop. They were engaged in trying to survive—again. The toad being had convinced him that they both needed knives before making the trek across the dusty plains and to the foothills of mountains Kinsolving saw struggling up into the cloud layer. Kinsolving hoped to scale those peaks, get above the omnipresent clouds and glimpse the stars. He had no reason to think he could figure out the planet's location, but he had to try.

Kinsolving had to admit that seeing the night's star field might not even help. He was no navigator or astronomer. The constellation might be entirely twisted from those he had grown up with as a youth on Earth. There had been few visible, thanks to the light pollution from the cities, but he had studied books. When he had been stationed on Deepdig he often lay alone outside his house to simply gaze at the stars. Those patterns had been slightly altered from the ones he'd learned, but not much. Deepdig was only a hundred light years from home.

But this prison world? Kinsolving had no way of knowing if what he'd see would mean anything to him. Trying, however, gave some imitation of purpose to his existence.

"This one's weapons make for good use," the Sussonssan said in its guttural tone. "See the knife on display? Such a fine working of a chain link into a double-edged blade."

"On display? You mean stuck in his belt?"

"Same thing."

Kinsolving had to admit that their intended victim did fine work. A humanoid lacking hair and a nose, the greenish-skinned being went about his work with an air of indifference that Kinsolving had come to associate with all those who had been on-planet longer than a few years. What mattered when escape was impossible, when even striking out at your captors proved beyond your abilities?

Kinsolving had been on this world only two months and this lethargy threatened to possess him.

"Now. We go. You wait and watch. There is much we do not like about this theft," the Sussonssan said.

"What? I don't see anything wrong." Kinsolving spoke to thin air. The toad creature hopped away, tiny hands waving in the air. The humanoid looked up, his tiny eyes showing no true intelligence; the Sussonssan struck. Heavily muscled legs powered its talons forward to rip and rake.

But the toad being had been right in its caution. The humanoid moved with a speed that belied its bulky frame. The taloned foot missed its target by centimeters. By the time the Sussonssan had recovered for another attack, the humanoid had drawn the knife they coveted and held it in a three-fingered, huge-thumbed hand. The humanoid's muscles bulged and he began sucking in noisy gusts of air, as if he had already run a long race. The hairless dome of the humanoid's head began to sprout thick, throbbing veins as the greenish pallor vanished and was replaced by a bright pink as the oxygen level required for fighting rose within the humanoid's body.

Kinsolving hesitated, then launched into the attack. Between the two of them, they could steal the humanoid's knife no matter how strong or agile the pinkly glowing being proved. Kinsolving didn't like this but resources were scarce. Without a weapon on the journey to the mountains, Kinsolving wasn't sure he could make it. The toad creature had shown him several small predators that abounded on the plains. Without more than a sharpened stick, Kinsolving had no chance against their ripping fangs.

He came in low, thinking to tackle the humanoid. Inhuman joints thwarted him. Kinsolving grabbed and found the humanoid lifting one foot and rotating ninety degrees on the planted leg. Like the Lorr, this humanoid had enhanced mobility because of differently hinged knees. Kinsolving rolled free and stared. He couldn't tell for certain, but it seemed that the alien had a universal joint instead of a more human knee. The humanoid swung about, knife flashing in search of a berth in Kinsolving's back. Only the Sussonssan's quicker reflexes saved Kinsolving. The powerful toad leg swept out and countered the slash.

Blood spurted and momentarily blinded Kinsolving. He hastily wiped it from his eyes, worrying that it was his own. It wasn't. By the time his vision cleared, he saw two bodies on the ground. The man dropped to examine the toad creature.

The humanoid's knife had severed a throat artery, killing almost instantly. But one taloned foot had raked along the humanoid's leg and up into the belly. Kinsolving thought a renal artery had been cut. He held down his rising gorge at the sight of so much blood. A shaky hand picked up the fallen knife.

Two lives had been snuffed out for this.

"The stars had better be there," he said softly. "Dammit, they'd better be!"

Crude knife clutched in his hand, Kinsolving rose and stared at the two corpses. The Sussonssan's fellow beings would know of its death; telepathic contact might be traumatic, but they knew. Kinsolving looked around for a soft spot in the ground to dig two graves and found only thin, rocky soil. The sound of approaching animals convinced him that doing what he considered a decent thing wasn't possible. The scavengers on this world were savage. A single man with only a knife stood little chance against a hungry pack.

Kinsolving abandoned the two to the pack of roving carrion eaters and ran as if his life depended on it—and it did. Seldom did the scavenger pack find enough to eat; they weren't above stalking prey and worrying it to death.

Into the night Kinsolving ran until exhaustion overcame him. He found a rough-barked tree and crawled onto the lower limbs, finding the vertex of two branches where he could lean back and try to relax. The Sussonssan had chided him often about his affinity for trees. The toad creature had claimed it came from racial memory, that only inferior beasts evolved from the arboreal. Truly superior ones, such as itself, rose from the primordial slime.

"Is it better to be a fallen angel or a devil risen from the muck?" Kinsolving mused. Was there any difference if both ended up in the same place, enduring the same conditions? He had no answer for this or any other problem plaguing him. The distant sound of the noisily dining scavenger pack in his ears, he eventually fell into a light, troubled sleep.

Barton Kinsolving kept away from other prisoners during the next month as he hiked toward the mountain range. The Sussonssan hadn't been a friend, but it had been someone to talk with, to keep from going crazy with loneliness and frustration. The passage of time helped Kinsolving come to grips with the isolation. He even came to prefer it. The others on this world were deadly criminals, locked away here and forgotten so that they would be unable to perpetrate future crimes on their societies. Kinsolving had given up hoping to find others like himself, others wrongly accused and sentenced. Trusting no one else—daring to trust no one else—had its drawbacks, but it also had benefits.

The meager food he gleaned from the soil kept him alive, adequately if not well. For two it would have been starvation or worse. Always sleeping with one eye open to trouble from a travelling companion didn't appeal to him.

Kinsolving stopped and cocked his head to one side, listening. The scavenger packs he had to avoid. He wasn't strong or quick enough to fight them. The smaller predators he might deal with using the stolen knife that had cost the toad creature his life.

"Meat," he said aloud, his mouth watering at the thought. "The predators taste like shit but are better than nothing." He had found little except for tubers to be roasted and swallowed as quickly as possible. But meat? Was that the meaning of the sound he heard?

Kinsolving dropped to his knee and allowed the high grass to partially hide him. Slowly scanning a full three-hundred-sixty degrees, he frowned. The sound grew louder, and he couldn't identify it. When it rose to a shrill whine, he clamped hands over ears in a vain attempt to block it out.

Seconds after Kinsolving thought the sound would kill him, he saw the lead gray clouds part and a starship come through, standing upright on its emergency rockets. Whoever was inside had to have incredible trouble to land a spacegoing vessel on a planet. Kinsolving knew that the emergency rockets were intended for a simple sit-down and nothing more. Any repairs that needed doing would have to be to the main engines or the ship would be permanently grounded.

Then the lethargy that had fallen on him evaporated and the fact hit him that escape lay at hand.

Even before the rockets had cut off and the high-pitched whine had died, Kinsolving was up and running for the ship. He recognized the lines, even from a kilometer away. He ran toward the most modern and powerful Earth-built speedster available for private use. Why they had landed on the prison world didn't matter to him. That they had and were probably human did.

He could talk his way off this world! And if that failed, Kinsolving's strong fingers brushed lightly over the knife slid through his belt. That knife had been responsible for two intelligent beings' deaths. Another wouldn't matter.

Not if it meant his freedom!

He reached the scorched area around the ship's base and slowed, cautiously picking his way through burning clumps of grass. A smooth whirring noise drew his attention upward to the emergency hatch. Someone stood there, waving to him.

"Hello!" he called. "Can you lower a line to let me into the ship?"

"There are natives!" came a delightful squeal. "I don't even know where I crashed. Oh, this is wonderful!"

"A line," he pleaded. "Or do you have a small elevator?"

"You seem very human. I didn't think there'd be many aliens who looked exactly like me." A giggle. "Well, you're not *exactly* like me. You're a man."

Kinsolving walked back a few paces and peered up at the hatch, squinting into the sunlight reflecting off the highly polished silver hull. "I'm from Earth."

"What a coincidence. So am I," came the voice. For the first time, Kinsolving saw more than the waving hand. A woman leaned far out and peered down at him. He frowned. The distance obscured her features but something appeared wrong. The

general shape was right, but the details seemed...
different. Kinsolving hadn't been away from human
society long enough to forget what a woman looked
like.

But it didn't matter to him if this one had a
highly contagious case of Buck-Babb's sarcoma. She
was human; she was a way off this prison world.

"I need to get into your ship!" he called again.
"Please!"

"Can you fix shift engines?" she yelled. "The main
drive went out. I have no idea how to even begin
fixing them."

"Yes, yes, I know how," Kinsolving lied. His hopes
for escape began to fade. Before he could fix the engines, the alien keepers in orbit would have homed
in on the grounded ship. Would they lob an atomic
and convert the entire area into radiant energy or
would they simply laser the ship to insure that it
didn't lift again?

Kinsolving had passed the point of mere survival.
If he couldn't escape, he'd prefer total destruction.

"Here's a line. Can you use it?" A slender loading
crane poked out from the hatch, a line attached. It
lowered—too slowly for Kinsolving's liking. But it
finally reached him. He tied a double bowline in the
end and slipped his arms through. He motioned to
the woman to get him back to the ship's hatch.

The trip up the side of the speedster dragged on
for an eternity. Kinsolving rotated slowly in his
sling, getting first a look at the barren plains he
had crossed and then the ship's hull. He preferred
the stargoing ship to the prairie. One held hope, the
other only death and evil memories.

"Hello," the woman said when he reached the
hatch. She reached out a dainty hand and helped
him swing into the air lock. "My, aren't you the bar-
barian? Are you some primitive warrior stalking
his prey on this world?" She giggled.

Kinsolving stood and stared for a moment. The woman was beautiful, short blond hair intricately coiffured with platinum wire and pearls. But Kinsolving had seen more gorgeous women in his time; that wasn't the cause of his speechlessness. She smiled and her cheeks changed from a natural hue to a pastel green. A broader smile when she saw his reaction caused swirling colors to flow in a kaleidoscope over her face, turning her into something both alluring and frightening.

"Do you like the dye job? I got it done just before I left Earth."

"Dye job? I don't . . ."

"It's all the rage. The dyes are injected just below the skin. Oh, the needles hurt a teeny bit, but not much. As my mood changes, so does the color."

"And physical movement changes the pattern," Kinsolving guessed. The woman's pout altered both color and design.

"I wanted to tell you that, but you already knew."

"Sorry," Kinsolving said, confused. "I'm—" He paused for an instant. Should he lie or should he give his real name. Kinsolving decided that his infamy wouldn't have reached Earth. He had been totally forgotten by now. He gave his real name.

"Charmed," she said, curtsying. "And I'm Lark Versalles. This is my ship. Do you like it?" The blonde struck a pose so that she turned and showed her profile to him. What had at first seemed a chaste blouse for a woman so daring in her facial makeup now changed. The sunlight struck the material and turned parts transparent.

"Do you like it?" she asked. "A little something I found on one of those alien planets. At one of their strange market places. I had the cloth made into a blouse. I have no idea what *they* intended it for. But the effect is stunning, don't you agree?"

Her breasts appeared bare, then covered, then partially hidden. Kinsolving had to agree.

"You seem confused," Lark Versalles said. "Are you ill?"

"Ill?" Kinsolving fought to regain his wits. He had expected only a staid captain and interminable argument about leaving the planet. He hadn't believed anyone like Lark could exist starside of Earth's upper classes.

"Sick. Possessed of demons. I don't know. I can see if the medibot is working. I doubt it. Oh, nothing on this horrid ship works for me. Daddy bought it for me and said it was the latest in self-repairing and all that, but it just doesn't work."

"Work," Kinsolving said. His plight came rushing back. They had to lift—soon. If they didn't, he would be stranded forever on the prison world. "What went wrong? Stardrives don't break down."

"Well, Mr. Kinsolving, this one did." Lark smiled almost shyly and moved closer, her hand resting lightly on his arm. "May I call you Barton?"

"Of course. But—"

"I've never been this close to a criminal before. I mean, a dangerous one. Daddy is hardly what you'd call honest. And no one who works for him is, either. But they're not dangerous, unless you have a company they want. Then they can be vicious with mergers and sinking fund debentures and all that."

"How do you know I'm a convict?" he asked.

"Those dreadful aliens in orbit sent a warning. You *are* a criminal, aren't you?"

"They convicted me, but—"

She silenced him with her lips. Her lush body crushed against his. Kinsolving started to push her away and then stopped. When Lark broke off the kiss, her face flushed blues and greens.

"You are *dangerous*," she said breathlessly. "This is going to be fun!"

"The aliens in orbit. What did they tell you?"

"This is some sort of prison colony. A Botany Bay. You know Earth history, don't you? Of course you do. You're from Earth." Her hand roved over his chest, his belly, lower. "Oh, yes, you're human. Very, very human."

"Lark, please. They might try to keep us here, to stop us from leaving."

"They wouldn't dare! Daddy'd never permit it."

"The ship's engines. Show me what's wrong with them."

"Oh, you think those ugly things in orbit might try to *stop* us? This is going to be great fun!" She grabbed his grimy hand and led him through the ship's narrow corridors to a work panel near the sealed engine room. Lark pointed to a single large red warning light.

Kinsolving had no immediate idea what might have malfunctioned in the engine. He'd always heard that the precision machines functioned flawlessly—or blew up. Seldom did a starship manage to limp into drydock to be repaired. It just wasn't the nature of hyperspace flight to allow even minor accidents.

"Where's the computer console?" he asked. Kinsolving looked around, trying to find operating instructions.

"Computer? Oh, it must be here somewhere. They put them all over the ship. So confusing, don't you agree? Let me try this one." Lark toggled a switch on the bulkhead.

A high-pitched, stilted alien voice echoed over a speaker. "You will not leave this world. You will remain where you are or your vessel will be destroyed. Respond or we will consider you a renegade and open fire."

Kinsolving and Lark stared at each other, his dark eyes locking into her light blue ones.

"Do you think they really mean it?" she asked in a tiny voice.

An answer to her question came with stunning suddenness. The ship rocked from side to side on its hydraulic jacks as the aliens in orbit opened laser fire.

CHAPTER THIRTEEN

BARTON KINSOLVING hit the button to cycle shut all air locks. The searing impact of the plasma against the side of the ship rocked the speedster on its jacks.

"Why are they doing this?" Lark Versalles asked innocently. "I haven't done anything."

"Not yet, you haven't," Kinsolving said. "But you will."

"I will?" she said, almost happily. "This is becoming more photonic by the second. What am I going to do?"

"Help a convict escape." Kinsolving staggered and went to his knees. A laser blast raked the side of the ship. The gunners in orbit had found their range.

"They weren't lying," she said. "You *are* a criminal. How exciting!"

Sweat poured down Kinsolving's face. He looked over the control console for the hyperspace engines. He knew nothing about such mechanisms, but he was an engineer, a good one, and his life depended on fixing the engine and getting into space.

"What happened? When the engines died on you?"

"Nothing. I was just trying to get a message through to Dinky and—"

"A message?" Kinsolving demanded, cutting her off. "What do you mean?"

"I turned on the com-unit and powered up to con-

tact Dinky. He's back on Earth—just getting ready
to leave, actually—so I made sure the power level
was at max."

"Didn't anyone ever tell you that you can't make
radio contact through hyperspace? That it'll overload the engines?"

"Oh, I suppose they have," Lark said. The dyes
under her cheeks turned a light pink, then suffused
with pastel blues and greens. "Everyone's always
telling me I can't do this and I can't do that. They're
wrong, mostly."

"Not this time," Kinsolving said, hurrying now.
Two more laser strikes rocked the ship. "There's in-
finite drain if you're in hyperspace and try to use
the radio. I'm no physicist and don't know why.
Usually there are cutoffs to protect the circuits.
Here!"

He pulled off the panel covering and found a
smaller board with a trio of toggle switches, all in
the Off position. Kinsolving flipped them to On.
Power hummed deep in the innards of the speedster's sealed stardrive engine.

"Why, you're a genius. You fixed it!"

"What did the guards in orbit tell you?"

"Oh, the usual warnings. Don't land, don't do this
and that. They didn't say they'd fire on me. Not exactly."

Kinsolving rushed to the cockpit, Lark trailing
behind and protesting that she didn't like being ignored. Kinsolving dropped into the comfortable acceleration couch and stared at the controls. Red
lights danced, each showing an onboard failure
from the laser barrage. But he had no trouble locating the launch sequencer. The elegant starship had
been equipped with only the finest.

"Wait, don't!" cried Lark.

Kinsolving didn't hesitate. The timer gave less
than five seconds before launch. Kinsolving found

himself crushed in the couch, pinned by not only his own increased weight but also by Lark Versalles'. The woman had stumbled and fallen across him when the rockets ignited. Kinsolving struggled to pull her into the couch alongside. He managed to get her squarely on top of him.

The dye patterns writhing just under the woman's translucent skin turned paler and paler as the strain of launch acceleration mounted, but Lark managed to lift her head and peer down into Kinsolving's face.

"Never done this before. This is fun!"

Her mouth crushed hard against his, both passion and acceleration bruising his lips. Kinsolving struggled but Lark held the high ground and controlled him until the rockets died suddenly.

She cried out in surprise, floating up and off, weightless. "We're in orbit already! That was over too soon!"

"Not too soon," muttered Kinsolving. "Just in time." He worked his way across the control panel, seeing that the fuel for the emergency rockets had been fully expended. There wouldn't be any maneuvering using steering jets, not now. But he didn't intend docking or even staying in orbit long enough to need them.

"Intruder starship," blared the speaker. "You will cease all attempt to leave this planet. You will be destroyed instantly if you attempt escape."

"Do they mean it?" Lark asked, one slender leg curled around a stanchion. "They *did* fire at us with their lasers, though they weren't good shots."

"Good enough," said Kinsolving. "Several external sensors are blown out." His fingers worked faster now.

"What are you doing?" she cried. "You're preparing for star shift. You can't do that!"

"Why not?"

"But we don't have time to compute a destination. You're launching at random. And they did warn us."

"They can't have us in their sights or they'd have vaporized us instantly. That's a bluff. They have to fire their lasers directly through the planet's atmosphere," he said, checking relative locations of speedster and space station. "Too much beam attenuation to do real damage—for another few minutes."

"You'd just *go?*" Lark asked, amazed at the concept.

"What's wrong with that? You want excitement, don't you?"

"Oh, yes!"

"Then that's what I'll furnish. Lost among the stars. A random destination. Think of the romance in that."

"A friend of mine was lost for six years," Lark said, dubious of the adventure Kinsolving offered. The colors moving just below the surface of her skin began a slow dance from light, pastel shades to darker hues.

As he spoke, he worked at the controls. His eyes kept darting to the sensor picking up the signal from the orbiting space station. Another few seconds would bring the speedster back into range.

He slammed his hand down hard on the sequencer again. This time the shift into hyperspace occurred instantaneously. Kinsolving's stomach turned inside out and a kaleidoscope of colors danced before his eyes as the stardrive worked its mathematical magics on the curvature of four-space.

The universe as he knew it vanished as light became too slow. His optic nerve refused to believe the lies this new universe told it. Kinsolving swayed dizzily, his ears roaring. A phantom song echoed through the din, more structured than electronic discharges from a gas giant planet but less ordered than true music.

Fingers tingling and his stomach tied into acid-filled knots, Kinsolving fought to regain control of his senses. He held on to the sides of the couch for several minutes until his senses quieted and he could sit up without an attack of dizziness. The distant music faded to nothingness and his eyes again believed the world around him. Only the churning of his gut remained.

"Lark?" he called. "Are you all right?" Kinsolving hadn't given the woman a chance to secure herself before the shift; there hadn't been any time left. The guard station had been preparing to turn this fine ship into molten aluminum and sublimated carbon.

"Fine. I'm fine," she said in a voice that betrayed that she wasn't.

Kinsolving swung out of the couch and paused for a moment to allow his legs to regain circulation. In the pseudogravity of hyperspace he could move about as easily as if he stood on the prison planet's surface—but he was free! He had escaped the planet from which no one had ever escaped before!

"Let me help you," he offered. His hands went under her slender arms. He heaved Lark to her feet. The swirling subcutaneous dyes provided the only color in her face—and he did not like the dark grays and ebonies intermixing. "Are you sure you're not hurt?" he repeated.

"Photonic!" she said. The woman's face began to glow with brighter greens and blues. When the decorative patterns turned crimson and silver he knew she meant what she said. "But I *loved* it in the acceleration couch." Her arms locked around him like steel bands. She kissed him deeply and long. Kinsolving found himself not only liking it but responding with all the fervor of a man lost to his own kind for long months.

"Um," he said, finally breaking off. "Nice, yes, but I've got to figure out where we're heading. It wouldn't do to get too lost."

"Moira was lost for six years, but she didn't have someone like you along to help pass the time." Lark's face radiated hot reds and purples that formed into tiny islands on her cheeks. Her arousal was obvious.

"Being lost isn't my intention," he said. "This is a fabulous speedster. Did your father buy it for you?" Kinsolving couldn't imagine the wealth that could purchase such an expensive ship for private use.

"Oh, not exactly. His company owns it, actually, but they give him anything he wants. And he gives me anything I want." She smiled and reached out, her fingers lightly caressing Kinsolving's cheek. "But that's boring. Where would you *want* to go?"

Kinsolving hadn't planned that far ahead. Only an hour earlier his plan had been to crawl up the side of a mountain, get above the ever present clouds and simply look at the nighttime sky to discover where the prison world might be in the cosmos. Escape hadn't been a part of his expectations, not after the first few weeks on the planet.

"Gamma Tertius 4, I suppose," he said. Kinsolving wondered if appealing to Chairman Fremont, explaining to the ancient man what had happened, would help. He had no idea. But something more than Interstellar Materials' headquarters lay on the desolate world. Kenneth Humbolt would be on GT 4. And perhaps Ala Markken would have been duty rotated there, also.

Ala! A void formed in Kinsolving's heart. How

much of his woe had come from the woman? Much? Little? Had Humbolt lied to her, too, and caused her to betray her lover? Was this part of the Plan she had told him of when she'd been imprisoned by the Lorr?

"Oh, tachyonic!" cried Lark. "I just *love* Gamma Tertius 4. The parties there are the best anywhere. IM knows how to make everyone feel so...good!"

"You've been to GT 4?" he asked.

"Many times. It's in the ship's nav-computer." Lark frowned in thought. "But if we don't know where we are now, that's not going to help, is it?"

"It might." Kinsolving wasn't adept at navigation. He knew so little beyond how to worry ore from reluctant rock that it bothered him now. His experiences had seemed broad until he had to face harsh reality. The toad being on the prison world had taught him more about survival than an upbringing on Earth had—and Kinsolving's childhood hadn't been easy.

Kinsolving settled down and began working his way slowly across the panel, making certain he knew the function of every control. It proved easier than programming a robominer. The starship's designer hadn't wanted to force crew and passengers into any hard work, either physical or mental.

"I have it," Kinsolving said, leaning back and staring at the board. "We're going to have to drop out to get a fix, but that shouldn't be too hard to do."

"Do we have to do it right now? Those awful guards might be following us." Lark pouted prettily.

Kinsolving considered. It wasn't likely that the prison world guards had followed. Only routine flights arrived and departed. Why try to trace the hypertrail of a starship? Kinsolving knew it was possible, but it required sophisticated equipment

not likely to be in the guards' arsenal. They orbited
the planet and did little. Their poor work with the
laser proved that, although Kinsolving knew that
he'd been very, very lucky. Beam attenuation had
robbed the laser of much of its destructive power.

And he had launched the speedster before the atmospheric shield could be pulled away by the space
station's orbit.

"They won't track us," he said.

"Are you *really* a criminal?" Lark Versalles asked.
Her eyes seemed to grow larger and shift colors.
Kinsolving blinked, wondering if this were a trick
of light or if the woman had surgically altered her
eyes, too. Since she wore her expensive finery just
beneath her skin, he couldn't discount that possibility.

"There's no need to keep digging at it," he said
irritably. "I was convicted for something I didn't do.
The Lorr court system is different from Earth's. I
had no chance to present a defense. They seem to
assume that any evidence given is evidence for conviction."

"So you're not a dangerous man," she said, lower-
ing her eyelids and smiling slightly. "I'm just no-
vaed at that."

"You don't seem mad."

"Let me show you how not-mad I am."

"The ship. Gamma Tertius 4."

"All that will wait. Daddy gave me a ship capable
of running without much attention. That's a good
thing, because my attention is usually elsewhere."

Lark turned and walked slowly from the cockpit,
one hand resting lightly at the neckline of her
shimmery, deceptively opaque blouse. Just as she
disappeared through the hatchway, the blouse came
free and drifted lightly to the control room floor.

Barton Kinsolving bent and picked it up, his

imagination running wild. He had been on the alien prison world for long, dangerous months. And he had been the only human. With the blouse in hand, Kinsolving left the cockpit and followed a trail of discarded clothing to Lark Versalles' sumptuous cabin.

CHAPTER FOURTEEN

"I FIND THIS distasteful in the extreme," Cameron said, nose wrinkling to emphasize his opinion. "Is there no other way to obtain the information?"

"I don't like dealing with Bizzies any more than you do," snapped Kenneth Humbolt, "but this is an extraordinary circumstance."

"Hardly," muttered Cameron. Louder, he said, "Think. These are the creatures who keep humans under their thumb. Such inefficiency they've shown! They cannot keep even a witless wretch like Barton Kinsolving imprisoned."

"Their vaunted prison world seems lacking, doesn't it?" said Humbolt. Only the idea of the aliens' vulnerability sparked a small hint of hope within him. Having to deal once more with Cameron did little to heighten this, though. He did not like the fop, yet the man had his uses.

Humbolt couldn't keep his eyes from darting away from the elegantly dressed Cameron to the small robot hovering at his side. The repulsor field had been turned to low and emitted a barely audible hum, but the deadliness of this machine was apparent in its every line, its every angle. Twin sensors blinked a baleful red like a living predator's eyes. The roving steel wire whips atop its head turned it into a large metallic insect; Humbolt had no idea what those sensors might detect—or if they were sensors.

He shivered slightly at the idea of this robot hunter on his trail. He had seen what it did to the Lorr, but he hadn't witnessed how it had accomplished the dismemberment. Were those antennae heated wires that slashed through flesh? Or had Cameron done something even more diabolical with them? Humbolt's mind ran wild, turning to electric whips and laser cutters and sonic disrupters.

"Discover what the Bizzie knows and I will act upon it," said Cameron. He reached into a brocaded vest pocket and withdrew a small gold box. With one finely manicured thumbnail he flicked open the box. Bending slightly, he put his nose near a tiny tube that had risen from inside. Cameron inhaled sharply and smiled.

"What is that?" Humbolt asked. "I don't want you drugged out of your senses. Kinsolving didn't seem to be the kind to escape from that Bizzie prison, but he obviously did. He might be more dangerous than we think."

"Have no fear, Director Humbolt. This is an innocent enough habit. It contains only pure cerium."

"What?"

Cameron smiled indulgently. "Cerium from your mines on Deepdig."

"You inhale pure rare earths? But those are metals. What—"

"It gives an ineffable response. You really must try it to understand."

"But it's a *metal!*"

"An expensive metal," Cameron pointed out. "Perhaps that is part of its appeal. Not everyone can indulge a gram or two a day. Or perhaps it is the reaction when it reaches the mucous membrane. It dissolves violently in dilute acids."

Humbolt scowled at Cameron, bent over and toggled an intercom switch. "Send the...gentleman in," he ordered.

When the alien walked into the room, Humbolt had to motion Cameron to silence. A second glance at the fop made him power down his robot. The machine had begun a deeper humming and the wire antennae whipped about with the frenzy of a trapped insect.

"Good day. It is kind of you to honor us with your presence, Warden Quonpta." Humbolt almost choked on the alien's name.

"Delete false sentiment," the alien said in a gravelly voice. "I find great trouble in my position. Never before has prisoner escaped. My place at the wardenship is now in question."

"As it should be," muttered Cameron. "You must perform your task well to expect continued tenure."

The alien swung at the waist, his feet remaining firmly fixed on the soft carpet. Twisted at this impossible angle, he said, "You are the hunter?"

"A crude description," said Cameron, smiling. "Think of me as the *man* who will save your reputation."

The emphasis in Cameron's words did not go by the alien unnoticed. He said, "Dealing with space debris such as yourself is similarly ugly to one of my station."

"Gentlemen, please," Humbolt said. "Let's not allow personal differences to cloud the issue. We have mutual interests. Let's explore how to best serve those interests."

"Why do you wish one of your inferior species returned to my planet prison?" Quonpta asked.

"You forget that this 'inferior' species escaped your world," said Cameron with some venom. "No other species has done that, is that not correct?"

"You wish him removed from some larger scheme," the alien went on. "This is the only reason you would consider dealing with me."

"Our reasons," cut in Humbolt, "are our own. If

both your and our reasons are served, where is the controversy?"

"I cannot authorize pursuit," said Quonpta, his gravelly voice turning basso. "We do not have the guards to spare, nor has this matter ever occurred to require such planning."

"I will see to the prisoner's return," said Cameron. "If he tries to find refuge in any human-settled world, I will find him."

"And if he attempts to hide among Biz...among alien populations," said Humbolt, "we require of you a permit for Mr. Cameron to enter those worlds, to pursue and capture."

"Individual worlds relinquish their rights with great difficulty," the alien warden said.

"It won't be easy obtaining the proper documents, you're saying," said Cameron, "but they can be furnished. They *will* be furnished, won't they, Warden?"

Quonpta bobbed his head and flapped long, slender arms as if they were wings. Both men took this to mean agreement.

"Tell us more of the escape," said Humbolt. "We've had only sketchy reports."

"I will not tell you the prison world's location," the alien said.

"We haven't asked. Although we have every hope in the cosmos that no other miscreant of our race is sentenced to this world, we have no desire to meddle in your judicial system, either. If secrecy of the world is part of that system, well..." Cameron spread his hands and smiled wickedly.

"A human starship entered the system, emitting a bogus distress signal."

"What sort of...bogus distress signal?" asked Cameron, his steel-gray eyes now half hooded and his concentration total.

"Engine malfunction. Indications of deliberate

overload were evidenced at many observation spots in the system. The pilot attempted radio communications while in shift space."

"That does seem suspect," said Humbolt. "Everyone knows that isn't possible, that it will cause an infinite drain on engines."

Cameron said nothing.

"The ship vectored directly for planetary landing, using emergency rockets."

"The main stardrive *was* out of commission, then?" asked Humbolt.

"That much is verifiable. Power levels were not at stardrive capability. The ship lands, prisoner Kinsolving enters and our orbiting guard station begins raying."

"Did your laser cannon damage the ship?" asked Humbolt.

"The landing was precise and occurred at the instant when our station could not adequately protect the integrity of our system."

"You're saying, Warden, that the beam dispersion in the atmosphere was so great that the ship escaped damage." Cameron's lips continued to move in silent speech long after he'd made this simple statement.

"That is so. The starship recovered power levels, launched and attained orbit. By the time the guard station had come into position to properly use its weapons, the starship shifted into hyperspace beyond our authority."

"Did you get a launch vector?"

"Inconclusive. There is nothing along that geodesic of hyper-travel. It is our belief that the starship shifted, when only a short distance, recovered orientation in four-space, then shifted toward some other location. The launch from orbit was either done to confuse us or in panic to avoid our laser cannon."

"Either way, they seem to have escaped neatly," said Humbolt. Real admiration rang in his voice. Any triumph over the aliens ranked high in his mind, even if it had been accomplished by one he'd rather see dead.

"Kinsolving's description has been circulated among all races using our prison world. He will find it difficult to escape should he be foolish enough to land on any of them."

"That still leaves human worlds—and those cultures not using your prison world. Which are those?" asked Cameron.

"I am not at liberty to divulge such information. Much of the prison world's efficiency is due to secrecy."

"It won't be secret when Kinsolving sits down and figures out where the world is—but then he already knows, doesn't he? Or someone working closely with him does. It couldn't be an accident that this starship happened by to pick him up."

"That is my thought, Director Humbolt. That is why I come in answer to your summons. If you will seek him, a reward will be offered."

"I ask nothing," said Cameron, "other than the planetary entry permits. Justice will be served."

"Do you hate this Kinsolving so that you send ones like *that* after him?" asked Quonpta of Humbolt.

"Mr. Cameron is a valued employee of Interstellar Materials. He will perform well. Now, Warden, there is one point you have neglected to mention which would be of immense value to us if we are to find Kinsolving."

Human eyes locked with alien. Quonpta finally said, "The recognition signal of the starship was recorded. It is probably false. Why risk such a daring mission and not change your signal?"

"Why have a signal at all?" asked Cameron. His

eyes had closed entirely now. "Why attempt a sneak to a prison world's surface blaring out any recog signal?"

"Here. This means nothing to us. Your registry might aid you."

Quonpta dropped a small metallic disk to Humbolt's desktop. Without another word, the alien warden swung about and left.

Humbolt heaved a deep sigh and settled back in his chair. "Glad he's gone. Those Bizzies give me the creeps."

"Know your enemy," said Cameron. "Consider this. He is panicked enough over Kinsolving's escape to come to Gamma Tertius 4. He came to a human-populated world. I think I can expect my entry permits onto any number of their worlds."

"Only the ones not alerted to Kinsolving's escape," said Humbolt. "Why allow you to duplicate their police forces' efforts?"

"Not so, Director," said Cameron. "The permits will be a mix of worlds. The Bizarres have no desire to make information available to us easily. They might fear we will find out their prison world's true location. Imagine recruiting their criminals for use against them."

"An interesting idea," said Humbolt. "But the danger posed by Kinsolving and the knowledge he carries about the Plan outweighs such speculations."

"What does he know that the Bizzies would believe?"

"Perhaps nothing. We cannot risk *any* leakage to the Bizzies of the Plan. Not at this stage." Humbolt folded his hands across his chest and leaned far back in his chair. "It's a pity we can't recruit Kinsolving."

"Is there any way to burn out his brain and reprogram?" asked Cameron.

"Hardly. The traits in him we'd most like to use would vanish with massive brain-burning. A pity."

"What of the source of his information? What of Ala Markken?"

"It was a lapse on her part," Humbolt said too quickly. "She won't make the same mistake twice."

"She has been rotated back to GT 4, hasn't she? Perhaps attached to your personal staff?" Cameron grinned wickedly.

"That does not concern you. The leak will not recur. Ala is a loyal worker for both IM and the Plan. I suggest that you match her diligence."

"Of course, Director." Cameron picked up the metallic disk left by the alien prison warden. He popped it into a wrist reader. Cameron's eyebrows rose in surprise. "This is an interesting deception on Kinsolving's part," Cameron said. "Such irony I had not expected from him."

"What is it?"

"The registry for the rescuing starship. It's registered to Galaxy Pharmaceuticals and Medical Techtronics."

"Coincidence," snorted Humbolt. "There's no way Interstellar Materials and GPMT could have been tied together in this."

"Unless our Mr. Kinsolving knows more of the Plan than you think."

"Ala doesn't know of GPMT's involvement. Just IM's. This isn't possible."

"Kinsolving appears more dangerous to the Plan than you had thought, Director. Perhaps I should begin my investigation at GPMT." Cameron smiled at the man's obvious discomfort.

"Get Kinsolving. Stop him."

"It would be in our best interests to find out exactly how much he knows of the Plan—and the source of his information. Your, uh, bed companion might know more of the Plan than you do, Director."

"Ala's..." Humbolt cut off his angry retort. Cameron baited him, enjoying the spectacle of a powerful director of Interstellar Materials floundering about.

"I'll start on our valiant, inventive Mr. Kinsolving's trail immediately," said Cameron. "I have a few ideas which might bring him to, uh, *justice,* soon."

Humbolt waved his hand to dismiss Cameron. The man left, the robot tracker following at his heels. Humbolt wished he could activate the robot for just an instant and dispatch Cameron with his own diabolical device.

But he couldn't do that. He needed Cameron. The Plan needed Cameron.

And Kenneth Humbolt needed to have a long talk with Ala. What *had* the woman learned of the Stellar Death Plan—and what had she told Barton Kinsolving?

CHAPTER FIFTEEN

BARTON KINSOLVING found himself talking to an appreciative audience. No matter what he said, even trivial matters dealing with mining, Lark Versalles hung on every word, adoration in her bright blue eyes. And Kinsolving found himself equally fascinated by the lovely woman. As he spoke, her skin tint changed, sometimes dramatically with sharp mood shift, sometimes subtly with highlights of a sparkling dust showing through her translucent skin.

The softer tones that mingled with the more passionate reds and purples he had seen earlier told of her current emotional state—she swung between outright lust for him and a less intense curiosity about his adventures. But both states produced electric, well-defined colors.

"Tell me more," she urged, "about the prison world."

Kinsolving took a deep breath. "The aliens simply drop their convicts on this world. There's not much else to tell."

"To live or die on their own," Lark said breathlessly. She found true fascination in such a sentence. The romance of it—and her part in aiding Kinsolving to escape—flushed her skin with a brighter scarlet and flaring purples that shifted form even as he watched. Kinsolving didn't know if

the woman or her cosmetic dyes intrigued him
more.

"I could never have made it, not even for a week,
without the Sussonssan's help. He kept me alive
long enough to learn how to survive on my own."

"You liked him?"

"I did, in a way. There were others I liked, too, but
I never got to know them as well. It's much like my
professor in graduate school said. The aliens have
different concerns but they are people, too. Learn
what is important to them and they become more
like humans and less...bizarre." This last word almost burnt Kinsolving's tongue. He had heard Cameron use it, and Humbolt, and even Ala Markken.
It had connotations of racial hatred in it that he
couldn't stomach. The short time he'd spent on the
prison world had convinced him that humans and
aliens could live together and even prosper. They
had no designs on humans or human-settled worlds.
They had vast ranges of space for their own, having
been stargoing centuries longer than mankind.

Hadn't he been treated more brutally by his own
kind than by the aliens, especially those like the
toad creature who had unselfishly aided him when
he'd needed it most? It had been Humbolt and Cameron who traded him for the ones responsible for
stealing the ore from Deepdig number two. The
Lorr had only reacted according to their own system
of justice. Even on Earth miscarriages of justice occurred that had nothing to do with racial hatreds.

"Do you know anything about the Plan?" he
asked Lark.

"Plan? Me?" She laughed, the emerald greens in
her cheeks showing sharp spikes as she did so.
"Daddy's always telling me I should plan ahead. I
never do. Maybe I can't. Live for the day. Carpe
diem is the old saying. Why should I bother thinking about the future when the present is so thrill-

THE STELLAR DEATH PLAN

ing?" Lark snuggled closer to Kinsolving. "After all, my renegade darling, you've brought more super-charged excitement into my life than anyone in the past six months."

Kinsolving didn't want to ask what Lark had found as exciting as aiding a prison escape. He wasn't sure he could handle it.

"Never mind. I just thought that you might have heard it mentioned. You travel in high circles."

"I *party* in high circles," she corrected. "Business is so boring. Daddy is always telling me I ought to get involved, that he'll start me out in something of my own. Why bother?"

"You can't simply roam the stars forever," Kinsolving pointed out. "You'll need money one day, a job, want to settle down."

"Never!" Lark Versalles denied vigorously. "Daddy'll leave me zillions and zillions, more than I can squander in a dozen lifetimes. Why work when I can do as I please, when I please, no matter where? And 'settling down' sounds more like choosing where I want a grave. There's so much to see and do."

"Parties to attend," Kinsolving said sarcastically.

Lark missed the insult. "Yes! And fun to have." Her cheeks and forehead flushed a light orange that should have been eerie but on Lark wasn't.

He started to protest, but Lark's arms were far stronger than he'd anticipated. She held him down firmly and by the time he wiggled free, he had no real desire to leave her.

"The nav-computer has located four RR Lyrae stars. That's enough to give us a precise fix in space," Kinsolving told Lark.

"We're going to Gamma Tertius 4?"

Kinsolving nodded. That seemed the only route open to him, even though he didn't know exactly what he would do once he arrived at IM's corporate headquarters. From Humbolt he could expect nothing but death. But what of Ala? Would she listen and help him?

"Do you know anyone in the Interstellar Materials hierarchy?" he asked. "Someone who might be able to petition Chairman Fremont for me?"

"I don't know any of the directors," she said almost sadly, "but I know a few of the junior vice presidents." A wicked twinkle came to her eye as she remembered getting to know them. "One of them will do anything I ask. I'm sure of it."

"Who is it?"

"I can't remember his name, but finding him once we get to GT 4 won't be hard. I remember exactly where his office is."

"How did you meet this unknown junior vice president?" Kinsolving asked, even though he didn't want to know the details.

"A corporate party, some sort of celebration about planning for their two hundredth anniversary celebration. Something like that. He struck up a conversation with me and then I—"

Kinsolving yelped as Lark showed him.

"You did that to him in public?"

"No one noticed. We went to his office and continued. He was quite smitten with me. He offered me a job and everything." Lark laughed at the memory. "He didn't know that I could buy and sell him and a million secretaries. I almost offered him a job as *my* assistant, but I thought better of it. No need to rush into anything."

Kinsolving pushed himself free of the woman and her questing hands. The nav-computer had a vector computed for Gamma Tertius 4.

But try as he might, Kinsolving couldn't activate the hyperdrive engines. A single red indicator light flashed whenever he tried. He cursed the "idiot lights" and wished real readouts had been installed to give some clue about the malfunction.

"You told me the lasers hadn't damaged anything seriously," Lark said. "Why aren't we starring off for GT 4? You know how I hate to waste time when there are more fun things happening elsewhere."

"Let me see," Kinsolving said wearily. He toggled the computer and studied the screen as line after line of instruction marched past his eyes. After an hour, he settled back in the chair, eyes strained and his neck muscles bunched. He hadn't even noticed that Lark Versalles had left the cockpit and had now returned.

"Well?" she demanded hotly. "Why isn't this silly ship going anywhere?"

"Safeguards have been built in, Lark," he told her. "We're going to have to make a shift of less than fifty light years to find a space dock that can repair the backup systems. We're limited until we get the emergency rockets refueled and some of those damaged sensors—unimportant though they are—repaired." He tapped out an inquiry and received an instant reply from the nav-computer.

"There's a facility about forty lights away. It's off the geodesic line going to GT 4, which means a longer trip getting there after repairs are finished, but the speedster ought to be up to a hundred and some odd light years."

"I've gone as far as five hundred in one shift," she said proudly. Kinsolving shook his head. Such a distance was reckless. Small errors at launch in the vector turned into monumental errors over five hundred light years. Most travel was accomplished by smaller shifts, often less than twenty light years, with course corrections at every shift back into four-space.

Kinsolving started to give the command to shift to the repair facility, then stopped.

"What's wrong, darling?" Lark asked.

"What am I going to use for money to fix the ship?"

"Oh, silly, don't worry. My credit is good everywhere. What's the world we're shifting to?"

Kinsolving checked. "Upsilon Triangulis 2."

"No need to worry. I know *all* the mechanics there."

Kinsolving didn't doubt her for an instant. He toggled the switch and the speedster surged into hyperspace, following a mathematically precise path through-past-around regular space.

"You *do* know all the workmen," Kinsolving said in amazement. Lark had greeted each one of the men and women by name—and they all seemed to know her, as if she had been gone only a few hours.

"When you travel like I do, it pays to know the people who can put your ship back together. The *Nightingale* doesn't need much work, usually." Lark shrugged. "But sometimes I get impatient and do things like trying to radio from hyperspace. That was dumb. I remember everyone, and I mean *everyone*, telling me I shouldn't do that. But it came out all right." She clung to his arm and rubbed herself against him seductively. "I did meet you, Barton. Anything that lets that happen couldn't be all bad, could it?"

"It might be." Kinsolving stayed in the background, trying not to let the workers see him clearly. He had no idea what hue and cry might go up for him. The aliens had boasted about no one ever escaping from their prison world.

Had anyone made it away and had then been killed? Or was he really the first to ever leave the planet's gravity well alive?

"Sweet ship," one technician said. "Sorry to see Lark abuse her so badly."

"Been rough," Kinsolving said, deciding not replying would attract more attention than speaking.

"Looks as if you've been in a battle. Laser melts on the side. Some of the aluminum exterior has spalled. Sensors overloaded, emergency rocket fuel gone, as if you've been maneuvering heavily." The tech turned and peered hard at Kinsolving. "You're not getting Lark into smuggling, are you?"

The shocked expression on Kinsolving's face made the technician laugh. "That was just a joke. I didn't mean it, though Lark would do anything once just for the experience."

"She's quite a woman," Kinsolving said.

"That she is. But I imagine you've found out in ways I never will." The tech looked around, then dropped into the couch and said in a conspiratorial whisper, "Lark and I did slip off together once. God, what that woman can do with a ten volt battery and some wires! She's a real inspiration to us. Not many ships come into UT 2. Not a one of them has a captain as gorgeous—or willing—as Lark, either."

"I wouldn't think so."

"Where you two headed when you leave?"

Kinsolving held back a sharp retort to tell the man to not ask such personal questions. Instead he said cautiously, "You know Lark. Just launch and wherever the prow points, that's where we go."

"What a life. Envy her. Hell, man, I envy you getting to go along. But you'll burn out. Every man she's ever brought to UT 2 hasn't lasted long. She burns'em out then finds another. But it's great while it lasts."

Kinsolving nodded and let the technician finish replacing the circuitry under the computer console that had tested bad.

"That's all I can do. If Lark destroys it again, bring it back and let me fix it one more time."

"Can you do the same for me?" Kinsolving asked. The tech laughed and slapped him on the back.

The instant the man left the cockpit, Kinsolving dropped into the couch and began running his own checks on the circuitry. Everything read out perfectly.

"They do such good work, don't they, darling Barton?" asked Lark.

"They do. Let's get going. I don't—" Kinsolving stopped when he saw the burly, armed man with Lark.

"This is Idi. He's station master. He's such a dear. He wanted to check out everything to make sure I'd be all right."

"Your crew did a fine job," Kinsolving said.

"Let me check it out. This is the only way I'll be satisfied." He motioned Kinsolving from the couch. Kinsolving reluctantly vacated so that the huge black man could begin his own examination.

Lark clung to Kinsolving, but the man grew increasingly uneasy. Idi had performed the same circuit check four times; each pass had resulted in a green light indicating nominal performance.

"Why is he stalling?" Kinsolving whispered to Lark.

Her eyebrows shot up and the colors under her skin swirled in crazy eddies. Kinsolving motioned her to silence when Idi's com-link sputtered into life. Kinsolving didn't understand much of what was said, but he caught his name—that was enough to galvanize him into action.

Fists closed and held together, he swung as hard as he could and caught the station master at the base of his massive neck. The jolt rocked Idi forward, but it was Kinsolving's second blow that laid him out on the cockpit deck.

"Why did you do that?" protested Lark. "He's a good friend!"

"I think I broke my hands," moaned Kinsolving. "Help me get him out. Didn't you hear the message that came in over his com-link? He was stalling until he got verification that I was a fugitive."

"Really?" Lark's angry expression faded and sunlight once more shone from her eyes. "How thrilling! We're running from the law! Just like in those old two-dee flickering things that Prinz projects against a wall. They're so silly, but fun!"

Lark helped Kinsolving drag the heavy man to the air lock. On impulse, Kinsolving stripped Idi of the com-link and a small stun tube tucked away inside his shirt so that just the handle had been visible. Then he rolled the man outside and started the lock cycling shut.

"Punch in the coordinates for Gamma Tertius 4," he ordered Lark. "I want an optimum course, minimum time."

"That's the only way I travel." She competently set the controls and let the nav-computer do its job. "This is so photonic!" she enthused. "I'm so happy I met you, Bart darling!"

Kinsolving wasn't convinced that he should allow her to continue with his dangerous mission. Lark had proven useful to this point, but any further might endanger her life. That she reveled in this had nothing to do with it.

But Kinsolving couldn't put her off the *Nightingale*. Not now. Not when the ship's sensors showed building EM fields around the newly repaired hull. The crew at the UT 2 station swung a laser cannon around in an effort to undo all they'd done.

"Hurry," Kinsolving said nervously. "They're getting ready to fire on us. That's their aiming field. That's what is causing the instruments to jump around."

"Don't worry," said Lark. "We'll make it." Her

hand descended to the launch button just as the starship gave a mighty shudder.

Barton Kinsolving wasn't sure whether they had shifted into hyperspace or the laser had found its target.

CHAPTER SIXTEEN

GAMMA TERTIUS 4 throbbed with activity. Even from parking orbit above the desolate world, Barton Kinsolving saw the vitality and energy in the single large city spreading more than ten thousand hectares across the bowl of a gigantic meteor crater. The planet had been airless and worthless to the other starfaring races.

Thaddeus McIntyre had arrived and seen more to the barren rock world than any of the others. His first duty had been to name the tall mountains, one rising at either side of the huge dish-shaped depression in the side of the planet. Mt. Abrupt at the far eastern end was taller than Mt. New Daisy Bates in the west. Then McIntyre set to work with primitive terraforming equipment. Over two hundred years, Interstellar Materials had taken over the work, added sophisticated devices to hold in not only atmosphere but also heat and had transformed the rocky bowl into a miniature paradise.

Kinsolving had been to GT 4 twice. Both times the sight of the green bowl set amid the brown and gray nothingness of the rest of the radiation-wracked world had made him think of Earth and Japanese bonsai trees. A miniature world grew and thrived in the pot of the meteor crater.

"Lovely," he said, not able to take his eyes off the speedster's forward vidscreen.

"Look, Barton darling. There's the corporate

headquarters building. Isn't it cosmic?" Lark fiddled with the vidscreen controls and zoomed in on the two-hundred-story-tall structure of gold and emerald splinters, each segment daring to thrust higher than the last until the upper floors extended beyond the dome of atmosphere and into the vacuum of space. "The entire top floor is executive offices."

Kinsolving tried to imagine the view from there and failed. Situated directly in the center of the huge crater, anyone on that floor had an unsullied view of hundreds of kilometers over the perfectly kept city below.

"That level, level one hundred one, is the party suite. The entire floor!" Lark didn't try to restrain her enthusiasm for once again being at the heart of serious fun.

Kinsolving saw the single flashing light on the control panel. GT Landing Authority needed information before allowing them to leave the *Nightingale*—and Kinsolving couldn't supply it.

He silently indicated that Lark should arrange for transport and care for the speedster while they were below. He swallowed hard and glanced around the small cockpit. He had grown used to the *Nightingale*. Kinsolving smiled ruefully. It hadn't been hard to do, either. Not with every creature comfort imaginable—and not with Lark Versalles aboard.

He knew he might be forfeit if he couldn't contact people willing to plead his case before Chairman Fremont. And even if he succeeded in getting his story to the chairman, that didn't mean Fremont would turn Humbolt and Cameron over to the Lorr for punishment. A director possessed immense power in IM, or any comparably sized off-Earth corporation. Charging Humbolt with the crimes of ore theft and murder and all the rest would cause trouble that might rock Interstellar Materials all the way to the foundations of its immense, beautiful headquarters.

Kinsolving had to rely on Chairman Fremont's integrity to take such risks. He didn't even want to consider the possibility that the rare earths had been stolen on the chairman's orders.

"Hello," Lark called in response to LA's identification request. "Here's the tape on the ship. It has all those silly numbers and things." She played out the registry tape.

"Welcome to Gamma Tertius 4, *Nightingale*," came the immediate response. "How many in your party will be shuttling down to the city?"

"Two," Lark answered without even glancing at Kinsolving. He had wanted her to say only one—he'd risk stowing away to avoid entry procedures. Now his chance for clandestine entry had vanished. "And this time get a *good* pilot. I was here six months ago and the landing was awful. It jarred my teeth it was so rough."

"You must have drawn Bone-breaker Benitez," came the cheerful reply. "We'll see what we can do for you this time. Good, good. How's Chairman Fremont's personal pilot sound? He's landing for the anniversary party, too."

"Oh, photonic! We're in time for it," Lark said. "I don't want to miss a single instant of the parties."

"You're in time, Lark. Treanna's on her way over. You won't have any problems with her landing. Always soft as a lover's touch."

"Thank you, LA." Lark smiled wickedly and toggled the call switch again. "Any chance that you'll be at the party?"

Laughter echoed from the speaker. "Sorry, Lark. No chance. LA's having a party of its own. Nothing as fancy as that on one-oh-one."

"I might come by if the one-oh-one party gets dull."

"Too bad we won't see you," the Landing Authority controller said. "That party'll never get dull. Not if it lasts till the three hundredth anniversary."

To Kinsolving, Lark said, "This is so much fun. I'm glad your orbit crossed mine."

"They'll be looking for me," Kinsolving said, more to himself than to Lark. Then he began to really think. This anniversary party atmosphere might be his saviour, if he proved bold enough to take advantage of it.

"You'll be with me, silly," Lark said, as if this made everything all right. Seeing his expression, she said, "As long as you're with me, who's going to look at you? They'll all be watching *me!*"

Kinsolving had to laugh. "I'm sure they will," he said. "Anyone as lovely as you has to be the center of attention."

"I've got to pack for the party. This Treanna person won't be docking for almost an hour. You keep watch, though, just to be sure. It never pays to keep one of those menials waiting long. I think that's why the landing was so rough last time." With that Lark Versalles vanished, on her way to pack for the anniversary party.

All Kinsolving could do was sit and worry. By the time the shuttle docked and he had helped Lark carry her cosmetics and jewelry cases into the cargo bay, he was keyed up to the point of explosion.

The shuttle down went quickly and smoothly; Kinsolving saw why Fremont had chosen this woman to be his personal pilot. Every move she made at the controls was precise and economical and the landing at the LA field near the edge of the city was over before he noticed they had even begun their final descent.

"All out," Treanna called back. "Don't worry about your cases, Lark. The handlers will take them to your usual suite. We're all glad you could make the party."

Kinsolving shot Lark a startled look. The pilot made it sound as if Lark was more than guest.

"Is your father going to make it?" Treanna asked.

"I don't think so. Daddy is always working so hard. I haven't seen him in over a year now. And he hates to travel."

"We're all happy his daughter doesn't share that trait," Treanna said. "You always brighten any gathering. See you on the way back!"

"Thanks," Lark said, distracted. She drifted from the shuttle, paying no attention to anything going on around her. Kinsolving followed at a discreet three paces, able to see everything and not be intrusive. He tensed as he walked out the passenger tunnel and into the main terminal, expecting armed guards to grab him.

Only the usual bustle of the Landing Authority greeted him. Lark walked through the clearance station without slowing. Kinsolving tried to do the same and was stopped by the clerk.

"Entry visa and travel papers," the clerk demanded. Lark had already vanished, off in search of new thrills, already bored with the bureaucratic demands.

Kinsolving glanced around and decided against using the stun rod he had strapped along his left forearm and hidden by his shirt sleeve. Too many guards prowled the corridors. None had focused on him yet. Any attack on the clerk would draw them like iron filings to a magnet.

"Lost my papers and visa," he said. The clerk's sour expression foretold a long and tedious wait. Kinsolving decided on a bolder approach. He couldn't be in any worse a position for the attempt —and the jumble of data entries might work in his favor. "My name's Barton Kinsolving, supervisor of mines, Deepdig, here as Chairman Fremont's personal guest for the anniversary."

"Supervisor?" the clerk said, one eyebrow rising slightly. "What happened to your papers?"

"That's a long story. I've filed the report with Director Humbolt. Kenneth Humbolt," he said, spelling it for the clerk. "He's my immediate superior." The names Kinsolving tossed around so easily impressed the clerk. Kinsolving thought his heart would explode from the effort of remaining outwardly calm while the clerk entered the data given him.

"Don't have an entry on your visa or travel orders, Supervisor, but the computer is backlogged over a week. The anniversary celebration is bringing in people from Earth and all over."

Kinsolving didn't want to point out that it was longer than this since he'd been convicted by the Lorr. He had taken the chance that Humbolt wouldn't attend to the personnel files himself. If left to any of the subordinates on Deepdig, his records might take months to arrive. Pumping out the mine would require shift-to-shift attention. With the trouble Ala Markken and the others had experienced, he didn't think record updates would rank high on their priorities. And if Ala had been returned to Gamma Tertius 4, that left only decidedly inferior workers in charge.

"Here are duplicates of your identicard and papers, Supervisor. You'll have to verify first. Press your hands here. Good. And for the dupes I need your retinal pattern, too."

Kinsolving lowered his face to the soft-covered ocular and blinked as the laser scanned his left eye and matched it with records hidden deep in the corporate computer. He heaved a sight of relief when no bells went off, when no guards came running after him.

"Have a great time, Supervisor."

"Thanks." Kinsolving turned to follow the course Lark had taken.

"Supervisor!" Kinsolving froze in his tracks. He slowly turned to face the clerk. "The blond woman that went through with Absolute Clearance. Was she with you?"

"Yes," Kinsolving said cautiously.

"Nothing," the clerk said. The expression of lust and envy on his face told the story. Kinsolving didn't have to be a telepath to know what the clerk's thoughts were, either. *Lucky bastard,* had to run through his mind.

Barton Kinsolving had acted with boldness and won. The company computer hadn't yet been flagged to record any use of his name or identicard. Until such time, he could live well and devote his full attention to reaching Chairman Fremont.

Kinsolving felt a cold wind across his spine as the thought came to him that the computer might be updated at any time. When it was, any use of his identicard would bring down company guards in droves.

He pushed the worry aside. If he dwelled on it, he might accomplish nothing. Courage had carried him this far. Courage would get him to Fremont and total absolution.

Outside the LA terminal, Kinsolving simply stood and breathed the fine, pure, cool air. A gentle wind blew from the north. That meant it was late afternoon. Every five hours, the direction of the wind changed by ninety degrees in a clockwise pattern, returning to any given direction exactly one GT day later. Kinsolving walked a few paces and turned. At his back rose Mt. Abrupt. In the far distance, hidden by the gleaming shaft of the headquarters building would be Mt. New Daisy Bates. Having his bearings, Kinsolving hailed a passing car, used his identicard and told the robot, "Supply."

He settled back as the quick spurt of acceleration thrust the car through traffic and toward the company warehouse. He needed more than a single change of clothing if he wanted to present a good appearance at Interstellar Materials' anniversary party.

Completely outfitted, he charged the bill against his accrued salary. Every use of his identicard caused Kinsolving to tense but the use was always authorized.

He knew it couldn't continue much longer. He had to reach Fremont—soon.

Going directly to the headquarters building with his newly packed cases, he entered the main lobby and looked around. Only once before had he been here. Then he'd had a guide to usher him up to the appropriate corporate office. Without such a guide, he didn't have any idea how to proceed.

He went to an information counter and toggled the Attention switch.

"How may IM be of service?" came the computer-generated voice. He had asked in one of his college courses why the information 'bots were never equipped with truly human-sounding voices. The professor had chuckled at the notion.

"Humans love being served," had been the answer. "You can dominate a robot, abuse it, insult it, walk away and feel better. A human treated similarly will make certain your request is never granted—or will be granted in the longest possible time."

"Efficiency," Kinsolving muttered.

"All IM employees strive for efficiency," came the robotic voice.

"I'm looking for Lark Versalles. She has a suite."

"That information is secured."

"I have some of her cases. Not all were delivered," Kinsolving said, changing his tack. The computer didn't care; a human would. Another count for machine over man when trying to dodge the system's rules.

"Leave them at the service entrance, northwest side, entry port five."

"They must be carried by hand. I will do it."

Kinsolving waited for the computer to make the proper decision. "One moment, please, while I contact the suite."

"Barton?" came Lark's immediate cry from the speaker. "Is that you? Where did you go?"

"Give me the entry code. I'm in the main lobby." Kinsolving looked around, certain that he would be detected at any instant. The feeling of paranoia grew inside until he wanted to scream. He felt exposed and was sure that every passing person would turn and point at him and begin to yell for guards.

"I'm on level forty-seven. Go to the lift shafts at the far side of the lobby and just give my name."

"You used your name as entry code?"

"Oh, don't be like that, darling. Daddy always chides me about such things. I know better, but it's so hard remembering silly codes and all that. This way I never forget and lock myself out and get embarrassed. Do hurry. It's so...lonesome in this big suite."

"Be right up," he assured her. Before he left the service robot, he said, "Send my cases to suite code Lark Versalles."

"Right away, sir." The tiny pop indicated that the order had been transmitted even as he gave it.

Kinsolving heaved a sigh of relief as he hurried across the wide marble-floored lobby. His fears had turned out to be irrational. So far everything had gone well.

He reached the elevators and pressed the summons button, stood back and waited.

The door opened—and out strode Cameron, a robot hunter-killer humming along on its repulsor field at his side.

CHAPTER SEVENTEEN

BARTON KINSOLVING felt the blood rush from his head. The dizziness assailing him turned into advantage. He turned to one side, hand hiding his face. Kinsolving bent over and went to one knee, facing away from Cameron. The man stopped; Kinsolving waited for the hand on his shoulder, the nerve-jangling impact of a stun rod, the shouted cry for guards, the robot to attack.

It did not come.

"Are you well?" Cameron asked.

"Too much t'drink," Kinsolving said, slurring. "Wunnderful party."

Cameron sniffed. "I dare say you've outlived your invitation at any party I wish to attend." The over-dressed man snapped his fingers and the hunter robot attentively followed.

Kinsolving chanced a look up to see the brightly dressed Cameron vanish in the crowded lobby. For long seconds, Kinsolving couldn't stand. His legs were too weak and shaky. He finally took a deep breath and forced calm on himself. He had almost come face-to-face with the man responsible for his woes. That he still lived spoke as much of pure luck as it did skill.

Kinsolving didn't lie to himself about escaping Cameron. Surprise had to be a major element. No one would expect a fugitive to return to the source of corporate power. And Kinsolving had to admit that Cameron and Humbolt might not even know he'd escaped from the prison world. Would the aliens sound an alarm and warn the human worlds —especially Gamma Tertius 4—of his singular escape?

He took a quick glance into the elevator cage and saw that it was empty. Only then did he enter and touch the code switch and say, "Lark Versalles."

The sudden rise of the cage drove him to his knees. Clumsily standing, Kinsolving was glad that he was alone. Explaining such behavior would be difficult—and it would make him memorable. The last thing he wanted now was to be memorable.

"Think small, think insignificant," he told himself.

The doors opened and all attempts to be insignificant vanished. A robutler hovered near the opened elevator door and said, "Welcome Master Barton. Lady Lark awaits you in her suite."

In addition to the robot, several human servants stood impassively along the walls, waiting for the slightest hint of need. Kinsolving tried not to gawk as he trailed behind the robutler. The carpets had to be Persian. No other design and texture felt this way beneath his feet. Paintings from renowned artists decorated the walls, with tasteful statuary placed so that the lines broke in unexpected spots. Most of all, the area was dominated by the panoramic view from the diamond-clear windows over the city, dots and squares of green betraying parks and browns and grays showing buildings.

Kinsolving walked along in a daze of wonder at such wealth. His prior visit to GT 4 hadn't revealed this aspect of Interstellar Materials' operations. He

knew that he had blundered into a world reserved
for only a select few.

A select few like Lark Versalles.

"Darling!" the woman greeted him. She threw
her arms around his neck and swung him about
as he walked into a room even more expensively
decorated than the area outside. He hardly noticed
the room's furnishings. Lark was gorgeously nude
and outshone even the most cleverly contrived artwork.

"Do you like it?" she asked, bouncing away from
him to display the canvas of her bare skin. "I had
some of the dyes redone and intensified the colors in
others." Nipples gleamed a bright blue, then faded
to gray-blue, only to change into hues Kinsolving
couldn't put a name to. Her breasts changed shades
to stay complementary to her nipples, and the rest
of her body coloring writhed with a pseudolife that
took away his breath.

"Fantastic," he murmured.

"I knew you'd like it. But do hurry. We've got a
reception to attend. Not a big one, just a few
hundred of the *top* IM execs."

"Lark, wait," he began.

"You're not going to vanish on me again, are you?
That was rude, disappearing like you did at the
LA." She stamped her foot in mock anger. The action of foot against carpet caused jagged edges of
coloration to rise in her left calf.

"I had to get some papers," he said. "My identicard." He swallowed and tried to look her squarely
in the eye. The effort proved almost more than
Kinsolving could achieve. The spectacle of her
body drew him powerfully, as it was designed to.

"But now that you've got all that you want," Lark
started.

"The party," he said. "Who is going to be there?
I've got to make contact quickly. If I don't ..." Kin-

solving let the words trail off as he remembered the
chance encounter with Cameron in the lobby. The
man might have been dressed like some courtier
from eighteenth century France, but Kinsolving remembered the look on his face when he killed the
Lorr agent-captain. Cameron had enjoyed it, truly
enjoyed the murder. Behind that fancy exterior lay
a cold and cunning mind.

"Oh, you can be such a bother," Lark said in
exasperation. "Just about everyone will be there.
Don't worry, my darling. I'll introduce you to
someone who can help. I promise." With that, she
spun, lifted elegantly on one toe to accentuate the
muscles in her legs and send new patterns arrowing up along those slender calves, then dashed off
to dress.

Kinsolving collapsed into a chair and simply
stared out across the city. He ought to be enjoying
the promise of Interstellar Materials' two hundredth anniversary. For the past hundred years the
company had been on GT 4 making this small segment of the world into paradise.

Kinsolving looked at the city and saw only bleak-
ness. His life lay shattered and the only hope of
piecing it together again was dressing in the next
room, more intent on choosing the right gown than
helping him. Kinsolving shook his head. He
shouldn't complain. If it hadn't been for the chance
landing of the *Nightingale* he would never have
escaped the alien prison.

Coldness clamped his heart. Had Lark's arrival
been pure chance? Did Humbolt plan something
more for him, something even more diabolical than
incriminating him in murder and theft?

Kinsolving couldn't figure out what that might
be. But one question that he'd never had a chance to
ask did come to mind. He called out, "Lark, will you
answer a question?"

"Certainly, darling, if you'll tell me which you prefer. This one or this awful blue monstrosity."

Kinsolving spun in the chair. Lark had turned on the glamour mirror and stood before it naked. Reflected was her face and lush body clothed in a scintillating rainbow of electricity. The fabric seemed to be more plasma than solid, shifting and shining, glowing and hiding.

"This? Or this?" She touched the frame of the glamour mirror and the rainbow vanished, replaced by a blue gown that seemed plain in comparison.

"The blue," he said without hesitation.

"But it doesn't *do* anything," Lark protested.

"What will the other women be wearing?"

The blonde smiled slowly as she understood. "Oh, yes, I knew there was a reason I brought you along." She danced over to him, bent and kissed him lightly on the lips.

"Lark, the question. Who is your father? Why does IM give you such a lavish welcome?"

"Daddy's so rich, he could buy and sell Interstellar Materials a dozen times over. That's why they fawn all over me. They're afraid I might say something nasty and then he'll actually buy them out."

"He's a stockholder?"

"Hardly. Don't repeat this, but Daddy would never have anything to do with a company whose revenue came from grubbing in the dirt. Nothing against you, darling Barton, but you must admit that it *is* rather primitive."

"But—" The door chimes interrupted Kinsolving. He sank down in the chair, letting the back hide him as the robutler glided over to answer.

"Lady Lark," the machine said, "the summons for the party has come. The opening presentations will be made in exactly five minutes."

"Oh, and I don't have anything to wear."

"The blue dress," Kinsolving said.

Lark touched the frame twice, then tugged at the glamour mirror's edge to reveal a cabinet. Inside hung the blue dress, specifically tailored to the measurements recorded in the mirror. Lark hurriedly dressed. Kinsolving hadn't thought the woman capable of such speed. She took his arm and almost dragged him from the room.

"We've got to be on time for the opening. That's when I'll be able to see who I can contact in your behalf." She squeezed tightly on his arm and guided him toward the elevator. The robutler obediently held the ornately wrought doors open. Again the sudden acceleration almost drove Kinsolving to his knees.

Before he could speak, the doors slipped away to show level one-oh-one and the party goers already filling the immense room.

"Time to go to work," Lark said, laughing. She pulled him forward and immediately began greeting elegantly dressed men and women in dresses so dazzling Kinsolving worried that he might need polarized goggles to keep from squinting. A few he recognized as junior executives at IM—he prayed that they didn't recognize him.

But Kinsolving need not have worried. If he stayed with Lark Versalles, he would never be the center of attention.

He quickly found, though, that he couldn't stay beside her. Not when the men clustered around her forced him away. He silently drifted to one wall and clung there, eyes scanning the party for anyone he might approach. A few junior vice presidents were in attendance but he didn't see Humbolt—or Cameron. He had hoped to find Chairman Fremont, but the frail man was nowhere to be seen.

Kinsolving hung back during the opening ceremonies. This was the first party of a month-long celebration IM planned to celebrate two hundred years of business off Earth.

"Friends of Interstellar Materials," a dark, pretty woman said from a small stage in the center of the room. "Welcome. Chairman Fremont regrets that health has prevented him from attending today, but he has entrusted me with the joyous duty of dedicating this status of Thaddeus McIntyre, the illustrious architect and builder of our headquarters, the man whose vision and foresight took us away from the planet of our origins and carved out a niche on Gamma Tertius 4."

The woman spoke of happiness and light, but a coldness about her made Kinsolving think of icebergs and the hard vacuum of deep space.

"Who is she?" he asked a woman standing by him.

"That's Director Villalobos."

Kinsolving said nothing more. Maria Villalobos was often mentioned as Fremont's successor. He had never seen her before, much less met her—but her presence convinced him that she was not the proper one to plead his case. The cold light from her eyes made it obvious that Cameron wasn't the only person at IM without scruples.

He might be doing Villalobos a disservice, but he didn't think so. Kinsolving looked around in time to see Lark leaving, arms linked with a young man dressed in an old-style tuxedo. Kinsolving started after them, then stopped. He didn't know what he would be interrupting—but he could guess.

Trying not to look too uncomfortable, Kinsolving floated around the periphery of the crowd. He felt a sense of forced merriment about them. These young IM executives were here for business, not pleasure. They worked one another, jockeying for power and influence, seeking information to use for profit and blackmail. Kinsolving watched in a mood approaching awe, remembering similar parties he had attended. His own actions hadn't been much different. Although he was a damned good engineer, he wasn't expert enough to be made supervisor at his age without also being good at trading information and influence.

He marvelled that he had once played this game. Kinsolving was now an outside observer; all was apparent to him. If only he didn't have to find someone to clear him, he might have enjoyed this revelation.

Some social sense caused him to jerk about in time to see Lark returning with the man. They parted and she quickly went to the side of another, older man. Kinsolving knew that Lark enjoyed this party, as much for the sexual opportunities it afforded as for the contact with wealth and power.

He moved quickly to within a few paces. The man she spoke to seemed familiar. When Kinsolving heard the blonde's words, he recognized his chance.

"Oh, Director Liu, this is such a *fine* party. You planned it, didn't you?"

The director of IM's financial division basked in Lark's praises. Within ten minutes, they left, Lark's fingers toying with the fastrip at the front of Liu's pants. The director playfully batted her hand away, but not too hard, not enough to discourage her.

Kinsolving followed at a discreet distance.

"Director, can we go to your office? I would ever so like to see it."

"No, Lark, not there. It's at the top of the building. Even with my private elevator, it would take too long to get there. I want you, my lovely. Now!"

Lark squealed in joy as Liu pushed her into a

small, intimately lit room. Kinsolving moved quickly, fingers curled around the edge of the door to keep it from closing and locking. He didn't have to worry about Liu or Lark seeing him. They were intent only on each other.

Kinsolving's uneasiness at watching vanished when he saw Lark toss the director's jacket across the room. It hit the floor with a dull thud that told Kinsolving something bulky was hidden away in a pocket. When the pair fell to the immense bed and began serious lovemaking, Kinsolving crept along the wall to where the jacket lay. He fumbled in the pocket and found a secure-case holding the director's identicard and at least a dozen other entry cards.

Kinsolving took the secure-case and left the room. It would be at least a half hour before Liu noticed the theft. If the man's power appealed enough to Lark, it might be longer than that. Kinsolving found another small room and went inside. It took him almost fifteen minutes to break open the secure-case and pull out the identicard. He pocketed it. The other cards were clearly marked for the security areas they granted access to.

All except one blank card. At first Kinsolving thought it was a spare Liu carried, one to be electronically imprinted. But his fingers ran along the edge and felt the dull nicks in the plastic. The card had been used often.

Kinsolving didn't worry about it. He sat down on the edge of a chair and thought about his windfall in obtaining these entry card keys. Somewhere within the IM computer must lie evidence that could clear him. Ala Markken had claimed that her thefts of the rare earth oxides had been condoned by someone higher up. He had assumed that she meant Kenneth Humbolt.

With Director Liu's identicard and access card

keys, Kinsolving hoped to be able to prove that. With evidence against Humbolt, he might be able to clear himself of the murder charges, also.

If nothing else, he could prove to Chairman Fremont that he had nothing to do with stealing from the company—and that the true culprit was still seated on the board of directors.

Barton Kinsolving left the room, seeking the executive elevators that would take him to Director Liu's office and the computer access available there.

CHAPTER EIGHTEEN

BARTON KINSOLVING thrust the stolen identicard into the receptor slot near the elevator. For a moment, he imagined alarms sounding in the heart of the headquarters building, armed guards rushing out to capture him, a million overlooked details tripping him up.

The doors silently slid open to reveal a spacious room; Kinsolving hesitantly advanced. The doors slid shut behind him. Only then did he realize this *was* an elevator.

"Floor?" came a soft voice. Kinsolving spun around, seeking the source of the sound.

He laughed ruefully. He had always wanted robot voices to sound human; he had railed about the information center in the lobby sounding so mechanical. The directors of Interstellar Materials shared his distaste and for their private use had programmed the computer properly.

"Director Liu's office," he said.

"May I check the authorization pass?" the computer asked. A single wall panel glowed a dull, cool blue in anticipation of reading the pass.

"This is a direct order. Take me to the director's office."

"Please, sir. I have been ordered to inquire of any unescorted passengers using this elevator."

Kinsolving glanced at the closed door and knew that he would be trapped if he couldn't produce the proper card key. He pulled out the stack of cards stolen from Liu and flipped through them, wondering which, if any, would be an appropriate pass.

A light blue card matching the panel seemed a good choice. He touched it to the panel and the light immediately vanished. The computer said, "Thank you, sir. Sorry for the inconvenience."

"Security is important," he said, wiping sweat from his forehead.

"I am happy you understand, sir."

Even before the computer had finished the apology, the doors slid open to show the directors' suites. Kinsolving left the elevator, cautiously checking every cross corridor. The anniversary celebrations had taken the staff from their usual posts. For that, Kinsolving heaved a deep sigh of relief. A stolen key card might get him past an elevator computer but it wouldn't work with a human guard or curious staff member.

Kinsolving wandered the lavishly decorated halls until he came to a door with Liu's name inlaid in gold and rubies. Using the identicard gained him entry.

He sat down in the chair behind the broad desk and shook. He wasn't used to breaking and entering. The strain of being keyed and ready for flight at the slightest noise had worked a toll on him both physically and emotionally.

Kinsolving settled his nerves and swung about in the plush chair and stared out over the city. This level of the gold and emerald building rose above the dome of atmosphere contained in the bowl of the crater. The ebon starkness of space allowed the stars to shine, even in midday, with diamond hardness.

"To work here," he muttered.

"May I be of service?" came the immediate response from a hidden computer.

"Yes. I need to view company files."

Kinsolving sat back when a computer console rose from the bare desktop. He moved the chair closer and hesitantly tapped at the keys. Surprise blossomed when he found that he didn't have to enter an access code. Liu was Comptroller of Interstellar Materials and had all financial records at his fingertips. Kinsolving realized again how lucky he had been to get into this office. The computer hadn't required passwords because of the impossibility of anyone reaching this point without being detected and stopped.

He jumped at every slight noise made in the outer offices. Kinsolving worked quickly, not sure what he wanted. From time to time he took notes on all that he found in the records of liftings from Deepdig. Other inquiries showed that the Deepdig shipping records had been altered to reflect not what had been lifted but what remained after a considerable portion had been stolen.

He found no evidence to show that Humbolt had been responsible. From the records available to Liu, he couldn't even show theft had occurred.

"If nothing is obvious, then they can't come back and say I was responsible. Whoever has stolen the ore has done a great job of covering up."

"Theft, sir?" came the attentive computer voice.

"Cancel," he said quickly.

Only the Lorr charge of murder appeared to be of any significance. That Kinsolving considered a mixed blessing. He had only this charge to disprove to clear his name. But proving his innocence would be difficult—more so if he couldn't show why Humbolt or Cameron would want to make it look as if he had committed the crime.

No theft, no motive to frame him.

He finished his probing with a complete listing of

destinations for the refined rare earths. He cursed under his breath as he handwrote all he saw on the console screen. Daring to ask for a hard copy might be his undoing if a notation were made internally. He doubted screen access would trigger such a counter.

He hoped that it wouldn't.

"Finished," he said, standing. He had been here too long and had gained little for his effort. Kinsolving went back to the elevator, lost in thought. He entered the spacious room, then looked up when the computer again asked for access card.

Once more the panel glowed a light blue, but this time Kinsolving accidentally pressed the unmarked card against it.

The elevator dropped precipitously, then came to a halt amid a mechanical grinding that made him worry about the machinery's safety.

"Is anything wrong?" he asked.

"Secured entry permitted," the computer said. Kinsolving stiffened when the computer added, "All success to the Plan!"

The doors opened. Kinsolving looked at the panel indicator inside the elevator but nothing showed. He poked his head out and looked around. The directors' offices had been luxurious beyond even a sybarite's dream. This floor proved as plain as an Earth office. Kinsolving slipped from the elevator and looked around.

No secretaries' desks lined these halls. No indication of any staff hinted at the importance of the few offices he found. Kinsolving looked into one office. It was almost empty. The next he found in similar condition. The last five had desks and computer consoles, but nothing as elaborate as that in Director Liu's office.

If the computer voice hadn't mentioned this mysterious "Plan" Kinsolving would have believed that a malfunction had dropped him onto a floor populated by minor, insignificant functionaries.

The office appearing to be used most drew him. He sat in the chair and tentatively touched the keys on the computer console. The screen glowed phosphorescently.

"What is the access code? Or is there one?" he asked, then clamped his mouth shut, waiting for the answering office robot. No robot. No sounds except for the distant creaks of the building heating and cooling. Kinsolving glanced out the window and saw that the view from the crystal windows was obscured by turbulence. This strange grouping of offices was positioned at the boundary layer between the dome of atmosphere sheltering the city and the harshness of space, almost as if by plan.

Plan. The Plan. *The* Plan.

Kinsolving worked at the console. His first attempts produced only restricted notations. Some codes were required, but general access had to gain him more information than he now had.

Under his breath, he mumbled as he worked. "What *is* the Plan?" he asked, putting this question to the computer, not expecting a response—and astounded when it began rolling across the screen.

Kinsolving sat back and read as fast as he could. The words reeled by with the precision of marching soldiers and he missed much, but he got more than he'd hoped.

Frantically, he scribbled notes on a scrap of paper. Again he wished he could send his captured output to hard copy, but that was out of the question. Kinsolving wondered that he hadn't set off alarms all over the building. Then he smiled wanly. The people responsible for the Stellar Death Plan wouldn't want to alert anyone else to their subversion, to their misuse of IM property.

He settled back and held his head between shaking hands when the scrolling had stopped. He knew where the stolen rare earth oxides had been shipped, how they had been stolen—and their purpose. He shivered all over at the magnitude of the Plan.

"Who's responsible?" he wondered aloud. "Who?" Nowhere in his search did he discover a listing of those at Interstellar Materials instituting such a diabolic plan for mass alien destruction.

A slight sound from the corridor alerted Kinsolving. He leaped from the chair and raced to the door. He pressed his ear against the panel but heard nothing. Kinsolving pulled the door open slowly against its mechanism until a slit allowed him a view of the hallway.

His heart almost stopped at the sight. Cameron patrolled the hall, his robot hunter hovering at his knee. As Kinsolving watched, the gaudily dressed man paused, head tipped to one side as if listening. Cameron turned ninety degrees, reached out and opened an office door.

"Go!" the man cried. The robot hunter dazzled Kinsolving with the speed of its departure. One instant it hung at Cameron's side, the next it simply vanished. He had no desire to find out its other capabilities.

He evaluated his chances. If he stayed, Cameron would find him. The tracking senses of the robot must be acute—why it hadn't already found him hardly mattered. It would. Soon.

Kinsolving acted before he thought through the consequences. He left the relative safety of the office and dashed into the hall. Cameron heard and spun to his right. Kinsolving's fist found the fop's nose. Kinsolving felt cartilage crushing and warm blood spurting. Cameron strangely did not emit any sound. He shifted weight and tried to counter, but Kinsolving still had the advantage. Instinctively, he used it. A hard shoulder caught Cameron high on the chest and sent the man reeling back into the office being investigated by his robot hunter.

Cameron crashed to the floor, momentarily shaken. Kinsolving slammed the office door and fumbled, finding his blank card. He pressed it into the key slot. A soft "snick" signaled the door locking.

Heart racing and breath coming in ragged gasps, Kinsolving stumbled back and dived into the waiting elevator.

"Your identicard is required, sir," came the soft, polite, human-sounding voice.

"Main lobby," he said, presenting Liu's blank card—the card that had unlocked the Stellar Death Plan for him.

"Thank you, sir." Kinsolving gasped at the speed of descent. He tumbled into the lobby, but no one noticed. They were too intent on their holiday, their own celebration of Interstellar Materials' two hundredth anniversary.

Barton Kinsolving had no idea where he ran, but he knew he had to get away from the headquarters, from Cameron, from the robot that would soon be sent after him.

CHAPTER NINETEEN

BARTON KINSOLVING tried to control his burgeoning fear. The thought of Cameron's deadly robot hunter coming after him made him want to run and run and run. To do so would attract unwanted attention. At points around the huge lobby stood corporate security guards. Their function was more ceremonial than enforcement, but Kinsolving didn't doubt that they would spring into action if Cameron—or any IM director—ordered them after a fugitive.

He was the fugitive. And he felt the pressure of time. He had rifled the files of Interstellar Materials and stolen a director's entry card keys. Those two crimes would send him to prison on Gamma Tertius 4, but Kinsolving knew that would be preferable to spending the rest of his life on the alien prison world.

But prison wasn't where he would end up if Cameron caught him. After reading the brief summary of their Stellar Death Plan in the tiny offices sandwiched between corporate floors, he posed more danger to them alive than he did dead.

"Who are they?" he muttered.

"Sir?" asked a guard. "Did you say something?"

"Nothing. Just talking to myself."

The guard eyed him curiously. Kinsolving swore under his breath. He hadn't wanted to attract attention. Now this guard would remember him when questioned. Kinsolving hurried from the lobby and stood looking directly west at the craggy spire of Mt. New Daisy Bates turning ochre in the rays of the too-distant setting sun. Did the rim wall around the city hold sanctuary for him?

Kinsolving didn't think so. The area encompassed by this artificial city had seemed immense when he had landed. Now it constricted, squeezed in on him, made him feel that there wasn't any room to run. With IM owning everything in the city—and on Gamma Tertius 4—he had no one to turn to. Everyone worked for the company in some capacity, even the smallest shop owner in the commercial section.

Most owed considerable devotion to Interstellar Materials, too, for getting them off overcrowded Earth, away from the pollution and ruin, and for giving them jobs.

Kinsolving held his head, feeling as if it would explode. His temples pounded like an ocean surf and the arteries in his throat throbbed and cut off his wind. He had to escape, he had to hide, he had to think.

Walking aimlessly would only work against him. Kinsolving took a few seconds and decided that a park provided the best chance for concealment. Anywhere that he might stay away from prying eyes gave Kinsolving that much more hope.

The park system of GT 4 had been designed by experts to give the maximum amount of privacy in the smallest possible space. The greenery helped the city air supply to a small degree, but oxygen and other gases for the atmosphere were artificially generated.

Kinsolving walked slowly along a path, then left it, going across a grassy sward to a rocky alcove with a scenic view of a tiny waterfall and stream meandering through the park. From this vantage he could see most approaches without being obvi-

ous. He settled down and tried to work out a real
escape.

Leaving Gamma Tertius 4 would be dangerous.
Cameron would immediately close off the Landing
Authority. He probably knew who he hunted—Kinsolving now believed that the aliens would have
alerted IM about the escape from the prison planet.
Even if Cameron had no idea who had broken into
the Plan offices and struck him, the LA would be
closed down tight. That might prove a problem for
IM in a few days when many of the guests started to
leave the parties to return to their duty stations
out-space. Until then, the LA could admit anyone
coming in from off-planet and not seem restrictive.

Or did anyone on GT 4 care about such things?
The company ruled the planet. Would they meekly
abide by any corporate decision, no matter how op-
pressive or in violation of Earth law?

Such as destroying entire planets and their alien
populations? Kinsolving shuddered at what he had
found in the computer files. The Stellar Death Plan
was nothing less than a blueprint for genocide on a
scale undreamed of before. A few million had died
at the hands of Earthly dictators.

Those fostering the Stellar Death Plan had
grander and bloodier dreams.

They would slaughter alien races down to the last
individual. And, from what Kinsolving guessed,
they wouldn't stop with just one. They wanted *all*
aliens dead. The paranoia about other species he
had heard in Kenneth Humbolt's words had been
translated into action on a scale so vast Kinsolving
wanted to think it was all a gigantic prank being
played on him.

He knew it wasn't. The look on Cameron's face
when he murdered the Lorr agent-captain proved
graphically that this was no joke. Cameron had
wanted to kill the alien, had *enjoyed* it.

Kinsolving's mind rolled and turned and spun and came up with no idea what he should do. Even escaping GT 4 would prove difficult. If he didn't, the best he might hope for would be death. The worst? Return to the alien prison world. Kinsolving had to chuckle at that thought, though. Cameron and Humbolt would be certain that he never left Gamma Tertius 4 alive.

Not after he had seen the broad outline of their vicious, racist Plan.

"What alien would believe me if I told them?" Kinsolving said aloud. The answer had to be simple: none. He had been convicted of killing a Lorr, a crime viewed as extreme by the aliens. They would assume he concocted details of the Plan to escape punishment.

Kinsolving stood and paced around the small rock enclosure, trying to find a way out, a way to alert the aliens to their danger without bringing horrendous retribution down on Earth and all humans, a way of stopping Humbolt before he carried out his savage scheme.

An electric tension in the air caused Kinsolving to stop his nervous movements and peer hard toward the entrance to the park. He saw only a few pedestrians walking slowly, some hand in hand. This was all he saw, but the man *felt* far more.

He knew in that instant how prey felt when sighted by a hungry predator.

Kinsolving held down the impulse to bolt and run for his life. Common sense prevailed. If he did, whoever sought him would be able to pinpoint him instantly. Who else in the park ran? Who else would emit the sweat of fear and the stench of panic?

He climbed to the top of the rocky cul-de-sac and got a better view of the trails leading to his high point. Kinsolving went into shock when he saw Cameron and his robot hunter slowly following his path up the hill. The robot swayed to and fro, as if swinging on a spring. The far end of each deviation from the path caused it to bob and bounce, then it returned, to repeat the procedure on the far side. It checked for spoor, both visual and odorous.

Did it also have sound and motion detectors? Could it hear the frenzied beating of his heart? See the way his chest throbbed under his shirt?

Kinsolving calmed. It was a machine and nothing more. Its senses might be enhanced, more acute than any human's, but it required constant programming. Without Cameron tending it, the robot hunter was nothing. Nothing but a dumb machine.

The fear remained but it no longer paralyzed him. Kinsolving started to plot how best to eliminate Cameron. The flashes off his bright clothing from the rays of the setting sun turned to blood before they reached Kinsolving. The man vowed that it would be Cameron's blood, not his own, spilled this day. Hadn't he already broken the man's nose?

That might anger Cameron, cause him to make mistakes he wouldn't normally. Kinsolving could only hope.

Seeing the way Cameron advanced, however, dashed any hope of the predator becoming careless because of rage. Cameron walked slowly along the path paying no attention to his robot hunter. His eyes scaled the heights for any trace of his prey. Once Kinsolving saw the man stop and cock his head, listening hard.

Cameron put his hands on his hips and rocked back, yelling, "There is no need to be tedious about this, Supervisor Kinsolving. Please come out. I bear you no malice for damaging my nose." Cameron reached up and ran his finger along its straight, hawkish length. "I've already gotten it tended to. Come down and let's talk."

He appeared foppish, but Kinsolving had seen

him kill without remorse. What weapons did Cameron have hidden? Kinsolving almost laughed aloud at his own stupidity. What weapon did Cameron need when he had that robot hunter coursing back and forth?

"Weapon!" Kinsolving exclaimed. He had forgotten the stun rod he'd stolen so long ago. He fumbled about inside his shirt and found the slender rod. Pulling it out and holding it gave him a small thrill of advantage. But he knew next to nothing about such things. What was its range? Glancing down at Cameron, he estimated the distance to be greater than a hundred meters. Kinsolving didn't want to test the weapon in this fashion.

"Supervisor?" came Cameron's call. "My robotic friend has your track now. It would have worked quicker except that it had no scent to compare with the trail. Now that it does, it will be able to follow you through even the densest population. Crowds will not shelter you or confuse my robotic friend, Mr. Kinsolving. Make it easy on yourself. Come down and let's talk."

From robot hunter's homing motions, Kinsolving knew that Cameron wasn't lying. The machine had found his scent and now worked quickly to close distance. Kinsolving scrambled down the far side of the hill, out of breath by the time he reached the bottom. Only open grassy meadows stretched in front. The curvature of the hill on either side offered scant protection.

Or did it? The robot would not attempt to outguess him. It would follow his track exactly, no matter how he dodged. In that might be his salvation.

Taking the rockier side, Kinsolving began working his way around the hill, slowing when he came to the side where Cameron had stood. The man had advanced in the wake of his robot hunter. Something warned Cameron. He pulled out a heavy rod—a weapon Kinsolving didn't recognize. Cameron started to circle the hill, as if he had some hint of what Kinsolving had done.

Kinsolving could run. Both robot and master would take long minutes to find what he had done. But that gained Kinsolving nothing. Flight only prolonged the inevitable.

He attacked.

Stun rod in hand, he started directly up the slope after the robot hunter. He hoped that Cameron had ranged far enough not to hear his somewhat clumsy assault.

Cameron didn't; the robot did. The metallic insect swung about its axis, repulsor field whining slightly with the exertion. Thin whips lashed back and forth like obscene antennae. Flat ceramic disks replaced the compound eyes of a true insect, but Kinsolving saw only the similarities and not the differences.

The robot hunter launched itself with the silence of a true predator on the hunt. Fat blue sparks jumped from its whip-antennae as it gained speed over the rough terrain.

Kinsolving stood still, waiting, waiting, waiting. He had one chance to survive. When the robot came within ten meters he lifted the stun rod and pressed the trigger button. A small hum sounded.

The robot hunter surged forward, unaffected. Kinsolving almost panicked and fled. To have done so would have meant his death. He held his ground and repeatedly triggered the stun rod. One antenna exploding from the ray was Kinsolving's only victory before the robot smashed hard into him, knocking him flat on his back.

He reached up and grabbed at the slippery metal body. No purchase. His hands locked behind the robot's back. With all the strength he had left, Kinsolving applied the bear hug. He yelped when he received a powerful electric shock. He felt flesh searing, his chest muscles jerking with the current. He dared not stop. He again twisted savagely to dislodge the robot. The robot rolled to one side, its repulsor field whining shrilly. As they rolled down the hill, the robot's other antenna snapped off.

This boosted Kinsolving's morale. He applied even more power to his death grip. Rocks tore at his skin, grazed his forehead, cut a portion from one earlobe. He clung to the struggling robot as if his life depended on it—and it did.

Grunting, Kinsolving got his knees under him. With all his strength, he twisted and smashed the robot hunter into a small boulder. The machine's repulsor field died. Through its casing, he felt the fading of its internal power. Kinsolving tossed the dead robot aside and leaned back to rest. He mopped off some of the blood oozing from a half dozen cuts, then realized he had no time for this.

Cameron still prowled the area. His robot might be deactivated but the human hunter remained at large and as deadly as ever.

Kinsolving bent and fumbled at the releases at the side of the robot hunter to get to its internal computer. He failed. On impulse, he pulled out Director Liu's identicard and touched it to the lock. The access panel slid open to reveal the robot's block circuit memory. Kinsolving plucked it free.

If the robot had "memorized" his scent as Cameron had claimed, a new robot would have to be used—and one without the benefit of that sensory imprint. A quick survey of the insides showed that his stun rod had been more effective than he'd thought. Small circuits had overloaded. The robot hunter hadn't been stopped, but it had been impaired enough for Kinsolving to wrestle it to death.

Kinsolving searched for his stun rod but failed to

find it. Rather than waste precious time hunting for it and possibly being found by Cameron, the man started down the path leading from the park.

The city was a trap for him. Nowhere to turn, nowhere to run. But boldness and courage had aided him this far. He had nothing to lose attempting another daring move. Feet pounding hard, he ran from the park. All the way he imagined Cameron's hand descending to his shoulder to stop him, to pull him around and administer the death blow.

It never came.

He returned to Interstellar Materials' headquarters. Liu's identicard still opened doors. With a little luck, he could even find Lark Versalles at the anniversary party.

But what then? Barton Kinsolving had no idea.

CHAPTER TWENTY

BARTON KINSOLVING smoothed off the dirt from his dress clothing and tried to minimize the wrinkles and tears by tucking what he could in under belts and behind a curiously buttoned jacket. The cuts on his face had to be left untended. He doubted anyone would notice—not yet, at least. When Cameron found his pet robot hunter destroyed, the city wouldn't be a fit place to be seen unless every identicard entry matched the one in Interstellar Materials' main computer banks.

Kinsolving fingered Director Liu's identicard and the other card keys he'd stolen. How much longer would these be useful? One careless moment using them and Kinsolving might call down the entire IM security force.

He entered the lobby and skirted the tight knot of people near the center by hugging the wall. It took twice as long to reach the elevators, but caution rather than speed ruled him now. He hoped that Cameron would scour the city for him. Returning to the heart of IM's power—and those who had concocted the Stellar Death Plan—would be suicidal.

Kinsolving hoped that Cameron thought along those lines. It was all that gave the man any chance for escape.

The elevator took him directly to the one-hundred-first floor where the party had become an orgy. Kinsolving's upbringing hadn't been prudish,

but such wanton behavior unnerved him. He had no
idea how to act, how to react when confronted with
licentiousness.

"Barton darling!" came a familiar voice. With relief, Kinsolving turned to see Lark Versalles hurrying toward him, a man and a woman in tow. "I want
you to meet two of my dearest friends. This is Dinky
and this gorgeous whiff of nebula dust is Rani du-
Long. Rani arrived just after we did but she's made
up for lost time."

Lark took a long, critical look at Kinsolving.
"Whatever have you been doing, darling? You
really ought to take your clothes off before doing it,
whatever it is."

"I agree," said Rani, moving close to Kinsolving.
Her fingers slipped through tears in his shirt and
stroked over bare flesh. She curled her fingers
slightly and began tugging. The ripping of cloth
sounded, even over the raucous music and the bois-
terous laughter from the party goers. "Such a nice
... friend you have, Lark."

"He's all mine, dear," Lark said, slipping between
them.

"What a pity. We've always shared before. Aren't
we friends?" Rani's hot gaze made Kinsolving increasingly uneasy. He couldn't tell if her dress had
been designed to reveal all that it did or if it had
been torn off by some overly amorous suitor.

Seeing the dark-haired woman's response when
she saw his own tattered finery, Kinsolving thought
she might enjoy ripping clothes before enjoying
other pursuits.

"I've got to talk to you, Lark. In private."

"Oh, all right. But just for a moment. Dinky
wants this dance, and I did promise." Lark looked
over her shoulder, reached out and lightly stroked
the man's strong, square chin. Kinsolving noted the

laser scalpel scars where cosmetic surgery had been performed to give a weak jawline solidity.

He spun Lark around and said quickly, "We've got to leave. I'm in real trouble."

"Didn't you find anyone to take your case to Chairman Fremont?" Lark frowned. "What a shame. I'll see what I can do. There are several junior vice presidents who owe me a favor. I'm sure one might take up your case. And if not, it will be fun trying."

"No, wait," he said. "There's been a change, a discovery." He licked his lips, not knowing how to phrase this. "I came across some records that people in IM don't want revealed."

"So promise not to divulge them. That's easy." Lark's bright blue eyes stared ingenuously at him. Kinsolving had to wonder if she were really this innocent or if it were a pose. He couldn't tell.

"What I found makes me more valuable dead than alive."

"Over some silly ore thefts?" Lark sniffed elegantly.

"The records have been altered. There's no way I can be accused of the rare earth thefts since it doesn't appear that they ever occurred."

"No one stole the ore?"

"The records have been changed to show that. The theft happened—and I know who is responsible. But Humbolt can't be indicted, and he's done such a good job, neither can I."

"Then there's no problem. What is *wrong*, Barton darling?"

"There's still the charge of murder. The Lorr agent-captain."

"Hmm, yes, that is serious, but they wouldn't turn you over to the aliens. Plead something-or-another. Do your sentence in an Earth prison."

"What would you say if I uncovered a plot by executives in Interstellar Materials to kill entire planets—entire races!—of aliens?"

"What do you mean?"

"The rare earths are being used to manufacture electronic devices that other species use as we do drugs. The difference is that the devices will first addict, then kill."

"They shouldn't stray from eng-drugs." Lark reached into a small sash and drew forth a tiny box. The top popped open and a tiny tube rose. At the bottom of the golden box Kinsolving saw a light purple powder, an engineered drug popular with those able to afford it. "I had this made for my own brain chemistry, but I'm sure it will do you a world of good. Try it, Bart."

He looked at the box and recoiled slightly. A quick sniff would alter his mood in whatever fashion Lark Versalles thought the most enticing. And it would leave no physical trace, being engineered for its nonaddictive nature. The electronic devices IM—or some at the company—proposed would do far more. Thrills, excitement, habituation, addiction, permanent brain damage, those were the results of their project.

"They mean to kill entire planets of people."

"Of aliens," she said. "They're hardly people. Well, they *are* but they're not our kind. You know what I mean."

"We don't have time to argue this. I've found out about their plan. They don't dare let me live to tell anyone about it."

"Who're 'they?'" Lark asked.

"I..." Kinsolving looked across the dance floor at the gyrating men and women. Which of these people *were* responsible? He couldn't believe that Humbolt alone conceived their Stellar Death Plan. A hand lightly brushed over the pocket where he had placed Director Liu's key cards. Liu had to be a part of the Plan, too. He had carried the blank access card.

But who else knew, who else in Interstellar Materials planned on a slaughter vaster than anything in Earth history? He saw the joyous faces, the taut faces, the strained, tense faces. Which of these also contorted in fear and hatred to order the deaths of billions of intelligent alien beings?

"We've got to go, Lark. Please, before it's too late." Kinsolving felt the noose tightening around him. Cameron had been careless twice. Expecting him to make the same mistake a third time seemed out of the question.

"I promised this dance to Dinky. Then we'll talk." Lark spun away, laughing and smiling at her friends. He watched her slip into the circle of Dinky's arms and glide away, gracefully moving in time with the music.

Kinsolving shifted nervously from foot to foot, wanting to leave, yet needing Lark. He had to get back into orbit to the *Nightingale*. No other escape opened to him. By the time Cameron finished his cordon, the Gamma Tertius 4 Landing Authority might not allow any vessel to shift from orbit.

"Shall we do it?" came a sultry voice. Kinsolving jumped.

"Shall we do what?" he asked, seeing that Rani duLong had returned.

"Dance," she said, her eyes challenging him. "Unless you can think of something more interesting."

"Later," he said.

"Then we dance." Rani took him in a surprisingly strong grip and whirled him to the center of the dance floor. Kinsolving had never considered himself a good dancer but with the sinuous grace shown by Rani, anyone looked better.

"Lark speaks well of you. She says that you're more exciting than anyone she's met in the past couple years." Rani rubbed seductively against him. "What are your hidden talents?"

"I keep her amused by my, uh, antics," Kinsolving said lamely. He almost stopped the dance and begged off when he saw Cameron enter. Fear surged. He held his rampaging emotions in check and whirled Rani into the center of the crowd.

"You're sweating," Rani said. "Am I that hot?"

"Yes," he said. Kinsolving whirled her around and around until the woman threw back her head and let her long midnight black hair sail forth in a wide circle. She laughed, a sound as pure and clean as ringing silver bells.

"You do have your moments," she said, dark eyes fixed on him. "I'd like to find out more about them —and see if I can't turn them into hours, or even days."

"After the dance," Kinsolving insisted. He kept most of the dancers between him and Cameron. Beside the gaudily dressed man hovered two robot hunters. From the occasional glimpses Kinsolving got, these robot hunters were different from the one he had destroyed in the park. With thicker casings and more heavily armored parts, these might have been war machines reduced in size for use within the city.

Cameron would relish the use of such deadly machines. Kinsolving might have defeated himself by destroying the lesser robot hunter. He had only given Cameron an excuse to use more powerful robots.

"Are you avoiding someone?" Rani asked.

"What if I am?"

"Oh, you men. You're all alike. I'm an expert at avoiding people I don't want to meet again. Or at meeting people I do." She moved slightly out of tempo with the music and slipped across Kinsolving's body so that he moaned softly in response.

"Now. Who is it you want to avoid? I'll show you how."

"The man in the emerald green jacket and pink ruffled shirt."

"Actually," she said, "it's salmon. But I do see him. He has a strange look about him. So cold, in spite of the radiance of his clothing."

"What's he doing?"

"How peculiar. He went directly to Lark. She's leaving with him. She and Dinky. No, Dinky's staying behind. Odd. I've never seen him give up a dance partner so easily."

Kinsolving swung about and got a quick glimpse of Cameron leaving with Lark. The two robot hunters flanked them. The robot nearest Lark emitted tiny blue sparks from one antenna. The first hint of escape would produce a nasty shock— or even death. Kinsolving couldn't discount Cameron's ruthlessness. But why take Lark? Had they somehow connected her with him?

"Cameron is arresting her," he told Rani.

"Lark? Arrested? Oh, this is cosmic! She'll have stories to tell for years to come. What did this Cameron arrest her for? Something you two are responsible for? Oh, yes, yes!" Rani cried. "You're a smuggler. How romantic. What did you smuggle, Barton?"

"You make it sound as if they'll let her go in an hour or so."

"Why not? She hasn't done anything. Not really. Smuggling is hardly enough of a crime to hold Lark Versalles!"

"What if they killed her? What if Cameron took her to the top of this building and shoved her off the roof?"

"But he couldn't. It's airless at the top. Lark wouldn't be able to breathe."

Kinsolving said nothing. The idea slowly penetrated that he meant what he said. Rani's expression changed from confusion to outrage. "He wouldn't dare harm her!"

"I saw him murder a Lorr on Deepdig. Cameron is capable of anything."

"But an alien is, well, an *alien*. We're talking about Lark!"

"A life's a life to Cameron—an alien or human one is equally as cheap."

"We'll see about this. Who's his superior?" Rani's anger rose now. One of her friends had gotten into real trouble. Kinsolving admired her loyalty but not her proposed method.

How could he know which of the IM executives knew of the Plan? All? Some? Which? Glancing around the room he saw none of the highest level. No director or senior vice president was in attendance, even though dozens of the junior executives frolicked and politicked.

"Director Liu," he said, realization coming to him. "That's why Cameron took Lark."

"Lark was with the director earlier," said Rani. "She bragged about it. But why should this Cameron object? Unless he and Director Liu..."

"No, not that," said Kinsolving. He had drawn Lark deeper into this intrigue than he'd intended. Cameron had checked the elevator record to see which identicard had been used. Director Liu had found his card case missing. The conclusion: Lark Versalles had stolen the key cards.

"What should we do?" Rani duLong asked.

"I don't know. I just don't know." Barton Kinsolving tried to hold back a rising tide of helplessness and failed.

CHAPTER TWENTY-ONE

"I'M CERTAIN it's all a misunderstanding. Lark will be able to talk her way out of it. Or maybe," Rani duLong said, leering slightly, "have something of a new adventure getting away from this Cameron. After all, he's only a man."

Kinsolving wouldn't have wagered on that. He had seen the demonic glee in Cameron's eyes when he had killed. The robots accompanying him were also killers. No one commanded such dangerous machines unless their use aided a mission.

Cameron's mission had to be killing. Nothing else fit. The foppish exterior hid a cold, cunning attitude.

"He's a supporter of their Plan," Kinsolving said. "He doesn't dare release Lark, not if he thinks she knows anything about it."

"Plan? What plan?" asked Rani. "Oh, I know."

"What? You do?" asked Kinsolving, his mind light years from all that happened around him.

"I've got the perfect plan. Let Lark suffer for a while, then rescue her. Until then, let's dance." Rani smiled wickedly. "Unless you can think of something else you'd prefer to do—together."

"Rescue," mused Kinsolving. He had to help Lark Versalles. Because she had aided him she now found herself in serious danger. He owed her his life for getting him off the alien prison world, if nothing else. She hadn't asked to be involved.

Rescue. How? No scheme surfaced. He allowed Rani to lead him to the dance floor. Mechanically moving his feet, hardly noticing the lovely woman in his arms, Kinsolving thought. Hard.

The card keys he'd stolen from Director Liu should be discarded. Their use would trigger alarms. Cameron would send a robot hunter to the spot of usage within minutes. Kinsolving didn't even know where Lark had been taken. To the barren suite of rooms devoted to the Stellar Death Plan? Possibly, though he doubted it. Most of the headquarters building was deserted today, the employees at parties or taking a holiday. Interstellar Materials was nothing if not generous in this respect.

A director's office? Kinsolving doubted that, too, unless Kenneth Humbolt personally conducted the woman's interrogation. From all that Kinsolving had seen of Cameron, the gaudy manhunter wouldn't want to share the task. He'd consider it a pleasure, even a thrill in some sexual way.

Kinsolving shuddered. His mind refused to grasp the fact that these people were capable of any atrocity. Any group able to contemplate the extinction of entire races wouldn't hesitate at the rape and torture of a single woman if they thought she had information they needed.

"Are you cold, Barton, or just anticipating?" Rani asked. He stared at the beautiful woman in wonder. She seemed oblivious to all that he'd said. She couldn't believe that Lark Versalles was in danger.

"Do you know the headquarters building well?"

"Not really. I've only been here a few times for parties. Dinky has a small place on the other side of the city, though. He spends a good part of his time on GT 4. He does. Why?"

Kinsolving already guided Rani off the dance floor. He scanned the crowd and found Dinky propped against a wall, leaning over a chair and trying not to collapse totally. Kinsolving dragged Rani after him. By the time they arrived at Dinky's side, the man had slumped over the chair and snored loudly.

"He's not much help." Rani stared at the man in contempt. "This isn't the only time he falls asleep, either."

Kinsolving sat down beside the unconscious man and shook him hard. Dinky groaned and mumbled something incoherent. Kinsolving steeled himself. He had been raised to avoid harming others. He took Dinky's earlobe and pinched down hard enough to cause a tiny crescent of blood to form. The pain lanced directly into the man's brain past the haze of the drugs he'd taken.

"Whatsit?" he demanded.

"Conference rooms. Where?" demanded Kinsolving.

"Director's rooms?" Dinky said, eyes still not focused.

"What level?"

"One-eighty, one-eighty-one."

Kinsolving sucked in a deep breath and held it for a long minute before slowly releasing it. This building was too immense to search floor by floor. He had to hope that Cameron had taken Lark to one of those levels.

"Do you want to play a new game?" he asked Dinky, talking to the young man as if he were a small child.

"Photonic!" cried Rani. "To hell with him. *I'd* like to play!"

"Great. The two of you can try it." Kinsolving fumbled out the stolen identicard and the card keys. "Here's how you play. Go to the lobby and wait for five minutes. Then try to see how many different places these cards will take you. Elevators, secured areas, everywhere."

"And?" prompted Rani.

"The one who gets into the most places, uh," Kinsolving stumbled here. What would be adequate prize for these jaded sybarites? "The one who gets into the most places wins and the other has to do anything the winner wants for one hour."

"Anything?"

"Anything," Kinsolving agreed solemnly.

Kinsolving fanned through the cards. He had five. He held them up for her to see. "You choose a card. And you, too, Dinky. And find three others to join in."

"You're not playing?" asked Rani, obviously disappointed. Her interest in this "game" extended only to winning Kinsolving for the promised hour. He looked at the card keys, then slipped the blank one into his pocket. It would be very dangerous to allow those besotted revellers to blunder into that special level—it might mean their instant death.

Kinsolving wanted confusion, not death.

"I'll play using the blank card. I'm not sure what it's good for, anyway," he lied.

"Morganna and Chakki will want to play. Come along, Dinky. Let's find them." She turned dark, blazing eyes on Kinsolving. "We start in the lobby in five minutes?"

He nodded, smiling now. Rani thought it was for her. She need not know that Kinsolving had no intention of playing and that there would never be a winner in this mad, dangerous game.

Except Lark, if he could find her.

Kinsolving watched Rani help Dinky to the elevator. Two others followed closely, engaged in animated conversation. The man—Kinsolving had already forgotten his name—seemed reluctant.

Morganna urged him along, and this was enough to get him to play.

They vanished into the elevator and Kinsolving went into action. Dinky had mentioned two possible levels where Lark might be. Kinsolving didn't dare spend the time searching those floors. He entered an empty elevator and ordered it to take him to the one hundred-eightieth floor. Kinsolving held his breath as the doors slid back silently. He expected to see a smiling Cameron waiting for him, both robot hunters hovering at his side.

The corridor stretching to a panorama of crystal windows at the far side of the building loomed silent and ominously deserted. Kinsolving listened for the slightest sound and heard nothing, but he had hardly expected to. All rooms in IM's headquarters were soundproofed. Lark might be screaming in a room only a few paces away and he would never hear.

He dashed to a receptionist's desk and scanned the control console. The complex array of indicators daunted him. It took a trained operator to use it to its fullest. But all Kinsolving needed was a moment's worth of information.

He seated himself and held the blank card key over the identi-slot. A sudden thought hit him. He smiled slowly and put the card back into his pocket and drew out the duplicate of his original identicard given him at the Landing Authority. Cameron hadn't had time to enter a lock on this card—he might not have learned Kinsolving had reactivated his employee card.

Kinsolving paused, then boldly acted. His personal identicard slid into the acceptor.

"How may I serve you, Supervisor Kinsolving?" the computer asked.

"I need to know the location of at least two directors. They must be in the headquarters building and they must be together."

"Three directors are present in room 18117."

Kinsolving wobbled a little in the seat. "Are two of the directors Humbolt and Liu?"

"Yes."

Kinsolving wondered who the third might be. He hesitated to ask for this information, fearing that the computer would alert them.

"Cancel all request."

"Thank you, Supervisor." The screen went dark again. Kinsolving fought down real fear as he reinserted the card and once more was greeted by the computer.

"Monitor restricted elevator usage from level one-eighty-one," he ordered. Kinsolving waited anxiously. Rani and the others ought to be using Liu's stolen cards all over the building by now. That would alert Cameron; Kinsolving hoped the man would personally see to this new problem and go chasing off in four different directions.

A minute. Two. Kinsolving thought he would die of frustration waiting. He jumped when the computer said, "Directors Humbolt and Villalobos, accompanied by one assistant and three robot servants are descending to level thirty-two."

"Cancel," Kinsolving snapped. He grabbed his identicard. It might never be useful again, but he could only hope. Slowness in cancellation thus far had been a boon to him. It might continue.

He took the elevator to the floor above. If Humbolt and the others had taken the director's private elevator, he need not fear discovery; that elevator lay on the far side of the building. Kinsolving entered the deserted corridor, a duplicate of the floor below. Slowly, carefully, he looked around each corner as he made his way to 18117. In front of the door, he paused.

Lark wouldn't be unguarded. Kinsolving guessed that the "human assistant" with Humbolt and Villalobos was Cameron. If that supposition proved wrong, he would be in serious trouble.

If he didn't act quickly, he would be in even more serious danger—and Lark's life would be forfeit.

Kinsolving touched the door frame and the panel slid open silently. Lark was held against a far wall by a single band circling her waist and fastened into the wall. Her blue eyes widened when she saw him, but Kinsolving didn't have to warn her to silence. She realized her only hope of rescue lay with him.

"But, Director," she said too loudly, "why are you doing this? I don't know anything. My daddy is going to be *extremely* upset with you. With Interstellar Materials!"

"I'm sorry for this, my dear," Liu said. "But even your father won't be able to solve your problem. Where is your companion? Where is Kinsolving?"

Kinsolving didn't give the man a fair chance. He folded his hands together in a double fist and swung as hard as he could. The impact on the back of Liu's head sent the director forward onto his face. He groaned once, jerked, then lay still.

"Did you kill him?" asked Lark.

"Don't think so. How do you open this?" Kinsolving searched for the release. Only a card acceptor looked promising.

"That. They used a card. The one with Director Humbolt. Cameron."

The steel band tightly held her to the wall. Nothing less than a cutting torch would free Lark—or Cameron's card key.

"Here goes nothing," Kinsolving said, pulling out the blank card key. He inserted it. A soft click sounded and Lark Versalles tumbled free.

"Thank you, Barton darling. I *knew* you'd come.

This has been ever so much fun. But Director Liu *did* make me mad. How dare he chain me like this!"

"Come on," Kinsolving said. He had a bad feeling about using the special card key. The use of the stolen cards had triggered alarms to alert Cameron. This one would, also. This card of all those taken would be most likely to draw attention.

"Where are we going?"

"To the directors' private elevator," he said. Something alerted Kinsolving just before they turned the corner to the elevator. He shoved Lark into an office and clamped a hand over her mouth. She struggled for a moment, then settled down, her arms around him and her head on his shoulder. He left a finger between door and jamb, giving a restricted field of view into the hallway.

Cameron and a robot hunter glided by silently. Kinsolving counted to ten, then slid two more fingers into the slit and tugged the door open. Cameron had just turned the corner. Kinsolving motioned for Lark to hurry. They went to the directors' elevator. Again Kinsolving dared to use the blank card key—for the last time. Any more usage carried too great a risk.

The door slid open and the pleasant voice asked, "Floor?"

"Lobby," he said.

"Thank you, sir."

The elevator sank swiftly to the lobby. He feared the worst when the door opened, but no platoon of security guards descended like vultures on carrion. If anything, the lobby seemed more deserted now than it had been earlier.

"This is *so* exciting," Lark cooed. "Picking you off that silly alien world has been such an adventure." Lark kissed Kinsolving soundly.

"No time for that. We've got to get away, get off Gamma Tertius 4. Cameron and the others will be looking for us. And this time they won't be so gentle if they catch you."

"I'm really very vexed with them," Lark said. "Director Liu acted so rudely. And I must say that the dark woman—the one pretty in a dark sort of way, if you like the type—insulted me. Imagine!"

"Villalobos?" he asked. Kinsolving had seen the director only at the opening ceremony.

"Yes, she's the one."

"They've locked the lobby doors," he said suddenly. "There's no other reason not to have guards patrolling everywhere."

His fears proved accurate. "Sorry, sir, access is denied," said the mechanical voice. "Only Class four and higher passed allowed."

"I'm a Class five," he said. "Supervisor level." Kinsolving put his identicard into the acceptor slot. He thought a thunderbolt had sounded; the door lock had opened.

"Come on," he said, dragging Lark behind him. He retrieved his identicard but knew it would be of no use to him again. Cameron still hadn't learned of the duplicate card being issued by the LA. But he would. Each of the stolen card keys would be tracked down now, no matter how much Rani and the others dodged and ran, trying to win the "game" Kinsolving had set up for them.

"Where are we going?" asked Lark.

Barton Kinsolving stopped and stared up into the starlit dome of atmosphere over the city.

"I don't know," he said.

All escape seemed cut off now. He had done well to this point, but luck had run out.

CHAPTER TWENTY-TWO

"IT'S COLD," complained Lark Versalles. "The wind is killing me." She pulled the skirt of the blue dress up and tried to hide behind it like a little girl might. Kinsolving had no sympathy for her. She was worried about trivial matters; he sought a way for them to survive.

"There's a small rocky alcove I know in a park," he said. Kinsolving cursed his lack of knowledge of Interstellar Materials' corporate city. He had been lucky to stay alive by doubling back, returning to the spots where Cameron wouldn't think to look. Did he try that tactic once too often? Would Cameron find Director Liu unconscious and Lark freed and immediately guess that Kinsolving returned to the park?

Kinsolving had no way of knowing what a true predator would think. But he would have to learn or die.

He shielded Lark from the wind as much as he could as they followed the hard-packed trail into the cul-de-sac. The view of the city surprised him. The lights shone clear, pure and distinct. No pollution marred an exquisite view. He wished that he and Lark had come to this spot under different circumstances.

"This is better," she said. "But it's even nicer when you put your arm around me." She burrowed close, her face almost hidden in the front of his battered coat.

"We need to get off GT 4," he told her. "We can't use the shuttle service. Cameron will have guards waiting for us."

"Director Liu accused me of stealing his card keys. You took them, didn't you?"

He admitted that he had. "I used them for access to a special floor." His eyes turned to the immense glass spire rising in the center of the city. "What I found there is why they want to kill me—us."

"Do you want to tell me? I deserve to know."

Kinsolving considered. Telling Lark did nothing to further jeopardize her. If Cameron or his robot hunters caught her now, they would kill her. The more who know of the Stellar Death Plan, the better the chance of stopping it.

"Someone—maybe all the directors—has worked out a plan to destroy entire alien populations."

"Why?"

Kinsolving shook his head. This went against the teachings of every instructor in college. Earth had adopted a policy of accepting its second-rate place in galactic society—temporarily. By work and application and learning to live with the scores of other, alien intelligent races Earth might rise and take its place as an equal.

That was what he'd been taught. That was what Barton Kinsolving believed.

"I've heard Humbolt say that the aliens are intentionally holding Earth back, keeping us a minor power."

"It seems that way at times," Lark said. "But there are so many of them and so few of us, why should they?"

"Exactly. We're a nuisance, but not a threat. We're the brash newcomer who has to find a spot to fit in.

I don't think any of the aliens seek to destroy us. They hardly even know we exist."

"What's the plan to get rid of them?"

"It's ruthless and dangerous," said Kinsolving, going cold inside. He hugged Lark tighter without realizing that he did so. "Humbolt has been pirating rare earths from the mines on Deepdig. After he fixed the records to show smaller liftings, the rare earths are sent to an assembly plant. I don't know where." Kinsolving heaved a sigh. "I thought at first their plan was just to rob the Lorr of taxes. It's more. The plants use cerium to build electronic devices that act like drugs do on humans."

"You don't mean these will help the aliens enjoy themselves?" asked Lark. She frowned. Kinsolving took that as a good sign. The woman understood.

"The devices are illegal. Humbolt and the others smuggle them in to planets like Zeta Orgo 4, the natives use them and become helplessly addicted. Eventually the device burns out their brains. I got the hint that it might even induce others near the unit to use it more until they, too, died, their brains turned to charcoal."

"This doesn't sound illegal as much as it does immoral," said Lark.

"The devices are engineered to addict and destroy. Imagine allowing the sale of drugs that only killed."

"This still doesn't seem *that* bad," said Lark. "The aliens don't have to use *any* gadget, much less the ones furnished by Humbolt."

"I think they do. The evidence I saw in the files is sketchy but the simple operation of the machine is addictive. Anyone within a few meters needs more stimulation. And then more and more until the brain is physically short-circuited."

"What would the aliens do if they found out about this?"

"I don't know. Among their own people, they

might send them off to that prison world." Kinsolving spoke without a quaver in his voice. "If they think there is a concerted effort by the part of IM employees—or Interstellar Materials itself—the consequences might be dire. They might decide to destroy Gamma Tertius 4."

"The entire planet?"

"Most of the alien races have that power." Kinsolving swallowed hard. "They might decide that Earth is the cause and destroy it."

"Maybe it's better if we don't tell anyone," suggested Lark. "If the aliens find out . . ."

"Is it better to let Humbolt and the others destroy billions of intelligent people for the sake of their xenophobia?"

"No," she answered. "How can we stop them? I mean, I'm no crusader. I don't want to do this, but it's so . . . wrong."

"We've got to get off GT 4," Kinsolving said. "How, I can't say. It wouldn't do to steal a shuttle, even if we could. I'm sure that there are defensive weapons in orbit around the planet. If Humbolt is crazy enough to think all the aliens want to destroy mankind, he's crazy enough to defend against a threat that doesn't exist."

Kinsolving held Lark even tighter as a blast of cold wind gusted around a rocky precipice. What would they do, even if they succeeded in getting to orbit? Locking the *Nightingale* would be too simple to do. Cameron might have overlooked deactivating Kinsolving's identicard and flagging it in the company computer, but that had been a small oversight. Cameron wouldn't make many more—if any.

"We can stow away," Lark said. "Oh, this might be fun! You see it all the time in the tri-vid dramas. We stow away, get into orbit and then find a starship to stow away in."

The woman made it sound so simple.

"Launch mass is carefully measured," he told her. "We might be able to get to orbit but the *Nightingale* will be ... watched."

"You mean locked and off limits." Lark sighed. "I love that ship. We've done so much together. But I imagine Daddy can get it back. All he has to do is ask."

"You make that sound easy."

"I've gone off with friends before and left the *Nightingale*. Then Daddy sends someone to ferry it to another planet. We always manage to make connections." Lark giggled like a small girl. "We can do it that way. Let Daddy worry about the *Nightingale*."

"What do we do once we get into orbit? I've got an idea on that score, but—"

"Oh, that's not hard. We just wait for Rani. She'd give us a free ride anywhere we want. She owes me. Besides," Lark said in a harsher tone, "she obviously wants you. That's all my fault, I suppose. I shouldn't have told her how much fun you are."

"Rani," he said. Kinsolving's mind raced. The dark-haired woman and her friends would be in custody by now. "Is she someone important?"

"Rani duLong? I should say so. Her brother is chief executive officer of TerraComp."

Kinsolving shook his head. TerraComp wasn't the largest Earth-based computer manufacturer but its market gave it incredible potential. He couldn't see Humbolt risking the life of the sister of Terra-Comp's CEO.

Besides, what had Rani done? She used a few card keys to run around IM headquarters, nothing more. It had all been a part of the anniversary party fun and games. Cameron wouldn't kill Rani or Dinky or the other two—he would just escort them off-planet.

Immediately.

"We've got to get to the Landing Authority, right now!" Kinsolving exclaimed. "I used Rani to create a diversion while I freed you. Humbolt and Villa-lobos will deport Rani without hesitation, anniversary party be damned. When they do, we've got to be ready."

"For what?" asked Lark.

Kinsolving had no answer. But when the opportunity presented itself, they had to be alert enough to take it.

"I can't walk another micron, Bart. I don't know why you're torturing me like this."

"There wasn't any way we could use public transportation without being noticed," he explained again to the complaining woman. "My identicard is flagged by now. And so is yours."

"Nonsense. My credit's good. Always has been. Oh, you mean Cameron would use it to trace us. I don't see why that's so bad. He knows we're heading for the LA."

Kinsolving had to admit Lark had a point. Simply hiding in the city gained him nothing. They had to leave Gamma Tertius 4 or be caught eventually. All Cameron needed to do was cordon off the Landing Authority and wait. Sooner or later they would blunder into the guards and be taken.

Kinsolving smiled wickedly. Catching them wouldn't be *that* easy. He had learned much.

He sobered. Too much rested on his escape. Humbolt had to be stopped before the mind-burn device was sent to alien worlds like Zeta Orgo 4. Discovery by the aliens might mean the destruction of Earth, but Kinsolving didn't want entire populations of alien planets to be destroyed, either. How he could walk this tightwire he didn't know.

But he had to try.

"The LA isn't fenced," he said. "There's no need

because everyone coming here is on company business."

"GT's hardly the garden and vacation spot of the universe," Lark said dryly.

Kinsolving watched as robotic sniffers worked on every vehicle entering the main entrance. At points surrounding the launch site robot hunters patrolled. He saw occasional metallic glints off heavy body casing and whiplike antennae. Getting past them would be impossible.

Getting past the sniffers would merely be difficult.

"Barton, look. Isn't that Cameron?"

Lark pointed to a vehicle waiting in the line for admittance to the LA. The vehicle immediately behind had four people huddled into the rear. Kinsolving recognized Dinky's head and assumed the other three were Rani, Morganna and Chakki.

He jerked hard on her hand and they walked briskly along the path paralleling the roadway. Kinsolving maneuvered around so that Cameron would have to crane about in his seat to see all that happened in the vehicle behind. Stooping, he picked up a large rock and handed it to Lark. She started to ask what he was doing. He gestured for silence, them came up beside the driver and tapped on the window.

"What is it?" demanded the driver.

"Those Mr. Cameron's prisoners?" Kinsolving asked.

"Who're you?"

"Landing Authority clearance," Kinsolving said, "Open the door, will you?"

"You don't look like an official," the man said, opening his door. "Let me check with Cameron."

He never got any farther. Lark hit him with the rock Kinsolving had given her. Kinsolving pushed the man back into the vehicle and stripped off his jacket. Time crushed down heavily on him. His fingers felt as if they had turned into stubby sausage. He was sure that Cameron would turn around and see what happened behind. Already the line of vehicles began to move.

"There," he said triumphantly, getting the jacket off the guard. Kinsolving slipped into it, wincing as seams split on the too-small garment. He grabbed the front of the man's shirt and heaved, tossing him out and onto the path alongside the roadway. In a few minutes, he would either recover or be noticed.

By then Kinsolving hoped to be in space.

"What's going on?" came Rani's curious voice. "Why, it's you, Barton. And Lark! Oh, this is ever so exciting. You didn't lie when you said it was all—"

"Quiet!" Kinsolving snapped. "Keep quiet until we're in orbit."

"They're taking us to our ships," said Rani. "Are you two going to stow away on the *von Neumann?*" Kinsolving nodded. "Photonic! Lark, dear, we're going to be the envy of everyone when we tell them about this. Escape from brutal guards on Gamma Tertius 4!"

Kinsolving edged the vehicle forward, keeping his head down when Cameron turned and pointed at them. Cameron gunned his vehicle and shot forward, toward a shuttle readying for launch. Kinsolving pulled even with the guards. The robotic sniffers emitted shrill warnings.

"Wait," the guard said as Kinsolving started to accelerate through. "The alarms went off."

"Of course they did, idiot," snapped Kinsolving. "Mr. Cameron told you that these people were being shipped out, didn't he? Deported?"

"Yes, but—"

"They're all in the computer as undesirables. You should worry if there *wasn't* an alarm sounded."

"He said there were four. I count five back there."

"You misunderstood him. Look, Mr. Cameron's a very impatient man, if you know what I mean. You call him back to verify something this minor, you take the blame."

The guard looked across the tarmac toward the shuttle. Cameron had already started to pace. He presented the perfect picture of a man ready to explode in anger. The guard motioned Kinsolving through without another word.

"Simply photonic!" cried Rani duLong. "Lark, this is wonderful. Wait until Tia and Pierre hear about our adventure!"

"What are you going to do now?" asked Lark, more concerned than her friend about Cameron.

"Keep in motion. No matter what, keep moving. You and the others get out and then run. Get into the shuttle. I'll be along in a hurry. When I do, we've got to launch. See if you can convince the pilot about that."

"Sounds like an interesting challenge," said Lark.

Kinsolving drove at high speed, then killed the repulsor field suddenly. The vehicle hit the pavement, slewed and sent up a curtain of sparks. Cameron bellowed in anger as he sprinted to get out of the careening car's path. Kinsolving's vehicle crashed into Cameron's and came to a noisy stop. Kinsolving gestured wildly, urging the others to speed. Lark followed instructions and herded them out and up the gangway into the shuttle.

Barton Kinsolving wondered what he ought to do now. In hand-to-hand combat he was no match for Cameron. Although the man didn't seem to have a robot hunter with him, he might be armed. Kinsolving couldn't stand against that.

Kinsolving cast a worried glance up and saw Lark waving from the shuttle air lock. Cameron had drawn the bulky tube from inside his jacket and stalked toward the downed repulsor vehicle.

Kinsolving waited, estimated, waited until he thought his heart would explode, then savagely twisted the repulsor field starter switch. The engine circuits overloaded and shut down almost instantly, but not before the vehicle lifted toward Cameron.

The front of the vehicle struck the man a glancing blow. Cameron screamed and triggered the weapon he held. The aluminum side of the car vanished in a flare of heat and a rain of molten droplets. Kinsolving abandoned the vehicle and scurried up the shuttle gangway, sometimes on hands and knees.

Lark dragged him into the air lock. Kinsolving spun around and sat down heavily. The last sight he had of the GT Landing Authority was Cameron lying facedown on the tarmac, his energy weapon a meter from his outflung hand.

"We did it!" cried Lark.

Kinsolving nodded numbly. The shuttle jerked as the heavy laser buried under the surface began pulsing, lifting them ever higher with every new lightning bolt of energy. They would be in orbit quickly.

What then? They hadn't yet escaped from Cameron. Kinsolving wouldn't believe it until they shifted into hyperspace.

CHAPTER TWENTY-THREE

"THEY'LL STOP US," said Barton Kinsolving. "I know they will. Cameron's not dead. Humbolt beamed out the message." He wrung his hands and sent himself tumbling head over heels in the zero gravity. The shuttle had launched and found its orbit, but Kinsolving worried over the turmoil on the planet below.

"We might not have much time," agreed Lark Versalles, "but we have enough to get to the *Nightingale*."

"No!"

"Why not?" she said petulantly. "I don't want to simply leave it here. I've done that too many times. Daddy is going to get mad."

Kinsolving's mind raced. "The orbiting defense system," he said. "We've got to get away from GT as quickly as possible. I'm sure that Cameron alerted the defense guards to laser the *Nightingale* if we try to get in."

"You're welcome to come with me," came a sultry voice. Kinsolving caught a stanchion and held himself in position to see Rani duLong floating in a hatchway. Her billowing skirt floated seductively around her thighs—an effect she worked hard to achieve.

"Am I invited, too?" Lark asked caustically.

"Of course you are, dear. It might be even more fun if the three of us are together."

"Perhaps not," sniffed Lark.

"Your ship."

"The *von Neumann*," said Rani.

"Is it nearby? Will we be able to board soon?"

"First on this taxi's route," she assured Kinsolving. "We can shift out of the system within, oh, a few hours."

"It takes that long for you to power up?" he asked, astounded. Lark's starship had been fully automated and virtually ran itself.

"Not really. That's the time I'm supposed to take to be sure everything is operational. My brother got mad at me once when I tried taking off too quickly. I did something to the engine. I don't know what. That's hardly my field."

"There's a safety override?" pressed Kinsolving.

"I suppose. I'm sure that you can figure out how to turn it off. You're so...capable." Rani rotated slowly, her skirt flaring around her body as she moved.

"Let's get to your starship as quickly as possible," said Kinsolving. The pressure of time sent his pulse racing. Every instant he thought might be their last. Cameron wouldn't take their escape easily. Turning this shuttle and everyone aboard into superheated plasma might not be company policy, but Kinsolving doubted if many of the directors of Interstellar Materials would complain.

Certainly Kenneth Humbolt, Villalobos and Liu would say nothing. And how many of the others were privy to the diabolical Plan?

"Docking in five," came the pilot's voice over the intercom. "Prepare for docking in five minutes."

"I'll need all my cases," said Rani. A frown marred her perfect features. "That silly Mr. Cameron didn't load them. I don't remember it. Oh, damn!"

"Don't worry," Lark said sweetly. "All your clothing is so out of style that it's better off left behind."

"What about Dinky and the other two?" cut in Kinsolving. "Are they going to be all right?"

"The shuttle will take them to their ships. Imagine being thrown off a planet like Gamma Tertius 4," said Rani. "The indignity." She smiled widely. "The utter *thrill* of it!"

Kinsolving saw that Rani, like Lark, spent her time seeking new sensations, new diversions. He had worked hard all his life. Simply having a job when so many on Earth didn't had been fulfilling for him. Lark and Rani were rich beyond his wildest, most avaricious dreams. For a moment he wondered how he would enjoy such immense wealth, money that allowed him to do as he pleased, roam where he would, see the galaxy firsthand.

Kinsolving found that his imagination didn't extend this far. All he could think of was getting free of Gamma Tertius 4 and trying to warn others of the genocides planned by those working for IM.

And Ala Markken. What of Ala? Her part in the Plan seemed innocuous. Or could anyone taking part in such mass slaughter be innocent? What had become of her after she left Deepdig?

Kinsolving held in his emotions when he realized that a spark still burned for the woman, in spite of what she had done on Deepdig, in spite of her part in sending him to the alien prison world.

"Docking...now!" came the pilot's command. A tremor passed through the shuttle as the hulls came into contact. A deep humming filled the shuttle passenger area; the magnetic grapples held their air lock to that of the starship.

"Do you think I should say good-bye to the others?" asked Lark.

The worry on Kinsolving's face made her abandon such a notion. "I'll see them soon enough. There's always an interesting party or festival where we can talk later."

Kinsolving had barely started the *von Neumann's* air lock cycling shut when the shuttle cut free. The pilot wanted nothing more to do with them. He might not know exactly what had happened at the Landing Authority but it had to mean trouble—and Kinsolving wondered briefly what encouragement Lark had offered the pilot for such a swift and un-questioned flight.

"Can you do something with all this?" asked Rani. She ran her fingers through Kinsolving's hair as he settled into the acceleration couch. Kinsolving looked up when he felt more fingers threading their way across his head. Lark hung suspended on the other side.

"This toggle is the safety override," he said. With a quick movement of the wrist, he freed the ship of the need for a lengthy countdown. His hands worked over the control console until Kinsolving felt as if he played some giant musical instrument.

"We're almost there. We're not supposed to go di-rectly into a shift from such a low orbit, but this is an emergency. We—"

Kinsolving squinted. The forward vidscreen flared twice. Tiny yellow and blue dots danced in front of his eyes.

"What happened? The safety switch? You broke my ship!" complained Rani.

"That was in space," said Lark. Realization dawned on her. She settled down into a couch, hand over her mouth.

"What's wrong?" asked Rani.

"The shuttle," Kinsolving said grimly. "They la-sered it. The first flare was the hull vaporizing. The second was the steering rocket fuel exploding."

"But Dinky and..." Rani fell silent when she un-

derstood that those on the planet below had ordered
the shuttle and all aboard murdered.

"Time to leave." Kinsolving didn't check to see if
Rani and Lark were secured. He toggled the stardrive. The compact ship shifted into hyperspace.

Through the vidscreen Barton Kinsolving got one
last look at Gamma Tertius 4. He was leaving behind those who would make themselves masters of
all space by brutal murder. They could not be allowed to succeed.

They would not!

"Ala," he said softly, then gave himself over to the
senses-twisting effect of the stardrive.

THE ALIEN WEB

For Sue Baker

CHAPTER ONE

BARTON KINSOLVING worked frantically to override the safeties on the starship *von Neumann*'s control panel. The owner, Rani duLong, had had the safeguard toggles installed by her brother to prevent sudden shifting into hyperspace and destroying the delicate mechanical and quantum mechanical balance in the superbly powerful engines.

"I don't see what the hurry is," Rani said. She floated upside down, her skirt swirling in a kaleidoscope around her tanned thighs. She spun about to be sure that Kinsolving got the longest look possible at what she considered her best asset.

Kinsolving worked feverishly to get the *von Neumann* away from Gamma Tertius 4 and the combat lasers being trained on them from below. The officers of Interstellar Materials Corporation dared not let him escape with the knowledge he had uncovered in their secret files.

Barton Kinsolving knew of the Stellar Death Plan. He knew how men and women in IM plotted nothing less than the genocide of an entire planet of alien beings.

He swore as he worked. He understood the frustration so many humans felt at the way the aliens treated them. Humanity was a newcomer among the stars, hardly starfaring for two hundred years compared to the thousands of most other species of intelligent beings. Why accept as an equal a race that had yet to earn that privilege?

Kinsolving understood and accepted the Earth governments' view that only by working slowly and diligently could humans be greeted as equals one day.

But the chairman of Interstellar Materials, Hamilton H.

Fremont, had chosen a different, quicker, more vicious path. Why wait to be accepted by the aliens who would always hate humanity and consider them intruders on their domain? Kill the "Bizzies," the bizarres.

Kinsolving was not certain that Fremont had authorized the genocide; he had been unable to contact the man directly. But other IM directors were intimately tied to the savage plan. Maria Villalobos, Kenneth Humbolt, Liu, Metchnikoff—those were guilty parties. Those directors had authorized the subversion of company property to further the mad scheme.

They had tried to kill him at the company-run rare earth mines on Deepdig, they had seduced away his lover Ala Markken, they had sent their assassin to remove him permanently.

Kinsolving enjoyed a moment of satisfaction. He had escaped Cameron and his robot killers on Gamma Tertius. He had escaped with information about the construction of electronic resonance devices that acted like narcotic drugs on certain alien species. And he would thwart their plan.

"Got it," Kinsolving cried. The safety relays were shorted out and now allowed manual operation of the *von Neumann.*

"That's not all you've got, if you've been around *her* for long." Lark Versalles drifted into the cramped cockpit and hooked one slender arm around a stanchion. Her blue eyes burned angrily as she glared at a wickedly smiling Rani duLong. Kinsolving was glad that the two women were friends. He would hate to be on the same planet with them if they were not.

"He's not yours, darling," Rani said with some venom.

"I saw him first. I rescued him—"

"Lark," cut in Kinsolving. "There's no time for that." He did not want her telling Rani about his escape from the alien prison world. The fewer who knew that most of alien-inhabited space hunted for him, the longer he would survive. Getting the information to alien authorities about the Stellar Death Plan concocted by Fremont and the others was too important to jeopardize in a petty argument. If the Lorr police found him before he contacted the aliens on Zeta Orgo, he would fail—and Fremont would triumph.

"Destination, sir?" asked the ship's computer. "There are programmed routes to most major starbases already in my data banks."

"Zeta Orgo 4," Kinsolving said. "Optimum course; no need to conserve fuel."

"Course is being plotted, sir. Do you wish to depart from orbit? We are within a ten-thousandth of a radian of exact launch."

"Do it," snapped Kinsolving.

"You broke my ship!" cried Rani when the forward vidscreen flared into eye-searing stars. "My brother's going to kill me for this!"

"It wasn't the override or the course setting," Kinsolving said, as stunned as the woman over what had happened. "They just lasered the shuttle we came up from GT4 in."

"But Dinky and the others..." Lark Versalles' voice trailed off when she realized that she had just lost friends needlessly. Ruthless people with a vision cared little for those in their path.

"They're gone. And we will be, too, if we can't shift out of here right now!"

His hand poised above the toggle that would shift the *von Neumann* into hyperspace. Kinsolving took a deep breath to steady himself. So much had happened to him. All he had ever wanted was to be a mining engineer, to experience something of the wonder of the universe by getting away from an overcrowded Earth and—what else?

There had been Ala. How he had loved her! He swallowed hard, his thick fingers trembling slightly. How he still loved her. If only they had been able to talk before he had been sent to the prison world. He had to find out the full extent of Ala's participation in the Death Plan. He could not believe she willingly went along with it; she had been a dupe, like him. Kenneth Humbolt had somehow deluded her into believing genocide was the answer to mankind's woes among the stars.

He hit the drive-authorization toggle and felt the *von Neumann* shudder as the powerful engines twisted the fabric of space and contoured new geodesic lines among the stars. A concussion rocked him away from the control panel and sent him flying off into the room, crashing into both Lark and Rani. The three ended up in a pile of tangled arms and legs. Kinsolving struggled to get free. Neither of the women seemed inclined to move.

"Don't fight it, Bart darling," said Lark. "This is fate." She giggled, then kissed him squarely on the lips.

"I knew there was a reason I didn't like you," said Rani duLong. "You're trying to keep him all for yourself. I always did think you were a greedy bitch, Lark."

Kinsolving twisted and got away from the women. The pseudogravity of hyperspace did not afford him the same weight as on an Earth-sized planet, but it was sufficient for him to gain his footing and scoot free. He spun around and stared at the two women, the blond and thin Lark and the dark-haired, lush Rani.

"How can you do this?" he asked, more angry than confused at their behavior. "Friends of yours just died. They were lasered into plasma by the GT Landing Authority. Doesn't that mean *anything* to you?"

Lark Versalles sighed and shook her head. "Bart, dear Bart, what is death? We all dance around like small children, reaching out and trying to touch it without really touching it because that means the end of the game. The only thrill life offers is getting closer than everyone else to dying—and bragging about it."

"That's not all there is," he said.

"No," Lark said. "There can be more." Her blue eyes misted over, and for an instant Kinsolving thought he saw a hint of the real person lurking within the shallow, hedonistic bitch that was Lark's usual facade.

The expression faded: But what had she remembered for that brief instant? *Who* had she remembered?

The *von Neumann* shuddered and threw Kinsolving back across the cabin. This time he collided with Rani duLong. The woman looked increasingly angry.

"Are you *sure* you didn't glitch up my ship? My brother's not ever going to speak to me if you did. Not after I wrecked the *von* trying to—"

Her words were abruptly cut off when all internal power failed, plunging them into total darkness. Kinsolving panicked. Never had he known such total and unexpected isolation. He reached out and grabbed, finding nothing. Robbed of sight, he had the sensation of floating aimlessly, falling down an infinite well, spinning around and around like a particle caught within a black hole's Schwarzchild radius. The omnipresent illumination in a starship served the purpose of orienting the passengers. Vision allowed them to maintain their sanity in a universe of twisted dimensions and no other sensory clues.

Kinsolving yelled. His own words echoed inside his skull, but he did not think anyone beyond arm's reach could hear. Flailing, he tried to find either Lark or Rani. He succeeded only in smashing his hand into a bulkhead—hard.

Cursing, he forced himself to calm. Panic gained him nothing. Something disastrous had happened to the *von Neumann,* and panic would only seal their deaths.

"Calm," he told himself. "Stay calm and find out why the power failed." He had often made his way through mine shafts as dark as the ship. He had lived underground, enclosed, crushed into claustrophobic quarters, and had not panicked. Kinsolving's fear faded and determination replaced it.

He edged around the cabin until he came to the well-padded contour couch in front of the command console. Kinsolving slipped into it. He tried to picture mentally where the controls had been. Each ship was slightly different, and he had never been aboard the *von Neumann* before their abrupt takeoff from Gamma Tertius 4. But he knew this space yacht could not be too dissimilar from Lark's *Nightingale,* left in orbit around GT4.

Cool plastic toggles marched in solemn lines across the panel. He had to guess what they controlled. The largest one he knew—that had launched them into hyperspace. To toggle it back now without knowing what had gone wrong might destroy the ship completely. Remembered stories of hyperspacial disasters sent icy jabs of fear through his chest. Even in an era when star travel was routine, accidents happened.

And they were usually catastrophic.

"This one must be the control for the lighting," he said to himself. He moved the switch slowly. The pneumatic couch sighed and lost rigidity. Kinsolving cursed anew. He had discovered the acceleration couch control. But the toggle next to the couch control returned a wan light to the cockpit.

Kinsolving swivelled around and found Lark standing in one corner of the cockpit, her face a pasty white. The chemicals she had injected beneath the surface of her skin lent an ever-changing pattern of colors that only accentuated her paleness.

"Bart," she said in a low, shaky voice. "I was alone!"

"We both were. We all were. Where's Rani?"

"I don't know I . . . the lights went out and I lost you and her and I was so alone. I don't ever want to be alone like that again. Never!" Lark stumbled forward and threw her arms around his neck, sobbing as she buried her face in his shoulder. He held her, understanding a part of her terror.

"We have emergency lighting only," Kinsolving said, his dark eyes flashing across the scanty readouts. Pleasure yachts ran automatically, with most troubles handled without bothering those humans aboard. "It looks as if we have a major power failure."

"Why?"

He shook his head. He could not discount the chance that the Gamma Tertius Landing Authority had gotten in a lucky shot with their combat laser and had damaged the *von Neumann*. But they had shifted without trouble. If there had been any malfunction before reaching hyperspace, he knew, the automatics would have aborted the shift. All starships were equipped with such emergency protection.

He swallowed hard at the thought that he had somehow circumvented the safety circuits when he had rushed their departure. Kinsolving dived under the control panel and spent long minutes tracing the override circuitry. He came back up, shaking his head.

"I don't think I caused the problem. Everything appears to be doing its job at nominal."

"What happened to Rani?" asked Lark in a pitiful voice. She hugged herself tightly and swayed restlessly. The colorful dyes swirling on her cheeks made her look sickly.

"No one's abandoning you," Kinsolving said as soothingly as he could. "Let's go find her. Together."

The flare of fear in Lark's eyes died. A weak smile danced on her sensuous lips. How like a small child she was in many ways, Kinsolving reflected.

"I'm photonic, Bart darling," she said. "Really and truly. Everything took me by surprise. I can deal with my emotions now." She straightened, pulling her shoulders back. "I've had to before."

He did not ask when. She had shown him only one facet of her personality, and it was not one that he appreciated. She had rescued him from the prison world by chance, doing it only to bring a quantum of excitement into her jaded life. Every action Kinsolving had seen Lark Versalles take had been directed toward· one thing: her personal amusement.

He took her arm and gently led her from the cockpit into the starship's main salon. The lavish furnishings of the *von Neumann* rivalled those on Lark's abandoned yacht. Kinsolving could not comprehend their gypsy lives, roaming from one party to another, seeking only pleasure, any more than he could the vast wealth it took to maintain such a life-style. A recreational ship such as the *von Neumann* would cost a thousand times what he might hope to earn as an engineer over a lifetime, even with off-Earth differential pay and danger bonuses.

"Rani?" he called. "Are you all right? Rani?"

Lark clutched his arm until she cut off the circulation. Kinsolving did not protest. He strained to detect the smallest sound that might give a clue to their problems.

"Those are the staterooms?" he asked Lark, pointing to a series of closed doors. She bobbed her head up and down so quickly that a long strand of her blond hair fell into her eyes. She did nothing to replace it; Kinsolving knew then how distraught Lark had to be.

He walked on, not bothering with the sleeping quarters. The galley functioned on low power, a simple meal sitting in the serving area.

"Is this automatic? Why did Rani fix food?"

"She didn't. She wouldn't," Lark explained. "She eats only plant proteins from Zenncon 1." Lark wrinkled her nose at the food. "She'd never even *consider* serving slop like this."

Kinsolving examined the galley computer, tracing back the leads to a junction box hidden in a bulkhead. Several connections inside the box had been fused.

"It looks as if someone ran a welding laser over this section," he said. "Or an overload came along the power feed from the engine room." For an instant Kinsolving stood and considered what he had said. "Damn!" he shouted. Pulling free of Lark, he spun and dashed down the corridor leading to the engine room.

He reached the outer door of the sealed chamber before he saw it.

Lark ran into him when he stopped suddenly. Kinsolving held out his arm to keep her back.

"What is it?" she asked. He silently pointed. She repeated her question.

The silvery blob clinging to the top of the door leading to the sealed engine chamber shivered as if cold, then extended tiny metallic probes and pulled itself a few centimeters up. A humming noise filled the narrow passage and the heavy, acrid odor of burning metal made Kinsolving's nose wrinkle.

"It's a robot. Very powerful from the way it's lasering into the engine room. Unless I miss my guess, another robot has already gotten inside and sabotaged the engines."

"What? How?"

"It can only be Cameron's doing. Robots like this are his specialty."

"Stop it, Bart! You can't let it ruin the engines. We... we'd be marooned between shifts!"

Kinsolving had no idea what that really meant. He'd never had the head for the abstruse mathematics describing faster-than-light travel. In ways that caused his brain to itch, the notion slipped around more than Einsteinian space-time considerations. It warped both space and logic. He had been content to be a mining engineer and nothing more. Now he was sorry for this decision on his part.

"I need something to stop it. A welding laser?"

"Bart, I don't know where anything is. Rani might know, but I doubt it."

"There's no telling where she is," he said, briefly wondering how the woman had managed to disappear on the small ship.

"Would any of this help?" asked Lark. She pried open a wall panel to reveal a variety of tools clipped into place.

"No power tools. Wouldn't want the ship's captain hurting herself," he said sarcastically. Sometimes the designers of such luxury yachts went too far in efforts to protect the owners. Kinsolving hefted a small hammer. In the pseudo-gravity he might not be able to direct as much force onto the robot as he would have liked.

Kinsolving braced himself against the bulkheads, pulled back and drove the rounded hammer head directly down onto the robot's silver beetlelike back. The light hammer slithered to one side, not even scratching the surface.

But Kinsolving provoked a reaction he had not anticipated. Like the insect it so closely resembled, the robot rolled over, wiry tendrils holding it in place. Kinsolving got a good look at the potent laser muzzle on the underside and realized that the robot had switched from offense to defense.

He kicked out and tackled Lark. They went down in the center of the corridor, the laser beam burning a millimeter-wide strip the entire length of his back. Kinsolving shrieked in agony as a second laser bored through his right shoulder and caused a tiny burn pit to form on the corridor floor.

"It's shooting at us!" Lark shouted.

Ignoring the obvious, Kinsolving rolled and smashed hard into the bulkhead. The sound of his impact drew the robot's attention. Another minute blue-white laser beam sought his flesh. But Kinsolving was already moving in the opposite direction. His thick, strong fingers closed around the hammer.

He dived forward, narrowly avoiding the laser that sought to gut him. Hair on the side of his head burst into bright flames. But Kinsolving knew he had only one chance to disable the deadly robot.

He swung the hammer, aiming it directly at the laser muzzle. Ceramics inside the robot cracked when he struck. The robot's laser melted a portion of the hammer. Kinsolving swung again. And again and again until he panted from the exertion.

The second or third blow had been sufficient, but the adrenaline pumping through his arteries refused to still and release him from the bloodlust he felt.

"Barton, please." He shoved Lark away and stood, drenched in sweat, his breath coming in ragged gusts. At his feet lay the silvered bettle of a robot, destroyed beyond recognition. By attacking its underside he had found the device's most vulnerable spot.

"I'm all right. All right," he repeated. Pain lanced into the side of his head. When he reached up, his fingers touched smoldering hair. His back stung and his shoulder turned into molten agony. The laser beam had burned completely through the fleshy part of his shoulder.

"You need to let the automedic work on you," Lark said. Gentle fingers probed his wound, but he pushed her away.

"There'll be time later," he said. "This one was trying to get into the engine room. Look."

Lark frowned and moved closer to examine the hole in the bulkhead that Kinsolving pointed out. "I don't understand," she said.

"Another robot's inside. This one was larger and more powerful, unless I miss my guess. But in the wrong place, even a tiny robot can destroy the ship."

"The stardrive," Lark said. "We haven't gotten rid of all . . . these things?" She nudged the fallen robot with the toe of her spun-gold dancing slipper.

"I don't think so." Kinsolving ran his fingers along the strip of sealant between hatch and bulkhead. Only the single needle-sized hole betrayed forced entry into the engine room.

Kinsolving opened a small panel and studied the keypad. "It opens only with an access code," he said in disgust. "Again, a way of keeping the owner from doing too much damage."

He smiled slowly. "There has to be a standard way of opening the engine room, though, when the ship's being serviced. It wouldn't be in the computer banks. Or a uniform code for all ships of this class." He reached into the panel and ran his fingers along the top of the recessed box.

"Victory," he said. "The code's imprinted just above the keypad." He tapped in the three numbers he traced out. The engine-room door slid back, revealing a darkened cavern.

Kinsolving held Lark back. "The floor. See? Those are Rani's footprints in the fluid."

"Why should there be anything on the floor?"

"A cooling valve has been opened—or damaged," he said, sniffing delicately at the strong odor. "That might be why the power shut down. The central coil began to overheat when the coolant pressure decreased. It lost superconductivity and shut down the entire ship's power."

"But Rani?"

Kinsolving slipped into the room, peering through the darkness. The faint light from the corridor lit only a narrow cone in front of him. The woman's damp footprints led to his right. Kinsolving worked along the wall, his every sense straining.

He cried out when he stumbled over something on the floor. He fell heavily.

"Bart, what happened?" demanded Lark.

"I've found Rani," he answered. In the darkness he reached out and touched the woman. She did not stir. He found her throat and pressed a fingertip into the carotid artery.

He found only cooling flesh and no pulse—and his finger came away sticky and damp with blood. Rani had been killed.

From the bowels of the engine room came a low-frequency power hum and the sound of a drill boring through stainless-steel tubing. The killer robot continued its work.

Unless Kinsolving could find and stop it, both he and Lark would end up like Rani duLong.

CHAPTER TWO

CAMERON WAITED patiently in the anteroom, studying himself critically in one of the shining windows looking out over Gamma Tertius 4. He moved slightly to get the light at the proper angle, forming a completely silvered mirror. He patted a lock of sandy hair into place, considered a color change and immediately discarded the idea. He turned from side to side to show off the expensive finery he wore, conscious of the secretaries watching behind him.

Did they envy him his position and power? Cameron doubted it. Their own power structures were vast and ran throughout Interstellar Materials. They might envy him his taste in clothing. The royal purple silk doublet with the flaring, fluted sleeves was offset just the proper touch by the real pearl buttons at wrist and throat. He wore a black velvet cape, weighted at the bottom with small lead pellets to make it hang straight from his broad shoulders. The tight patterned yellow-and-chartreuse trousers might be an angstrom too much, he knew, but what the hell? If he could not make his own personal fashion statement, who in this sedate dreary company would?

Let those watching envy him his good taste in clothing. Or let them fear him.

Cameron smiled into the mirrored surface. Yes, let them fear him. That pleased him most of all.

A slight shift in position returned the lights of the city to his view. The two-hundred-story tower dominated the crater in which the city had been built. Terraforming had given a dome of atmosphere to the city—but it did not extend to this altitude. On the other side of the cool glass lay only the vacuum of space.

Cameron touched a small silver cylinder at his belt. A simple command and the robot would burrow directly through the glass. The explosive decompression would kill all those within the room. Did any know the power he held so close? Cameron thought that they did. They knew and they feared.

How could a man find a better job than the one he held at IM?

"Mr. Cameron, the chairman will see you now," announced the secretary Cameron had singled out as the one wielding the most power in this tight little group. "You'll have to leave your weapons with me."

Cameron sneered slightly. Not too much, he decided. Just enough to show contempt and yet remain genteel.

The secretary blinked, nonplussed. He said to Cameron, "You can't go in until you've removed your weapons."

"Which ones?" asked Cameron, suddenly alert. He had noted the scanning when he entered the outer office, but how accurate it had been remained a question of some importance. Although IM could afford the finest in detection equipment to protect Hamilton Fremont, those in charge seldom extended themselves. Not in the manner Cameron would, had he attained such an exalted position.

"Chairman Fremont is waiting, sir," said the secretary. "Do you wish to anger him with refusal of a standard and reasonable request?"

"Of course not," said Cameron. He pulled out a half dozen different robot devices, most intelligent, most capable of independent action once programmed for a mission. Cameron retained another dozen implements of varying degrees of sophistication.

"Is that all, sir?" asked the secretary. Several of the others exchanged glances, anticipating the confrontation.

"One more," said Cameron, smiling broadly.

"If you enter the room with any more, sir, you won't like the result," warned the man.

"Not to worry, not to worry," Cameron said airily. He swung about, the velvet cape swirling dramatically. He walked toward the door, his stride long and certain. Cameron never hesitated as he passed through the door and into the boardroom where Fremont and the others waited for him. The retained implements of death passed through whatever scanners were trained on him. He could kill anyone within the room in less than a second.

The feeling of power buoyed him. How fragile a thing life was, and he held the assembled board of director's lives in his hand. A simple touch on an activator would send out a dazzling array of robotic death no one could stop.

Cameron bowed elegantly in Maria Villalobos' direction. The woman sat at the far end of the oval conference table, her dark complexion even darker today with barely restrained anger. Of those in the room, Cameron admired her most. She never let petty things like conscience stand in her way.

For the others, Cameron held varying degrees of contempt. Metchnikoff had once been a contender for the ultimate power at Interstellar Materials Corporation. No longer. The money-man, the cautious accountant, Liu, had replaced him. And for Kenneth Humbolt, Cameron did not even attempt to hide his ridicule.

His quick eyes assessed the situation. The directors' emotions ranged from Villalobos and angry to Humbolt and terrified. Cameron turned to Hamilton Fremont, chairman and chief executive officer of IM.

Fremont's frail hands reached out and touched the table in front of him. Watery eyes tried to focus and failed. At Fremont's side stood a statuesque nurse. Cameron's interest in her extended far beyond the sexual, though she was physically beautiful. She controlled the automedic that prolonged Fremont's life—and she prepared the drugs that brought the doddering fool back to the realm of the living.

She bent over and pressed an injector into the side of Fremont's throat. Veins pulsed and the peculiar transparency of his skin vanished as the blood flow improved. A hint of steel returned to the old man's bearing. He did not move or speak but became the center of attention, like a consummate actor making a stage entrance.

"She cannot be bought with anything you can offer," said Fremont.

"Sir?" Cameron said, startled.

"Poisoning me through Mella's treachery is not possible."

"I am sure that you are adequately protected, sir." Cameron did not like the way this session was progressing.

"Further, eight items you brought into this room violate my dictum against weapons and have been rendered useless. The other four I allow you to keep as a token of admiration for your audacity."

Fremont coughed. His nurse gave him another injection. She looked up, her hot, dark eyes burning with . . . what? Cameron could not tell. He would have to inquire of this Mella and see what her weaknesses were, what vices would bind her securely to his will. Control over Fremont would place him in a very favorable position with the other directors, especially Villalobos.

"I admire audacity," Fremont rambled on. "Once. Disobey my direct order again and you shall be terminated. Is that clear, Cameron?"

"Sir, I meant nothing—"

"Shut up. I know what you meant to do. Do you think you are the first—or the brightest or most talented—to enter this room? Hardly." Fremont spat out a thick, green gob. Mella obediently wiped it off the table and disposed of the tissue through a port on the back of the automedic.

"Sir, time is of the utmost importance. Can we get on with this?" Villalobos looked as though she had swallowed something that disagreed with her.

"Very well, Maria. I concur with your appraisal of this sorry situation. Mr. Humbolt has botched everything terribly and order must be restored. Secrecy must be protected. The Plan must advance."

Cameron noted the difference in the way Fremont referred to the two directors. A quick glance across the table at Humbolt confirmed it. The director stared straight ahead, a nervous tic deforming his cheek.

"Report, Cameron. Tell us how you allowed a major breach in our security to occur," said Fremont. Nothing of the frail, feeble man remained. Whatever drug Mella had sent coursing through his ancient veins worked miracles.

"I am not in charge of security, Chairman Fremont," Cameron said. "I only tend to matters assigned me by Director Villalobos."

"This supervisor, this Barton Kinsolving, comes to Gamma Tertius from a mining planet and invades our most highly protected computer files. He discovers the broad outline of the Plan, if not specifics. He was your special project, was he not?"

Cameron shot Humbolt a look of pure hatred. Humbolt had tried to push the blame off onto Cameron's shoulders for the way he had handled Kinsolving on Deepdig.

"Director Humbolt received some small cooperation on my part," said Cameron. "I arranged for Kinsolving to be sent to the Bizzies' prison world. He proved cleverer than anticipated and became the first convict to ever escape."

"Kinsolving is human, dammit. Why did you think to trust the Bizarres in this matter? Kinsolving should have been removed permanently, not shipped off to some planet where he could simply walk away."

"We are still looking into the method of his escape," said Cameron. "He had aid, of that we are sure. He came to GT4 in the company of Lark Versalles."

"You let them escape," accused Humbolt. "No matter what happened on Deepdig, *you*, Cameron, you let them escape Gamma Tertius."

"Not true," snapped Cameron, irked at the way Humbolt fought to preserve his own position. The director ought to show more restraint. "The resources were not given me. I had no idea why Kinsolving was to be stopped."

"You have been briefed on the Stellar Death Plan since that time?" asked Fremont.

"I have, sir. To the extent that Kinsolving has learned of the Plan, that is. The specifics have not been told to me, but all that Kinsolving knows I also know now."

Fremont said nothing. His eyes had turned into chips of flint. To betray Interstellar Materials, Fremont or the Plan would be unwise—it would be suicidal.

"This Kinsolving got off-planet. Explain, Cameron."

"I am sure that he has been destroyed, sir. I secretly placed small robotic devices aboard each of the ships in parking orbit. Any ship lifting from the planet without first obtaining a disarming code would find my robots...most deadly."

"The *von Neumann* shifted without authorization. Are you saying that it is definitely destroyed?" demanded Fremont.

"Each ship contained two of my robots programmed to destroy the shift engines. Whoever is aboard the *von Neumann* will not exit into normal space."

"Sir," spoke up Liu. "I have checked the registry on the ship. It belongs to Aron duLong, CEO of TerraComp."

"Damn," muttered Fremont. "We kill off those in our own rank instead of the Bizzies."

"Explaining to duLong how his sister came to die after leaving GT4 might be a problem," said Humbolt.

"The hell it will be," snapped Fremont. "Accidents happen in hyperspace. Even to the families of well-placed Earthmen. What involvement does TerraComp have in the Plan?"

"Very little, sir," spoke up Liu. "A few of their lower-echelon executives have provided valuable service to us, mostly supplying computer security codes for other companies, but we have concentrated our major effort on the larger computer-manufacturing firms."

"There's some consolation in that," said Fremont. "But we must be assured that the damned ship is destroyed and all aboard will never report to duLong or anyone else who might ask embarrassing questions. Mr. Cameron?"

The gaudily dressed man shrugged. "My robots will not fail. They cannot. The *von Neumann* will not exit from hyperspace. Was Kinsolving aboard, also?"

"We can assume that he was," said Liu. "Humbolt ordered the Landing Authority to laser the shuttle. We have recovered some small pieces but have been unable to determine how many were aboard, much less their identities."

"A pity," Cameron murmured insincerely.

"Your part in Kinsolving's escape has not been ignored, Cameron," said Villalobos. "You failed to prevent him from leaving the planet. He and this space-brained bit of party fluff Lark Versalles slipped out from under your thumb much too easily."

Cameron said nothing. He had been remiss and might now have to pay dearly for it.

"She's the daughter of a colleague," said Fremont. "I've met her only a few times, but her father was once a good friend. How did she come to get involved with Kinsolving?"

"Unknown," said Villalobos.

"Too much surrounding Kinsolving's escapade is unknown. I want all the details, Cameron. You will work directly for me until this matter is resolved."

"What else do you require, Chairman?"

"Everything. Kinsolving's background is in the company data banks but flagged with a secrecy code to prevent further prying. Humbolt will give you the code. Find the location of the Bizarre prison world and discover how Kinsolving became the first to escape—check that claim, also. I doubt the Bizzies are *that* efficient."

"What else, sir?"

"Everything else, dammit! Make certain that Kinsolving did not pass along the information about the brain-burner devices. Go to Web, if necessary, to ensure that the Plan proceeds there. If we can wipe out the bugs on schedule, we stand to make great inroads into their trading empire."

Fremont's color changed radically. He turned white, then translucent. His hands shook and he appeared to wobble and fade. Mella moved quickly to his side and administered another injection.

"The Plan must be served. See to it, Cameron," Fremont ordered.

"As you wish, sir." Cameron bowed slightly in Fremont's direction, then deeper in Villalobos'. He totally ignored the others at the large conference table. The woman shot him a fierce look hot enough to sublimate carbon.

Cameron was harder than that. He smiled faintly, pleased that he had disquieted her without angering her. He quickly left, his mind turning over hundreds of new facts as he wondered how he could twist them to his benefit.

"Mr. Cameron," spoke up Fremont's secretary. "Director Humbolt will see you in one hour."

"Fine," said Cameron. "Tell him I'll be in my office."

Before the secretary could protest, Cameron left. Let the chain of command be established early, let Humbolt know where he stood.

Humbolt could come to him. There was no need for Cameron to go to Humbolt. Kenneth Humbolt's days on the board of directors of Interstellar Materials were obviously limited.

Cameron went directly to the suite of rooms he maintained as offices on the thirtieth subfloor. Most of those in prominence at the company struggled to work their way ever upward in the tower. Such obvious status was not for Cameron. He insisted—and got—offices in the lowest level of the basement.

The cavernous rooms could not have been better for him. Two of the rooms he had outfitted as laboratories where he worked on robotic designs. Another room he had equipped for the specialty manufacture of unique robotic microcircuitry, both by ancient amorphous sputtering furnace techniques which produced bulky circuits virtually impervious to varied levels and frequencies of radiation and by more sophisticated modern methods.

Cameron walked directly into the lab he had outfitted to withstand explosive testing. He began working through his clothing, pulling out the hidden robot devices. One by one he examined them and laid them aside. As he worked, Cameron's frown deepened. The eight devices Fremont had said were useless had fused circuitry.

"How did he do it? My detectors showed nothing out of the ordinary." He puzzled over this. When he came to the four that Fremont had "allowed" him to retain, Cameron's wrath boiled over.

He touched the side of a slender tube. The rocket blast from the end singed his hand. Cameron jerked back and threw up an arm to protect his face. When the expected explosion failed to occur, he cautiously looked at the mannequin target.

The tiny device had embedded itself in the center of the mannequin's face, as it had been programmed to do. But the explosive had failed. The other three devices were also partially disrupted.

"I could have killed him," muttered Cameron. "But it would have been messy." He moved, his hand making a small circular gesture. Two tiny robots, hardly larger than grains of sand, shot outward and collided at chest level on his target.

The mannequin melted, cut in half.

"The old man has some resources, but he could not have stopped me completely." Cameron smiled and began recording his observations, on Fremont's security devices, on the possible ways that the old man had disabled the robotic devices, on avenues to thwart future embarrassments.

Finished, Cameron went to his office. He settled into a formfitting chair and lounged back. Tiny finger motions alerted a robot to lower the illumination level. Soft minimalist music played and a gentle breeze blew across his face. Carried on the breeze came scents both exotic and common, overpowering and subtle.

The office robot had been programmed to offer up a symphony of scent. It produced a masterpiece.

Lost in the world of fragrances, Cameron allowed his mind to drift. Underestimating his opponents had proven dangerous, but the information he'd gained thrilled him.

He had been little more than Maria Villalobos' pet assassin before the Kinsolving assignment. Although Barton Kinsolving had proven a true and fortunately rare embarrassment, he had also been responsible for Cameron's learning of the Stellar Death Plan.

Such audacity! To remove the alien influence, not by millimeters but by light-years!

He slipped into a deeper sleep state thinking of how his robot legions could march on Bizarre worlds and destroy the aliens by the millions. By the billions! To command computer armies!

Or to be in charge of a project such as that which would destroy all the Bizarres on Zeta Orgo.

"Web, they call it," he said softly. "A death web filled with billions of Bizzies gibbering and cavorting about, their minds completely shorted out!"

Cameron liked the prospect. The only flaw he could find

in the scheme, as it had been revealed to him, was that he had not been the architect of death drafting it.

Lost in the quiet world of perfumed air, he drifted even deeper into sleep, where he dreamed of conquest and personal glory.

CHAPTER THREE

"WE CAN'T LEAVE her here. Not like this!" Lark Versalle's voice rose until it threatened to break with strain.

"Quiet," cautioned Kinsolving. He looked around. The light filtering in through the opened hatch provided too little illumination for his liking. The boring sounds continued unabated. What would happen if the robot saboteur were disturbed in the middle of its work? Had it been set to explode? Or was it worse than the silver insectlike robot that had been working its way through to the engine room?

"They can't hear. Do you think a damned robot can hear? They're deaf. They aren't anything but hunks of animated metal."

Kinsolving grabbed the woman and shook, gently at first, then harder until Lark's teeth rattled.

"Calm down. You'll get us both killed if you keep this up. Of course a robot can hear—if that's the way it's built. I saw some of Cameron's tracking robots." The man shivered involuntarily at the memory of fighting one of the devices. Only luck had allowed him to destroy it. "He can even put a scent attachment onto the machines. They can track like a living bloodhound, if he wants them to."

"But Rani."

"She's dead. Nothing either of us can do is going to change that. Go back outside and wait for me."

Lark sucked in a ragged breath and slowly exhaled. "What if you don't come back out? What do I do then?"

"Die," he said harshly. Kinsolving had no time to coddle her. She might have rich parents who heaped every possible luxury on her, but they could not help her now. Only he could, and Kinsolving did not want to be burdened. To his surprise, Lark nodded and silently left.

He watched her shadow on the floor vanish. Kinsolving wondered if he had done the woman a disservice. Her entire life had been a never-ending party, one pleasurable event after another with no significant thought about danger or death or even the day-to-day problems of earning a living. He doubted if Lark had ever faced true adversity. Now a single mistake would doom them both to a slow death sandwiched between dimensions comprehensible only to a demented mathematician.

Kinsolving bent closer to Rani and studied her neck. The wound was not burned. However the robot had killed, it had not been with a minute laser. Kinsolving tried to put himself in Cameron's position, to guess how the robot master might think.

There could not be any way that Cameron would know that Kinsolving and Lark would choose the *von Neumann* for an escape. That meant that all the orbiting space yachts had been similarly booby-trapped with robots. Two per ship?

What would Cameron use? The one laying crushed out in the corridor was only large enough to carry the laser and the equipment powering it. Smaller robots with lasers were feasible, but Kinsolving had a gut feeling that Cameron had placed only one laser robot on each ship.

If he had sensitive enough equipment, Kinsolving knew, he could detect the power leakage from a robot's energy unit and pinpoint each of the invaders. The laser added to the chance of its being found accidentally.

"He'd have a second robot, smaller, much smaller," Kinsolving said, thinking out loud. "This one wouldn't be vulnerable to detection by power leakage. No laser."

The drilling sounds continued—and seemed to verify what Kinsolving suspected. A final glance at Rani du-Long's neck showed the ragged edges around the wound, torn bits of flesh such as might be left by a rotary drill.

Kinsolving thought that he would find a robot hardly larger than his finger equipped with a drill as fine as a human hair. He closed his eyes for a moment and tried to force down the fear he felt. The robot had attacked Rani

and swung its drill bit around and around until it gouged
out a large enough hole in her neck for her to bleed to
death.

He tried to reconstruct the chain of events. He and Lark
had been in the control room when the power failed. The
emergency lights came up and Rani was gone. Had she
heard something in the corridor and gone to investigate?
Yes. She had tracked down the robot, perhaps hearing it as
it drilled through the door seal and into the engine room.
She had entered, either knowing the access code or finding
it in the same manner that he had. Then the robot had
killed her.

Kinsolving almost backed out of the engine room. This
meant that it had attacked the ship's circuitry elsewhere
before moving into the engine compartment. What other
problems lay ahead for the *von Neumann?*

He stopped. The robot had to be destroyed before it
permanently crippled the engines. Rani had followed it into
this room and it had killed her from ambush, from the
darkness of a ledge or bulkhead. Or had Cameron equipped
it with propellant to fly?

"Something less demanding, something smaller," decided Kinsolving. He slipped around a tall cylinder containing the engine-control computer. No indicator lights
showed. There was no need for them here. The drive either
functioned perfectly or it did not. The latter case meant
either complicated work in dry dock or . . . death in space.

"It doesn't fly," he said to himself. "It might have tracks
like a tank." He mentally discarded that notion. Although
pseudogravity existed during the hyperspacial shift, the
ship had hung in orbit around Gamma Tertius and had been
at zero grav.

Using his ears more than his eyes, Kinsolving homed in
on the busily boring robot. The deck under his feet became
slippery with the fluorocarbon coolant leaking from the engine casings. He twisted and his feet shot out from under
him. Kinsolving landed heavily, cursing—and then noticed
that the drilling sound had stopped.

In the dark he got to hands and knees and crawled toward the coolant sheath. He found a tiny geyser of the

high-pressure fluid. The hole could not have been more than a millimeter in diameter, probably less than that.

The clumsiness on his part proved lucky for him. He reached up to find other holes and felt a hot wire rammed into his hand. Reflexively, Kinsolving closed his hand and jerked away.

The burning increased. He squeezed down harder, then crushed his tiny attacker against the coolant-smeared deck plates. He felt a giving, then heard a *snap!*

Fumbling in the darkness, Kinsolving made his way back to the hatch leading to the main portion of the ship where Lark waited. When his eyes adjusted to the light, he opened his hand and stared at the tiny machine he had destroyed.

"That's it?" asked Lark. "But it's so small!"

The entire device was less than a centimeter long and hardly four millimeters thick. The drill bit, as he had already surmised, looked like a stiff hair protruding from one end.

"Cameron's doing," he said. "See how these tiny cilia along its sides move it? The robot can't travel fast, but it can move, with gravity or without."

"What does it do?" asked Lark, fascinated.

"It bores. That's all its programming can handle. Cameron gave it a minimum of commands, then let it decide how to carry them out. Hide, don't be found. That must be its primary defense. There's not much way it can protect itself."

"It killed Rani," pointed out Lark.

"It caught her by surprise. It had to. That would be a second command. Kill, if necessary. And the third command? Find the coolant sheath and drill through it repeatedly. From the size of the drill bit it sports and the amount of coolant on the floor in the engine room, it must work fast."

"That seems like a lot to put into such a tiny device," said Lark, frowning.

"The block circuit forming its CPU is probably measured in molecules. Most of the robot is motile and drill capacity." Kinsolving stared at the machine, wondering at its workmanship. Such a robot was not necessary; it showed that the maker lavished exquisite care on it.

That had to be Cameron. No one else would put in such effort to make a device designed strictly to kill.

"What are you going to do about the engines?" the blonde asked. Some color had returned to her face. The swirling dyes just beneath the skin, however, continued their Brownian motion, some colors forming tiny islands that spun like hued snowflakes in a blizzard.

"Fix them, though I don't know if there's much I can do. If I can put a patch on the steel tubing, I'll do it."

"Why should that be hard?"

"Because of the pressurized coolant inside those tubes," he said. "We don't have the facilities to drain the coolant, then fix the damage, then repressurize the cooling coils."

"It's not explosive, is it?"

Kinsolving did not want to take the time to explain the problems he faced. The high-velocity stream of coolant might only be fractions of a millimeter thick, but it made repair difficult. He was not sure he could turn off the Tesla turbines, either—not while they were hung in hyperspace. The ship might drop back into normal space.

Or it might not.

"Are these the only tools available?" he asked. The panel they had pried open held a few items, such as the hammer he had used to destroy the first robot and a variety of screwdrivers. Little in the way of electronics test gear was available. Most repairs could not be done by the captain while in flight.

"There might be a welding laser somewhere," said Lark. "This isn't my yacht, you know."

"Please." Kinsolving took her and held her at arm's length for a moment, staring into her blue eyes. A spark of concern burned there, the first hint that Kinsolving had that she truly understood the depth of their problem. "This might mean our lives."

"So?" Lark shrugged and pulled free. "This isn't very much fun. I want to get back to where I can enjoy myself."

He shook his head. At the moment, he did not care what her motives were for helping him. Limping to a port where the *von Neumann* could be repaired mattered. Nothing else.

Still, Lark Versalles disturbed him. So much went on in the universe and it seemed to pass by her as she and her friends sought hedonistic experiences. Kinsolving snorted. He might be the other side of the equation. Ala Markken had always told him he worked too hard, took life too seriously.

A lump formed in his throat when he thought of the woman who had betrayed him. Or had she? Kinsolving found his thoughts wandering. Humbolt might have duped Ala into doing something she had not intended. She might not have understood the import of what Interstellar Materials did. They might have lied to her.

He could not believe any woman he had loved so could condone destroying entire planets filled with intelligent, living, breathing beings—even if they were aliens.

"Here," said Lark, shoving a small red box in his direction. "I found this in the airlock. It might be what you're looking for. It's heavy enough to hold an entire repair shop."

He hefted it and agreed. He opened the sealing seam and found a small handheld welding laser. Inside the case he read yellow-painted letters showing that the last servicing crew had carelessly left this kit behind.

"The *von Neumann* went to Gamma Tertius from Earth," he said. "That's where this was left."

Lark nodded. "Rani's brother liked her to check it now and then to be sure the *von* was in good shape. Terra-Comp's not got a lot of off-planet sales. Most of them are local."

Kinsolving remembered his schooldays on Earth. Terra-Comp had seemed like the largest computer corporation in the universe. It had come as a mild shock to him to find that a dozen others, all operating away from Earth and trading with the larger alien markets, were many times larger in both sales and profit.

"This will do the job," he said. "If I can do it at all."

Lark started to say something, bit back the words, then shifted her weight nervously from one foot to the other.

"What is it?" he asked her.

"Can I, well, do you need me to help? I don't know

much about machines, so you'd have to tell me what to do."

"I'm going to need light. Find a flash and come in." He placed a hand on her shoulder and smiled. "Thanks."

Lark smiled weakly and hurried off to find a portable light source.

Kinsolving went into the engine room. The coolant had continued to pool on the deck plates, making every step treacherous. He slipped and slid to the spot where he had found the drilling robot. Six holes spewed forth the vital coolant in a microfine spray.

His nose began to twitch almost immediately. He considered finding an oxygen mask, then put it out of his mind. The coolant was not noxious, just irritating. Then Kinsolving stopped and peered at the sprays. The fluorocarbon coolant was not dangerous as long as it was liquid. What would happen when he applied the welding laser to the metal? Was the resulting vapor lethal?

He slopped through the puddling coolant and went to the cockpit, leaving a sticky trail of coolant behind him. Leaning over the pilot's acceleration couch, he touched the computer toggle.

"Sir?" came the immediate reply.

"Engine collant. Is it dangerous when vaporized?"

"If heated to a gas, the coolant is instantly lethal to human life-forms. The vapor is a chemical analog to nerve gases used on Earth during the Twentieth Century. The phosgenelike gas burns the eyes and sears the lung tissues. It is not recommended that any repairs be made to the ship's cooling system while in transit."

"Status report on engine coolant system," Kinsolving asked.

"Pressure loss one percent. Rate of loss is accelerating."

"What is the maximum loss permissible that will keep the engines running?"

"Fourteen percent. At the current rate of loss, this level will be reached in four hours."

"How long until we shift back to normal space?"

"Seventeen hours."

"Report on full status," Kinsolving said.

"Power levels have been reduced to maintain drive field

energy," said the ship's computer. "There is a damaged circuit in the main power branching, origin of damage unknown. This caused the lighting level to drop to zero lumina."

"Can you pinpoint the problem?"

"No."

Kinsolving shrugged this off. He could worry about finding the severed power cable later—if there was a later for them. The leaking coolant had to be fixed first. Otherwise, in only four hours they would never be able to shift back into normal space.

Kinsolving stopped at the airlock and found a spacesuit that almost fit. He would have to hunch over slightly and be careful not to straighten up suddenly, but Kinsolving thought he could do the spot welding necessary while wearing the suit.

"Bart, why are you wearing that silly thing?" asked Lark. She had a small light on a gooseneck in her hand.

"The gases formed when I heat the coolant sheath will be poisonous. You're going to have to wait outside while I work. And make certain that the vent fans don't exhaust from the engine room into the rest of the ship."

"How do I do that?"

"Put on a spacesuit and check with the ship's computer."

She frowned. This did not seem glamorous enough for her, but Lark silently went to find a spacesuit that would be both chic and protective.

Kinsolving heaved a deep breath, sealed the helmet and went into the engine room. He closed the door and lightly touched the spot where the robot had bored through the seal with the welding laser. It hissed and popped, then melted enough to close the hole. Only then did he turn his attention to the problems facing him.

Shining the light across the surface of the tubing showed each jet clearly. Nine holes. More than he'd seen on the first examination. Kinsolving peered closely at the tubes, wondering what type of stainless steel had been used. He was expert at fixing bulky, rugged mining equipment. Usually a sledgehammer sometimes proved as useful as delicate electronic probes. But such repair techniques would not do now.

He sighted through the welding laser guide, then lightly touched the trigger. A moment's flare almost blinded him. The suit helmet did not have polarizers built into the visor. He blinked through tears and got rid of most of the dancing spots in front of his eyes. Then Kinsolving tried again.

This produced a spurt that looked like steam.

He moved away and ran a gloved hand over the faceplate. The coolant had vaporized instantly—and it had become corrosive. Even if it had not been poisonous, Kinsolving saw, he would have needed some form of face protection. The brief contact with the gas jet had eaten into the plastic and frosted it over.

"Careful, now," he said, moving back into position. More carefully, he aimed the laser and squeezed the trigger. The geyser of droplets stopped. "And again and again," he said, talking to himself.

Slowly, carefully, Barton Kinsolving fused the holes that had been drilled by Cameron's diabolical robot. He could only hope that he had begun the work in time.

Being lost in hyperspace was not something he enjoyed thinking about. Being lost forever was even more frightening.

CHAPTER FOUR

A SOFT CHIME sounded. Cameron's eyes blinked in the proper direction. The slight movement caused robotic devices throughout his warren of rooms to come alive. No one sought him out here in this subterranean vault except for assassination.

Cameron had survived several attempts. His work for the board of directors of Interstellar Materials did not make him many friends—even among those he served so well.

The annunciator at the door leading to his outer office gonged louder, more for the effect it had on any callers than to alert him. Cameron swung around behind his large desk, a small gesture bringing up the light level and turning off both the electronic scent organ and the music that allowed him to concentrate.

"Come in, Director Humbolt," Cameron said in a booming voice. A dozen different machines studied his caller, evaluated the information, processed it and came to a conclusion in a fraction of the time it took for the chime to die.

Kenneth Humbolt stalked into the dimly lit room, hardly glancing around. Cameron considered this sheer folly on the man's part, but his opinion of Humbolt had never been high. Without preamble, Humbolt said, "We've got real problems, Cameron."

"We, Director?" Cameron smiled at the other man's discomfort. His quick mind worked through the possibilities. Humbolt ranked high enough in the corporation to summon a menial, yet he had personally come to confront Cameron in his office.

Why? Several ideas came to Cameron. Humbolt might

feel his offices were not security tight and that Fremont—
or more likely Maria Villalobos—spied on him. The director might feel more comfortable .here. But that struck Cameron as farfetched. Although these offices *were* cleaner
of spy impedimenta than any of the other company suites,
that did not mean Humbolt should feel more secure here.
Quite the contrary.

Cameron discarded this notion in favor of Humbolt's ass
being in grave danger.

"What can I do for you, Kenneth?" he asked quietly.
Humbolt's eyes flashed at the lack of respect. When he did
not chastise Cameron for it, the robot master knew his appraisal had been accurate. Kenneth Humbolt's days as a
power in IM were limited.

"It's Kinsolving. We don't have any indication that he's
dead."

"My robots were aboard the *von Neumann*. The ship
would be destroyed after shift. There has never been a vessel recovered that had drive problems."

"Fremont needs positive proof. The Zeta Orgo business
is reaching a crucial point. We must attain deep penetration
into that market if IM is to keep pace with other companies."

Cameron nodded, taking all this in. He had wondered if
Interstellar Materials had devised the Stellar Death Plan by
itself or if others were involved. The possibility now existed, from what Humbolt said, that IM's role was minor,
that the other Earth-based corporations were the real
powers behind the Plan.

"What exactly is it that IM is supposed to do on Zeta
Orgo? On Web, I think they call it."

"You know damned well what the planet's called, Cameron."

"Would you like to sit, Kenneth? A drink to steady your
nerves? Something stronger? A tranquilizer?" Cameron
fought back a broad smile. He saw the anger reaching a
deadly point in the other man. To goad Humbolt too far
now would require the use of force to restrain him. Cameron preferred to get as much from the director as he
could without resorting to violence.

But if it proved necessary, ten different devices would burn/laser/stab/cripple Humbolt where he stood.

"It was your mistake that allowed Kinsolving to escape. You're the one who is going to correct it. God, what a glitch this has turned out to be. It's taking up all my time!"

"My fault that he escaped? Come, come, Kenneth, that's not so. He did get through a checkpoint I established at the Landing Authority, but it was *not* my order that lasered the shuttle when an intercept was possible. Such an interception would have neatly captured Kinsolving, preserved the lives of valued company employees, not created unfortunate shock waves among those privileged enough to be invited to the celebration—and it would have given proof that he had been stopped."

Cameron studied Humbolt and watched the sweat beading on the director's upper lip. How he had attained such an exalted position in IM's power structure lay beyond Cameron's imagination. Humbolt was completely unlike Villalobos or Liu or Fremont. Those powerful people shared the traits that so attracted Cameron to his robots. Emotion never clouded their decisions. They worked relentlessly. They might be hurt but they continued on. Only total destruction would stop them.

But Kenneth Humbolt? What a sorry figure he cut in their rank!

The director started to pace nervously. Cameron had to deactivate several of his robots to keep them from flying into action when Humbolt entered their sphere of influence.

"That's all behind us now. We've got to make sure that nothing goes wrong on ZOo."

"ZOo?" Cameron asked mildly.

"What else do you call a world filled with animals?" snapped Humbolt. Cameron allowed the man an instant of superiority. Let him ridicule the arachnoids and their planet. It mattered little to Cameron.

"Tell me about this project," said Cameron. "After all, if I'm to help you—and further the Stellar Death Plan—I need information."

He saw that Humbolt was torn on this point. Such an audacious strike against all aliens had to be kept quiet.

Cameron knew that the merest hint of such a plan might trigger massive reprisals against all humans.

He closed his eyes and pictured Earth turning into a white blossoming flower of dust and death as the alien fleets destroyed it. That might be the least of their woes. Human interests stretched across the galaxy now, no matter how tenuously. The entire human race might be removed if the aliens reacted in that fashion.

"All right," Humbolt said, caving in to Cameron's pressure. This acquiescence proved how desperate Humbolt's position was on the board of directors.

"Web. Tell me about it."

"The aliens are arachnoid. We have conducted extensive studies and learned that they are immune to most drugs we might use to subvert and undermine their governmental authority. However, this form of Bizarre can become addicted to a device."

"Yes, yes," Cameron said impatiently. "That was what the unpleasantness on Deepdig was about. You need the pure, unstressed single crystal of cerium. It resonates at a frequency the Bizzies find utterly captivating."

Humbolt looked sourly at Cameron. "That's right. More to the point, they cannot control their need for this specific electromagnetic radiation. We have built the brain burners with such power that any Bizzie within a hundred-meter radius will also be affected."

"But following an inverse square relationship. I should suspect," cut in Cameron.

"I ... yes. We can be sure of burning out the brains of only those within a few meters. Usage of our device will turn them into vegetables in a week or less of addiction."

"The more who come within the field of the resonating device, the more who will become addicted—and the more who will be destroyed. An elegant solution. Why was Web chosen to begin the Stellar Death Plan?"

"I don't know. Fremont never told me, the old..." Humbolt's voice trailed off and he looked around, suddenly suspicious. "We're not being tapped, are we?"

"There are no spy devices within these walls." Cameron smiled. "Except those of my own construction, that is."

"Fremont's got the finest engineers working on his spy devices," said Humbolt.

"I have no doubt. I've done some work for him myself."

Humbolt did not seem to hear. "That old fart. Imagine him and Mella together in bed."

Cameron raised one carefully plucked and formed eyebrow. The idea had never occurred to him. He waited for Humbolt to continue.

"The drugs he uses. They do things to his metabolism, speed it up, change him all around. He can't relax unless he's made love to her a half dozen times after an injection."

"That many?" asked Cameron.

"He's a maniac, but God, what a genius!"

"He devised the Stellar Death Plan?"

Humbolt shook his head. "Fremont is only one of the cabal. I don't know who the others are, but they're the most powerful men and women off-Earth."

"It seems a shame that Earth governments are so... conservative," Cameron said. "No one on the planet of our species' birth has the nerve to fight for supremacy."

"They all want to live peacefully with the Bizzies. Look at the schools. Look at the type of men they turn out."

"Like Kinsolving," goaded Cameron.

"Yes, like him. He'd betray his own kind. He wants us to continue being little more than slaves to the Bizzies. Humans have the right to rule, to be more than servants. So what if the aliens reached the stars first?"

"Yes, they should give us whatever we want."

"They shouldn't stand in our way. It's mankind's destiny to expand. If they stand in our way like they're doing, they should know we'll blast over them!"

Cameron wondered if Humbolt's feelings of inferiority fueled his devotion to the Plan. Cameron understood the drive for power, for supremacy. The dozens of alien races prevented humanity from gaining that power. But the need to rule was not in Humbolt. He shrugged off the director's true motives. Humbolt would provide a convenient stepping stone and little more.

"We can neutralize Web within a year—if we can get enough of our brain burners onto the world," said Humbolt. "There are other aspects of the Plan going on simultaneously. We can cripple all the Bizzies, no matter where they come from, within ten years. Then nothing will stop us. They won't be able to deny us entry onto their worlds, won't be able to stop us from exploiting mining planets or sending our ships wherever we want."

"Arachnoid creatures, the natives of Zeta Orgo 4," mused Cameron. "Unpleasant to look at. Why were they chosen for this experiment in death? You said other races also fall victim to the lure of the brain burners."

"I don't know, dammit."

"I wasn't asking you. I was thinking out loud," said Cameron, already tiring of Humbolt. He had learned as much as he could from the director. He needed to work out as much of the Stellar Death Plan as possible to see how to personally benefit from it.

The Plan required the utmost in caution. A mistake meant racial suicide. Worse, a mistake at this level might mean his own death. Those ruthless enough to obliterate an entire race would not hesitate to kill a faltering individual.

"Would proof of Kinsolving's demise be of any use?" he asked.

"What? Oh, yes, that's what Fremont wants. It's what he's ordered us to produce."

"Us?"

Humbolt tried to stare down Cameron and failed. He averted his eyes. Cameron's contempt grew without bounds.

"If I provide it for you, what might I expect in return? It's all well and good to further the Plan. What human wouldn't want to remove such a stumbling block from humanity's path? But there ought to be more."

Humbolt ran his hands up and down his pants legs in a gesture Cameron found infuriating. He held his tongue, waiting to see what Humbolt offered.

"Mella. I can offer you Fremont's nurse."

"In what capacity?" This puzzled Cameron. Women as lovely as the nurse attracted him, of course, but simply to bed Mella without other gain struck him as pointless—and dangerous.

"You can learn about the drugs she gives Fremont. And

more. Remember what I said about Fremont's cravings after the drug injections."

Sex, marvelled Cameron. This was all Kenneth Humbolt offered him. Was this the full extent of what the man considered life had to offer? Cameron ran a finger along the intricately embroidered lapel of his jacket. A slight pressure would cause a relay to close. The activated robot would reduce Humbolt to a greasy, smoking spot on the rug in less than a microsecond. Cameron seriously considered the director's permanent removal. He did not think anyone on the board would censure him for such an abrupt action.

He might even receive a promotion. Villalobos would back his election to the board. This dangerous woman still found him useful. Liu might, also. Even Hamilton Fremont might rejoice at having a weakling like Humbolt disposed of.

Cameron stayed his hand. Humbolt had not outlived his usefulness. Yet.

"I will go to Web and oversee the distribution of the devices," he told the director. "Along the way, I'll collect the evidence of Kinsolving's death."

"Good. You won't regret siding with me in this, Cameron. You won't. Remember Mella."

"I will," Cameron assured him.

Kenneth Humbolt left, thinking he had forged a strong bond and gained an ally. Cameron could only bide his time and see how best to destroy the inept director and thus increase his own influence within Interstellar Materials.

He blinked in the proper direction. Gentle fragrances again drifted on a warm breeze. Cameron closed his eyes, savored the exotic scents and plotted.

Very soon IM would have a new director on its board.

CHAPTER FIVE

BARTON KINSOLVING left the engine room, the space-suit in acid-soaked ruins. The poisonous, corrosive gas formed during welding the small holes in the steel tubing had turned the once-flexible fabric brittle and had completely frosted over the faceplate. But Kinsolving smiled. The repair work was finished.

"What about the lights?" asked Lark Versalles.

"One step at a time," he told her, irritated that she had not praised him for the work already done, the risks he had taken. He pushed past her and entered the cockpit.

Flopping onto the couch, he asked the ship's computer, "Engine status."

"Coolant levels four percent below nominal. No significant impairment of engine function."

"Have you run a self-diagnostic on the lighting system?" he asked the ship's computer.

"Circuit or circuits out in the galley. It is impossible to isolate the exact location of damage."

"That's good enough. Thanks." He swung up and out of the couch and almost collided with Lark. The blonde stood, staring at him. Tears beaded at the corners of her eyes.

"What's wrong?" he asked. "The engines are in good shape. We're not going to be stranded in hyperspace. And the lights will be working again in a few minutes."

"Bart darling, I'm not used to this. I mean, all this danger. The people I orbit with are used to excitement, but it's never *really* dangerous. Oh, we play like it is, but mostly it's all pretend." Her blue eyes misted over and the tears did spill. "I'm not like you. You know how to do everything."

"Not everything," he said. Awkwardly, he took her in his arms. "I just do what I have to do."

"You know how to fix the engines."

"I'm an engineer. I spent most of my time tinkering, getting machines to work properly, finding glitches in electronic circuits, figuring out why the cutting lasers never worked just the way I intended."

"But you know how to do those things. I don't know how to do anything. Except have fun."

He was not sure Lark was complaining or simply stating a fact. Or if it mattered to her at all.

"Did you go to college?" She shook her head. "Did you want to?"

"I suppose," Lark answered. "But why bother when there's nothing to gain? My daddy is so rich I could never spend a fraction of his money if I spent ten lifetimes trying."

"There's more than money, more than just having fun. Do you ever get a sense of accomplishment for anything you do?"

"Not really."

"When have you been the happiest?" Kinsolving asked, taking a different course to get to his point.

"Maybe when I was with—" She cut the words off abruptly and shook all over. "It's hard thinking about him, but I do when I'm with you. But you're so much different. Not like him at all."

"Someone you loved?" Lark nodded. Kinsolving let the matter drop. He had repair work to do on the yacht. They could not continue at this twilight illumination for long. The internal lights carried a full spectrum of radiation to maintain health, both mental and physical. For a short time, it would not matter, but over longer spans it had to.

"What are you going to do when you reach Web?" asked Lark.

"I've told you what Fremont and the others at IM are planning. I've got to stop them."

"But it's so dangerous, Bart. And why bother? What do the aliens mean to you? I know Daddy is always saying that they're in the way, that they hold us back from freely trading, but are they worth the risk? Really?"

"If you don't see anything wrong in what Fremont and the others call their Stellar Death Plan, there's nothing I can say."

"It's wrong to kill, but they're just weird-looking and they don't care for us. Why should we care for them?"

Kinsolving did not answer her directly. "Intelligence, no matter what form it takes, is precious. There's so little of it in the galaxy, at least as far as we've explored. The aliens might not like us because they think we're inferior and haven't evolved enough, but killing them off doesn't prove we aren't the animals they think us."

"So we have to fight them on every front, face to, uh, beak or antenna or whatever, to prove we're their equal? That doesn't sound like 'people' I'd ever want to know or call friends."

"Why not? Has mankind backed down from a challenge before? I believe we can meet and match their best, no matter whose rules we're playing by. My professors at the university thought so, too. I remember Professor Delgado saying as much."

"There are some things that maybe a university shouldn't teach," Lark said. She pulled her arms in tightly around herself and stared at the forward vidscreen. The patterns dancing on it were those randomly generated by hyperspace and meant nothing.

Kinsolving saw that argument would not work. He said, "I'll fix the lighting, if I can. You want to help me?" She shook her head. He heaved a deep breath and then went to the galley to find where Cameron's robot had started its sabotage.

The man worked in silence. Finding the problem proved more difficult than he had thought. Whether he worked ineptly because his mind kept turning over everything Lark had said or the robot had done its work too well, he could not say. Eventually he found the almost microscopic cut through the power cable. A single strand had been severed by the robot's boring tool.

Once found, the break proved simple to repair. Kinsolving finished and waited. Slowly, the ship's computer powered up the lights. In less than five minutes the yacht seemed its normal self.

All except for Rani duLong's body and the puddles of coolant still on the engine-room floor. Kinsolving did not ask Lark if she wanted to help with this depressing chore. He lifted Rani's corpse and pulled it through the coolant to a vacuum locker. He levered the woman's body into the coffin-sized glove box and sealed the lid. Through the plastic window he saw her face peering up, almost as if she would open her eyes and speak. But she was dead as surely as if Cameron had personally fired a laser or driven a knife deep into her heart.

Kinsolving slipped his hands into the gloves and worked around the body until he found the evacuation valves mounted inside the ship's hull. He turned them and waited until the indicator lights flashed red. Then he pulled his hands free of the gloves, flipped the toggle that powered open tiny jets inside. The atmosphere gusted into hyperspace, going wherever anything from four-space entering this peculiar realm went.

Rani duLong lay in peace now, preserved by a vacuum harder than any generated in a planet-bound laboratory.

Kinsolving stood and stared at her, thinking how tranquil she looked now. Life had been frantic for her—as it was for Lark—and she had lived an existence Kinsolving could not appreciate.

Rani had drifted like a piece of spacial debris, blown wherever the protonic solar winds willed. Kinsolving could not exist with such little purpose.

He settled down, perched against the side of the vacuum locker. Was he pursuing the problems created by the Stellar Death Plan just to give his life meaning? He had lost Ala Markken and his job and had been branded an outcast by most of society, both alien and, he imagined, human. Word would pass slowly through space and in a few years he might be forgotten, but until then he was a fugitive.

"Tilting at windmills," he mused. Then Kinsolving laughed. "Hell, I don't even know what that means."

He slopped through the coolant, found a control pad for a service robot and tapped in orders to clean the floor. He waited until the ankle-high robot slipped from its berth in

the wall and began sucking up the coolant. It made gob-
bling noises and whined as the thick fluid entered its storage tank, but other than this it seemed to do well.
Kinsolving left it to its task. He did not think the fluid
would harm anything if not tended to, but any further malfunction in the engines might heat it.

He did not like the idea of having an engine room filled
with poisonous gases.

Kinsolving paused in front of the door leading to the
spacious sleeping quarters that had been Rani duLong's.
Lark lay sprawled on the massive bed, eyes open and staring straight at the ceiling. Kinsolving glanced up; she was
watching herself in a magnifying mirror. He left her to her
thoughts, whatever they might be, and entered the cockpit.

He sighed as much as the couch when he lowered himself into it. The strain had been more than he had expected.
Barely escaping the lasers on Gamma Tertius, the troubles
with Cameron's hidden robots, Rani's death—everything
had drained him.

Before he dozed off, he checked the few simple indicators on the control panel. Less than twelve hours until they
reached Zeta Orgo 4.

And then what? Barton Kinsolving was not sure he
knew. He slipped off into heavy, dreamless sleep.

Kinsolving came instantly awake when the sirens
sounded. Heart pounding, he gripped the edge of the
couch, ready to spring out and fight. The blinking red light
on the control panel at first panicked him; he thought the
engines had again failed. Then he realized that he had slept
up until the instant of shift back into four-space.

"Twelve hours," he muttered.

"I didn't want to wake you. I thought you needed the
sleep," said Lark Versalles. He looked over his shoulder.
She stood in the entryway, leaning heavily against the
doorjamb. She had changed her clothes, probably going
through Rani's until finding something that fit. The two
women had been similar enough in size—as if it mattered
when most of what Lark wore was stretched skintight.

"Just as well. It's going to be dangerous getting landing

permits. I don't know much about Web, but I doubt if they appreciate or encourage human sightseers."

"I had the ship's computer feed what it knew into this." She tossed him a small data recorder. The screen had been cracked but the device seemed intact otherwise.

"Thanks."

"You won't have much trouble getting down. I'll vouch for you. A visa for prolonged stay might be hard, though. That's up to you."

Kinsolving felt a momentary loss when he understood what Lark was saying. He had assumed that she would go with him, be a part of his crusade to save the aliens from Fremont and the others who had concocted their Stellar Death Plan. But the way she spoke told him gently that she wanted no part of it.

Why should she? This was not her fight. All he had brought her was misery and death. Her friends back at GT4, Rani, her lost luxury ship, notoriety that might make her as wanted on alien worlds as he was.

She had, after all, rescued him from the aliens' prison worlds. That should be enough.

"Is there anything else aboard the *von Neumann* that might be of use?" he asked. "I haven't had time to inventory the stores."

"There's a can of those salty fish eggs that Rani liked to eat with her plant proteins. Imported from Earth. Everything else is pretty ordinary."

Kinsolving started to thank her, but the words jumbled and caught in his throat when the *von Neumann* slipped back into regular space. The colors twisted and turned in a mind-dazzling vortex in front of his eyes and his stomach threatened to come out his ears. Kinsolving recovered and immediately found the Zeta Orgo 4 approach control demanding clearance codes.

The ship's computer supplied the basic information. It did not satisfy the controllers.

"You had better answer something fast, Bart," the blonde told him. "Part of that data block I gave you says they have an elaborate orbital defense system. The spiders don't like visitors. They armored four moons and have roving killer satellites scattered throughout the system.

Even if you get away from the planet, the satellites can be activated to lock onto the ship and hunt us down."

"Even through a shift?"

Lark shook her head. Kinsolving decided that he did not want to find out if the aliens had developed a detector capable of tracking through the multidimensions of hyperspace.

"Yacht *von Neumann* requesting landing for..." Kinsolving looked at Lark. Her face had been chiselled out of stone. No expression betrayed whatever emotions raged within her. Only the quick pulsing of a vein on the side of her forehead told the strain she felt.

"Landing visa for one required," he said. Kinsolving felt a tension flow from his muscles when he spoke. The decision had been made. Lark would be free of him and his absurd quest to keep fellow humans from killing beings who held only scorn for his kind.

"Denied."

"Diplomatic mission," he said.

"Denied. Earth has full component of diplomats on-planet. Our weapons are trained on your ship. Do not attempt to flee."

The tension returned. "I am an employee of Interstellar Materials," he lied. "We control mining rights on this world, in addition to a considerable import-export trade." He had no idea if the latter was true, but if IM intended smuggling the brain-burner devices onto Web, some prior formal agreement had to have been transacted to hide the perfidy. From all Kinsolving had seen, sneaking to the surface of Zeta Orgo from space might be impossible.

"Full Identification required," came back the immediate response.

"Supervisor Barton Kinsolving," he said, adding his employee ident code. The distances were too great between planets for anyone from IM to have beaten him here from Gamma Tertius 4, and, as far as he knew, no device for communication without physical transfer existed between the worlds. Rumors had abounded for years that the aliens had an interstellar radio, but these were only rumors.

If they were not, if the authorities from the prison world had notified all species of his escape, he would find himself sent back so fast that there might as well be instantaneous communication.

"Your trade commissar knows nothing of your arrival," came the harsh reply.

"But yours does," Kinsolving snapped. "Do you want me to turn around and return to headquarters? If you do, valuable trade concessions will be lost. I will make certain of that."

"Do so," said the controller.

Lark put one hand on his shoulder. His thick, heavy hand covered her more fragile one. He motioned her to silence. The controller seemed disinclined toward friendly commerce, especially with a human. Or perhaps this was only the arachnoid's way. Kinsolving had never even seen a tri-vid of a Web native. Their psychology, their way of conducting business, were total unknowns.

The communicator crackled after a few minutes and the controller spoke. "Landing allowed for one human. The ship will dock and be held under the authority of the Supreme Web."

"The ship is shifting immediately after I disembark." Lark's hand tightened on his shoulder. "There is no need for servicing or other amenities."

"You will be blown into plasma if you attempt to flee."

"Send an orbital vehicle to shuttle me to the planet's surface. The *von Neumann* will shift immediately."

"What is its destination?"

"This is of no concern to you."

Lark moved closer and whispered, "Should you be so rude? Look." She pointed to the forward vidscreen. The knobby protrusions on the two closest moons showed the heavy space artillery trained on them. One miscalculation on either side's part and the *von Neumann* would be turned into a thin fog of expanding ions.

"I'm only treating them as they're treating me."

"But they have such big guns."

Kinsolving had no answer for that.

Lark's grip tightened until he thought she would draw blood with her fingernails. A sharp, bright point blossomed on the vidscreen, then grew in size. Dopplering factors showed on the bottom of the vidscreen. Whatever it was came directly for the *von Neumann* at high speed.

Weapon? Shuttle? Barton Kinsolving knew of only one method to find out.

He waited.

CHAPTER SIX

BARTON KINSOLVING put the small data recorder into his pocket. He had little else to carry with him when he left the *von Neumann*. One quick touch to another pocket reassured him that his identicard and the card-keys he had stolen from Director Liu were safe. How often he could use them—if at all—before being tracked down by Cameron depended on his confidence and audacity.

At the moment, he felt anything but audacious. Lark stood silent and closed, her eyes occasionally darting but never meeting his directly. Kinsolving had not thought it would be difficult leaving the woman and her mindless pursuit of pleasure.

It turned out to be harder than he had ever believed.

"Be careful, Bart," she said. "It . . . it's been fun. Some of it anyway."

"Lark." He took her in his arms. She felt cold and stiff and stony. He released her. "I'm sorry I've disrupted your life so. What are you going to do now?"

She shrugged. "I might go home for a while. I may take a quick trip to Earth and see if I can find Aron. He . . . he ought to be told about Rani. This is her ship, too."

Kinsolving did not ask what Lark would tell Aron du-Long about his sister's death. Whatever was said, Barton Kinsolving would play a large role in the tale. And he would have still another enraged hunter on his trail.

The aliens who tended the prison world wanted him for both escape and the crime that had put him in exile. Interstellar Materials must have Cameron seeking him out. Hamilton Fremont did not seem the sort to believe in remote-control death. He would demand proof of Kinsolving's death. A mere "accident" in hyperspace would not satisfy the chairman of IM. Kinsolving smiled wanly. It would not satisfy *any* of the directors. Any group able to conceive of and begin executing a plan to wipe out an entire race had to be ruthless.

"Tell Rani's brother that it was an accident, that there wasn't anything we could do about it." Kinsolving knew how lame and hollow this sounded. He was trying to think of something more to say when the ship shuddered slightly.

The docking shuttle had attached itself to the magnetic ring surrounding the air lock. It was time to leave.

"Good-bye, Bart," Lark said.

She turned and hurried off before he responded. The lock cycled open to reveal a strangely fragile alien inside. The creature's space suit consisted of a large clear plastic bubble with four protruding gloves, each containing a hairy leg. The spider head with its parody of a human face rocked from side to side. Kinsolving interpreted this as impatience. He quickly donned a suit from the rack beside the lock; this one proved even smaller than the suit he had worn when repairing the coolant coils.

Kinsolving rocked forward in an awkward gait and pressed past the spider being and into the shuttle. He looked around and saw nothing resembling an acceleration couch. The arachnoid lifted one leg and pointed to rings fastened in the deck plates.

It took several seconds before Kinsolving realized that he was supposed to lie down and grip the rings. The spider lumbered back and locked all four free legs through metal rings. Within the confines of its bubble, the spider held a remote controller in curiously tiny pink-fingered hands that appeared from a flap on its underside.

The airlock cycled shut. The decks quivered with power. The shuttle jerked free of the *von Neumann* and started down to the planetary surface. Kinsolving marvelled at the differences in approach to transferring passengers from orbit to the planet. No human world used unpressurized shuttles. The inhabitants of Zeta Orgo 4 seemed to find nothing wrong with keeping both pilot and passenger in hard vacuum for the trip's duration.

Kinsolving lifted his chin and toggled the suit radio. "How long until we ground?" he asked.

For a few seconds he thought the spider had not heard him or did not understand. Kinsolving started to repeat when the arachnoid said, "No talking. Distracts pilot."

A surge pressed Kinsolving flat. He struggled to keep from blacking out under the intense acceleration. As suddenly as it had come, the weight left his chest. Only a frantic grabbing of the rings kept him from floating free. Then came the deceleration.

All the while the spider stood, taloned claws hooked through the deck rings. Its legs bowed slightly, but other than this small sign, Kinsolving had no hint that the spider felt any of the abrupt maneuvering or the forces vectoring in on it from first one direction and then quickly shifting to another.

A loud hissing noise sounded and buffeting increased. The cabin's sealing failed—or the shuttle's design allowed heated atmosphere to gust in. The air temperature rose until Kinsolving's spacesuit strained to radiate enough heat. Even conduction through the deck plates failed to remove the heat boiling the air around him. Sweat poured off his face and tickled, then itched and finally burned.

He shook his head to clear the sweat from his eyes. The arachnoid had no such problems. It stood stolidly and piloted.

The bump indicating touchdown came as soft as a feather settling on a pillow. Kinsolving moved painfully, his joints refusing to function after the abuse they had taken in reaching this point.

"Out," said the arachnoid. The spider creature shrugged twice and freed itself of its spacesuit. Leaving the deflated plastic skin on the deck, it wobbled out the airlock.

Kinsolving shook his head to clear it. The arachnoid walked as if it were weak and unable to support its own weight, yet he had seen it withstand acceleration that had pinned him flat. Stretching, moaning as jabs of pain drove into his joints. Kinsolving got out of his suit. A cool breeze blew through the opened hatch.

He got to the edge of the airlock. No ladder or steps provided easy exiting to the ground.

"Any way for me to get down?" he yelled to one of the ground crew. The drop might be as much as five meters. He did not want to kill himself. Others would be more than willing to do it for him, if suicide should ever enter his mind.

"Come. Hurry. This ship must space again soon. Do not hesitate. Come!" The arachnoid on the ground waved a furry leg in a gesture shared with Earthmen. Kinsolving sat on the brink, turned and dropped, fingers locked on the sharp edge of the airlock. Dangling, he paused for a moment, then let go. He fell heavily, rolled and came to a sitting position. Gravity here matched what he was used to on both Earth and Deepdig, and he had judged well enough not to harm himself.

Kinsolving brushed himself off and started walking. He caught up with the arachnoid who had called to him.

"Do I need to check into Landing Authority?" he asked.

The spider turned and rotated its head up. For the first time Kinsolving got a close look at the alien. It stood almost shoulder level to him. The head had a face of sorts, but nothing the man could call human. A distinct nose protruded over the top of chitinous mandibles that moved constantly, as if pulling in food to the mouth behind. The eyes startled Kinsolving the most. They might have been human eyes. More warm emotion in those light purple orbs than he had ever seen in Cameron's eyes.

"It is such a nuisance dealing with humans," the arachnoid said in a voice an octave too shrill for comfortable listening. "You have been granted clearance. You would not be standing on this planet if you were not fully authorized. Do not annoy this one further."

"Where do I go, then?"

The head rocked around and the eyes blinked slowly. Kinsolving saw an extra set of eyelids, transparent membranes like those on Earthly alligators, close over the eyes. "Why do you come to Web? To annoy this one with stupid questions?"

"There're no forms to fill out? The controller was able to grant me a visa? Where do I pick up the visa if anyone asks to see it?"

"You are on-planet. That is enough. No one lands without full clearance. Do whatever chore you must, but do not antagonize those of higher station. Do you understand, human?"

Kinsolving indicated that he did. He kept walking beside the spider creature, finding his own gait changing as he unconsciously mimicked the rolling motion required for the arachnoid to move on eight legs.

"Why do you follow this one?" the arachnoid asked peevishly. "Go on your way. Do what you must and do not bother this one."

"Sorry. I just don't know where to go."

The spider hissed like a snake, then jumped. Kinsolving dropped to one knee, arms coming up to shield his face. The arachnoid had not attacked. It had jumped, its powerful, springy legs sending it almost two meters into the air to catch a dangling line. Like its smaller Earthly cousin, the spider being made its way up the line with incredible agility. It vanished over the top of the crane holding the cable.

"On my own," said Kinsolving. The lack of security at the landing field astounded him. The natives put full faith in their space defenses to prevent illegal entry. He saw how this made the smuggling operation of the brain burners even more insidious. If the arachnoids refused to believe anyone could penetrate their defenses, they would be doubly adamant that such illicit devices could not exist.

Kinsolving walked and watched and tried not to get in the way of the ponderous trucks moving freight from one section of the field to another. He got no clear idea of where the freight was stored, where it came down in shuttle or where it was launched into orbit for transshipment. All motion seemed random.

He dropped onto a bench and simply watched. Somewhere on this field Interstellar Materials must house its shipments. If Fremont smuggled in the brain burners with legal cargo, Kinsolving might be able to find evidence that would convince the arachnoid authorities.

He chuckled to himself at the ease with which he had landed on Zeta Orgo. On Earth or any other human-run planet, the forms to be filled out would stretch a dozen AUs. It seemed that on Web a decision made by one was binding on all—or accepted by all. Kinsolving wondered how often bad decisions were made and how often others' decisions were simply ignored.

For all that, he wondered how the spiders governed themselves. He knew so little of the planet and its people. As he watched the chaotic activity around the sprawling landing field, he pulled out the data recorder Lark had given him. He played through the audio portion of the information, learning little more than he already had gained by direct observation.

But one part furnished information that held his interest. "The Supreme Web is the ruling body," he mused. "How do I reach them? Who are they? And how are they chosen?"

He started to stop a passing spider when he spotted a truck with the blue-and-green trident on the star background that identified it as belonging to Interstellar Materials.

Kinsolving's hand brushed lightly over the pocket containing his identicard. He had no idea how long he could hope to use it to gain entry to IM facilities. It had worked —briefly—on GT4. The card-keys stolen from Director Liu had bought him a few extra minutes of freedom before they had been cancelled.

Would those same keys work on Web? The director had to have access to facilities everywhere, being in charge of finances for the star-spanning corporation. But would the key cards be recoded on-site, or would they carry the master code and not depend on local approval?

Kinsolving bet on the latter. He remembered only too well the inspection tours from corporate headquarters. As supervisor of the rare earth mines on Deepdig he had never been informed of the purpose of the inspections—or when they would occur. Such matters as access had never bothered him then. He had changed greatly in those few weeks since Deepdig.

He began walking after the truck. Over an hour and ten kilometers later he found it hovering outside a warehouse similarly marked with the IM logo. Kinsolving dropped to the ground and rubbed his feet. He was not used to this much foot travel. And it had proven more dangerous than he would have thought. No one else walked. Trucks hovering on their repulsor fields, strange vehicles rolling on multiple wheels, small scooters barely large enough for their arachnoid drivers, all had been aimed at him. Or so it seemed. He had dodged well and finally found what he sought.

Kinsolving hoped he had found it.

The information he had uncovered on the Stellar Death Plan had been brief, a mere outline without details. He would not know a brain-burner device if he saw it. But if distribution across Web was to be a reality, it had to start somewhere. Kinsolving thought it would be here at the warehouse amid the legal cargo bought and sold on-planet.

Kinsolving rubbed his feet, then his stomach. It had been too long since he had eaten. And he had no way of obtaining local money or credit. Kinsolving touched the data recorder Lark had given him. Even in what might be comprehensive analysis of Web, nothing had been said about the arachnoids' economy.

Humans devised plans to totally annihilate entire planets of aliens and had so little information about them that they did not know if they even used money. He shook his head sadly. It made it all the more imperative that he stop Fremont's mad plan. What might be learned from the arachnoids? What might be taught them?

Kinsolving studied the entrance to the warehouse and decided against a bold approach. Armed guards stood at ease on either side. If two sentries waited outside, how many more were just inside the door? The arachnoids appeared to appreciate blatant security measures. The heavy fortifications on the planet's four moons showed that.

"Show of force is guarded against," he muttered to himself. "That might mean more subtle means of entering are never tried." The arachnoid mind might lack such deviousness.

Kinsolving trooped around the building, studying its high walls and finding a lack of windows. The huge doors allowing entry for the hovertrucks seemed the only way inside.

No other buildings were nearby for him to scale and look down on the IM warehouse. Aircraft might be able to take off and land from the roof, but getting there would be a problem beyond his resources.

"If not on the ground or in the air, then how?" Kinsolving smiled. The years he had spent as mining engineer stood him in good stead. Where others might consider the warehouse impenetrable, he immediately thought of burrowing underground. There had to be sewer and electrical conduits and possibly more. As paranoid as the executives at IM were about aliens, they would not allow their warehouse on a planet slated for destruction to have only one entry point.

Underground. There must be tunnels. Kinsolving went to explore. Less than an hour later he found small outbuildings marked with radiation danger warning signs. The card-key lock appeared unused, which immediately aroused his interest. The building had the look of a refueling kiosk—but unused. Why? He pulled out Liu's cardkey and thrust it into the lock. For all the disused appearance, the lock and door mechanisms worked smoothly and silently.

"This is it," he said. Kinsolving paused just inside the door, looking around for security cameras. A tiny bead in one corner of the small room drew his attention. A vid lens hardly larger than a grain of rice monitored the room. He quickly smeared it with dirt from the floor. He doubted that the circuit ranked high on the priority list for the guards to monitor. But he knew he would have to work quickly. The smallest hint of intrusion would bring down a platoon of armed men ready to kill.

Kinsolving worked his way around the room and found nothing to indicate that it had ever been used to refuel nuclear piles, on surface craft or the heavier suborbital hypersonic wings favored by IM for on-planet use. What he did find was an unmarked slot in the wall. Again he used Liu's card-key.

As silently as the outer door had opened, a section of floor parted to reveal stairs leading downward. The tunnel beyond headed in the direction of the warehouse. He had found the way into the heart of Interstellar Materials' operations on Web.

Would he find enough to convince the arachnoid natives that IM intended genocide, or would he find only death?

Kinsolving pushed that thought out of his mind. He had already accomplished the hard part of his self-appointed task. He had learned of the Stellar Death Plan and how Fremont intended to kill the spider creatures.

He descended the stairs and peered into the inky blackness. For a moment he hesitated, worrying about security along the tunnel. But when he started to go back into the shed to find a way of lighting his progress, the door closed, plunging him into total darkness.

Barton Kinsolving fumbled about, seeking the card lock that would open the door. He could not find it, try as he might. He settled down. He didn't want to go back into the shed. He wanted a path into the warehouse. Carefully, one hand on the wall and the other in front of him to prevent running into an unseen barrier, Barton Kinsolving started down the tunnel toward the warehouse.

Or what he thought was the warehouse.

CHAPTER SEVEN

BARTON KINSOLVING edged along the pitch-black tunnel, testing each step before planting his full weight. The walls dripped and the overhead roof, in the spots where he could reach up and touch it, felt like concrete. He might be only a meter under the surface of the landing field.

He continued his slow pace, hardly daring to breathe. Once, he stopped and listened intently. The muffled sounds confused him. Kinsolving tried to decide if it was a hovertruck going by on the surface or something moving about in the tunnel. Or even evidence that he was nearing the end of the long, straight tunnel and would emerge into the warehouse.

No light showing made it seem unlikely that he neared the warehouse, unless they kept the door sealed. Over and over he touched the pocket with the stolen card-key, assuring himself that he had not lost it. His mind kept turning to problems other than those immediately confronting him, though.

The card. The code magnetically imprinted. If he could read the code, he might be able to alter Liu's ident number and make a generic card. For IM to change all their farflung codes would be a chore not easily done. He would have access for months or even years with such a falsified card-key.

Kinsolving screamed when his left hand brushed over something that felt like a wire brush. A living wire brush.

He jumped back in the darkness, lost his balance and fell heavily onto his back. Instinctively, he brought his knees in close to kick out with his feet.

"Do humans always adopt such peculiar greeting positions?" came the shrill query. "Or are you of their perverted sex maniacs and desire to mate with this one?"

"What?"

"This one is not good enough for you, is that it?"

"What are you talking about?" Kinsolving scrambled to get his feet under him. In the dark tunnel, he felt as if he swam in molasses. Although he knew this was purely psychological, that did not make the sensation go away. "Who are you?"

"This one has been shown your tri-vid dramas. There is nothing but peculiar mating in them, sometimes with orifices not even evolved for sexual use. We must view these as part of indoctrination when work is near your kind."

"You work at the Landing Authority?"

"This one is a worker, class three." Pride came in the squeaking voice.

"I'm honored to meet one of your station," Kinsolving said, not knowing what else to say. He tried to keep the sarcasm from his voice. "I apologize if I damaged you."

"You could not harm this one. Your progress down the corridor was peculiar, but then this is to be expected from a species engaging in perverse sexual rites."

"What did they show you?" demanded Kinsolving.

"Only your standard tri-vid fare." Kinsolving had the feeling that the arachnoid shuddered in horror, even though he could not see him to be certain.

"You watched me coming down the tunnel?"

"Yes. Although illumination is slight, it is more than adequate for advanced species such as this one's."

Kinsolving heaved a deep breath and tried to calm himself. "You aren't a guard posted in this tunnel," he said deciding even as he spoke.

A long silence. Then came a tiny squeak that Kinsolving thought meant "no."

"Why are you here? Trying to break into the IM warehouse?"

"You perform a similar task," accused the arachnoid.

Kinsolving reached out and again brushed over wiry bristles. He tried to picture the situation. The spider being's legs would almost fill the tunnel. To fight past would be impossible. The creature saw, however dimly, and he did not. Besides, Kinsolving had determined that the spider was here for some clandestine reason.

"You seek to steal something from the warehouse," he said.

"And you, do you not also seek the Box of Delights?" demanded the arachnoid.

Kinsolving considered this. The brain burner had been described as contraband, an outlawed device much like chemical drugs on most human-settled worlds. The attraction was illicit and thrilling—definitely narcotic and addicting—for the inhabitants of Web.

"Yes." Kinsolving did not trust himself to say more. The spider being might be Web's equivalent of a policeman trying to stop the importation of the "Boxes of Delights" or he might be an addict. Until he knew more, Kinsolving did not dare comment.

"We can share. It takes only a few minutes for me to achieve the strands."

"What do you mean?"

"To . . . to feel superior to all others," the arachnoid said, as if lecturing a dim-witted child. "Why else use the Box of Delights, if not to attain the uppermost strands?"

"Good point. Have you been into the warehouse? Do you know where the brain b—where the Box of Delights is?"

"Many have come this way. We must tread softly. Those of the Web Will slay many careless seekers."

"The Web Will? You mean police? Law-enforcement officers?"

"Law? This one fails to understand your words. Those of the Web Will do what is proper, what is right."

"And they would prevent you from using the Box of Delights?"

"Of course. It is dangerous to become wrapped in one's own fantasy world and exclude all else, especially the commands of the Supreme Web."

"Where are Those of the Web Will?"

"You are not of them. You are a human. Why deal with them? Why ask? Is this more of your species' perverted sexual deviance?"

"No, no, I just want to be able to recognize them, to avoid them." Kinsolving lied.

He recoiled when a hairy leg brushed over his face.

"You lie," said the arachnoid. "But you are not with Those of the Web Will. They would never accept a human in their ranks."

"Let's just say I have my own reasons for finding the Boxes of Delights."

"There are many?" The unrestrained eagerness in the arachnoid's voice told Kinsolving of the unavoidable, addictive lure contained in the reasonating single crystal of cerium.

"I think so."

"They charge so much for them, but there are quiverings in the web that the price will fall like a spastic youngling."

"Lead the way," said Kinsolving. "Together we might be able to find the Boxes."

He heard the *click-click* of hard talons on the concrete floor. Other than the sound the man had no way of telling anyone else travelled the tunnel with him.

"Are there sensors?" he called out.

Almost in his ear came the reply. "This one has removed the devices from their circuit. Such primitive equipment."

"You know of security cameras?"

"This one is of Web. Of course. This one is a level-three worker."

Kinsolving fell silent. It seemed that even the lowlies of arachnoids possessed knowledge of IM's most sophisticated equipment. He stumbled and would have fallen if the spider being had not slipped a talon through the collar of his jacket and held him erect.

"The steps lead up," the arachnoid said, again in the tone of a parent lecturing a wayward child.

"Is the door at the top locked?"

"That has thwarted this one's efforts. An alarm will sound every time the door opens, with or without proper access codes."

Kinsolving could only depend on the captured card-keys. A director would not want his presence known always. Perhaps the card-key would disable the alarm.

Kinsolving knew that was not likely, but he had little choice but to try.

Fumbling in the dark, he let the arachnoid guide his hand to the tiny slot that would hold the electronically encrypted card. He boldly thrust it into the lock; he had nothing to lose. Entry into the warehouse from the surface looked impossible.

The sudden ray of light lancing through the opening door blinded him. The spider creature shot past him, mandibles clacking. By the time Kinsolving's eyes had adjusted to the bright lights, the arachnoid had dismantled the entire electronics system controlling the door.

"No alarm," the spider said.

Kinsolving nodded numbly. He had not clearly seen the creature before. Although he had spoken to several and had taken the shuttle to the surface with an arachnoid pilot, the nearness of the alien sent an uncontrollable shudder through his body.

"You are cold? The impossible lights above sear everything. This one does not understand the internal heat for this building."

For Kinsolving, the warehouse was pleasant. It had been the sight of a mottled gray-and-brown spider able to stare him in the eye that had produced the reaction.

"I'm fine. Where do we look?"

"They are your species, perverted and sick though they are. You choose a likely starting venue."

"The most recent arrivals. Where?"

The arachnoid took off, the lumbering gait making Kinsolving slightly motion-sick following. He found himself unconsciously duplicating the side-to-side, up-and-down movement. The man shook himself free and concentrated on the crates. Most labels told of Interstellar Materials shipments of single-crystal and strain-free crystals for scientific studies. The crates were hardly large enough to hold many brain burners.

"There," Kinsolving said. "The crates marked mining equipment."

"There is no mining allowed on Web," the spider said. "These are being shipped though to other planets, human-settled worlds called Acheron and Cocytus." The arachnoid stumbled over the names.

"The rivers of woe and lamentation," muttered Kinsolving. Louder, he told the spider being, "There aren't any such worlds. Those were written on the crates to give the appearance of transshipping."

The spider tensed his legs and shot to the top of the crates. Quick talons jerked open one of the plastic crates. Kinsolving would have had to use a cutting laser to equal the creature's speed in spilling out the crate's contents.

"Whatever's in there, it's not mining equipment," he said.

"Boxes of Delights!" cried the spider.

Kinsolving whipped around, fearful that the arachnoid had alerted guards with his shrill outcry. The noise of heavy equipment moving freight in other parts of the warehouse drowned out the alien's shout of joy. The creature pulled out a small red plastic cube with indentations on either of two opposing sides. Talons thrust into the depressions.

A quiver shook the spider. It settled down on the crate, oblivious to everything else in the world.

Kinsolving reached up and grabbed one hairy leg. He shook it hard. The creature did not respond.

"I should record this," he said, still astounded at the quickness with which the Box of Delights worked on the arachnoid. Kinsolving fumbled in his pocket and pulled out the data recorder Lark had given him. The information on Web had proven useless. He recorded over it, aiming the tiny lens at the arachnoid lost in a private universe of rapture.

Kinsolving shot the spider from all angles, making certain to change the focus to include the IM imprint on the crates, the dozens of other red boxes inside, everything he could.

From a vantage point beside the arachnoid, Kinsolving slowly panned the entire IM warehouse. Through the tiny aiming display, he caught sight of two burly men rounding a stack of crates. He ducked down before they spotted him.

"Damnation," cried one man. "Another of those Bizzies

got in and found the brain burners. The boss isn't going to like this."

"Hell, let's just get rid of it. Nobody'd be the wiser. And in a few weeks, who'll be on-planet to care?".

"Not the Bizzies, that's for sure."

Kinsolving recorded it all, the two men pulling the a-rachnoid off his perch, their attempts to tear the brain burner from his talons, their failure.

"Let it die happy," said the larger of the men.

"Seems a shame that they got to die that way. I wish they'd suffer."

"Won't be long before we're in charge," the first said. "The Bizzies that're left, well, hell, we can do as we please with them."

They began exchanging increasingly improbable ways of murdering the arachnoids who had not succumbed to the brain burners. Kinsolving felt his stomach churn.

The men's savagery did not make him very proud to be a human. Kinsolving quietly slipped back to the tunnel entrance. No one had noticed the door standing ajar or the electronics panel that the spider being had dismantled. Kinsolving hurried inside, struggled to pull the door shut and was instantly plunged into Stygian darkness.

As he made his way back to the shed set on the side of the landing field, he thought about what he might do with the evidence he had collected.

"Those of the Web Will," he mused. Alien police, even though the spider had trouble with the concept. Find Those of the Web Will, show them his evidence and...then what?

Barton Kinsolving went cold inside. What would the arachnoids do? He had already sampled alien justice on another world. The Lorr had given him a life's exile on their hidden prison world.

What might the spiders do to him? To Interstellar Materials personnel who knew nothing of the brain burners? To other humans on-planet? To him?

CHAPTER EIGHT

"CHAIRMAN FREMONT thinks I should go with you," said Kenneth Humbolt.

"Oh?" Cameron smirked at the idea.

"To make sure nothing goes wrong, that you are able to guarantee a flow-through on the brain burners."

Cameron watched Humbolt begin to fidget nervously. The director knew as well as the robotics expert why Fremont wanted him along on this trip. It was not to guide Cameron's deft hand. It was punishment. Cameron might be lower in title and status, but everyone knew who would be in charge of the mission.

"Really, Kenneth, I can deal with the distribution problems on my own. I've done similar jobs, though at the time I hadn't realized how important they were. I didn't know that there even was a plan. Not that Fremont and the rest of IM's board has taken me into their confidence. I'll do all I can to . . . achieve maximum results."

"I'm sure," muttered Humbolt. "That does not change my orders. I'm to go to ZOo and oversee the project."

"You'll have to hurry," said Cameron.

"What? Why?"

"I'm shifting for Web in exactly one hour." Cameron lifted a small box and tucked it under his arm. The precision tools inside would be put to excellent use on Web. He had designed several unique tracking robots. Testing them required prey, victims. Cameron had no doubt that any number of worthy targets might be found on that distant world.

He eyed Humbolt. Perhaps even a director of Interstellar Materials might find himself on the receiving end of a

hunter-killer. Orders had not come in from Fremont—or
Maria Villalobos—but they might at any instant. Cameron
had the instincts of both a killer and a vulture. He *felt* the
nearness of death in others.

Kenneth Humbolt was not long for either IM or life.

"An interesting array of weaponry," commented Cameron. "The Bizzies must find it necessary to maintain
such an awesome battery on their moons. Do they engage
in numerous wars? I saw no evidence of destruction or use
of the lasers."

"I don't know why they armed so heavily," said Humbolt. The entire trip had been spent worrying over his op-
tions, how he could regain lost power and position in IM,
how he could turn this disgrace to his own advantage.
Damn Kinsolving!

"I've studied company files on Web. It seems that they
have refused repeatedly to grant mining rights. A major
disruption of their society would allow Interstellar Materials to make a strong bid for those privileges."

"The Plan must be served. The Bizarres are everywhere
and they keep us down. They have united against humanity. We must stand firm against them. The mining question
is a minor one."

"You recite the litany well," said Cameron, his mocking
words stinging Humbolt out of his self-pity.

"It's not litany. I believe it."

"Of course you do," Cameron said soothingly, but the
sneer on his lips turned the words like a knife thrust into
the belly. "And the billions IM stands to profit from
disruption on Web is incidental."

"Trillions," Humbolt said sullenly.

Humbolt winced as Cameron's hot eyes burned him.
"You lack the instincts of a true killer, Kenneth," said Cameron.

"I'm a businessman, not an assassin like you."

"What's the difference? Both require a certain ruthlessness and tenacity. You shy away from doing what is
needed. Kill off a few billion bizarrely shaped aliens? Why
not if it gives profit? They compete unfairly by blocking
human trading on their worlds. Cut off the parent world

and their colonies must seek supplies and equipment and revenues from other sources. Why not human sources, no matter how distasteful they might find this?"

Cameron chuckled at Humbolt's growing uneasiness. The roboticist added, "Why not human sources, when we *know* that disaster is about to befall Web and have prepared for it?"

"There's more than monetary gain at stake," snapped Humbolt.

"Oh, yes, there is, there is," said Cameron. Humbolt rubbed his lips, more worried than ever. Cameron had been a few minutes late reaching the starship. From what Humbolt had seen of the assassin and had read in his company psych-profile, punctuality ranked high with him.

Cameron had been detained on Gamma Tertius by someone important, someone powerful. Fremont? Villalobos? Another director? What had been said? And why wasn't he, Kenneth Humbolt, a director of IM, also given those last-minute instructions?

Humbolt worried until he thought the veins in his temples would explode.

"A good, serviceable security system, Mr. Rogoff," Humbolt complimented. "The warehouse is impenetrable from either the air or the ground."

"Infrared scanners at work all night, one hundred percent overlap on the visual cameras, motion sensors and roving robot guard designed by Mr. Cameron." Rogoff turned and nodded in Cameron's direction. Cameron's expression did not change. He cared little what this fool of a supervisor said, good or bad, about security. The brief examinations he had given the warehouse showed a hundred ways to enter unobserved. There might be more, but he tired of figuring them out.

"You realize, Mr. Rogoff, that we are not dealing with stupid creatures," said Cameron. "The Bizzies on Web are extremely adroit at microelectronics."

"They're nothing but goddamned spiders. Who can take a king-sized bug seriously?"

"You might be onto something there," Cameron said

dryly. Such an attitude explained the lax security around the warehouse that Humbolt foolishly praised so highly.

"Glad you think so, sir. I really admire the work you do with those guard robots. Bring any new models to test?"

"A few," said Cameron, his mind elsewhere. "Just experimental models. Nothing for routine use." He wandered through the stacks of plastic crates, alert to every nick and scratch. Cameron drew a pair of goggles from inside a pocket in his flowing purple velvet cape. He pushed back the cape and settled it on his shoulders, fox-fur collar snuggling gently around his neck. Cameron adjusted it; the core of the soft fur carried a thick, flexible inertial plastic that turned instantly hard if anything should impact it—like a bullet or garrote wire.

A similar vest rested beneath the mauve silk shirt. Cameron accepted the risks of fieldwork and considered his possible adversaries. Humbolt and Rogoff might denigrate the Bizzies on this planet. Cameron had only admiration for their electronics skills. Until he learned otherwise, he had to assume their skills at assassination were similarly well developed.

The cape settled, he adjusted the goggles, moving the lenses around to give a polarized visual light view. The scratches became instantly apparent. A different set of filters and new setting on the variable spectrum generator set in the goggle rims gave IR readings. Still another set showed unexpected drops that fluoresced on the floor. Cameron walked in what appeared a random fashion.

The drama that had occurred atop the crate laden with brain burners unfolded and revealed itself to him.

"Anything wrong, Mr. Cameron?" asked the supervisor.

"When did this shipment of, uh, equipment arrive?"

"You mean the brain burners? Got them in a week ago. We're about done forging the transshipment papers to show them being sent on to other planets."

"Nonexistent planets?"

"Why not? Somebody back on GT thought up the names."

"Archeron. Cocytus." Cameron's nose twitched.

"What's wrong, Cameron? You find something?" demanded Humbolt.

To the supervisor, Cameron said, "There's been one in-truder, possible two, who has opened this crate within the past few days. What happened to him?"

"Intruder?" Rogoff's expresssion shifted from confusion to fright to an emotionless mask in the flickering of an eye. But Cameron saw. So did Humbolt.

"Who got through your security, Mr. Rogoff?" de-manded Humbolt. "A Bizzie looking for a brain burner?"

"That would certainly indicate that the Bizzies are aware of the source of the devices," mused Cameron. "A definite breach of security. Unless one of your own men has been rummaging about in the crate." Cameron tugged at the lace ruffles on his cuffs. An index finger lightly brushed a tog-gle that recalled and armed an aerial robot he had sent forth to reconnoiter the warehouse.

"That's it," said Rogoff, his face still impassive. "A worker mistook this for one of the real shipping cases and accidentally opened it. But it was all right. He was cleared."

"How badly was he hurt?" asked Cameron. His fingers touched another toggle hidden in the lining of his cape.

"Hurt? What are you saying? He wasn't hurt."

"No, I suspect not. Not unless you employ natives to work inside the warehouse. You were inept in removing the droplets of blood on the floor. The natives' blood fluor-esces under UV. A distinct trail leads off in that direction, no doubt where you disposed of the body."

Rogoff snarled. His hands slid under his light jacket toward the small of his back. A tiny hum sounded. Ro-goff's face went slack even as he toppled forward.

"What happened?" asked Humbolt, stepping away from the fallen supervisor.

"Mr. Rogoff chose an infelicitous course of action. He attempted to draw whatever weapon he carried in a holster in the middle of his back." Cameron touched his hidden toggle again. The buzzing came again, louder. A five-centimeter-long robot shot down and hovered just above Rogoff's unmoving shoulders.

"What is that thing?"

"A friend, Kenneth, a friend. I sent the robot on patrol. When Rogoff so unjudiciously attacked, the robot obeyed a

command to protect me. It launched a small needle laden
with a poison developed by a friend of mine who works for
Galaxy Pharmaceuticals."

"Galaxy? GPMT?" Humbolt's eyes widened. Cameron
made a mental note of the reaction. Galaxy Pharmaceuticals and Medical Techtronics must be involved in some
way with the Plan to cause such a violent start in Humbolt.

"A friend in research. But the basic design of the elec-
tromagnetically driven steel needle is mine. The robot contains a small magazine of the magnetized needles. The
needle is launched much as you would expect a particle in
a mass driver to be."

"That small thing contains a miniature mass driver?"

"And a score of needles, should one be insufficient. My
next model will be more elaborate, with a magazine of
needles ranging from relatively harmless to instantly fatal."
Cameron poked a brilliantly polished boot toe into Rogoff
and turned the supervisor over. An expression of stark pain
had been permanently frozen on his face. "I use only the
instant-acting poisons for this model. Seems to be painful,
doesn't it?"

Humbolt glanced from Cameron to the robot patiently
hovering, then back to its creator. "Call it off."

"It only protects us, Kenneth. Don't worry. Unless you
have a weapon and make a sudden movement. Its discrim-
inator circuits are very sophisticated for such a small
robot."

"What—" Humbolt took a deep breath and calmed himself. "What happened here? With the crates?"

Cameron looked innocent. "I can only reconstruct the
incident, now that Rogoff has committed suicide on us.
Damned inconsiderate, don't you think?"

"The crate. What of it?"

"Ah, yes, the crate with the brain burners. I suspect a
Bizzie gained entry, took a device out and used it. Some
workers found him. Rather than handling the matter in an
efficient, sane manner, they beat the arachnoid to death."

"The stains on the floor?"

"And the crate and in several other unlikely spots, many
very high up."

Cameron craned his neck back, felt the inertial collar

hidden beneath the fox fur and stopped his inspection. "They dragged the Bizzie over there, possibly putting the body in the plasma torch for disposal. The corpse, at any rate, is no longer on the premises."

"That was smart. No trace of the body left."

Cameron snorted derisively. The body might have been reduced to atoms but the evidence remained, evidence they had been too stupid to remove. The entire operation on Zeta Orgo teetered on the verge of disaster. It was good that Chairman Fremont had ordered him to take whatever measures led to success.

"This is a bit of good luck for you, Kenneth," said Cameron, watching the director closely.

"What? How can you say that? Rogoff might have breached security on this part of the Plan so badly that the Bizzies have learned about it!"

"Hardly," said Cameron. "Careless, yes, that he was. But the Bizzies would have lasered the warehouse to the ground by now if they suspected. No, you are lucky. You can assume Mr. Rogoff's duties and personally ensure the completion of the Stellar Death Plan on Web."

"Become supervisor? A director?"

"It would be only a temporary assignment, of course. But to promote a local employee who might have been responsible for this..." Cameron's hand swept the scene that glowed brilliantly when he shone the ultraviolet light on the alien blood spots.

"I see what you mean. I'll find out who's responsible and take care of them."

"Good," said Cameron, his mind already diverted to other matters. "I'll continue my inspection. Have someone see about removing the late Mr. Rogoff. He'll begin to stink soon. That's an unfortunate aspect and one which will have to be researched further. The poison accelerates decay, I fear."

Cameron strode off, his goggles constantly being adjusted to new and different frequencies. The Bizzie had penetrated Rogoff's security. Who had accompanied the spider being? Cameron found minute traces of another. But another Bizzie?

Cameron did not believe so.

He stood in front of the hidden doorway leading to the underground tunnel and simply stared at it.

"Ah, my good friend, you *do* live!" Cameron said. He spun and returned to see what trouble Humbolt had created. After dealing with it, there would be time to track down Barton Kinsolving.

CHAPTER NINE

BARTON KINSOLVING clutched the data recorder close to his body to keep it from being knocked from his hands as he pushed through the crowd. The arachnoids wobbled and cavorted but never—quite—touched him. This did not keep him from jerking away when a heavy body or a hairy leg seemed to be on a collision course with his face.

He studied the recording he had made inside the Interstellar Materials warehouse. "Proof," he muttered to himself. "This is enough to launch an investigation, enough to show that IM is trafficking in illegal electronic devices."

Even as he spoke, Kinsolving heard the hollowness of his words. Investigation? Who would investigate? Those of the Web Will? Kinsolving had no idea how to contact them, or even if they were policemen in the strictest sense of enforcing interworld laws. The arachnoid had spoken of them more as priests, as those beings responsible for maintaining the righteousness of the web and the spiders dangling from it.

Kinsolving put the small data recorder safely into his pocket and stared around. He had left the landing field and walked for what seemed hours. The weather proved suprisingly mild for what he assumed to be midwinter. The heavy storm clouds in the sky, the sudden chill from a gust of wind, the condition of the plants had all hinted at winter. But along the city streets he found only warm breezes and not a single snowflake falling on him.

He openly gawked at the tall-spired buildings as if he had never seen anything like them before. Kinsolving smiled wryly. He felt like a child brought into the big city from out in the country. The buildings he had seen before, on Earth, on Gamma Tertius, on several other planets. But never had he imagined the way the natives of Zeta Orgo used those buildings.

Huge cables dangled between the uppermost spires, swaying in the wind until Kinsolving got dizzy watching. Along those cables scurried the arachnoid inhabitants of the world. Now and then he would see a spider, hardly more than a dark dot, release from a cable and plummet down. The first time Kinsolving saw this happen, he thought the spider being had somehow slipped or been blown off by the high winds.

The creature deftly played out web behind it, coming to a gentle halt at a window entrance three stories above ground level. The spider swung about, paused for a few seconds to cut free of the strand, dropped through and vanished from sight.

A coldness began in Kinsolving's belly when he realized that elevators might not exist on this world. He craned his head back to stare up at the sky-gutting spires. If the people he sought had their offices high up in the immense buildings, he might never be able to reach them. Waiting on the street until they chose to descend did not seem a good course of action, either.

The way the arachnoids went from one building to the other along their aerial highways hinted that some might never descend to the ground. Like the gods in Valhalla, they ranged across the sky and seldom deigned to notice human endeavors.

"Still," Kinsolving said to himself, "there are enough of the natives who do choose to walk." He wondered why. Very few vehicles were in use, and those carried cargo too heavy for a single arachnoid to carry easily. Finding out the reasons for a society doing what it did lay far beyond his ability. A xeno-sociologist might spend a lifetime studying these strange beings and never get more than an inkling of why the aliens built and acted and lived the way they did.

"And we're as strange to them," Kinsolving said. As if to prove his point, a passing arachnoid stared at him curiously, the head moving in impossible directions. The spider creature lumbered on, mandibles clacking and talons whispering along the hard pavement.

Kinsolving slipped down a wall, his back aching and his feet ready to give out. The spiders managed to step over him. Most never seemed to notice the human obstacle in their path, getting all eight legs around him without touching.

He had been running too long. It was time to think. He did not have money or credit on the planet, he could not remember the last meal he'd eaten, and worst of all he did not know how to proceed with the damning evidence he had accumulated in the Interstellar materials warehouse.

Finding Those of the Web Will might be an approach, but Kinsolving knew that the arachnoids would not accept his unsubstantiated word for anything. Even the recordings he had made of the spider shaking and quivering as he activated the brain burner would not be convincing enough for alien authorities. He cursed himself for not having brought along a few of the illicit devices as evidence.

Then Kinsolving realized it was for the best that he had not. To be caught with contraband on Web would reveal that he had escaped the prison world. Even if the authorities on Web did not find him guilty of a crime, they would probably notify the Lorr, who would take him back to exile on the prison planet.

"No alien police," he said. "Forget Those of the Web Will." Then who might aid him? Kinsolving sagged. He had run through most of those likely to want to stop the importation of the deadly Boxes of Delights. That left only the humans on Web.

He could not run to the IM planetary supervisor. It seemed impossible that supervisor level would not know of the smuggling. The details of the Stellar Death Plan might not be revealed fully, but the supervisor had to authorize the fake shipments and doctor the records. Kinsolving had heard hints that other corporations gave aid—or had a hand in formulating the Plan—so he dared not seek out help from that quarter.

"The Earth consul. That's the only choice left." Kin-

solving heaved himself to his feet and started off, alert now
for a city guide that give directions to "alien" businesses
and consulates. He found it, a small mushroom-topped
kiosk less than a meter in diameter, but hunt as he might,
no controls were apparent.

Kinsolving jumped back when the kiosk suddenly lit.
He saw the top flicker—and above this hung a spider on a
web strand. Whatever the arachnoid saw on the top satisfied him. The alien continued his swing and vanished
through a fourth-story window.

Kinsolving looked around and decided that the controls
must be on the top. He scrambled up the smooth-sided
pillar and stared at the rounded dome.

A high-pitched squeaking drew his attention. Five
meters above him swung another spider being chittering at
him to get out of the way. The legs worked against the
strand of web stuff while the tiny pink hands made gestures
at Kinsolving that could not be anything but obscene.

"You, silly human thing. Get away from the guidance
device."

"This?"

The arachnoid squeaked until Kinsolving's eardrums
threatened to burst. But he saw how the information
kiosk worked. The display rose in a tri-vid column, a
golden arrow pointing. Strange runelike markings floated
in the air above it. The arachnoid chittered again. The
arrow altered direction slightly, sank, and a new set of
runes appeared. A final screech sounded at a frequency
only an Earthly bat could appreciate and the entire display vanished.

Kinsolving slipped to street level and watched in fascination. From this vantage point, he could not see any of the
hologram. Only from above could they be read.

He again climbed the kiosk, balancing precariously on
the dome. A few arachnoids avoided this information
kiosk, but enough others ignored his antics for him to get
an idea how the guide worked. The golden arrow pointed
in the direction. The elevation of the arrow—above the
kiosk or above the ground?—showed what level of building. The writing must tell distance.

None of this revelation helped him use the kiosk.

"Out of my line of vision, human one." Another arachnoid dangled above Kinsolving, ready to use the information kiosk when he got out of the way.

"Can you help me?" called up Kinsolving. "I can't activate the computer."

The arachnoid shrieked and got his directions, then paused. One eye studied Kinsolving. "Where do you wish to go, voiceless one?"

"The Earth consulate."

Chirping. Squeaks. A bark. Kinsolving saw the golden arrow appear level with his knees as he stood atop the dome.

"That direction. Travel for one-ninetieth of a planetary rotation."

"Is it ground level?"

"Of course." The arachnoid's tone left little to wonder about. The alien ridiculed any other beast unable to make use of the cable system hanging between buildings.

"Thank you." Kinsolving wanted to ask more, but the spider creature spun away, sucking in the web he had spun and ascending with a speed more terrifying to Kinsolving than the descents he had witnessed. He had noted the direction shown by the golden arrow, but had no idea how far to travel. Dropping to the ground, he set out grimly toward the consulate. How long he would have to travel, he did not know. For the first time, Kinsolving regretted having erased the information that Lark had copied onto the data recorder.

He patted the pocket with the device and shook his head. No, he did not regret it. He would walk for a year, if necessary. The spiders were abrupt, curt, intolerant of humans, and why not? He had learned so little of their ways. Why should any of them take the time to instruct him when he had failed to provide for his own education?

In less than an hour of weaving through the buildings and trying to maintain the proper vector, he found a small blue-and-silver crest mounted on the door to what appeared to be a store.

"This is the consulate?" he wondered aloud. It might have been a specialty store for its size. Kinsolving stood and stared and worried anew. Would he find help, or would the consul side with Fremont and the others involved with the Plan? Kinsolving made the decision. He had no choice. Without allies, without resources, he had to trust someone. In general, the tone on Earth was not that he found among the corporations. The educators, the governments, even the general populace looked on the aliens with neutrality if not favor.

That did not mean the consul was not in the pay of IM. That didn't mean that he might not agree with the Plan's purpose.

Kinsolving forced such thoughts out of his head. He had no way of checking; he needed help in stopping the distribution of the brain burners. If nothing else, he would determine quickly where the Earth's representative stood on the matter.

He strode up to the door, then went inside. For a moment, Kinsolving thought he had been transported back to Earth. A green valley stretched in front of him. The Shenandoah? Fog-shrouded purpled mountains rose on either side. A blue ribbon of river traced its way through the valley floor. Most convincing of all was the soft breeze blowing in his face carrying the scents of Earth, of the Appalachians, of growing trees and spring and times long past.

He shook himself out of the reverie and looked out of the corners of his eyes for a hint about what he had gotten himself into. Peripheral vision showed a small com unit on a plain desk. The tri-vid display was so real, though.

"I'd like to see the consul," he said, toggling the com unit.

"You're from Earth!" The voice sounded startled. Kinsolving smiled. Well that the consul should be surprised. He had bulled his way onto Web without the proper visas and notification.

"This is a matter of the utmost importance. How do I get past the tri-vid?"

"Sorry. I'm alone most of the time. The view keeps me from going crazy." The display winked off, showing a plain room barely wide enough for Kinsolving to walk through without brushing his shoulders on the walls. At the end of what amounted to a wide corridor stood a plain door, again bearing Earth's blue-and-silver crest.

In the room lounged a smallish man with graying hair and a harassed expression on his face.

"Mr. Consul?" asked Kinsolving.

"Name's Andrianov. Garon Andrianov. Pleased to meet you." Kinsolving introduced himself. The consul took Kinsolving's hand and pumped it until the circulation faded. "Sorry, sorry. Didn't mean to do that. Gets lonely here. I mean, there's the paperwork and all, but nothing more. Seldom see another human, unless I go to the landing field. And they don't want much to do with me. Think I'll meddle in their affairs, I suppose."

"You don't have a staff?"

"All computerized. Not much to do on Web. Not much."

Kinsolving had the sinking feeling in his gut again. This consulate ranked so low that Earth sent only one diplomat?

"Don't remember processing you through. I flag the files of all Earthers who land. When did you land?"

"Not long ago," said Kinsolving. He stared at the small, intense man. No option remained. He had to trust Andrianov.

Andrianov silently motioned him to a couch. No desk existed that Kinsolving saw. He guessed that most of Andrianov's work went through the computer and the consul did little but approve the programming.

"This isn't easy for me to say," Kinsolving started.

"Tea?" asked Andrianov. "Sorry for interrupting, but I have so few human visitors. And I do get tired of dealing with the natives. Their ways are, well, odd to one from Earth. I'm from Novosibirsk. It's our turn to supply personnel for the consulate. I replaced an Argentinian who left the lovely tri-vid you saw when you came in." Andrianov sighed. "Wish I could have one of the Ob River. Such loveliness."

He shook himself from his memories of distant Earth. "Sorry. So sorry. I hope you *do* understand. Seeing only the arachnoids..."

"Do you like them?" asked Kinsolving.

"What? Well, yes, of course. On the whole, I must or

I'd go quite crazy. Lonesome job, this one. Lonesome.
And tedious. So seldom do I see anyone from the field.
There's not much of a human community here, as there is
on other alien planets."

"The Bizzies—" Kinsolving started.

"Please, sir. That is an offensive term. I understand that
human palates cannot form the proper name for Web's inhabitants, but do try to remain civil."

"Good." Kinsolving relaxed. He launched into his story,
showing Andrianov the data recorder of the arachnoid and
the brain burner, of how he had stumbled onto the Stellar
Death Plan, of how Hamilton Fremont and others on the
board of directors of Interstellar Materials had concocted
the genocidal scheme, everything—except the problems he
had encountered on Deepdig that had resulted in his exile
to the prison world. Kinsolving knew that revealing this
would prejudice his case.

"You are in a dangerous position, Barton," said Andrianov. "IM certainly wouldn't like you snooping about
their warehouse, no matter what the circumstances. This is
not evidence acceptable to a court, you know."

"I understand. What I have to do is convince you that a
problem exists, a serious one threatening billions of lives.
Then we can worry about legality and proof."

"Must stop the spread of these brain burners, as you call
them. Boxes of Delight the natives call them. Terribly addicting. They can starve to death using them. Goes right to
the cortex and stimulates the pleasure center. Ugly death,
ugly, wasting away and smiling the entire while. Or what
passes for a smile."

"Mr. Andrianov, is there any way you can impound the
contents of the warehouse?"

"None. I have little authority over humans on-planet. I
issue permits. I grant visas—never turned one down in
three planetary years of service—I go to the occasional
formal governmental function. That's all I do."

"Is there an ambassador? Someone with the power to
investigate IM's actions on Web?"

"No ambassador. Always going to be exchanged but
never done, that sort of balls-up mess. Been a decade or

longer since an ambassador resided on Web. Or one from
Web went to Earth. Think it's a mutual decision. Neither
wants to maintain the pomp and ceremony and expense of
a full embassy."

"Those of the Web Will," said Kinsolving. Andrianov's
pale eyes snapped up and held Kinsolving fixed like a bug
on a pin. "What of them?"

"How do you know about Those of the Web Will?"

"The arachnoid I met in the tunnel mentioned them."

"We dare not seek them out. All humans would be
killed. All. They are terrible creatures. Reactionaries. They
are the arachnoid counterpart of those authoring the Stellar
Death Plan."

"Who do we contact? If you can't stop the flood of the
brain burners, someone in the Web government must be
able to."

"The Supreme Web. They have the authority, but reaching them is difficult." Andiranov made a funny coughing
noise. "In all my years on Web, I have never seen them
assembled. Don't even know *where* they meet. For all I
know, the Supreme Web might be a rumor or a joke played
on gullible humans."

Kinsolving sank back in the chair and closed his eyes. A
terrible pounding threatened to blow apart his skull.

"Direct indictment," Andrianov said unexpectedly. "We
need to show that IM officials are responsible. Your data
shows only that the Boxes of Delights are stored in their
warehouse. If we can implicate someone in the company,
that might be enough to get action."

"From whom?" Kinsolving asked tiredly.

"From the Supreme Web. They *must* exist. Or a group
like them. There's government on Web. It's just that I've
never had a matter important enough to seek it out." Andrianov made the coughing-laughing noise again. "Fact is,
they discourage such things. No ceremony, no sense of
decorum."

"How do we do it?" asked Kinsolving. He dared hope
again. A little.

Andrianov shook his head. "This is new for me. I process paperwork. But we'll think of something. We must, or all arachnoids on Web will die."

Barton Kinsolving looked at his newfound ally and shivered slightly. Andrianov was better than no ally at all.

He had to be.

CHAPTER TEN

GARON ANDRIANOV leaned back in his comfortable chair and thought—hard. For three years he had been stranded on this miserable planet surrounded by miserable bugs while waiting for another assignment that would be equally miserable elsewhere.

He turned slightly, his hand lightly brushing over a control. The vidscreen flowed from the idyllic scenes of Earth to a sleeping Barton Kinsolving. The man lay on his stomach, head turned toward the camera. He slept heavily. Andrianov saw that nothing less than a major quake would disturb that slumber.

Andrianov toggled another screen and played through at high speed the data recording Kinsolving had brought. He gusted a big sigh. A miserable assignment, a miserable post, now miserable problems. The small man tried to find where his sympathies lay.

With the spiders? Somewhat. They were not too bad if you got to know them as individuals. However, so few ever *wanted* that kind of contact that Garon Andrianov had only two whom he called friends among the native populace. His business and diplomatic dealings hardly extended farther than that pair.

He owed the inhabitants of Web nothing. But Earth? What did he owe the plant of his birth? Andrianov toggled on a recorder.

"Diary entry, current date, the usual format." He took a deep breath and composed his thoughts. The recorder would take appropriate action later, eliminating the stutters and mistakes and leaving only a perfect report. "Evidence has come into my hands showing illicit importation of what the natives of Zeta Orgo 4 call 'Boxes of Delights.' Append the recording given by Barton Kinsolving."

He did not owe Web anything, but he did owe Earth the report and he did owe it to himself. Such a discovery—and its successful resolution—would get him a double-step promotion, perhaps back to Earth, or at least to a more suitable planet.

"I fear that this scheme by the chairman and the previously named directors of Interstellar Materials will endanger Earth security. Should the Supreme Web learn of this so-called Stellar Death Plan, military retaliation on human bases and worlds is both possible and likely. See prior reports on military capabilities of Zeta Orgo 4 and append appropriate sections."

Andrianov sipped at his tea as he thought. The danger to Earth outweighed all else. If he thought that Fremont and the others stood even a small chance of succeeding, he would do nothing. But how could they triumph? The billions of arachnoids on Web worked against their scheme, even one this subtle.

Addiction was a problem, yes, but when it reached epidemic proportions, the spiders would find ways of halting it. They were not bound by Earthly laws. Andrianov had read of times in Web history when hundreds of millions had been sacrificed for the good of the planet. How those decisions were reached—and by whom—he had never discovered, but it proved that the arachnoids had a ruthlessness about them that made the worst of human tyrants pale in comparison.

He swallowed hard. They made the worst of humanity pale in comparison—until now. Fremont would slay billions. Planets. Entire species!

"I do not believe," he said, picking up his report once more, "that only xenophobia drives the Stellar Death Plan. Financial gain figures prominently in the reasons for this mad scheme. Mining concessions on Web are minimal now. See appended report. Massive catastrophe to the native populace would open the way for extensive exploitation."

Andrianov ran his finger over the toggle. "Finish and seal the report, put it in diplomatic queue and transmit at the first opportunity." He thumbed the toggle and leaned back, feeling as exhausted as Kinsolving looked.

He had done his duty. No one expected more than a report from a minor consul without staff. But Garon Andrianov wanted to do more. To find the Boxes of Delights, to get the hard evidence implicating local IM officials, those were the ways to promotion.

Andrianov glanced up once more at the vidscreen and saw that Kinsolving had not stirred a muscle. He might be dead for all the signs of vitality he showed. Knowing his uninvited guest would not awaken for hours, Andrianov stood, adjusted his short, waist-length black, properly diplomatic jacket and left. He had more than enough time to gather the evidence he needed.

Andrianov shrugged his shoulders and made certain that the recording devices built into his jacket were ready for action. His heart pounded faster, and he stopped for a moment to wipe the sweat from his forehead. Only when he had once more fallen into the diplomatic, expressionless calm taught in school did he stride up to the door of the Interstellar Materials warehouse.

Two guards exchanged puzzled glances. Andrianov noted with some apprehension that both carried weapons of some sort hidden under their jackets.

"What can we do for you?" asked the guard on the right.

"I wish to see the supervisor. Mr. Rogoff, I believe, is the name." Andrianov ran his fingers along the lapel of his jacket and recorded both men's responses. The standard-issue diplomatic equipment had lain unused in his wardrobe since he had come to Zeta Orgo. It felt good to use it.

It felt good to be doing something that would aid Earth —and his own career.

"Rogoff's been rotated," the leader of the pair said. "Got a new super."

"Indeed. I don't have any record of Mr. Rogoff's departure."

"Why should you? He's an IM employee."

"And I am consul for this world. Exit visas are required. We need to know how many Earth citizens are on-planet at any given time." Andrianov remembered the unpleasant repercussions on Angel 2 when the natives rioted and began killing indiscriminately. It had taken him weeks to get an order of magnitude estimate of the Earthmen on-planet. He had never been able to identify them all.

Andrianov tried to push that from his mind. In part, his handling of the aftermath on Angel had led to his assignment here.

"You're the consul?" asked the subordinate, his eyebrows arching. "Never saw you around here before."

"My business is with Rogoff—or whoever has assumed his duties."

"That'd be Humbolt."

Andrianov stiffened. From Kinsolving's account, Director Kenneth Humbolt figured prominently in this so-called Stellar Death Plan. He tried not to keep from grinning broadly and giving away any element of surprise he might bring to bear on Humbolt.

"Director of the company, isn't he?"

The guards eyed him suspiciously. "Let me put in a buzz for him," the leader said.

Andrianov jumped when a soft voice at his elbow said, "Thank you, men. I'll see to this."

Andrianov spun about to see a gaudily dressed man, easily half a head taller, standing beside him. He had not heard anyone approach. In some way, he had the feeling that this peacock of a man had been summoned. But how?

"I am Mr. Humbolt's personal assistant," Cameron said. "He's told me so much about you, Mr. Andrianov."

The consul swelled with pride. Here was proof that his position mattered with some people.

The smile faded and was replaced by a frown. "I don't believe your visa was processed. Nor was this Humbolt's."

"A slight problem, no doubt. Come, sir, come into the offices and we'll discuss the matter at greater length, if you can spare the time from your busy schedule." Cameron took Andrianov by the elbow and guided him into the warehouse. "The stack of authorizations can be piled a light-year deep at times. Takes a certain amount of time to filter down to your desk, I'm sure. You must be busy, very busy."

"Not that busy," Andrianov said. Something about this

brightly bedecked man bothered him. "I didn't catch your name."

"Cameron." Andrianov forced himself to maintain diplomatic calm. This was the man Kinsolving had accused of the most vile crimes imaginable. Andrianov glanced around, then lightly brushed his fingertips over another toggle hidden in his clothing. No responding warmth came to his upper arm to signal the presence of robotic spy devices. His diplomatic sensing equipment was the finest the diplomatic corps could provide. Not even a demented genius like this Cameron was made out to be could thwart Earth's most advanced microelectronics.

Andrianov relaxed, secure in the knowledge that his spy devices worked—and that Cameron had none trained on him.

"What do you have in your latest shipment, Mr. Cameron?" Andrianov asked, looking around to find the crates Kinsolving had recorded. He saw nothing suspicious.

"The usual. Quite a few cases of strain-free single crystals. We work mines on a dozen different worlds. The most profitable are those on Deepdig." Andrianov tried not to respond to this. Kensolving had mentioned being supervisor on this planet. "Rare earth crystals." Cameron went on, not noticing the nervous jerk Andrianov had made when Deepdig was mentioned.

"The locals use a great deal of the rarer products in their equipment. You wouldn't know what that use is, would you?"

Cameron shook his head sadly. "No, Mr. Consul, I don't. Our trade agreements with Zeta Orgo 4 require us to deliver and not pry. I have been told that the natives are superb with their applications work. Just a rumor, mind you, since we've never seen their products. That would be a violation of myriad other agreements, of course."

"Yes, yes, the interlocking trade agreements."

"Those do hold back humanity," Cameron said. "Think how we might progress if we could get the most recent of every world's products for study instead of being relegated to only furnishing raw materials like colonials."

"We're well compensated," said Andrianov. He stopped and gawked. A plastic crate lay open, its top pulled back.

"Come along, sir. Director Humbolt will—"

"A moment. Let me look." Andrianov toggled his recording cameras as he peered into the open crate. He let out a pent-up breath he had not known he was holding when he found the inside empty.

"Are you looking for something in particular?" asked Cameron. "I'm certain we could provide it if you'd only let us know."

"Part of my job is to regulate trade. I fear I've been lax. Not enough time . . . you realize how that can be."

Cameron made a neutral noise that might have been agreement or derision.

An office door opened and a man Andrianov recognized from Kinsolving's description looked out.

"You must be Mr. Humbolt." Andrianov thrust out his hand. "I'm planetary consul, here to check on some paper-work problems I've encountered. Too many people coming and going without visas."

"Cameron, what is this? A joke?"

"Oh, no, sir," said Cameron. "He *is* consul."

"Get rid of him. We've got work to do."

"Sir, that wouldn't be wise."

"No," cut in Andrianov, "it wouldn't. I am the duly appointed arm of Earth on this world. I can revoke your operating permits and see Interstellar Materials thrown off-planet if you fail to comply with my lawful requests."

Humbolt looked as if he were working on some medical disorder deep within his gut. He gestured. Andrianov followed, head high.

The office lacked even the modicum of civilization found in his own. Andrianov began to feel superior. Kinsolving had overstated the problem, he was certain now. These two were not the cunning, ruthless geniuses he had made them out to be. They were just like him—harried bureaucrats.

They might do a bit of smuggling on the side, but Andrianov could not see them doing anything more danger-ous. However the brain burners entered Web society, it was not through these men's efforts. Andrianov's recording devices had found nothing to hint at illicit storage in this warehouse, and he had specifically set his detectors for purified cerium used in the Boxes of Delights.

"What is it I can do for you, uh—"

"Andrianov," supplied Cameron.

"What can IM do for you, Consul Andrianov?" Humbolt had regained his composure and smiled winningly. But Andrianov had been in diplomatic circles long enough to see through such superficial bonhomie. He had relied on it himself enough times at social functions not to recognize it instantly.

"There have been massive movements of personnel on and off this world unreported to my office. Cargo has been delivered and removed without my official seal being affixed."

"Sir, there has been some confusion in our office. Explain to him, Cameron."

"Yes, of course, Kenneth."

The use of the director's first name made Andrianov sit straighter in his chair. It blossomed like a nova in his belly. Cameron toyed with the director—a man supposedly his superior. For the first time Andrianov experienced a pang of fear. The situation here was not as he had thought. If he had missed the power structure so completely, what else had he missed?

"You see, Consul," Cameron said in an unctuous voice, "IM has had a small disaster to contend with. Supervisor Rogoff died. We acted in the best interests of humanity. We returned his body to Gamma Tertius 4 for burial. This left the position of supervisor open, but promoting someone to such an important post is not something done without thought. Chairman Fremont sent Kenneth to fill in, until a permanent appointment can be made."

Again came the jab, the use of the director's first name. Andrianov knew that every word Cameron uttered was a lie. He toggled all his recording and sensing equipment. Whatever went on in this room must be fully documented so that he could study it at leisure.

"Quit outgassing, Cameron. He's not buying a word of it." Humbolt sank into the chair behind the simple wood desk.

"I wonder where we went wrong," Cameron said.

"Look here, you—" Andrianov squawked when Cameron savagely struck him. His head snapped back and for an instant he blacked out. He regained his senses slowly. A trickle of blood ran from a cut lip.

"The consulate is a solitary post on Web," said Cameron. "He doesn't even have a human secretary. Possibly he has a Bizzie mistress. Do you?"

"Sir!"

"Cameron, let that be. Who cares? What are we going to do with him? He obviously suspects something. Otherwise he wouldn't have come here with all his electronics flashing."

"What are you saying? Look, Director Humbolt—" Again Cameron battered him to silence.

"Your standard-issue diplomatic surveillance equipment is woefully inadequate, Consul." Cameron began a detailed description of every device Andrianov carried, including two that bore confidential ratings. "I designed better sensing devices when I was still a student in undergraduate classes."

"Forget the bragging, Cameron. What are we going to do with him?"

"That's easy," replied Cameron. "The real crux of the matter is how he learned that anything was amiss. I suspect that Chairman Fremont was right in sending me to be sure of our Mr. Kinsolving's demise. Was it Barton Kinsolving, Mr. Consul?"

"By all space, it is!" gasped Humbolt. "How did that bastard escape?"

"He's a very capable man. More than I thought."

Andrianov forced his way across the room and put his back against a wall. "You cannot harm me! I'm an emissary of Earth! There'll be hell to pay if you touch me again!"

"Mr. Consul, that is ridiculous. If you vanish, who cares, save those filling out the necessary forms? We might even be able to make it appear that the Bizzies killed you."

"That's not wise, Cameron."

"No, Kenneth, of course it isn't. Not when we have the brain burners to distribute. Attract no unwanted attention."

Cameron laughed and motioned Humbolt to silence. "Isn't it apparent that Mr. Andrianov knows of the brain burners, that this is the reason he's come trooping into the warehouse, his silly cameras grinding away? Kinsolving. Kinsolving has told him everything."

"He wasn't lying. This is all true. You and Fremont and the Stellar Death Plan!"

"Get rid of him, Cameron. Now. We don't dare let him make a report."

"I'm beaming every instant of this back to my office. It's being put under diplomatic seal!"

"Your voice cracks when you're under pressure," said Cameron, smiling broadly. "No transmission is possible. My little friends assure that." He blinked twice. Four silvered cylinders appeared in midair.

Andrianov started edging for the door. Cameron held out his hand, then pointed. One cylinder hummed, then spun about its axis.

"What?" Andrianov reached up to touch his face. He was dead before the hand got halfway.

"Is this undetectable?" asked Humbolt.

"The needle went into his eye. There might be small amounts of bleeding, but I do not think so. The poisoned sliver bends easily to slip around the eyeball and go directly into the brain. Only a detailed autopsy will reveal the cause of death."

"Put him in his vehicle."

"Really, Kenneth, how unimaginative."

"Do whatever you must, but do it. I've got work to do."

"I'm sure you do, Kenneth, I'm sure you do." Laughing, Cameron snapped his fingers. Larger robots held just off the floor by their repulsor fields came in and grappled onto the consul's dead body. Amid muted hums, they dragged Garon Andrianov from the office, Cameron following closely.

Humbolt watched, thinking how easily that corpse could have been his. He turned to the work at hand, but his heart was not in it.

CHAPTER ELEVEN

BARTON KINSOLVING stirred, smiled in the limbo of his half-sleep and then came suddenly awake. For a brief instant he could not separate the soft world of dreams from reality.

And the reality confused him until he remembered coming to Garon Andrianov, talking with the consul, presenting what evidence he had indicting Interstellar Materials in the contraband smuggling, then eating a big meal and falling asleep. Kinsolving yawned widely, stretched and sat up.

"Consul?" he called. No answer. Kinsolving stood and stretched a bit more, getting blood flowing through his veins. Only then did he go exploring the consul's office. He looked around, not wanting to disturb anything. When he came to the entryway tri-vid, he stopped and admired it. But the initial impact had passed.

Kinsolving saw small problems with the pastoral scene, spots where the artist had ineptly erased and redrawn from an actual hologram. He sighed. Earth had been like this once, or so they were taught in school. But how long ago had that been? Five hundred years? Possibly more. Now most of the surface was a honeycomb of living quarters to house the seventeen billion inhabitants. Parks and other open spaces existed, but nothing as lovely as the tri-vid.

Who could see them? Not the majority of the populace, not when the daily entry fees to the nature park might equal an entire year's dole. When most did not work, when most were supported at subsistence level by the robot factories, when most did not care, nature became unimportant. Most existed, not lived.

"So lovely once," he mused. Kinsolving's attention

came back to matters closer at hand. "Andrianov? You working?"

He explored further and found the suite of offices smaller than he had thought at first. Clever use of mirrors and tri-vid walls of larger rooms enhanced the illusion. But nowhere did he find Garon Andrianov.

Kinsolving seated himself in Andrianov's couch and found the controls close at hand. Idly, he worked through the toggles and found a computer control sophisticated enough to run Earth's affairs on Web—and little more.

"Tell me about Web," he commanded the computer.

"You do not have authorization from Consul Andrianov," the computer complained.

"I am his guest."

"I am programmed to divulge information only to those with appropriate access codes."

"What can you tell me about Andrianov?"

An almost human sigh came from the computer, startling Kinsolving with its realist mimicry of a human. "I am glad you inquired, sir. Consul Andrianov wore the diplomatic suit when he departed four hours ago."

"Diplomatic suit? I don't understand." Visions of proper attire to meet the arachnoids on matters of state came to mind, but only laughable images formed. He could not picture Andrianov wearing a suit with eight hairy legs sewn onto it simulating the spiders'.

"This is classified information," said the computer. Kinsolving turned slightly in the couch to make himself more comfortable. Dealing with the machines often proved tiring, but he considered this a necessary task. Something was wrong and the computer knew what. Deep in its electronic mind it worried—and that worried Kinsolving.

"If the consul is in danger, not revealing parts of this might result in further harm to him. You must evaluate the damage caused by telling me of the diplomatic suit and the harm that might befall the consul if you do not."

The computer took several seconds to decide, convincing Kinsolving of the seriousness of the matter.

"Standard-issue diplomatic suits contain extensive electronic surveillance equipment, including visual and audio recorders, sensors in a width spectrum of EM radiation, jamming devices to prevent counterintelligence tapping of suit-recorded data, plus . . . other innovations."

"Classified?"

"Consul Andrianov wore such a suit," the computer said, nimbly sidestepping a direct answer. "It has proven ineffective in protecting him from even more sophisticated devices."

Kinsolving jerked upright. "Cameron?"

"That name was mentioned within the limits of the sensory equipment used by the consul."

"Other names. Itemize."

"Rogoff, not located within detection radius, presumed dead. Humbolt, Kenneth, director and now acting supervisor on Zeta Orgo 4. Cameron, assistant, in command of IM robotic surveillance and disposal."

"Describe the last data transmissions."

"Consul Andrianov's body temperature has dropped below the point where the suit automatically powers down. The last transmissions constitute an exchange between Humbolt, Cameron and the consul. From the information gathered, an assassination device of unknown type and action might have been used to murder Consul Andrianov."

"Did Cameron order it?"

"There is some indication that he was responsible for issuing a nonverbal order. Many hunter-killer robots are activated by simple gestures, winking of the eye and even the tensing of certain muscles, usually on the face."

"Why do you know about hunter-killer robots?"

"A diplomatic field computer must know all aspects of statecraft, including those more illicit ones likely to be employed against human employees."

"How is this office protected?"

"A minimum of defensive devices are activated."

"This is classified and I don't need to know, is that it?"

"Yes." A pause. "You are safe within the confines of these offices. Assassination has never been an arachnoid method of state diplomacy. Their murders are restricted to personal disputes—and disputes of law."

"Such as war."

"That is correct. Also, they consider protection of the

Supreme Web their highest calling. Any means to achieve this worthy end is permissible."

Kinsolving nodded. This told much of the way the spider beings thought. As a government, they were honorable in the strictest human sense. They would not rely on underhanded means to attain their goals. However, if they did not like the way a negotiation went, they saw nothing amiss with declaring war and destroying entire planets.

The messenger bringing the bad news might be safe, but only until he returned with their response. Then everyone died.

"You believe that Andrianov has died?"

A long pause. Kinsolving imagined the computer working through every data input until it reached a conclusion. He jumped when the computer answered. "There is a high probability that this has happened. It is an assumption more likely to be true than the opposite."

"What should I do?"

"You are not empowered to act in any capacity."

Kinsolving considered this. Although the computer was right, it did not go far enough in considering the problems.

"Cameron might have killed the consul. Is there anyone who can be notified able to act?"

"Not on this world."

"Send the message to the person best able to act."

"That requires a message packet. I need proof that Consul Andrianov has been severely injured or incapacitated before sending the packet in a diplomatic communiqué."

"Use your sensory equipment to study the IM warehouse," Kinsolving ordered. "Record everyone entering or leaving."

"I have already been ordered to do this by Consul Andrianov."

"Show me the recordings."

"These are classified."

Kinsolving settled back, his head throbbing. He did not think it would be possible to get the information he needed from the computer if Andrianov had put a security block on its data banks. But he had to do something. Sitting and waiting for Cameron to stride through the door would only mean his death, in addition to Andrianov's.

"The arachnoids," he said. "They do not want the Box of Delights smuggled onto Web. Who works against it?"

"The arachnoids do not have a police force as humans understand the term. A defender of the faith attempting to stem the tide of such illegal importations is Quixx."

"Where can I find Quixx?"

"I have no information on that. However, he is often seen patrolling the periphery of the landing field. He uses sophisticated microelectronic equipment of unknown function to monitor every cargo."

"Describe Quixx. Or show me a tri-vid of him."

The computer obeyed. Kinsolving stared at the life-sized spider with rust-colored stripes on gray fur. He moved around the image, studying the creature. The small hands that folded up and into the thorax fascinated him. The fingers were tiny, more like a human baby's than an adult's. How the spider used these hands for precision work without rolling up into a ball to be able to see, Kinsolving was not sure. Or perhaps the spiders did curl up, their legs protecting head and hands as they worked, resting their products on their bellies. He had no doubt that the digits were flexible, strong and capable of minute, close work.

"Do many arachnoids have the same coloration?"

"To the natives, such patterns provide identification. However, Earthly eyes are unable to routinely distinguish in hue and pattern."

"What does this coloration say about Quixx? Is he a high-status citizen?"

"Coloration means little when correlated with governmental position or power."

Kinsolving nodded, his head already racing far ahead. "Can you go to full-alert status after I leave and admit no one except the consul?"

"That requires a priority alert condition."

"Death of the consul would qualify, wouldn't it?"

"Only if it were shown that Consul Andrianov had perished."

"Go to maximum alert permissible. I'll return with the evidence that Cameron killed Andrianov."

"Very well," said the computer. Kinsolving put some

food into a small pouch and slung it over his shoulder. It might be some time before he had the opportunity to eat or sleep this comfortably again.

"One moment," the computer said, when Kinsolving reached the outer door. "You have no money."

Kinsolving said nothing. He did not even know what money on Web looked like.

"You, as a displaced citizen from Earth, are permitted to draw against a special account. Please accept this temporary identicard for the equivalent of one planetary week's living expenses."

An identicard dropped into a small cup beside the door. Kinsolving took it.

"Thanks."

"You are welcome." The computer unlocked the outer door for him. "Please find Consul Andrianov and determine his fate. I have grown fond of his ways."

Kinsolving nodded. He had not expected human emotion from the computer; it had not seemed to be large enough. As he stepped into the street, the door securely locked behind him. He stared up at the building. How much of it belonged to the consulate—and how much of it did the computer inhabit? Its programming might prevent him from obtaining all the information he needed, but it had come to his aid.

That was more than he could say about others of his own species.

Barton Kinsolving started walking briskly in the direction of the landing field. Even with the temporary identicard securely in his pocket, he did not know how the arachnoid transit system worked—or if they even used one.

CHAPTER TWELVE

AFTER THE TIRING walk from the consulate, Barton Kinsolving rested at the edge of the landing field. Occasional shuttles shot into the sky, some leaving tails of condensed vapor behind, others firing clean and cool with a propulsion system he did not recognize. He heaved a deep breath and sat down, his feet hurting. It had taken only a few minutes for him to discover that Web had no public transportation system—or none that a human might use with a temporary identicard.

Not for the first time, Kinsolving wondered if his crazy mission to save Web from Fremont and the Stellar Death Plan was worth his effort. He knew that Interstellar Materials would profit through the resulting chaos on Web, and it was in this confusion that inroads to both trade and power would be made. Let the arachnoids take care of themselves, one part of his brain said.

They are intelligent beings, said another, and you must help them.

"Maybe I should just help myself," he said. IM—and Cameron—had done so much to destroy him that he wondered if he could ever recover his good name. By the time Cameron finished poisoning human minds against him, Kinsolving knew, he might be unable to find refuge on any inhabited planet, human or alien.

That started the fires of anger burning again. What had Humbolt told Ala Markken? Kinsolving could not believe that his lover would follow a plan of genocide. He knew her better than that. She had been subverted in some way. And if not by Humbolt, then by Cameron and his infernal robotic devices.

Kinsolving heaved himself to his feet, moaned at the aches and pains, then started walking. The consulate computer had said that the arachnoid Quixx prowled the landing field.

But it was such a *big* field.

Kinsolving had no idea where to begin. A few abortive attempts to ask passing arachnoids discouraged him from further questioning. He wandered for almost an hour before seeing a small cluster of vehicles and a dozen arachnoids huddled in a circle near a shuttle servicing hangar. Kinsolving headed for the group. Perhaps one would answer his questions, to get rid of the annoying human if nothing more.

His pace quickened when he saw a vehicle turned on its side and a human leg sticking from inside.

"What happened?" he demanded, pushing his way through a forest of hairy legs. The spider beings bobbed and jerked, moving away from him. Kinsolving stopped and stared. He had prepared himself for Andrianov's death. Preparing for it and actually seeing the consul dead in the middle of twisted wreckage were two different things.

"You know this unfortunate one?" came a soft voice, a full octave lower than most of the shrill, chittering arachnoids.

"Yes." Kinsolving turned to face a spider who came up to his shoulder. For an instant, Kinsolving had a strange sensation that he knew the being. "Are you Quixx?" he asked.

"Not only do you know the victim of this sorry accident, you also know this one. How interesting a human thing you are. How is it you have acquired such knowledge?"

"That's Consul Garon Andrianov."

"This one has learned much from a diligent search of the dead human thing's identicards. He even has card-keys enabling entry to the Earth consul."

"He was murdered!"

"An odd allegation from another of his species to one most likely to have committed such a vile crime."

"I'm not accusing you," Kinsolving said hastily. "Cameron. With Interstellar Materials. And Kenneth Humbolt."

"The new planetary supervisor and his assistant. You are of their hatching to know them so well?"

Kinsolving looked around and saw only peculiar arachnoid eyes on him. But speaking in public of Cameron and his deeds did not seem too bright. Kinsolving looked up and tried to find a hint of a spy camera, one of Cameron's robots reporting back to its master. He saw nothing. That worried him even more. Had he missed it? Or did Cameron hold the "Bizzare" police in such low esteem that he did not waste the efforts of even a single robot?

"We are unobserved," said Quixx. "You appear troubled on this matter."

"Cameron's a genius with robotic devices. Hunter-killers. Spies. There's no telling what other uses he puts them to."

"The area is secure. This one is competent to such interdiction of unwanted eyes, both organic and otherwise."

"You're a policeman?"

"This one's function is less than that, if this one's understanding of the human thing's job is precise."

"We need to talk."

"There will be more than simple talk. You *do* know the consul?"

"In private. Let's talk in private. Long-range lenses can record everything we do and say."

"Those of Interstellar Materials?"

"Yes."

Quixx hunched over and rolled his head down. Kinsolving saw how the spider worked around to use his hands, but he could not see what Quixx did. The clicking of fingers working on control keys sounded above the rising howl of the wind across the tarmac. After several seconds, Quixx straightened.

"Much has been learned. You are not on this planet legally, although you were permitted to land. Why do you take this risk when it is well known that we punish severely such crimes?"

"The Box of Delights," Kinsolving said. "Brain burners. Call them what you like. Those are what bring me here. Hundreds, even thousands of them."

Quixx bobbed up and down on strong legs. His head

turned from one side to the other, as if trying to bring Kinsolving into sharper focus. "These surrounding us are drones. No hearing, no thought, only obedience to this one's whim. They study the wreckage and the human thing's body. What do you believe the conclusion is?"

"Nothing, if they're that mindless. But I know what *yours* has to be. Garon Andrianov was murdered."

"You admit to this heinous crime?"

"No!"

"You speak of the Box of Delights. You confess to knowledge of Consul Andrianov's poisoning."

"Poison?" This rocked Kinsolving. He had thought that Cameron would use a hunter-killer robot to electrocute the consul.

"Cleverly administered. A slender, flexible metallic sliver laden with a quick-acting neuron-disrupting protein entered the side of the ocular cavity, slipped around the eyeball and pierced the retina. An autopsy will confirm this."

"I didn't know how he died."

"This seeming accident with the clumsy vehicle drew my immediate attention. The murderer did little to convince this one that the vehicle collision caused the death. It is as if the murderer wished for this one to probe more deeply."

Kinsolving went cold inside. Cameron had to know that Kinsolving and those aboard the *von Neumann* had escaped Gamma Tertius 4. Cameron would never assume that his robotic killers had left a lifeless hull drifting in hyperspace.

Kinsolving turned cold when the thought hit him that Cameron might have found evidence of his spying in the IM warehouse when the arachnoid had broken into the crate and taken the Box of Delights. A faint outline of a footprint, a small thread, even a whiff of pheromone might have been enough for Cameron's hunter robots to lock onto his presence and follow his trail through the escape tunnel.

"This will look like my doing," Kinsolving said in a dull voice.

"A partial fingerprint has been lifted from the door panel." Quixx seized Kinsolving's hand and lifted, peering intently at the middle finger of the left hand. "The print and yours match."

"How can you—" Kinsolving stopped. He had no idea about the arachnoid's senses. If the spider being meant to frighten him, he had succeeded.

"You claim you had no knowledge of Consul Andrianov's death?"

Kinsolving explained how he had been in the consulate resting when the computer had alerted him to the drop in Andrianov's body temperature. "I know nothing more than this."

Quixx nodded. "This one believes your story."

"What? But you said my fingerprint was found on the doorframe. I've never touched his vehicle!"

"This one is aware of such. The print was chemically etched by a process not unknown to those of this planet. Reconstruction: An unknown one made a photo template of your print and etched it into the metal. The chemistry of your skin oils does not match precisely that of the print, indicating to this one that the print was not made by you."

Kinsolving tried to absorb all this, but some sixth sense kept him from fully concentrating on Quixx's words. He turned and stared at the arachnoid drones. They worked skillfully and silently. The wind had died down a little, but a distant whirring sounded.

Machines?

Robots!

Kinsolving jumped when he caught the flash of a silvered flying robot. But before he could shout a warning, ten emerald-green laser beams converged on it in midair. Not even a trace of dust floated to the ground from the destroyed assassination weapon.

Kinsolving simply stared. Each of the drones had pulled a weapon and fired simultaneously.

"How..." His voice trailed off. Quixx held a tiny weapon, also, the arachnoid's pink fingers delicately curled around it. He had rocked back and supported himself on his four hind legs to give better sighting.

"This attack confuses me. It is either very astute or very stupid."

"Cameron knows you don't think I killed Andrianov. He tried to kill me."

Quixx said nothing to this.

"Are you going to arrest him?"

"This Cameron of whom you speak with such fear?"

"He's responsible for Andrianov's death."

"Another reason this one does not believe your print on the doorframe is real: No other print exists. Such purity of purpose would erase a print in such an obvious location."

"There are no others?"

"Only those of the consul."

"The brain burners," Kinsolving said with emotion. "Cameron knows where they are. I'm positive he wouldn't keep them in the IM warehouses. He'll have moved them, but he's in charge. No matter that a company director is on-planet. Cameron is the mastermind."

"Ah, the Box of Delights. It is this one's need to learn more of the source of such evil machines."

"I don't know much about how they're built. The electronics causes a single crystal of cerium to oscillate. When it hits resonant frequency, it does something to your species' brain."

"That is a succinct description of its functioning," agreed Quixx. "The cortical membrane of our brains becomes excited by the resonance. This produces intense yearning."

"Yearning?"

"Box of Delights is imprecise but colorful as a description. Those who use the device are prone to romanticize it." Quixx bobbed up and down. It took Kinsolving several seconds to realize that this motion directed the drones pulling apart Andrianov's vehicle.

"It's part of a master plan. The Stellar Death Plan, they call it," Kinsolving hurried on. "They intend to get everyone on your planet to use the brain burner. These devices are stronger, more powerful. Everyone within a certain radius will be affected. When enough of your populace is brain-dead, chaos will reign."

Quixx looked at Kinsolving with a quizzical expression in his face. "This one has seen your entertainment tri-vids.

Are you engaged in producing one? Such a fantastical story!"

"It's true! The Stellar Death Plan. They hate all aliens. They call you Bizarres. Bizzies."

"And this planet is known as ZOo."

"What?"

"Your astronomical name for it is Zeta Orgo 4. Many human things shorten it to ZOo. This one has studied the odd word. Your zoo is a place to imprison animals that once roamed free. This reasoning is not understood, but calling us 'animals' is common, especially among those who control work robots loading and unloading freight."

"Chairman Hamilton Fremont is behind the smuggling. He's responsible for ordering the Box of Delights onto Web, and Cameron is carrying out his orders."

"The Box of Delights presents problems to society other than the fanciful one you pose." Quixx clacked mandibles together, lifted one taloned leg and scraped at the serrated edges, then tucked his chin down, the mandibles closing into his mouth.

"What problems? Fremont intends to destroy all intelligent life on this planet by burning out your brains!"

Of this Quixx could not conceive. But the arachnoid did say, "The social structure on this world is extremely rigid. The Box allows those of the wrong class to shift status, for a brief time."

"This isn't status we're talking about!" shouted Kinsolving. "You'll be a lump of protoplasm. No thoughts. Nothing going on inside your skull! The damned brain burners will have short-circuited every synapse in your head!"

"Our brains do not rest within the head, as do yours." A leg came up and tapped the abdomen. "The seat of our reason lies here."

"I don't care if you carry it in your hands! It'll be turned into a cinder!"

"Such emotional outpouring," said Quixx, startled at Kinsolving's outburst. "Do you human things always carry on in this unseemly fashion?"

Kinsolving tried to control himself. He had found Quixx, and the arachnoid seemed to have the power of a policeman. Quixx could stop Cameron. Quixx could save his entire race, if only he would listen to the facts.

"Look," said Kinsolving, "what difference does it make why you stop the flood of brain burners? Do it for preservation of social structure, do it to prevent your entire species from being slaughtered. But do it!"

"This one is unable to understand your interest. Other humans would cheer our demise. Their taunts fill this one's hearing cavities. Why are you different?"

"I don't like what they're trying to do. I don't like the idea of genocide."

"You do not enjoy the status gained in your own society," added Quixx. "You will prepare for deportation. There is no need for your presence during this time of searching for truth."

"Deportation? Where?"

"To what planet will we send you? Your identicards, although in several names, say you are of Gamma Tertius 4. It is to that human planet we send you."

"No!" Kinsolving dared not be sent back to IM's corporate headquarters planet. "Send me to Earth, anywhere else."

"Why do you carry many different identicards?"

"How do you know?" Kinsolving touched the pocket containing them.

"Our scanners are able to work at distances greater than yours. We do not allow clues to go untested. This one works to find a murderer."

"Cameron. Check him out. Use your probes. But watch out for his robots."

"Deportation," Quixx said firmly. "As quickly as possible. You will report to the Hall of Leave-taking immediately." The arachnoid turned and stared at the drones still going over the consul's vehicle, their taloned legs moving the heavy wreckage with ease.

"Wait, Quixx. You're not putting me into jail until then?"

"No." The arachnoid sounded puzzled. "This imprisonment psychosis of you human things. This one has noted it in other species, but not to this degree. Where would you like to be locked up? This one might be able to find another to watch over you. This one cannot also provide perverted sexual congress to go with this imprisonment, if that is your intent in asking the request."

"You'd trust me to go to the, uh, Hall of Leave-taking on my own?"

"You have been notified of deportation. You will obey, of course."

"Of course," said Kinsolving.

"Wait!" called Quixx. "In your voice is rebellion. There is nowhere on this world for you to go. You will leave."

"I'll leave," said Kinsolving.

Quixx's mandibles moved soundlessly and the arachnoid's legs all twitched, as if extreme consternation shook his entire body. Kinsolving walked away, trying not to look back—or break into a dead run. Quixx could not understand his motives.

Kinsolving was not sure he understood them himself. But he was not going to be sent back to Gamma Tertius 4. And he was not going to let Cameron sear the brains of a planet filled with unsuspecting aliens.

CHAPTER THIRTEEN

"THEY BLEW IT UP! They stopped your invincible robot!" cried Kenneth Humbolt.

Cameron nodded and idly ran his fingers along the hem of his cerise and orange cape. Small, hand control toggles passed under those knowing, dextrous fingers. The slightest touch on any one would remove Humbolt permanently. Cameron had scores of his obedient, intelligent robots stationed around the office and warehouse.

The question that Cameron could not decide was whether to use a large robot to crush the life from Humbolt or use a smaller one that gave instant death.

He activated neither waiting robot. As much as the assassin hated to admit it, he still needed Humbolt. For a short while, but the need remained.

"The Bizzies are more adept at detection than I thought. A sensor on the robot reported back ten laser hits before destruction."

"Ten! But that'd mean one beam from each of them."

"True." Cameron frowned. "From observation of how they approached the wreck, only the one with mottled red legs had any intelligence. The others simply obeyed his commands."

"Slaves?"

"Possibly. Or a modified life-form. They might even be inferior species."

"They're all inferior."

Cameron said nothing. At times it amazed him that Humbolt seemed to believe every detail of the Plan's credo. Cameron was too new to it to accept it as anything other than a way of gaining power—and he had been off-planet more than Humbolt. He had seen much, learned more from a wide variety of aliens. But he obviously had not learned enough. His probe had been well armed, installed with the smartest block circuit programming he could devise and had sensors enabling it to avoid detection by all but the most sensitive equipment, yet the Bizarres had destroyed it easily. Their form might be strange, but Cameron vowed not to underestimate their talent with microelectronics.

"Why did you send the robot killer anyway?" asked Humbolt. His voice rose until it almost broke with strain.

"The consul's death was nothing more than a lure, a trap. When Kinsolving appeared, I wanted to be certain he did not slip away again—as he did from *your* laser barrage."

"He's here," said Humbolt, shifting to attack. "That means your robots failed to blow up his ship in midflight. You failed, too. And now you've failed again!"

"I prefer to look at this as an experiment. We know Kinsolving is alive and on-planet. The consul has been removed as a source of aid. There isn't another human he can turn to."

"I've checked the ships in docking orbit," said Humbolt. "You were right. The *von Neumann* shifted away soon after it arrived. But the Landing Authority didn't know its destination."

"It matters little. The women with him—Rani duLong and Lark Versalles—are not significant."

"Lark Versalles is," said Humbolt. "You know that she's connected to GPMT. And the duLong woman's brother heads TerraComp."

"They are nothing," Cameron said, dismissing them totally. "It is Kinsolving who poses the true problem. He has been lucky. That will stop."

"Send your damned killing machines after him, then. He couldn't have gone far after the Bizzies blew up your robot."

"I don't want to send out my hunters prematurely. If the police official investigating Consul Andrianov's death sees them again, he might decide to pursue the matter further than blaming Kinsolving. Their microelectronics technology is superb."

"They're Bizzies."

"And inferior to you?" Cameron's cold stare caused Humbolt to look away.

"Stop him. Stop Kinsolving. That's an order."

"Yes," Cameron said in a soft, venomous whisper. "Chairman Fremont's order."

Quixx stood beside the wreckage while his drones finished their meticulous sifting. No scrap had gone unseen. No clue had been missed. The human consul had been killed cleverly, then placed in the vehicle in such a way as to mimic an accident.

Why? Quixx's mind turned over the possibilities. The human things did not function in an orderly fashion. Their thoughts must be jumbled heaps of emotion and ideas and primitive superstitions. But they usually followed some logic, no matter how twisted.

Quixx had many hypotheses, a few facts, no conclusions. He watched as the human Kinsolving walked away. The human had said he would go to the Hall of Leave-taking and depart the planet immediately, but Quixx had seen the signs of falsehood in the man's posture. He would check later with the exit drones to be sure that Kinsolving found the proper vessel to take him away.

Quixx had to believe that the consul's murder had been inspired by Kinsolving. Had Andrianov died as bait for a trap? With Kinsolving as the prey? That presented a likely hypothesis since the futile attack by the aerial robot had been launched. But the attack was so poorly conceived and executed. Quixx clacked his mandibles in frustration. Did the consul's killer believe that such a device would not be instantly detected and destroyed?

Even his drones had reacted to it. A simple robot, hardly worthy of the name. Yet Quixx knew little of the human things' mores and beliefs. He knew even less of their pitiful technology. It was time to report on this dire matter to the Supreme Web. He left the drones to restore order on the landing field and walked off, clacking to himself.

How primitive the humans were! How truly primitive!

CHAPTER FOURTEEN

THE BACK OF Kinsolving's neck itched as he walked
away from Quixx. The arachnoid had some reason for not
sending guards with him, Kinsolving thought. A test? Kinsolving did not want to arouse the spider being's ire by
openly arguing to the point of belligerence, yet he was not
going to let himself be deported. What worried the man the
most was the apparent understanding on Quixx's part that
Kinsolving was not going to obey—and yet nothing had
been done to enforce the edict.

Or had there? Kinsolving's eyes worked along at ground
level seeking anything unusual. He slowly worked upward,
straining for a trace of a killer robot arrowing in at him.
Nothing. As he rounded the corner of a building he hazarded a glance back. Quixx had returned to the work of
directing his drones.

No pursuit. No guards. Kinsolving ducked low, spun
and waited, thinking that Cameron might use this instant to
attack. He felt silly when nothing had happened after five
minutes.

He wondered if Quixx was testing him, if the arachnoid
had surveillance sensors scattered around the landing field.
Kinsolving took a deep breath and decided that he had to
act. Standing and waiting for someone to catch up with
him would only ensure that someone *would*.

Kinsolving kept the squat, massive rock-melt building
between him and the spot where the consul's vehicle had
been destroyed. He set a brisk pace toward the shuttle landing pits, infrequently looking back to see if anyone followed.

"'The wicked flee when no man pursueth,'" he quoted. "'But the righteous are bold as a lion.'" Kinsolving did not feel especially bold, and he was the wronged party and had to flee.

He stopped and stared into the peculiarly tinted blue sky when he heard the rumble of landing rockets. The arachnoids did not use launching lasers for their shuttles; they depended on what was, to him, a less sophisticated system of rockets. But the spiders showed no lack of commerce across the immense field. Everywhere he looked he saw shuttles being unloaded as they came down from the massive cargo ships in orbit. And almost as many shuttles were being loaded to lift into orbit before starring off for other worlds.

One shuttle coming down on a pale blue flame caught his attention and held it. As the rocket shuttle turned slowly in descent he saw the Interstellar Materials logo on the side. The shuttle touched down gently less than a kilometer away.

Kinsolving started toward it, then stopped, indecision freezing him. "Will they be that stupid?" he wondered aloud. With Quixx openly investigating Andrianov's death, would Humbolt bring down more brain burners?

"Humbolt wouldn't, but Cameron would," he decided. Nothing would be too daring for the roboticist. The man would see it as a challenge, a chance to show his superiority.

Kinsolving watched as a fleet of heavy equipment converged on the grounded shuttle. Squinting from the sun, he made out the hatches being sprung and work robots beginning their programmed task of unloading. IM brought much to Web. But hidden in there, he felt, would be more.

As a small vehicle driven by an arachnoid scooted past, Kinsolving reached out and grabbed a convenient handle on the back. He swung himself up and behind the spider being. By the time the arachnoid noticed and shoved him off using four hind legs, Kinsolving was within a hundred meters of the IM shuttle.

Acutely aware that he exposed himself to unnecessary danger, Kinsolving looked around for a place to spy without being seen. Nothing large enough existed. The crates stacked around were in constant flux, being shifted from one spot to another. Nowhere did he see a human overseer, though. The robots did not mind if he watched—unless they had been ordered to respond to his spying.

"'Bold as a lion,'" Kinsolving said. He walked directly to the opened hatch and peered into the belly of the immense cargo ship. Prepared to run if any human accosted him, Kinsolving tried to make out the action within. Only robots worked inside; they had no need of illumination.

Kinsolving walked up the conveyor ramp and slipped to one side, back against the outer hull of the shuttle. He took out the data recorder and began photographing what he could in the poor light. The tracked robots lumbered back and forth, dragging crates bearing the IM sigil. A few crates carried markings of other companies, but only a few. If he found the brain burners anywhere, it would be here.

"Where to begin?" he muttered. Thousands of metric tons of IM cargo moved out of the shuttle and to the distant warehouse. Which of the crates carried the contraband?

"Robot!" he called out to one painted in yellow-and-green stripes. "What color is your leader?"

"Red and blue," came the immediate response. The yellow-and-green machine never slowed as it pulled at a pair of immense crates floating a few centimeters above the deck. These boxes were so heavy that repulsor units had been installed.

Kinsolving glanced outside into the warm sunlight, then back into the hold. He felt as if he moved from the realm of the living into some vast and desolate underworld populated only by the souls of the dead. The robots worked tirelessly, their programs solving both simple and complex scheduling problems, their computers interacting to produce the most efficient unloading possible. Kinsolving dodged them as he sought the red-and-blue leader.

At the back of the cargo deck he found the machine. Pale light shone on the floor around the robot. Puzzled, Kinsolving moved closer. Someone had worked on the robot and had failed to properly secure the access panel. The heart of the robot's programming had been exposed.

"Robot, halt," commanded Kinsolving.

"I am not authorized to obey you," came the machine's

immediate response. "Your vocal pattern is not within range of my recognition circuits."

"You are a menace to humans and other machines. A panel on your side is dangerously open. Allow me to fasten it securely."

The robot said nothing as Kinsolving approached. He knew he had reached it on the most elemental level in its complex computing unit. Danger to its assigned mission could be removed if the human fixed the panel. The robot would temporarily obey as long as the imperilling condition persisted.

Kinsolving pulled open the panel and looked inside. The pale access light shining inside allowed for easier repairs. The toggles controlling the robot's functions were scattered throughout the interior.

He did not recognize all the controls, but the loading robot was not unlike the mining robots he had used to get ore from the stoops and into the refinery storage bins. A few minutes of tinkering had circumvented the machine's defense programming. Another minute gave him the servile condition he needed.

"Where are the crates containing the brain burners?" he asked.

"These are not words in my vocabulary," the robot responded.

Kinsolving changed his tack. He had not been thinking. Humbolt would not program a robot by listing the contents of the contraband crates. "Crates were set aside for special handling. Which ones are they?"

The robot swung on its vertical axis and faced four large plastic crates to one side of the hold. The leader robot had been standing guard—if these were the crates he sought.

Kinsolving ordered the robot to remain where it stood, then opened the nearest of the large boxes. He let out a low whistle when he saw the contents. Not a hundred or even a thousand of the brain burners rested inside, neatly packed and wrapped against thermal and mechanical shock. If his guess about their number proved accurate, this crate contained no fewer than five thousand of the insidious devices.

And he had found not one but four crates. Twenty thousand packages of mind death!

"Robot," he called as he dug through the crates, making a data recording as he went. "How many other special-handling crates were aboard this shuttle?"

"Fifty," came the startling answer.

Over a quarter of a million of the machines had reached Web in only one trip! How many other shuttle loads had already been sent across the face of the planet? Kinsolving shuddered at the thought. He had seen the arachnoid caught in the throes of his Box of Delights. All volition fled an otherwise sentient being. The only thing of worth in the entire universe came from the electromagnetic radiation from these boxes. Starvation. Loss of will. Physical damage to the higher regions of the brain causing untold suffering, not only for the victim but, for the rest of a society having to support the brain-dead hulk. All those awaiting millions of arachnoids within the operating radius of these infernal machines.

Kinsolving shook from reaction to the evil the brain burners would create. The entire arachnoid world would be torn apart. And Quixx had hinted at a special social problem caused by the devices that Kinsolving could not fathom.

"Where," he asked the leader robot, "have they been taken? To the warehouse?"

The robot did not respond. Kinsolving fiddled with the toggles and removed even more of the machine's programming, reducing it to little more than a binary computer.

"Yes," it croaked out in a voice that sounded like metal scraping metal.

Kinsolving studied the robot's inner workings and began tinkering with the control toggles. In less than ten minutes he had reprogrammed the robot to forget any intrusion by a human into the cargo hold. Kinsolving lifted a brain burner from the crate he had opened and tucked it under his arm.

"Seal this crate," he ordered. "Then continue your assignment."

Kinsolving hesitated for a moment, waiting to see if his tampering had been adequate. If a small blue light appeared on the robot's control panel, it meant that he had failed and an alarm had been sent.

No light appeared.

Kinsolving heaved a sigh of relief and hurried from the shuttle hold and back into the bright light of day.

"Fifty-four crates," he said aloud. "Enough to destroy an entire city. More!"

Kinsolving looked at the small brain burner, turning it over and over in his hands. He did not—quite—dare to stick his fingers in the depressions on either side to see if he could activate it. The cerium-crystal resonance might have been chosen to affect only the arachnoids, but he did not want to take the chance. He needed clarity of mind to stop Cameron and the others.

He walked, aimlessly at first, then with more determination as a plan evolved. Alerting Quixx would not be enough. If the arachnoids had a system of government similar to most of those on Earth, it might take days to get the proper documents through the courts to search the IM premises. Kinsolving did not dare wait that long. Visions of explosions and fire danced in his head, then faded.

IM was not likely to allow explosives into the warehouse. Sensors would detect anything Kinsolving was likely to find around the landing area to use as a weapon. And fire? He did not remember the equipment inside the warehouse, but he knew that the crates containing the brain burners had been standard shipping plastic. The fire would have to rage at temperatures over five hundred degrees Celsius before the contents would be damaged. Long before that happened, he knew the fire-fighting robots would extinguish his feeble efforts.

"There's a way," he said to himself. "There must be. There always is." He circled the immense imposing block of windowless warehouse, studying it. Kinsolving came to the same conclusion that he had before. Entering undetected from either the surface or the air was impossible. The nubs of sensor heads poked up everywhere along the roofline. Vibration, sight, scent, heat, Doppler shift, all went to the master security robot for processing. Any slight variation from established norms and hell would break loose.

He returned to the small shed with the radiation-warning sign on it. Kinsolving knew the risk he took following the same subterranean route into the warehouse that he had used before. Although he had not set off alarms then, the odds were much greater this time that the tunnel had been closed off to his intrusions. Cameron was not the type to leave an entryway unprotected.

Kinsolving slipped inside the empty shed and carefully studied the dust on the floor. He saw no indication that anyone had been inside since his last entry. His footprints cut sharply into the layer of dust and a fine powder of newly settled dust lay atop the marks. Closer examination showed the talon marks of the arachnoid who had preceded him down the tunnel. Nothing else.

Kinsolving held his breath as he used Liu's card-key again. The trapdoor opened again. No alarms. He glanced up at the rice-grain vid camera; the dirt he had smeared on its lens had not been touched. Kinsolving slid into the stairway and descended, testing each step, every sense alive for the slightest hint of danger. His heart almost exploded before he reached the tunnel floor. Kinsolving forced himself to relax. He needed to be keyed up, but too much adrenaline would be worse than none at all.

Cursing himself for not bringing a flash, he blundered along in the darkness. Occasionally stopping, Kinsolving strained to hear. Hovertrucks that whispered by on the surface produced a bass rumbling in the tunnel. A tiny dripping hinted at more moisture in the tunnel than he might have expected. But no other sound came. The darkness began to affect him. Kinsolving had spent much of his life in mines—but he had usually carried three or four different light sources. Infrared to study ore veins, UV to check for luminescence, white light to see by, sometimes even a polarized light to check for strain in supporting members.

Now all he had was the sense of touch.

Kinsolving stopped suddenly, then smiled. He had come to the end of the tunnel. How he had known this lay beyond conscious thought. A foot placed tentatively on the lowest step of the spiralling stairs leading to the warehouse produced no obvious alarms. Kinsolving ascended until he came to the metal door keeping him from his goal. A faint yellow light from above showed the tiny alcove well enough for him to move with more confidence.

The cold metal door resisted efforts to open it. He found

the lock. It had been changed—replaced with one more complex and difficult to open after the arachnoid had tampered with the previous one.

Cameron obviously had discovered how the arachnoid had entered the warehouse. Had he also detected Kinsolving's prior entry?

Kinsolving worked in the twilight, fingers tracing the door's frame. The door seemed too secure to blow apart, much less knock down. With heavy laser drills and a work robot he might be able to make a dent in the refractory material. Maybe. But the frame fitted into a plastic wall. This seemed more vulnerable.

He left the door and slid along the plastic, tracing out the small room's four walls. Nothing seemed promising until Kinsolving stopped moving and simply stood. A faint draft crossed his face—and it came from above, not from the stairwell leading to the tunnel.

Reaching up, Kinsolving grabbed the small ledge over the doorframe. Straining with effort, grunting and feeling the skin peeling off his fingers, he pulled himself up until he braced one elbow on the tiny ledge. Twice he slipped and almost fell. The third time he secured a better berth by finding a small grate half a meter above the top of the door. It was this grate that let the small amount of light into the alcove.

Fingers on his right hand locked through the grating, Kinsolving was able to explore with his left hand. He found another tiny grate mounted in the ceiling. Tugging gently on the ceiling grate pulled it free. A steady gust of air met his face as he worked around.

Brighter light shone through a slowly rotating plastic fan blade. He almost shouted in triumph. The fan and the grate were small; the unit itself was mounted in a meter-square plate. It took Kinsolving another minute to unfasten the wing nuts holding it in place and only a few seconds to push it away.

The warehouse was his!

Kinsolving flopped through the opening and onto a ledge overlooking the floor. It took several minutes for him to regain his strength and examine his bloodied fingers. He had not cut himself too badly on the grates, but he left a trail behind that even a poorly designed guard robot could follow. Kinsolving tried to tear strips from his shirt to wrap his hands, then stopped. The fabric did not tear well and he did not want his hands turned into useless clubs. Better to leave blood markings than to lose dexterity.

He had to find a way of destroying fifty-four crates of brain burners. He was not likely to do it with bandaged hands.

Strength back, he dropped to the floor. The locking mechanism on the door proved even more complex than he had thought. Although he did not have the time to trace the circuits, Kinsolving guessed that any attempt to open the lock would have set off alarms and brought every guard robot in the warehouse.

He was lucky to have found the vent fan.

"Lucky," he said to himself. "I'm not the lucky kind. That was too easy. Cameron would not overlook an easy way in like a fan unit. Not if he installed this bank-vault lock."

A soft sound, a whispering of silk on silk, alerted Kinsolving. He spun.

Cameron stood next to a mountain of shipping crates, a smile twisting his lips. "I really expected you to have a handflash. Removing the fan would have been even easier then. You made it harder than it should have been, Supervisor Kinsolving."

Kinsolving looked left and right, frantic to find an escape route. Killer robots hovered at knee level wherever he turned. He could not pass them, nor could he hope to elude them.

"Will your death be equally difficult, Kinsolving?" Cameron asked in a voice laden with quiet menace. "Or will you make it easy on us all and die quietly?"

Cameron threw back his cape and gestured dramatically. The killer robots, flailing metal tentacles glowing with blue electrical death, advanced on Barton Kinsolving.

CHAPTER FIFTEEN

"ALL YOU HAVE to do is die, Kinsolving," said Cameron.

The robots hummed quietly as they advanced. When they got within arm's reach, Kinsolving heard the crackling of high voltage off the metal antennae whipping about. He yelped in pain when one tentacle lightly brushed his thigh. His entire leg went numb. Kinsolving sank down, clutching the burned spot, trying vainly to regain use of the leg to run.

But where could he run? The killer robots had him hemmed in. Everywhere he looked, he saw robots. A frantic glance over his shoulder showed that the door leading to the tunnel was too securely locked to open in a hundred years, much less seconds.

More from reflex than thought, Kinsolving pulled out the brain burner he had taken from the cargo shuttle's bay and held it in front of his face to block another high-voltage whip aimed at his face.

The robot's flexible death probe rebounded harmlessly from the plastic case. Even so, Kinsolving felt the muscles in his arms jerk in response to the nearness of the high-voltage discharge.

"Isn't this much more interesting than a simple laser?" asked Cameron. "I have a few guard robots equipped to fire on sight, but there have been problems. Alas, we inadvertently lost two human workers during field tests."

"And the supervisor? Rogoff?" Kinsolving asked. He sagged against the wall. The brain burner would not shield him from all the robots. The machines coordinated their attack too well for that. One shot in to touch him while the others waited. If he responded to block the attack, the others surged forward. Better to let only one touch him than the entire deadly pack.

"They are rather like hunting dogs," said Cameron. "I fancy myself something of a sportsman. That's why I didn't program any of them for a fatal shock. But together, who can say? Two, three, a half dozen? I'm afraid you'll have to discover the precise number it takes to die, Kinsolving."

Kinsolving learned the hard way that two robots would not kill him. The stench of burned flesh rose and hung in his nostrils. He was not sure whether the odor was worse than the pain each wound gave.

"But I am ever so rude. You mentioned Rogoff, our late supervisor? He is departed from this miserable world."

"Dead, you mean."

"That, also." Cameron swirled his cape and moved to get a better view of the slow torture his robots inflicted. "I read about bearbaiting during ancient times on Earth. A fascinating hobby. It is a true pity that we've lost our taste for real enjoyment. A penalty of civilization, some might say."

Kinsolving saw no need to revive such a custom. Three electrified probes touched him simultaneously. He fought grimly to keep from blacking out. Try as he might, he could not block all the robots with the plastic box. One, yes; two, seldom; three, never.

His bloodied fingers began to slip on the box's smooth surface. The only way Kinsolving could maintain his grip was to shove his fingers into the small indentations. The force of the brain burner activating threw him back against the wall so hard it knocked the wind from his lungs.

Through a veil of darkness, he peered out at the killer robots. In his condition, it could only be a matter of seconds before they closed in and killed him.

The seconds passed and Kinsolving's vision cleared. He sucked in painful lungfuls of air until he could stand.

"What did you do to them?" shrieked Cameron. The gaudily dressed man had dropped to his knees beside a killer robot. The machine lay on its side, the flickering blue haze of electric discharge gone from its tentacles.

Kinsolving spun and saw that all the robots had been disabled. One's repulsor field had vanished and it had driven directly into the ground, turning the concrete floor to dust with the force of its failure. Another had blown apart; Kinsolving had been so close to unconsciousness that he hadn't heard the explosion. It had destroyed three other robots in its mechanical death throes.

"You son of a bitch! What did you do to them?" shouted Cameron. The assassin pushed the inert metal carcass away and rose, hand reaching under his cape.

Again Kinsolving reacted instinctively. He threw the brain burner at Cameron. The edge of the box caught Cameron on the side of the head. The glancing blow caused him to stumble. He reached up to touch the slight wound and his hand came away blood-smeared. The instant of hesitation on his part allowed Kinsolving to drive forward, his numbed legs barely responding.

Kinsolving stumbled over a fallen robot and fell head-first into Cameron. The pair went down in a pile, but only Kinsolving rolled free and sat up. Cameron lay still, his head canted at an awkward angle.

"Killed you, you miserable son of a bitch," Kinsolving cried. He moved painfully to hands and knees and went to be sure that Cameron had not been stunned. He wanted him *dead*.

Before Kinsolving could wrap his fingers around Cameron's throat and squeeze any life remaining from his body, he heard a popping sound. Of the killer robots disabled by the action of the brain burner, one remained functional. Its repulsor field had been destroyed but it crept forward, using its steel-whip tentacles like fingers. Fat blue sparks leaped from each tentacle tip as it bored into the concrete to pull itself toward Kinsolving.

"Stop," he said. "Deactivate. Erase program." No matter what Kinsolving ordered, the robot continued its slow, crippled progress toward him. The sensor lights ringing the circumference of the robot gleamed reds and yellows, showing extreme malfunction. But still it came on.

Kinsolving took a step toward Cameron to search the fallen assassin for a weapon. He doubted that Cameron went anywhere without a dozen lethal devices, in addition to the activators for his robot legions.

But the motion alerted another robot, one posted high above in the warehouse. It dived down so fast that the air whined past its cylindrical body.

Jerking away, Kinsolving avoided the stream of steel needles the robot shot at him. He took scant pleasure in watching the robot crash into the floor, destroying itself. Its dive had been too steep, its speed too high, to avoid collision.

Kinsolving moved away from Cameron. Even fallen, the man maintained a wall of death around himself. Kinsolving shrieked in pain as electricity volted through his leg. He stumbled away from the punishing pain. He had forgotten the killer robot making its slow way to him to complete its program.

"Die," the robot croaked. "Must kill you. Stop. Kill."

Dragging his injured leg behind him as if it were made from wood, Kinsolving got away from the struggling robot. He looked around and found a short steel rod used to brace crates. He limped back toward the killer robot that still pursued him. He had learned that, without the proper cancellation code, there was only one sure way to stop one of Cameron's robots.

He judged distance and swung the rod. Kinsolving connected, felt the mechanical shock of impact, then experienced an even more severe electrical shock as the robot discharged itself fully along the conducting steel. Kinsolving blacked out. When he recovered, he was not sure who had gotten the worst of the fight.

The robot lay smoking, no emergency lights showing. It had been returned to the realm of inert metal, but Kinsolving's arms and legs felt equally inert. He moaned and fought to keep moving, to get blood flowing, to push back the red waves of pain hitting him from every direction.

He pulled himself onto a crate and half lay across it, regaining a modicum of strength. He still felt more dead than alive, but looking around convinced him he had won this battle. The killer robots were scattered around the warehouse, some metallic corpses and the rest only marginally functional. He eyed Cameron again, wondering how he might reach the man to see if he had a broken neck—and if not, to finish the job.

The occasional humming from overhead stopped him. Cameron's aerial sentries still protected him, dead or alive.

Kinsolving picked up the fallen brain burner and used the steel rod to pry open the lid. The microelectronics inside had been fused beyond recognition.

"Positive feedback," he said to himself. "I triggered the brain burner and it set up feedback in the robots." He laughed harshly at the irony. The device IM hoped to use to destroy Web had turned on their robotic assassins and had given him another chance to rescue the arachnoids from the Stellar Death Plan.

He dropped the plastic box and went to find the other crates containing the infernal devices. It took almost an hour of dodging robot loaders before he found them. A mountain of the shipping crates rose. He scaled the cliffs of plastic and fought off the top to a crate. Inside rested more of the brain burners. Hundreds more.

From his vantage point atop the mountain, Kinsolving looked down. A mountain of death. But how could he destroy it?

He could not. As he had prowled through the warehouse scheme after scheme had come to him—and each had been discarded in turn. Some had been impractical, others fanciful, still others suicidal. And not one had a chance of success. With a small atomic he might remove the threat permanently from the face of Web, but Interstellar Materials had other warehouses, other shuttles to bring down the brain burners, all the time in the universe to manufacture more of the cerium-crystal resonators.

Kinsolving took two of the devices. He could not carry more and hope to get down from his precarious perch. By the time he reached the bottom of the stack, he felt the pressures of time mounting. It had been long—too long—since the fight with Cameron and his robots. Although most duties in the warehouse were automated and required no human supervision, Cameron's failure to report back would bring human guards. Or a new flock of the flying robots.

Kinsolving looked above and saw the speed-blurred

streaks as they patrolled. He sat for a moment, trying to decide why he had not been attacked. The only explanation that came to him was that Cameron had laid a trap and had wanted his prey firmly in the jaws before closing it. Kinsolving had the eerie feeling of being watched, evaluated, made ready for the kill if he attempted to leave the warehouse.

He tested his theory by moving toward the main doors. More of the flying robots gathered. Beside the doors stood a pair of killer robots, powered down but obviously on duty. Kinsolving tossed a bit of debris between the robots.

The flash dazzled him. These were not equipped with electric-shock whips. They carried lasers powerful enough to vaporize a piece of resilient plastic packing material. He slipped back to stay out of their detection range. For a few minutes, he fingered a brain burner and considered his chances of escape by using it to short-circuit the robot guards. But he hesitated. These machines were significantly different in design. That he had not also taken out the flying robots when he triggered the first brain burner showed that this weapon had a limited effective range.

Design, range, uncertainty—and knowing that human guards patrolled outside—stopped him. He returned to the massive steel-plated door leading to the underground escape tunnel.

The deactivated robots still littered the area. But Cameron was gone. Kinsolving cursed. Was the man dead and only dragged off by robotic slaves? Had Humbolt blundered in and found Cameron?

Kinsolving pushed that from his mind. A human would have sounded the alarm immediately. Kinsolving counted on a robot rescuing its master. Although the robots carried out even complicated orders, none truly thought. They were too small for the electronics needed for independent and innovative action. Kinsolving smiled grimly. Cameron had thought himself invincible. That fit the facts well.

The man's arrogance had prevented him from giving all the robots orders to hunt and kill an intruder, under any circumstance. Cameron had wanted to personally issue the order to kill Kinsolving—and had. But only those hunter-killer robots nearby had received the order. Others prowled and worked only to prevent exit. Anyone's exit.

"So a robot's dragged him off," said Kinsolving. That took some pressure off him. But not much. He saw no other way out of the warehouse than through the tunnel. He considered crawling back up and dropping through the fan-unit hole. The leaden weight in his arms told him he wouldn't be able to make it. In his current condition, he had to find an easier exit.

Kinsolving studied the door and traced the circuits controlling the lock. When he had first come through the door with the arachnoid, it had been well hidden, an obvious escape path for the supervisor and chosen assistants should danger require flight. Cameron had refurbished the door and left it visible and obvious. Kinsolving found the control keypad and idly punched in a few numbers. Nothing. But he had not expected it to respond without the proper coded sequence.

"Here's where your experience pays off," he said, dropping down and pulling off the access panel. Kinsolving studied the workings. He had jury-rigged enough equipment in his day to have some inkling about where to start. The installation had been made to prevent entry, not exit. A double strand and a small transmitter showed the alarm system to detect tampering with the lock. He disabled this. No flight of steel needles or diving robots or laser-spitting guards appeared.

Heartened, Kinsolving worked on. He finally came down to one small block circuit that had to contain the coding for lock. Input went through the ceramic block, and if everything matched, a signal came out to power open the door.

Kinsolving shorted out the power lead and applied the sparking ends across the block circuit.

A grinding noise came as music to him. The massive door shuddered and the locking mechanism opened.

"At last!" he cried. Kinsolving had been in the warehouse too long. He had no idea how long ago Cameron had been moved or what action the robot had taken on discovering its master. The entire building might be surrounded, or nothing might have occurred. Cameron might have sta-

tioned no backup guard robots or ordered them to do more
than simply prevent exit.

Kinsolving strained to pull the door open far enough to
slip through into the darkness of the small room and stairwell beyond. It was then that he heard the telltale hum of a
repulsor field functioning at overload.

"God, no!" he shouted. Kinsolving's muscles bulged
and strained against the sleeves of his shirt as he struggled
to close the heavy door behind him. The patrolling aerial
robots had been activated by the door lock. He had thought
he had disabled the warning transmitter. Had he missed a
backup, or had Cameron given the robots other orders? To
attack if anyone opened the door? Possibly. Probably. He
knew it was no consolation thinking about the vent-fan
unit—any exit would have triggered the robot.

The first stream of steel needles bounced off the side of
the door and ricocheted out into the room, whistling as
they went. One came through the door and pinned Kinsolving's shirt to the plastic wall. He jerked away, ripping
the fabric. He did not want to risk touching the needle. He
remembered what Quixx had said about Garon Andrianov
being killed. Poison. It seemed like something Cameron
would do. Simple steel projectiles of this size would not
stop a full-grown, determined man. Not unless those needles carried fast-acting poison.

Kinsolving looked through the small crack left between
door and frame and saw scores of the aerial robots hovering outside, looking like a school of killer fish homing in
on its prey.

He could not get the door closed. The projectiles came
in a steady stream through the small opening and kept him
in constant fear for his life. When he looked up and
through the opening where the vent-fan unit had been,
Kinsolving knew he had to run. The robots had found the
gaping hole and were shifting their efforts from the metal-
plated door to the easier highway he had made for them.

Headfirst, Barton Kinsolving dived down the stairs. He
hit the bottom and lay for a few seconds, dazed. It took
him another few seconds to regain his sense of direction
and realize that escape lay along the pitch-black tunnel and

not back up the stairs to the faint light filtering down from the warehouse.

A sharp glint of light off a silvered robot body convinced him that only death lay at the top of the stairs now. He plunged through the darkness, careening off the left tunnel wall and colliding with the right. Several times he stumbled and fell, but always he kept moving forward, either crawling until he could find his balance or running until his lungs felt as if they would explode and his legs would fall off.

Panting harshly, he reached the end of the tunnel and stared up into the shed.

"Made it!" he gasped out.

Kinsolving went cold inside when he heard a roaring sound, caught up by the restricting walls of the tunnel and magnified a hundredfold. The repulsor fields of countless aerial robots!

He swung around the spiralling stairs in time to avoid a flight of steel needles that turned the walls and floor into an alien life-form sprouting deadly spines. He moved to get back up the stairs. Another barrage of death.

And the humming of the repulsor fields came ever closer. He had escaped the warehouse only to be trapped in the tunnel. He could not climb down behind the stairs without being turned into a pincushion. And to stay hunched down behind the stairs meant that dozens of the robots would have an easier time killing him when they arrived.

Trapped!

CHAPTER SIXTEEN

BARTON KINSOLVING had only seconds left to live. The robots had followed too well down the stairs and the tunnel. He did not dare guess at their programming. They might follow him across the face of Zeta Orgo if that was the instruction given by Cameron.

Another flight of needles caused a shower of dust from the concrete wall behind him. Kinsolving did the only thing he could. Once again he activated a brain burner.

He stiffened and fell forward onto the floor, momentarily stunned by the resonance shock running through him. His head felt as if someone had driven burning sodium spikes into it and he was sure that he had gone blind.

The effect of the brain burner wore off and left him weak and shaking. His vision returned, but the pain hammering at his temples lingered. But strewn about on the floor, casting back dim reflections from the light above, were the flying robots. One spun in crazy circles, shooting out a steady stream of needles until its magazine emptied. Another tried to bury itself in the floor. Still others crashed repeatedly into one another, their sensors fused.

Kinsolving pulled himself to his feet and fought against giddiness to avoid the deadly, poisoned needles embedded in stair and wall and ascend to the shed. Caution returned. He studied the footprints in the dust. No sign of another having been in the shed since he had entered showed on the floor. Staggering as if drunk, Kinsolving went outside and into the fresh air.

The too-blue sun sank below the horizon, casting sharp shadows all around him. He went around the shed and stared at the Interstellar Materials warehouse. The setting alien sun turned it into a looming box of darkness, only occasional glints showing off sensors mounted along the roof.

Kinsolving lifted the brain burner he had triggered in the tunnel. He did not have to pull the lid off to know it, too, had been destroyed. The acrid stench of burned electronic components almost gagged him. He tossed the cerium resonator aside and checked to be sure he still had the second one he had stolen from the shipping crate. It bulged in his pocket.

"This is it," he said. "This is all the proof I've got. And what do I do with it? Turn it over to Quixx?"

Kinsolving immediately discarded that notion. The arachnoid policeman—or whatever Quixx's position actually was—would not necessarily believe everything an off-world "human thing" told him. Simple possession of the Box of Delights might be grounds for imprisonment or worse.

Kinsolving vowed to never return to the alien prison world, even if it meant his life.

"What now?" he asked himself. The brilliant landing-field lights winked on here and there, but offered no answer to his question. The brain burners were in the warehouse, but Kinsolving did not know for how long. If he were Kenneth Humbolt and had found Cameron killed —or at least wounded—and an array of sentry robots destroyed, he would clear out any incriminating cargo.

Kinsolving had no idea about the time scale for the distribution, either. All quarter million of the devices might be sent out tonight. Or tomorrow or in the next five minutes. He could sit and watch—but so what? What could he do to stop them? And an incredible amount of legitimate cargo entered and left the warehouse daily. How would he recognize the contraband?

Another tack had to give a better chance for stopping the Plan.

Kinsolving started walking back to the city, the consulate fixed in his mind more as a direction than a destination.

* * *

The city streets turned into an alien and exciting wonderland after dark. Stangely colored lights shone everywhere, moving like beacons, dancing, shifting, emphasizing, hiding in glare and shadow. Kinsolving felt like a tourist come to the metropolis, gawking as he blundered through the dense crowds of arachnoids.

Their wobbling gait caused him little trouble after the first hour of jostling. He adjusted his own and avoided most of them. And he quickly found out that most of the foot traffic bounced and headed aloft, following dangling cables, spinning strands of their own, clambering up the sides of sheer spires like the spiders they were.

Kinsolving wondered if he attracted any attention. The way the arachnoids held their heads, turning at angles impossible for a human neck, made it impossible to tell. His clothing hung it tatters and blood seeped from numerous cuts and scrapes he had acquired. The burns on his legs and arms were apparent to anyone examining him in even a cursory fashion. And he could do little to hide the Box of Delights since his jacket had been reduced to rags.

But not a single arachnoid stopped him. None showed any interest in him at all. For that Kinsolving thanked what little luck he still had.

He settled onto what he took to be a park bench and stared across a grassy area dotted with tall trees. The cool wind rustling through the leaves soothed him and let him relax.

"What to do?" he murmured.

"How much?" came a shrill voice from behind. Kinsolving jumped to his feet, spinning to face an arachnoid almost able to look him squarely in the eye.

"How much is what?"

"The Box of Delights. You carry it boldly. This one's has succumbed to fatigue and no longer produces the joy it once did."

"The battery is dead?" Kinsolving asked in surprise. The one in his hands had been built with an internal power supply powerful enough to overload a dozen or more killer robots. How much use had this spider being put his Box of Delights to? Or had he used only a feebler version? To hand over the one he had might mean the arachnoid's brain death, Kinsolving realized.

"Don't last long. Go dead in a few days. This one yearns for recharging Boxes of Delights." The spider shifted restlessly from one side to the other, mandibles hanging loosely under his mouth orifice.

"What's it worth to you?" asked Kinsolving.

"Four days."

"A week—seven days," counted Kinsolving, not even sure what they were bartering.

"Done. Give this one your identicard."

Kinsolving fumbled out the identicard the consulate computer had furnished. The arachnoid took out a similar one and placed his on top of Kinsolving's. A quiet, barely audible hum sounded and the arachnoid handed the identicard back. He had transferred a week's food and lodging in exchange for the brain burner.

Kinsolving handed over the plastic box, guilt burning brightly as he did so. He sought to stop the distribution of these insidious devices, not to help in their spread. But as the arachnoid rocked back on his four hind legs and eagerly took the box in his tiny pink hands, an idea came to Kinsolving.

"I can charge your dead Box of Delights," he said.

The spider eyed him and finally shook his head. "No need, no need. This is enough." With that, the spider being walked off. Kinsolving took a deep breath, then followed. This might prove more difficult than he anticipated if the spider took to the strands dangling from virtually every spire in the city of towering heights.

Kinsolving sagged when he saw the spider grab a strand and spin off and upward, vanishing into the trees. He started at a jog, then broke into a run, gasping as he went. Above his head, the spider made good time sliding from strand to strand in the trees, then started up and across a web bridge between the tree at the edge of the park and a ten-story building some distance away.

The man watched and took note of the window where the spider vanished. He dashed across the busy traffic-filled streets and entered the ground floor. It was not as hopeless as he had feared. Although the arachnoids had no need of personal elevators, they did use freight lifts. Kinsolving took the cargo elevator to the fourth floor and burst into a corridor completely strung with webs. He brushed several away—or tried. The sticky strands clung and burned where they touched bare flesh.

Kinsolving ripped away more fabric and freed himself. He oriented himself, found the side facing the park and decided that this window—or aerial doorway without door panels—had been the one where the arachnoid addict had entered.

The bare, brightly lit corridor had hundreds of small tunnels leading from it. Kinsolving frowned as he moved along, studying each tunnel. None seemed large enough to accommodate a being as large as the one he had sold the brain burner to, yet there seemed to be no other explanation for his abrupt disappearance. Kinsolving stared at the far end of the corridor and worried that the arachnoid had only passed through, using this as an aerial terminus. He shook such a notion out of his mind. The spider had to be here somewhere. He just had to, or Kinsolving's entire plan had failed miserably.

Careful study of the passageway showed minute, fresh scratches on one plastic-lined tunnel leading off at an angle. Kinsolving summoned up all the courage he had, then wiggled head first into the tunnel. The tunnel narrowed and cramped his shoulders, but he kept on.

A sudden turn brought him to an unfurnished room large enough to hold four of the spiders. They had gathered around the Box of Delights. Kinsolving recognized the one who had purchased the cerium-crystal resonator. He hunkered down and chittered loudly, the other arachnoids listening intently.

Kinsolving braced himself when the spider being reached out with two taloned legs and activated the brain burner. The surge of power assaulting him lasted for only a few seconds, then diminished rapidly. Kinsolving blinked and cleared his vision. The impact of using the brain burner had thrown all four arachnoids back. The one whose talons had activated it had collapsed into a heap against a far wall. A sickly smell that Kinsolving associated with death permeated the room.

But two of the spiders stirred weakly, their legs waving about as they tried to stand. Neither succeeded.

Kinsolving kicked forward and moved in the tunnel to where he could roll free into the room.

He examined the nearest spider. The being's light purple eyes were open and glassy. He saw no hint of life remaining. The two trying to stand made squeaking noises that soared past the limits of his hearing. From the way they thrashed about, Kinsolving did not think they would ever be useful members of arachnoid society. Their minds had been seared by the electronic blast.

Kinsolving knelt beside the arachnoid who had triggered the Box of Delights. Small clickings came from the mandibles.

"Are you able to speak?" he asked.

At first the arachnoid answered in his native language, then shifted to a slurred speech that Kinsolving translated with difficulty. "Web. This one ruled the Supreme Web."

"The Supreme Web?" Kinsolving prompted. "What of it?"

"This one decided for the world. Vibratory debates won. Strands of Power, all under this one's power!"

"Would you like to do more?" asked Kinsolving, hating himself for what he had to do. "You can rule the Supreme Web for all time. You need another Box of Delights. This one can be recharged and give even more intense pleasures."

"Recharged?"

"Take the Box of Delights and get it recharged. Think of the Supreme Web. Think of the, uh, vibratory debates!" Kinsolving's voice rang with urgency and cut through the fog permanently burned into the arachnoid's brain. Talon-tipped legs slid under a bulky body and lifted.

Kinsolving silently handed the spider creature the box, not trusting him to find it without help.

"More? How? Where does this one get another chance along the glorious strands of the Supreme Web?"

"Take it back to the one who usually supplies your Boxes of Delights. The one who gives you the chance to attain the Supreme Web." Kinsolving had no idea what he promised, but it motivated the arachnoid. The spider wobbled and bobbed around but headed for the tunnel that had brought it into this cubbyhole. With surprising agility considering its disability, the arachnoid vanished through the tunnel.

Kinsolving fought down his rising gorge as he glanced around the room one last time. One spider had perished. The other two would never use the brain burner again—or do anything else for themselves. This was a scene that would be repeated millions of times unless the Plan could be stopped in time. He turned and followed the spider through the tunnel, listening to its chitinous talons clacking on the floor and walls ahead of him. Kinsolving tumbled into the outer corridor in time to see the arachnoid vanish out the window-door where he had entered from the park.

At the window, Kinsolving stared down at the ropy strand of web stuff hanging in a catenary between the sill and a third-story window on the next building. The strand from the park almost drew Kinsolving like a magnet. He could slide down to the firm ground and not worry about falling. A ten-meter fall would not necessarily kill him but it would severely injure him, especially in his condition.

"No time to think about it," he said, looking across at the window-door where the arachnoid had disappeared.

Kinsolving pulled off his shirt and wrapped it around his right hand, then threw the free end over the strand and grabbed hold of the cloth with his left. He never hesitated. He jumped.

"Aieee!" The cry came out in reaction to the falling-sliding-speed sensation. Kinsolving barely had time to recover his senses when the window-door came rushing up at him. He got his legs up and braced before he crashed against the wall. The impact stunned him, but Kinsolving clung to his shirt. He dangled from the spider strand for a moment, then pulled himself up painfully.

The friction from the slide had burned almost entirely through his shirt. Another few meters would have cut the cloth in half and sent him plunging to the street.

"Luck," he sighed. "So far, the luck's been with me tonight."

It continued to hold in his favor. The arachnoid had negotiated its aerial walkway easily but found it almost impossible to navigate along the corridor. He smashed into the wall and simply stood, trying to forge ahead through solid plastic.

Kinsolving put on the remnants of his shirt and hurried to the arachnoid. "The Supreme Web," he whispered urgently. "Yours, if you find the one who sells you the Boxes of Delights. He can recharge it. Go. Find him and enter the Supreme Web!"

This brought the arachnoid around. He made a start back toward the entryway, then continued listing in a tight circle until he found a small tunnel rimmed in dark orange plastic. He plunged into it, Kinsolving following closely.

The arachnoid outpaced Kinsolving in the tight tunnel. Kinsolving came to the verge of the tunnel and peered into a room identical to the one in the other building. No furniture, plain gray plastic walls faintly luminous, several other entryways dotting the perimeter.

The Box of Delights fell to the floor with a clatter. Shrill chittering sounds filled the air, giving Kinsolving a headache. From the way the other arachnoid held himself, Kinsolving knew that he did not enjoy being harangued. He imagined he knew what was being said.

"Recharge the Box of Delights," the addict demanded.

"Impossible," said the supplier.

"Do it! I must attain the Supreme Web!"

"For a price!"

"Any price! Do it!"

The arachnoid supplier took the brain burner and turned it over in his pink hands. From somewhere that Kinsolving could not see the arachnoid produced a long, thin cylinder and inserted it into the brain burner. The device hissed like a snake.

More shrill chittering. The supplier handed the brain burner back to the addict, batting one taloned leg away when it was apparent that it would be immediately used.

Kinsolving wondered if the supplier realized the danger in the new resonators. IM needed to maintain its network of distribution as long as possible.

He had found a supplier. From this arachnoid he could learn where IM made contact, where it hid the brain burners after they left the warehouse. But how? Kinsolving had no idea how to interrogate an arachnoid, especially a criminal living on the fringes of society.

A quick move carried Kinsolving into the room. He came to a squatting position. Neither arachnoid had noticed him. They continued their shrill argument. The addict did not worry Kinsolving. The initial contact with the resonator had burned out too many nerve centers for the being to present any real danger.

But how was he to tackle the supplier?

Kinsolving acted rather than thought. He dived forward, arms outstretched. He gathered in an armful of hairy legs and jerked as hard as he could. Five legs trapped, he dumped the arachnoid to the floor — hard.

He rolled and tried to weave the legs into a tight knot. Almost instantly he realized this was not going to work. The legs kicked independently and with greater strength than he would have thought possible. He found himself flying through the air to crash into a wall.

The arachnoid noisily complained and came to all eight legs. The mandibles clacked ferociously as the spider creature faced Kinsolving.

"The Box of Delights!" Kinsolving called out to the addict. "Use it!"

The supplier batted the brain burner from the weakened being's hands. Then he advanced on Kinsolving, death etched on every feature of his alien face.

Barton Kinsolving's death.

CHAPTER SEVENTEEN

BARTON KINSOLVING edged along the gray plastic wall, his eyes fixed on the arachnoid's front legs. Those long, chitin-tipped weapons swung back and forth in a pattern that prevented Kinsolving from diving back into the tunnel. But even as this thought crossed his mind, he knew to try an escape like that would mean instant death. The spider being moved too quickly—and one long leg with the hardened tip would spit him before he wiggled a meter along the tunnel.

"The Box," he called frantically to the addict. "Use it. Return to the Supreme Web! You can leave behind all your misery. Do it, damn you, do it!"

The arachnoid advancing on him reached out with a third leg and scooped up the brain burner, pulling it to a safe spot beneath his heavy body. Another leg pushed the addict away. The arachnoid shrilly voiced his displeasure with this treatment, but the brain burner had done its evil work; the spider addict could not control his legs properly. Kinsolving's only hope for survival lay in getting the addict to activate the resonating device—and the chance for this had passed.

Kinsolving feinted to the right, dodged left and tried to grab the Box. He would willingly kill both spiders in return for the massive headache using the Box of Delights gave him.

His groping fingers missed the edge of the box by millimeters. A casual sweep of a powerful leg sent him reeling back, helpless, unable to even stand without support from the wall behind his back.

"You will die, weakling human thing," the advancing

spider said shrilly. "Why do you meddle where you are not wanted?"

"I need to reach whoever supplies you the Box of Delights."

"You disrupt trade. You disrupt this one's serenity!"

The arachnoid launched with incredible speed. Kinsolving could not have avoided the pouncing being had he been in top shape. The fights, the flight, the chase after the addict to reach this hidden warren all told on him. Summoning all his strength, Kinsolving barely moved his head to one side to avoid the heavy, talon-tipped leg that came smashing toward his face.

He grabbed a middle leg and tried to wrestle the arachnoid down again. A blow on the top of his head sent him spinning across the room. He fell heavily. When he tried to rise, every muscle in his body refused to obey. He had been pushed beyond the limit of his endurance. Kinsolving collapsed and stared at the arachnoid bringing death to him.

Chittering so loud it threatened to rupture his eardrums echoed in the small room. Kinsolving put his hands over his ears to shut it out. At first he thought it was the spider's hunting cry. Then he realized that the supplier had frozen as if terrified.

Legs shaking, head turning back and forth, the arachnoid gave every indication of fear. Kinsolving glanced toward the addict he had followed. This arachnoid also cowered.

Kinsolving pushed himself to a sitting position, his sweating back against a cool plastic wall. The insane chittering rose in intensity, giving him a ringing in his ear to match the headache hammering like an ocean's surf in his temples. As suddenly as it had begun, the shrill noise stopped. Kinsolving felt drained, as if someone had relieved him of the burden of life.

From a tunnel on the far side of the room came a mottled red body and hairy legs. The new arrival shook several times, as if smoothing ruffled fur.

"Quixx!" Kinsolving called.

"Ah, the human thing who should have left this world and has not."

"I'm glad to see you. This..." Kinsolving's words

trailed off. Quixx ignored him and waddled over to stand directly in front of the Box of Delights supplier. Quixx lifted his two front legs and brought them together sharply —with the other arachnoid's head caught squarely between. The impact dropped the supplier to the floor where he lay, not even twitching.

"You didn't kill him, did you?" asked Kinsolving. "He could have led us to the source for those damned things."

"The Box of Delights? Its source is of no concern to you. This miserable destroyer of our culture is all that matters."

"Cut off the supply and people like him won't have anything to sell," protested Kinsolving. He saw that this argument got nowhere with Quixx. The arachnoid's values were too alien. Or were they? Realization slowly dawned on Kinsolving. He saw only an isolated incident in what would be a long investigation.

"Yes, human thing, we know the source of the Box of Delights. We are not the uncaring animals you seem to think we are."

"I never—" Kinsolving bit off the words. "I wanted to help. You didn't seem to be investigating."

"Your exploits are remarkable, especially for one acquainted with trees and not webs."

Kinsolving did not bother telling him that he had barely seen a tree until he had left Earth for the off-world colonies. Humans might be fallen brachial tree dwellers, but that did not mean he practiced his heredity as the arachnoids did.

"What are you going to do with them?"

"That one," Quixx said, pointing to the addict, "will be executed."

"What? Wait, why? He was a victim."

"He murdered friends with this device. Do human things not consider murder a crime against the web?"

"He didn't know it would kill them. He's lucky it didn't kill him."

"He's unlucky that it didn't kill him," Quixx corrected. "Those remaining behind with irreparable brain damage have been removed from the web of society. Those deaths fall on him, also."

Kinsolving remembered stories of the ancient—and not so ancient—Chinese ways of dealing with opium addiction. Death. For using, for selling, for trafficking. This arachnoid savagery appalled him, but there were precedents in human history.

That didn't make it right.

"You might be able to care for them, help them recover. This craving can't be natural."

"Our finest neurosurgeons have seen numerous cases before this day's counting. There is nothing to do for those who use the Box of Delights. The higher functions vital to acceptance in the web are gone. They have exchanged a place in society for a fantasy world of belonging to the Supreme Web."

"That's the common delusion?"

Quixx shook all over, then settled down until his face was level with Kinsolving's. "The resonance activates the portion of our brains that matches oneness with the Supreme Web. Use of the Box of Delights can achieve no other delusion."

Kinsolving did not understand what Quixx meant. "When you reach the rank of Supreme Web, there's some neural trigger in your brain that is toggled?"

"Imprecise words for a being without the proper concept of true attainment and glory." Quixx's head rocked from side to side. "Accept those thoughts as truth. They are close; they are distant. They must do you."

"You knew that Interstellar Materials has been supplying the brain burners?"

"There could be no other source."

Kinsolving swallowed hard. "What are you going to do about it?"

"All humans on this world might be destroyed."

"You'd lose valuable trade with human worlds."

Quixx made a rude noise, then shifted position, getting his long, hairy legs settled around him like a living star. "We trade with human worlds out of pity. There is little you supply that we need. Certainly nothing in electronics."

Kinsolving stared at the arachnoid. He had never thought of trade with the alien planets as being a form of aid, the more advanced helping the lesser beings achieve status. Humans were newcomers to the reaches of space; most suitable planets had been appropriated by other races.

"Those in control at IM, including the chairman, have formulated what they call the Stellar Death Plan. It's designed to leave Web in confusion, to kill billions. This will enable the company to move in and assume your markets."

Quixx repeated his rude noise.

"There's more," Kinsolving went on. "Fremont and the others feel that you and the other alien races are deliberately holding back mankind through trade barriers."

"Racist," Quixx said, the word sounding strangely sibilant as he spoke it. "This one does not understand the concept any more than you appear to embrace the oneness of the Supreme Web. This one has encountered the word often among you human things."

"You don't feel inferior to other races, or to more advanced ones?"

"We are superior beings. It is our destiny to aid those who are inferior to us."

"Surely, another race does something better, easier, quicker. You must envy someone."

"No."

The alien concepts—Kinsolving was not sure whether he or Quixx was the alien—refused explanation. The arachnoids of Web seemed secure in their knowledge that no one could be better. Kinsolving wondered if they denied the achievements of others, or if they were truly disinterested.

"Do you ever compete with others? For planets, for commodities you need?"

"Yes, of course. That is the nature of interspecies contact. Social friction with those not of the web. If it becomes too great, we fight. Or we do whatever else is required to reduce friction."

"You wouldn't try to subvert another race, if you thought that was the only way to reduce friction?"

"If the other species is of any intelligence, they will discover such meddling."

"As you have done," Kinsolving said bitterly.

"Humans are peculiar beings. Never before have we found such unformed creatures among the stars." Quixx cocked his head to one side, then added, "Perhaps once. This one's memory is faint and distant on the subject."

"What happened?"

"We ate them. A particularly succulent species a few years' travel toward the galactic center."

"Are you going to do that with Earth? With humans?"

Quixx spat. "No." Kinsolving relaxed. Then he almost cried out in horror when Quixx added, "You taste bitter. There is no food value in your race. We must deal in other ways."

"Look," Kinsolving said earnestly. "This is all Interstellar Materials' doing—the company and its leaders. Earth as a planet is innocent."

Even as the words slipped out, Kinsolving wondered if he had spoken the truth. He did not know if this were true—but he *hoped* that it was. Earth's official policies had always been to win acceptance from the other starfaring species. How far did the conspiracy of the Stellar Death Plan go? Through the various Earth governments? What other star-spanning corporations believed as Fremont and Humbolt and the others at IM and had joined forces in the Plan?

His professors in school had been adamant about mankind finding a niche among the stars and in harmony with the others already there. Kinsolving could not believe that this was all a farce, a misdirection, a travesty.

"We can interdict all cargo brought to our world," Quixx said. "We need not do this, however, if the Supreme Web achieves oneness on a solution."

"You're not going to hold Earth responsible for the actions of a few of its citizens, are you?"

"This one has worked many strands," Quixx said. "Never is it possible to predict how the Supreme Web will react."

"What about Andrianov? I know who killed him."

"The consul is of no importance, other than how his death reflects on others of your species. This one remains neutral on punishment to be meted out."

"Others demand severe punishment?"

"Is this not the way with your race?" asked Quixx. "You do not have unanimity of opinion. You work against this

Fremont and others loyal to his faction. And you do this without support of a strand." Quixx shook his head. "Alone. You work alone, is that not true, Kinsolving?"

"It is."

"This one cherishes the moment."

"What?"

"Of knowing you," explained Quixx. "Although none of this one's race would be so foolish, your actions show determination and a savagery to be savored."

"I only wanted to help. It's wrong to kill off an entire species."

"We have done it. There is nothing wrong with it. But the reasons for the action are important. Your Fremont and Interstellar Materials have failed to find good reasons. For that, then, they must be stopped. The Supreme Web will act."

A hairy leg reached out and pulled Kinsolving to his feet. Barely able to stand, Kinsolving wobbled toward the tunnel leading out of the small gray room.

"What of the brain burner?"

"Leave it. Others will come for this doomed fool." As he passed the supplier, Quixx cuffed the arachnoid again.

"Where are we going?"

Quixx snorted and pushed Kinsolving ahead of him into the tunnel. The shrill words coming from behind froze Kinsolving's insides.

"We go to the Supreme Web. Judgment must be passed. On Interstellar Materials, on Fremont, on you."

Judgment must be passed. The words rang over and over in Barton Kinsolving's head as Quixx shoved him along the larger corridor outside and to an elevator that dropped them to ground level.

CHAPTER EIGHTEEN

CAMERON STIRRED when he felt himself moving. He thrashed about weakly, the pain more than he could bear. His arms refused to move properly and his head had been filled with exploding stars and a huge black hole in the center dragging in all his strength. Cameron stopped fighting for a moment and tried to remember what had happened, how this sorry state had come about.

He tried and failed. His thoughts jumbled like a lasered building, tumbling down into ruin, dust obscuring vision, noise drowning out real thought.

"Dammit," he heard someone say from light-years away. "Fix him. He can't die."

Humming and clicking noises came that Cameron—almost—recognized. Robots. He knew the sounds came from robots. Those were what he did best. His fingers worked miracles. He was a genius in programming and design. Yes, robots. His. His!

He tried to hold that thought and failed. The pain overwhelmed him and a numbing tide seized him. He fell into the black hole, not even trying to fight its fatal attraction.

Cameron's awareness returned slowly, but his memory refused to give up the facts of what had occurred.

"Is he all right?" demanded a querulous voice. Cameron forced open an eyelid and peered into bright lights. The pain at the back of his retina caused him to retreat once more to the safety of closed eyes.

Memories rose within his mind, forcing away the black pit that continued to suck at his consciousness. He remembered his life on Earth, the orphanage, the abuse, his vows to never allow that to happen again, how he escaped.

"No!" Cameron moaned out. "Get away. Let me be. I can do it myself. What do I need you for?"

Strong hands gripped his shoulders and shook. Pain almost robbed him of his precarious grip on the world.

"Do not," came a metallic voice. "You are harming the patient."

"I don't care if I kill the son of a bitch. I've got to find out what happened in there."

Cameron remembered bits. Humbolt. Director. Director Kenneth Humbolt. And the robotic voice? An automedic. Injury? Had he been injured? It must surely be that he had. Humbolt showed no sign of weakness. Cameron groaned as the pain escalated from Humbolt's shaking.

Transcending weakness, Cameron reached down inside and pulled up the indomitable willpower that had freed him from his masters at the orphanage, the power that had brought him to the pinnacle of power at Interstellar Materials. He grabbed Humbolt's punishing hand and wrenched as hard as he could.

A loud shriek of agony fed his strength. He twisted harder, feeling the bones giving in the wrist, the fingers folding back in unnatural directions.

"Dammit, Cameron, stop that!"

Cameron dared to open his eyes. A smile danced on his lips. He held Humbolt's hand in a deceptively gentle grip. The director could not know that Cameron was expending all his precious, jealously garnered strength to keep from fainting.

"Am I hurting you, Kenneth?" he asked. His voice sounded weak. He must never show weakness. Not to a worm like Kenneth Humbolt. Not to anyone.

"What happened in the warehouse?" demanded Humbolt. Cameron released his grip and let the director back away. The man rubbed his wrist.

To the automedic, Cameron said, "Director Humbolt's wrist is damaged. Scan it and repair, if necessary."

"Cameron," protested Humbolt, but he subsided and let the automedic do its work.

"Only a minor sprain, sir," reported the obedient robot. "However, you have sustained a dangerous injury."

"Detail," he snapped. Cameron's cold eyes fixed on

Humbolt, daring the director to protest this shift in authority. Humbolt said nothing. He sat, rubbing his wrist.

"You have sustained a hematoma of the dura mater."

"Further," Cameron prompted. His head pulsed and throbbed until he wanted to scream. Only Humbolt's presence prevented such an outburst on his part.

"You have sustained a concussion that bruised the fibrous membrane covering your brain. Treatment has progressed well."

"I feel like debris," complained Cameron.

"There is little more that can be done without proper attention. It is recommended that you return immediately to Gamma Tertius 4 where proper medical facilities can be brought to bear on your medical emergency."

"It couldn't be much of an emergency," said Cameron. "I can still move."

"There is certain brain damage to correct. Facilities do not exist on this planet for such precision work. I am only a mobile automedic unit, not a hospital unit."

"We'll get you back to Gamma Tertius," said Humbolt. "After we've talked. What happened? Who hit you?" The sneer in Humbolt's voice hurt Cameron worse than his head.

"I . . . I don't remember. Not exactly. It's all twisted around like a swirl of dust."

"Amnesia, both partial and complete, is often the result of such a serious head injury. You may find memory returning slowly, or not at all," said the automedic. "It is my diagnosis that, upon receiving proper treatment, you will regain fully your memory and suffer no ill effects of the blow."

"Damn!" raged Humbolt. "You don't know if you got Kinsolving or not, do you? He might have slugged you, then left untouched."

Cameron could not remember. He began reconstructing most probable outcomes, just as he would program a patrol robot to check all contingencies.

"It was Kinsolving," he said. "He must have escaped with a brain burner."

"What? Why?"

"I can only assume that something happened to destroy my killer robots. It wasn't possible to escape the trap I set for him without total deactivation of the killers. How he did that, I don't know."

"The burned-out remains of your precious robots have been packed away."

"I'll examine them later. There must be something to show how he—"

"The unit. Why do you think he's got a brain burner?"

"I was knocked unconscious," said Cameron, his mind working more efficiently now that it had a definite problem. "He could roam at will through the warehouse with me unconscious. There were only a few aerial robots patrolling above, and those were programmed to prevent anyone from leaving."

"We shipped the crates with the brain burners hours ago. You mean Kinsolving might have put something into them? A bomb? A tracer?"

"Calm yourself, Kenneth." Cameron had recovered enough to again feel distaste for the director's emotional outburst. "He might have, but if any robots did not detect anything as the crates left the warehouse, I doubt that they contain sensors or bombs. No, he took one. For evidence."

"The Bizzies didn't even inspect the crates when we shipped them out."

"Beginning distribution of the more potent units now is dangerous, Kenneth."

"I've already ordered it. We've got to get them in circulation as fast as we can. The Plan demands it!"

"The Plan demands only success. You're jeopardizing it."

"A fine one to talk. Look at you: injured. A concussion. And who did it? The very man you were sent here to kill."

"You've examined the premises? How did he leave?"

"Through the emergency tunnel. He opened the locking mechanism and returned the way he came."

Cameron settled back, relaxing. "Then my robots took care of our mutual problem. Anyone leaving would draw their attention. He might have deactivated the killer robots, but no device could also disable the aerial guardians." Cameron worried about that point. His killers should have been invincible, and had been deactivated. The flying robots might have suffered a similar fate. But how could he admit this to Humbolt?

"We didn't find his body."

"No matter." Cameron's head began to throb.

"Director Humbolt," interrupted the automedic. "Mr. Cameron's vital signs are showing distressing irregularity. He must be placed in a life-coma until better-equipped units on Gamma Tertius 4 can operate."

"Life-coma?" said Cameron, eyes opening. "No, not yet. Not yet. Only when you lift me to orbit."

"We've got a pair of cargo ships waiting to shift out," said Humbolt. "We'll get you out right away on the *Pluto*. I'll wait to verify distribution and follow on the *Persephone*."

"Go tend to it, Kenneth," said Cameron, an edge to his voice. "I'm not sure how much longer I can hold on."

"Let the damned robot put you under. The next thing you'll know will be at headquarters."

"See to it, Kenneth." Cameron's voice turned icy. The director muttered to himself and hurried from the room.

Cameron lay back, the room spinning in crazy orbits that changed constantly. When the procession of the walls died down to a bearable movement, Cameron said, "Bring my workbox."

"A life-coma is recommended. You are in no condition to override my medical opinion. Your cognitive abilities are impaired."

"The workbox, then you can put me into the life-coma."

"No." The automedic's programming had reached the conclusion that Cameron was no longer responsible due to the head injury.

"'We have fed our sea,'" quoted Cameron, "'for a thousand years and she calls us, still unfed.'"

"Programming override accepted," said the automedic. Cameron nodded and immediately regretted the action. Something came loose inside his head.

"My workbox."

The automedic beeped and hummed. From beyond Cameron's line of sight came a small loading robot carrying the electronics box. He motioned. The robot placed it within reach. Cameron pressed his thumb to the lock and opened the lid. Inside lay an aerial robot hardly ten centimeters in length and five millimeters thick.

"Activation code: Et tu, Humbolt." Cameron watched through blurred eyes as the minuscule robot powered up. The box quivered and then stilled when the robot lifted up and quietly hung, suspended in the air.

Pride of supreme achievement welled up within Cameron. This silent killer carried death in four forms, programming that permitted it to carry out its task in the most complicated situation conceivable and a special set of instructions that allowed a complete tri-vid report to be returned after it had finished.

"Do you understand your instructions?" Cameron asked.

The robot was too small to permit it to carry a speaker; almost unseen green flashes from its laser signalled that it desired only the final command to be on its mission.

Cameron forced his eyes open and stared at the flying sliver. He knew a minute laser scanned his retinal patterns, waiting for the command that only he could give. His eyelids sank, rose and sank again. When Cameron looked again, the air was empty.

Cameron toggled six less sophisticated but still capable aerial robots to protect him on his way off-planet and to the orbiting cargo ship. He did not trust Humbolt not to assassinate him, especially in this weakened condition.

He smiled. Humbolt would soon cease to be a problem. Chairman Fremont's orders had been carried out.

But what of Barton Kinsolving? Cameron's smile soured. If only he could remember what had happened in the warehouse. Kinsolving had to be responsible. He was the only one capable enough.

"Automedic," he called out.

"Yes, Mr. Cameron."

"The life-coma. Do it. Now."

Cameron winced as a panoply of drugs burst through his skin and poured into his veins. Then a coolness settled over him. He stopped fighting the pain and found himself relaxing, drifting, able to think clearly, if not to remember.

"Good-bye, Humbolt," he said softly, the words inaudible.

But Cameron's final thought before the life-coma totally possessed him was of Kinsolving.

CHAPTER NINETEEN

BARTON KINSOLVING looked nervously at Quixx. The spider loped along, his eight legs moving in a smoother rhythm now that they had left the building and travelled along the ground. Kinsolving sped up, his breathing coming in shorter gasps now. The spider being took no notice of the human's discomfort. If anything, he lengthened his stride and put even more strain on Kinsolving.

Kinsolving wiped sweat from his eyes and doggedly kept up. Quixx might be testing him, seeing if the puny human with only a quarter of the proper legs could compete with a "civilized" being. Or, Kinsolving thought, Quixx might not even think in such terms. He had no idea how the arachnoid saw the universe or humans or even himself. None of the spiders used a personal pronoun. Kinsolving wished he could decide what that meant. It might give him some insight into the character of the aliens he dealt with. He stumbled when they reached rougher terrain. The paving inside the city gave way to gravel, the gravel to dirt and finally to a rocky slope that took every ounce of energy he had left to scale.

Once on top of the hill, Kinsolving paused, not caring that Quixx continued on. He turned and looked back at the city bathed in lights every color of the spectrum. How did Quixx see his city? As this rainbow palace of soaring spires and delicate arches spanning hundreds of meters, all true architectural masterpieces, or did the spider being think of it only as a dirty, overcrowded city?

"Quixx, wait," Kinsolving called out. "I need rest."

"We are almost there. We must not keep the Supreme Web waiting. It is not done."

"Do you want to bring me to them dead?"

Quixx trotted back up the hill and faced Kinsolving. "It does not matter. If you perish in the next few minutes, the knowledge locked within your mind can be extracted. For a short time only, but it can be if death is recent."

"You'd do that?"

"Not if you refuse to die until after the Supreme Web has made its decision."

Kinsolving looked at the fairyland of towers, the shifting radiance and hues, the stark majesty of the city created by the arachnoids. Could any race capable of such beauty fail to show compassion in their system of justice?

He had ample evidence that they did—that they would. The laser cannon on the moons, the small items Quixx mentioned of eating their enemies and showing no quarter when fighting.

"I'm ready," he said. Kinsolving took several deep breaths and prepared to begin running again. Quixx reached out a long leg and tripped him.

"Where do you go?"

"You said . . ." The soft whisper of a repulsor craft danced along with the wind. Kinsolving scanned the darkened sky and caught glints of light off the hull of a large vehicle descending at the foot of the hill not fifty meters away.

Kinsolving picked himself up and dusted off his tattered clothing. Glaring at Quixx, he said, "If you'd tell me what's happening, you wouldn't have to treat me like a prisoner. I'll gladly tell your Supreme Web all they want to know."

"Of course you will," Quixx said. "You will not be given a choice. This one has guaranteed your voice."

"Where is the Supreme Web?" Kinsolving asked. "Near? Or will we be in the aircraft a long time?" He studied the vehicle hovering a few centimeters off the ground. Travelling long distances in this machine did not thrill him. The pilot had a windscreen. The passengers huddled in the back, hanging on to the metal rings mounted on the open deck. If the vehicle reached a speed of even two hundred kilometers an hour, Kinsolving thought, he might be blown out. He had been through too much to have the strength left to fight against wind and gathering cold and untold hours of flight.

"Near," said Quixx. The spider herded him forward and somehow lifted him using four legs. With a jump that made it appear that the arachnoid had springs for legs, he dropped beside his human captive. Quixx's legs stretched out. He scooped in four rings, his taloned legs securely holding him down. Kinsolving remained sitting. He held on to the rings on either side and faced forward.

The sudden surge as the pilot put full power to the repulsors crushed Kinsolving flat. When the vehicle started forward, Kinsolving knew he could not hang on for more than a few minutes. The wind ripped at his face. Cold fingers tried to pry loose his hands, and his eyes began watering. Risking his life, he swung around until he faced the rear of the vehicle. Taking the brunt of the wind across his back helped clear his watering eyes. Nothing warmed his hands.

"You are in pain?" asked Quixx.

Kinsolving could only nod. He was positive his fingers had turned gray with frostbite.

"We are near to joining the Supreme Web. Very near." The arachnoid's voice carried more than simple reassurance with it. Kinsolving heard the excitement, the sense of achievement and pride in what Quixx said. Appearing before the Supreme Web must be a significant honor, Kinsolving thought.

He huddled over, trying not to feel too miserable. He quickly decided that if he did not lose himself in misery, he would only dwell morbidly on his fate.

Still, Kinsolving thought, he had not done too badly. Interstellar Materials would never again be able to smuggle the brain burners onto Web, not with the arachnoids aware of the source of the diabolical devices. Cameron had been killed.

Kinsolving swallowed hard. He *hoped* Cameron had been killed. He had no proof. But Humbolt and the others would never escape Quixx and the spiders' justice. For that Kinsolving was happy.

But for himself? He shivered and worried and finally let his mind go completely blank. The numbness, both physical and mental, helped quell the panic and pain assaulting him from every side.

Kinsolving almost fell from the deck when the vehicle banked suddenly, then dropped vertically. Only Quixx's swift reactions and a pair of grasping legs saved him. The repulsor craft settled to within a few centimeters of the ground. Kinsolving tumbled out, thankful that he had arrived safely.

He looked up and, for a brief instant, stood speechless. "The Supreme Web," he said in a small voice. He felt as if he were in a library or a hospital and had to whisper. Loud talk would be sacrilege.

"This way," ordered Quixx. Kinsolving noticed the change in the way Quixx spoke. Authority boomed out now. He could believe that the arachnoid was a policeman in charge of the situation. Kinsolving rubbed his hands and returned some circulation. He followed as closely as possible while trying to grasp the full extent of the aerial immensity of the spiders' web.

Four spires had been erected on low hills over a shallow, lush valley. Everywhere he looked in that valley glowed dim lights of all colors. Singly, no light appeared bright. The untold thousands taken together gave a soft illumination brighter than daylight.

Each spire rose a lofty five hundred meters and swayed slightly as the winds whipped around the tops. One spire shone with an inner ruby light. Another glowed a dull emerald. A third burned with a yellow light almost too intense to stare at directly. The remaining spire stood black against the blackness of night.

But the web! The strands of web running from each of the spires were fully the thickness of Kinsolving's thigh. And from the major cables ran an eye-confusing array of smaller ones forming the pattern over the valley. The web looked like any of a thousand he had seen growing up on Earth—the difference lay in the immensity of this one.

"Why are the pylons colored like that? How are the webs spun? Artificial? What's the significance of the pattern?" he asked. Kinsolving wanted to know it all. He had the feeling that too few humans had ever seen this aspect —this vital part—of arachnoid culture.

"Tradition rules the Supreme Web," was the only answer he received.

They walked to a spot where Kinsolving saw the door inside the spires. The green spire nearest them showed a black spot that spread and grew until six spiders walked out abreast. With an agility no human could match, the arachnoids climbed unseen strands of web stuff and mounted to the web suspended between the four spires. Wave after wave came from the spire until Kinsolving wondered if any spider being remained on the face of the planet. He turned and saw a similar exodus from each of the other three spires.

Along the suspended web moved the dark wave of arachnoids.

"How long does it take?" he asked, fascinated.

"Each node will be occupied within a few minutes," said Quixx. "We must go now to our place. It is not allowed to be late. This one has the honor of being on the Web for only the fourth time. Status rises with each decision."

Kinsolving ran to keep up with the hurrying arachnoid. Quixx reached the lowest spot on the major web strand dangling between the green and ruby spires and caught a tiny cable. He began ascending almost as fast as Kinsolving could run on the ground. Kinsolving reached the spot directly under Quixx and stared. Even if he'd had a web to climb, his progress would be painfully slow in comparison.

"What do I do?" he called up to Quixx.

Kinsolving yelped as a cable whipped down and snaked around his waist. His feet sailed into the air, and Kinsolving found himself hanging upside down. Then he screamed as the cable around his waist jerked, tightened, and Quixx began reeling him in. Kinsolving flailed about before realizing that he only made it worse by struggling. He closed his eyes, but this only caused his gorge to rise. His imagination outstripped reality.

Kinsolving forced his eyes open. The ground whirled about below him as he was pulled further and further up into the Supreme Web. It took ten minutes before he came to rest just under a major strand. Quixx worked on the cable with his tiny, weak hands.

"Stand on the web. Or sit," Quixx amended, when he saw that Kinsolving had trouble just hanging on to the strand.

Kinsolving kicked and pulled up, getting one leg over the edge of the immensely thick spider strand. It took another minute of careful maneuvering before he sat beside Quixx.

"Do not shake so," the arachnoid ordered. "You disturb all within the Supreme Web."

"It's a long way to the ground." Kinsolving should not have looked; he did. Quixx had pulled him out over the valley. The ground, dancing with its parti-colored lights, was visible a kilometer below. Too visible for Kinsolving's peace of mind.

He forced his attention off the ground and onto the Supreme Web and the spider beings on it. Quixx had hinted that every intersection in the web would have an occupant. Kinsolving lost track of how many he counted. Thousands. Perhaps as many as a hundred thousand. Those nearest did not stare at him as he did at them. Their full attention focused on the distant center of the web.

"Is the arachnoid there the most important?" asked Kinsolving, gesturing toward the confluence of the web strands. He closed his eyes for a moment. The gentle, warm wind caused the strands to lift and drop precipitously. When his stomach quieted, he again looked.

"All are equal within the Supreme Web," said Quixx. "The Web is greater than any strand."

Kinsolving had the feeling that Quixx recited a catechism. He also saw the tenseness in the arachnoid's body. Quixx stood poised, as if to leap into empty space.

"The inquiry begins," said Quixx.

The reverential feeling that Kinsolving had experienced on seeing the Supreme Web heightened now. All those around him stood silent and motionless. The only faint stirrings in the web came from natural disturbances. Kinsolving fidgeted uneasily. He was acutely aware that he introduced vibrations along the strands that the others instinctively avoided.

"I am to ask you these questions," said Quixx in a voice strangely different from his normal tones.

It took Kinsolving several seconds to realize that the differences were more than simple pitch and deeper timbre. Quixx had, for the first time, referred to himself as "I."

"I need to know your involvement with those present at the Interstellar Materials warehouse, those who bring the Boxes of Delights to my planet."

Kinsolving began his story, telling of his work on Deep-dig in IM's rare earth mines, how he discovered the cerium-crystal thefts, how his inquiry had led to Gamma Tertius 4 and Chairman Fremont. Kinsolving carefully avoided mention of how Cameron had maneuvered him into a spot where he looked guilty of murder to the alien Lorr who owned Deepdig. Kinsolving definitely avoided mentioning his exile to the Lorr prison planet and his escape. Any hint that he was less than a law-abiding citizen would reflect badly on his story.

Kinsolving fell silent after concluding with the encounter with Cameron in the warehouse. He had no idea how his recitation had been received. The only sound across the vast valley was the hint of wind through the strands. Not an arachnoid moved. None spoke.

"Why do you risk your life for the natives of the planet you call Web?" asked Quixx. "I see no reason for a human thing to do such a selfless deed."

Kinsolving swallowed hard. He hardly knew where to begin. "Intelligent life, no matter its form, is important. It should not be taken lightly. It should never be taken for reasons of prejudice."

"I do not understand. All intelligent beings, by definition, must have prejudices."

"Opinions are not prejudices," Kinsolving said hotly. "Fremont and Humbolt and the others feel those races who reached the stars before humanity are deliberately holding us back. They think this is a war between all aliens and mankind." He took a deep breath and added, "They see immense financial and political gains if they can eradicate life on Web. Importation of the Boxes of Delights and their widespread use will cause immense death and debility. Genocide. They will profit from the vacuum formed by the passing of so many of your kind."

"You do not approve?"

"No. Most of those on Earth believe we can achieve equality with you and the others already among the stars through our own efforts. We can *earn* it, not *steal* it."

"Most. I need more information. Not all those human things of Earth share your feelings? Some feel as those from Interstellar Materials and Gamma Tertius 4?"

"Humans are known for diversity of belief. I do not know how many think like Fremont and the others. Some, not many. The Earth governments do not support Interstellar Materials in this mad scheme."

"I am confused. There is not a consensus of opinion of Earth beings binding to all? Peculiar. But I have experienced similar reactions in worlds nearer the rim of space controlled by me." Quixx continued, as if arguing with himself. His words came in a rapid stream and he began slurring.

Kinsolving watched as the arachnoid quivered. He glanced out over the Supreme Web. No other participant behaved in such a fashion. Kinsolving at first thought Quixx had become the focus of all the others' thoughts, a vortex for telepathic transmission. Then he discarded the idea. His hand rested on the web strand. The more Quixx rattled on, the more distinct came the vibrations in the web.

Kinsolving's eyes widened as he understood. All those on the Supreme Web communicated their opinions through minute quiverings in the strands. Some quirk of design focused those wavelike disturbances, some adding, some subtracting, until a consensus by resonance was formed. The arachnoid chosen to be the center for the responses— Quixx—spoke for the entire web.

A flash of insight told him what it would mean if the Supreme Web were disrupted. Their decision-making capabilities would be diminished. The more arachnoids using the brain burners, the fewer would actually appear on the strands.

He saw the lure of the Box of Delights. To always be on the side of right, no matter what your opinion. To be an absolute ruler in a world governed by democracy. No matter how strange the thought, to always have the mass voting with you—that was the diabolical promise of the Box of Delights.

Kinsolving doubted if Fremont or the others like Humbolt understood the impact of introducing the brain burners into the world. If they did, they would rejoice. Not only would they be destroying or crippling huge numbers of arachnoids, they also undermined the government by removing those taking part in the consensus.

"I have reached a decision in this matter," said Quixx. Kinsolving pressed his hand against the strand. He could no longer detect the high-frequency vibrations. The Supreme Web had voted and decided. "Interstellar Materials will be barred from future trading on my world. Kenneth Humbolt, Cameron and the others cited by Kinsolving will be executed. Further, all humans will be denied entry to my world for fifty revolutions."

Kinsolving felt no surge of triumph at this. He felt drained, hollow inside. Condemning those of his own world gave him no pleasure.

"I have also decided what will become of you for your part in this Stellar Death Plan of your kind, Kinsolving."

Kinsolving looked up sharply. Quixx stood and stared at him, no discernible expression on his alien face. Carefully, Kinsolving rose. If he were to be sentenced to death along with Humbolt and the others, he would accept the punishment of his feet.

Balanced on the thick strand, Barton Kinsolving waited to hear the alien condemn him to death.

CHAPTER TWENTY

BARTON KINSOLVING prepared to die. He looked at the ground and fleetingly considered jumping. The idea vanished instantly. He had not come this far to kill himself. If the arachnoids chose to execute him, let them. He had done all he could. He had saved them. His part in the Stellar Death Plan had been nothing but total opposition. Let the Supreme Web condemn him and all humans for what Fremont had done. That did not change his beliefs.

"Kinsolving," said Quixx, speaking for the entire web laden with arachnoids, "I wish to commend you."

Kinsolving almost fell as he turned in surprise. "Commend? Not condemn?"

"I do not understand how an individual can oppose the will of the majority. It is never done on Web. I am always in control as the result of careful deliberation with all of high enough status chosen to be part of the Supreme Web. However, other races can be perplexing. You have acted independently and provided me with valuable information."

"But Humbolt and the others will be executed?"

"I differ from other starfaring races in this regard. I believe that the only method for dealing with such action must be of a permanent nature."

"Death."

"Of course," said Quixx, speaking for the entire world.

"What will happen to me?" Kinsolving asked, hardly believing his good fortune. The arachnoids appreciated all he had done! Of all the aliens he had dealt with, they appreciated his sacrifices!

"I ask that you leave the planet. Quixx had rightfully

158

ordered your deportation earlier. You avoided this command. I will not punish you for this wrongful act since it is part of this peculiar independent behavior pattern you human things enjoy."

"Thank you." Kinsolving moved cautiously and regained his balance on the thick strand of web stuff. "I must be free to choose the planet. I don't want to go to Gamma Tertius 4."

"You have violated the Supreme Web of that world," said Quixx. His face screwed up in a totally inhuman expression of concentration. "But you have no such order in your pitiful life. There is much I do not understand. I must consider."

Throughout the Supreme Web the arachnoids began to ponder this strange turn. Tiny ripples moved along the strands, magnified and came rushing in to Quixx's eight legs firmly planted on the strand.

"You may not choose the planet," came the answer. "I will not send you to Gamma Tertius 4, however."

Kinsolving nodded. He did not have the strength to pursue the matter further. Just being free of Interstellar Materials' influence might be enough.

But the Stellar Death Plan still existed. One small aspect had been thwarted on Zeta Orgo 4. What did Fremont and the others plot for other worlds populated by aliens—by Bizzies, as Fremont and the other bigots called them?

Kinsolving knew that he could never stop until every last scheme had been rooted out and exposed. It might destroy IM. It might destroy him. Kinsolving did not care. This had to be done.

"Will you help me to expose IM's schemes on the other worlds?" he asked Quixx, knowing that the arachnoid still spoke for the Supreme Web.

The answer came back faster than anticipated.

"No."

"But why not?"

"That is beyond the authority of the Supreme Web. I aid other worlds if possible but do not meddle in their internal affairs. I have no certain knowledge that the Supreme Web can be of service on any other world."

"Others might need help. They probably don't know

about the Plan." Kinsolving did not add that he had no knowledge of future efforts Fremont might take now that Web lay secure and beyond the reach of the Plan for fifty years.

"Then let them learn."

The finality in Quixx's voice cut off any further protests. Kinsolving did not pretend to understand how the arachnoid mind worked. They were savage, yet had more than a streak of compassion. They came to decisions in a democratic process but could not understand individual effort and action. Kinsolving smiled wryly. They were as mysterious to him as he must be to them.

But they were all intelligent beings. They had to learn to work together.

"Down," came Quixx's usual shrill voice.

Kinsolving looked around. The spider beings left the Supreme Web by dropping down cables until it seemed that the air rained arachnoids. In a few minutes all would be gone.

"Where are we going?"

"To carry out the wishes of the Supreme Web. This one is pleased with the decision. It is to our best interest."

"What would happen if you weren't satisfied with it?"

Quixx looked startled. "Nothing. This one would not like the decision, but it would be executed, as decided by the Supreme Web."

A cable flashed out and curled around Kinsolving's waist. He tried to keep from screaming as they fell precipitously. He tried but failed. Never before had he dropped to his knees and blessed the soil for its firmness under his body.

"Come along. We go directly to the Interstellar Materials warehouse. Those responsible for introduction of the Boxes of Delights to this world are imprisoned there."

"Already?"

"There is no need to hesitate. The Supreme Web does not make mistakes. It cannot. We have penned up the human thing responsible. This one, as observer for the Supreme Web, desires to be present when the sentence is carried out."

"Is Cameron among them?"

"Identifying a particular human thing is difficult. If this is a matter of importance to you, this one shall allow you to verify before your deportation."

"Fair enough," said Kinsolving. They hiked back to the open-backed repulsor vehicle. This time Kinsolving started with his back to the wind. It helped keep down the windburn on his face, although his ears burned hotly by the time the vehicle silently descended a dozen meters from the main doors leading into the IM warehouse.

"Where are your guards?" Kinsolving asked, frowning. He saw no patrols or any other sign that Quixx had effectively cordoned off the warehouse. "You know about the escape tunnel that leads to the shed?" He pointed.

"Our electronics are superior to yours," said Quixx. "We have pinpointed the movement of everyone within. The tunnel is permanently closed."

"Electronics can be confused or even lied to."

"Yours, not ours."

Kinsolving had doubts. Cameron was a genius. The arachnoids might be advanced in microelectronics to a point he did not understand, but Cameron would. After the robotic assassination attempt after Andrianov's murder had failed so miserably, Cameron would have learned much. Kinsolving did not see the sneeringman making the same mistake twice.

No matter how much it hurt his pride, Cameron would never again underestimate the abilities of the arachnoids. And they seemed oblivious to this threat.

Kinsolving heard faint whines. He ducked down and saw Quixx's tiny pink hands working the controls of a tiny box. The whines modulated into a more melodious sound. Only then did Quixx lift two front legs and issue the order to enter the warehouse.

Kinsolving thought he had good eyesight. He gasped when hidden arachnoids rose up all around and moved in what appeared to be an undulating black carpet toward the doors. The sophisticated electronic locks never slowed their advance. Dozens—hundreds—of arachnoids boiled into the warehouse.

Straining, Kinsolving heard a tiny *beep!*

"The planetary supervisor, Kenneth Humbolt, has been

apprehended," said Quixx. "Come. This one wishes to confront him before the orders of the Supreme Web are executed."

Kinsolving had to follow at a dead run. Quixx's rolling gait had smoothed to a sleek movement faster than any human could run. Panting, Kinsolving came to a halt just outside the supervisor's office.

Inside he saw Humbolt banging his fist on a desktop. Kinsolving opened the door and heard the director's loud protests.

"You damned Bizzies have no authority to do this! IM will restrict this planet! You'll be cut off from all our rare earths. Where will your electronics industry be then? What will happen to your damned stardrive engines? They need lanthanum to operate. We'll shut you off! We'll isolate the entire damned planet!"

"They know all that, Humbolt," said Kinsolving. "They also know about the brain burners and the Stellar Death Plan. I told them."

"You—" Humbolt saw Kinsolving for the first time, then screamed and tried to throttle him. Quixx batted the director away with a front leg, almost as a human would flick a spider off his shoulder.

"I told them everything. You can't hope to kill every alien in the universe."

"Traitor," seethed Humbolt. "You're a traitor to your own species. Your name will be—"

"Forgotten," cut in Kinsolving. "But yours will be remembered. Along with Hitler and Kubioshi and even vander Leeuw. Genocide isn't the way to stop them from keeping us down—they *don't care about us.* We're nothing to them, Humbolt. We've got to earn the right to even matter. Until then, we're nothing."

"Burn in hell for this Kinsolving!"

Kinsolving settled his mind. "Quixx wanted to see the person responsible for bringing the brain burners onto Web. You're it. He's going to execute you."

Fear flashed across Humbolt's face. "The Bizzie doesn't dare! He can't! I'm an employee of IM. We have immunity!"

"He will. Where's Cameron?"

"On his way back to GT4."

Those words caused Kinsolving to sag. His worst fears had been realized. Cameron had not died. And he had passed beyond the arachnoids' power to bring him to justice.

"It might be easier for you if you're willing to confess everything, tell them how you distributed the brain burners, everything about the operation of the Plan on Web."

Humbolt opened his mouth, then froze. He held this ludicrous pose for almost a second before he began to shake uncontrollably. Humbolt fell face forward across the desk, features rigid.

Quixx's reactions carried him to Humbolt before Kinsolving could even reach out to catch the man. "This one is curious," said Quixx. "The criminal human thing has died strangely."

"Cameron!" cried Kinsolving. He did not know how, but the assassin's long, deadly hand had reached across light-years to touch Humbolt. "Check the room for robot killers."

"There is no . . ." Quixx's voice trailed off. The sudden flare of burning white light blinded Kinsolving. Tiny bits of metal stung his face and hands. He simply sat down heavily.

His vision slowly cleared. He had to rely more on hearing. The silky soft whisper of the arachnoids walking told him that many had crowded into the room.

Quixx's voice finally reassured him about the arachnoid's personal safety. "This one destroyed an electronic device—a robot. You detected its presence; this one did not. How confusing."

"What was it?" asked Kinsolving. His eyes watered.

"Unknown. Barely detectible, ultralow power use, it sent a pellet of self-contained poison into Humbolt."

"Cameron did your work for you, then," said Kinsolving.

"The Supreme Web entrusted that chore to me." Quixx sounded irritated at being robbed of the chance to execute Humbolt.

"The others are still handy," said Kinsolving. "Do it to them."

"They are already dead," came the chilling words. "This one wanted only to satisfy himself that Humbolt acted in the manner you claimed. He did. How curious."

"What now?" Tiredness flooded over Kinsolving.

"The Lorr starship arrives in orbit within seven-nineti-eths of a rotation. You will be placed in their custody and returned to their prison world."

"What?" Kinsolving shot to his feet. "But the Supreme Web, you commended me, you said I could leave, choose where I went."

"That is not so. It was agreed that you would not be returned to Gamma Tertius 4. Your lawbreaking against the Lorr is of no matter to the Supreme Web. You have received your commendation. Be content with it. We do not wish to debate the issue of your criminality with the Lorr, who have requested your return."

Kinsolving went cold inside. Better that he had dived off the web strand a thousand meters above the Supreme Web's valley.

Quixx turned and waddled from the room.

"Aren't you placing me in custody?" asked Kinsolving.

"You will go the Hall of Leave-taking for the shuttling to orbit by the Lorr. This one's task is completed satisfacto-rily." Quixx vanished without another word.

Kinsolving left the warehouse. Stacked neatly were the bodies of the humans who had worked for Interstellar Materials on Web. Kinsolving held back the impulse to fling himself on the nearest pile and just wait. He had vowed to never return to the alien prison world, but he saw no path for escaping that sorry fate. Every IM employee on Zeta Orgo 4 had been executed—and Cameron crossed the stars alive and successful in his assassination of Kenneth Humbolt.

"But they failed. Dammit, IM failed to kill everyone on Web!"

Kinsolving started walking, not caring where he went. To passively await the loose-jointed Lorr was not possible. But to fight? He had no resources.

He sank down, back to a wall, and closed his eyes.

Kinsolving's nose twitched as a gentle wind blew a strange, pleasing and familiar scent to him. His eyes shot open.

"Lark!" he cried. Not ten meters away stood Lark Versalles. Her hair had been recolored and blazed like a multi-colored beacon in the night. The photochemicals swirling just beneath her perfect skin had taken on new intensity. But it had been her distinctive perfume he had smelled.

"Hello, Bart," she said. She walked to him, almost shyly.

"What are you doing here? You shifted for Earth, to return the *von Neumann* to Rani's brother, to get away from here, to—"

"Shush," she said, placing a slender finger against his lips to silence him. She stood on tiptoe and kissed him. "I got into hyperspace and I was all alone. I missed you, so I told the ship to come back."

"You'd have to finish the trip."

She shrugged her elegant shoulders and smiled. "The ship obeyed. It's supposed to, isn't it?"

"Must have been an emergency override I missed. It brought you back to the nearest planet—Zeta Orgo 4, in this case. But what did you tell it? No, never mind."

"You're a perfect pile of debris, Bart darling," she said, stepping back to look at him. "You never did dress well, but this is disgraceful. The Earth Gala would heave you into a plasma torch if you showed up looking like this. Although I remember once when Dinky tried to—"

"Lark, we've got to leave. Now. Can we get back to the *von Neumann* and out of orbit?"

"There's nothing wrong with the ship," she said. "And the shuttle is about ready to go back. The pilot said something about not lingering, that they were chasing all the humans off-planet. I don't like their shuttle. You have to hang on to metal rings and the spacesuits aren't comfortable and the pilot is terrible."

He dragged her behind him as he ran for the shuttle. With any luck at all, he could get away and aboard the *von Neumann* before the Lorr ship attained orbit.

With a fabulous amount of luck, he could shift from Zeta Orgo 4 and leave behind the arachnoids and the Su-

preme Web and Quixx and a thwarted Stellar Death Plan.
And he could again elude the Lorr.

"Here, Bart," said Lark. With every movement, her skin
changed colors. Somehow, her hair found a complementary
shade within seconds. Her flushed face had brought out
corroded-copper green highlights in her hair. As she caught
her breath, icy blues and cool purples swirled beneath her
cheeks; the carefully shaped ends of her hair mirrored these
and then turned orange and shining gold. "Here are the
awful, smelly spacesuits,"

They looked wonderful to him. He kissed her and then
hurriedly dressed.

Lark hugged him tightly. Over the suit com she said, "I
missed you so, Bart darling. It was so *dull* without you!"

Barton Kinsolving knew that whatever happened, it
would not be dull. Not with the Lorr after him, not with the
full might of Interstellar Materials turned against him, not
with Cameron still alive. It would not be dull. Never!

A PLAGUE IN PARADISE

For Gwynne Scholz,
the naked DEA agent
falling through the ceiling,
the $13,000 kidney, being fed to
alligators,
and all the other great stories

CHAPTER ONE

"IT'S NOT POSSIBLE," Barton Kinsolving muttered to himself as he struggled with the luxury yacht's simple, foolproof controls. "The Lorr police vessel is homing in on us."

"They're following us?" Lark Versalles brushed back long strands of her fine blond hair and revealed her forehead. The glamour dyes she had injected subcutaneously whirled about in complex eddies just above her eyebrows and slowly turned different shades of purple. Kinsolving tried to decide if this color change meant the woman was agitated or if she felt only annoyance at the delay in leaving the system.

For Kinsolving, having the alien spacecraft homing in on them meant more than simple irritation at being detained. He had escaped the planet of Zeta Orgo 4 and its arachnoid inhabitants only minutes ahead of the Lorr police. It mattered little to the spiderlike creatures that he had thwarted a plan—the Stellar Death Plan—of his former employers that would have destroyed the aliens' minds. In their oddly twisted way of looking at the world, the arachnoids had not betrayed a benefactor by turning him over to the Lorr.

Kinsolving stared at the vidscreen and the dim image of the approaching Lorr spaceship. When he had worked for Interstellar Materials on the planet Deepdig as a mining supervisor, he had been wrongly implicated in the death of a Lorr agent-captain. The trial and conviction had been swift, and alien justice required exile to a prison world.

He had escaped—the only sentient being to do so. And Barton Kinsolving had become the preoccupation of every Lorr peace officer.

Even worse, those in power at IM eagerly sought him, too. They wanted nothing less than the total extinction of hundreds of alien races populating known space. Genocide. Even thinking of their hideous scheme on Zeta Orgo 4 made him shudder. He had stopped them this time. He had seen one of the IM directors killed and, for all he knew, the assassin Cameron had died, also. Kinsolving shuddered. He dared not take the killer's death as a fact. Cameron had proven himself too wily in the past to succumb to an ambush while guarded by his specially designed robots.

"They're getting closer," Lark said. The purples swirling beneath her skin faded and became light yellows, giving her a jaundiced, diseased look. Kinsolving had to interpret this as increasing dread on her part. He felt as ill as she looked.

"I'm doing all I can. The overrides on the ship make it hard to work." Not for the first time, he cursed the safety features that prevented casual access to the controls. Its former owner, Rani duLong, might have been able to get around the safeties but she had been murdered by Cameron's infernal robot killers. Kinsolving and Lark had escaped only through good luck and a small bit of skill on his part in fixing the ship's hyperspace shift engine electronics.

Kinsolving dived under the control panel and found the spots where he had shorted out the safeties once before. Small charred areas marked his successes. What might fail because of his efforts he dared not think about.

"Lark," he called out from under the panel, "what's the course indicator reading?"

"Something about, oh, it's set for Paradise!"

"I don't care where we jump as long as we do it soon. Is that the lowest numbered reading?" He had no time for complex alignment. The first star system that matched in the navigation computer would be their destination.

"Yes."

He thrust his hand upward, putting his thumb on one exposed contact and his thick index finger on another. Kinsolving screamed as pain assailed him—but the pain came not from the minute electrical current finding a least resistance path through his sweat-dampened skin but from the impact of the hyperspacial shift.

He felt as if he were falling down an infinite well. Colors more vivid than any in Lark's cosmetic arsenal spun in demented kaleidoscope patterns before—behind—his eyes, through his brain, deep into his very soul. And the sounds! He always heard phantom music, haunting, alluring. He tried to turn to face its source, but it changed as he moved. Always, it came from a different direction, a place beyond sight and hearing. Kinsolving struggled to make out the eerie tune, to put a name on it, to be able to remember it.

As always, he failed. The churning in his gut subsided. The music drifted away. The wild vortices of color collapsed and normal sight returned. With it came the light pseudogravity of shift space and an odd stench.

It took Kinsolving several seconds to realize that the skin on his fingers had burned. He jerked back, breaking the contact.

"Bart, darling, what happened?" asked Lark. Her voice carried the plaintive quality which demanded that he respond and make everything right again in her spoiled, rich universe.

"I probably ruined the control circuits." He sucked on his burned fingers to cut off the oxygen to the wounds. Crawling from under the panel, he looked up at the woman and, not for the first time, felt a surge of emotion. Putting a definition on what that emotion really was proved even more difficult than identifying the phantom music of pipes and synthesizers created during shift.

Love? He doubted it. Lark had inadvertently rescued him from the Lorr prison world. For that he owed her much. No one else had ever escaped that cruel exile. But what he felt for her transcended simple duty. He had assumed an obligation when he had allowed her to accompany him. For her, he provided a new and exciting diversion. Kinsolving wondered if Lark understood how truly dangerous it was being near him. Possibly. She was not a stupid woman.

Duty and gratitude, yes, and more: these he felt for her. And friendship. He liked her in spite of the differences in their backgrounds and outlooks. She had seen the horror Interstellar Materials sought to create by their genocidal Plan and had aided him. Deep down, though, she did not feel the commitment he did, the outrage, the stark revulsion at Cameron and IM's Chairman Fremont.

Lark Versalles skimmed through life, sampling daintily, tasting the sweet wines and never finding the bitter.

"The ship's going to need a long time in dock to fix," he said.

"Don't worry about it. My credit's still good. Especially on Paradise!"

"What is this world?" he asked, pulling himself up and buckling himself down in the pilot's acceleration couch. He only half listened to her gushing explanation as he scanned the limited controls. Most were nothing more than warning lights. The ship's on-board robot repair crew toiled to fix most minor problems. The major ones he had created required human attention and the complete equipment of an orbiting dry dock.

A quick glance at the vidscreen showed only the jumbled patterns of hyperspace. The Lorr had tracked them too quickly back in the Zeta Orgo 4 system. Something— someone—had alerted them to his presence. They had no reason to suspect this luxury yacht of harboring their prime fugitive from justice.

By choosing a world at random, Kinsolving knew he had eluded the Lorr—unless their technology far exceeded that of the humans. Could the aliens follow a starship through a shift and pinpoint its destination? Kinsolving shuddered again, a mental picture forming of them coming out of hyperspace and finding the Lorr police vessel waiting.

"... spent months there. It's photonic, Bart, darling. *Anything* you want, and I mean *anything!*"

"Paradise?"

Lark swung about and snuggled close, her long arms circling his neck. Her face blocked out the vidscreen and control panel. It wasn't a displeasing situation, but Kinsolving experienced a pang of uneasiness at being unable to watch the control panel telltales. Too many circuits aboard ship had been destroyed to grow careless.

Lark's bright blue eyes bored into his dark ones. Her lips parted slightly, sending waves of light greens radiating from her mouth in a delicate spiderweb. The woman's cheeks flushed a bright pink, then turned a more passionate red.

"We're free of them. The Lorr, IM, all of them. Let's relax and enjoy ourselves, Barton, my dearest."

She bent forward and kissed him. Kinsolving resisted slightly, thinking he saw a flashing red light on the control panel. He took a quick look and saw nothing. He had seen Lark's cheeks blazing crimson as her desire mounted. He reached out and put his strong arms around her, drew her closer. There might be better ways of passing the time in the infinite expanse of hyperspace, but Barton Kinsolving could not think what they might be. Not with a woman like Lark so close.

"Again, Bart, please," begged Lark. She knelt behind the couch and put her arms around his neck. Her soft blond hair brushed the side of his face, the sunlight-gold strands floating up in the breeze to tickle his nose. He brushed them away and reached out to press the appropriate controls on the panel.

"Time to shift back to normal space," he said.

She brightened at the idea of again being on Paradise. She swung about and dropped into the acceleration couch beside him, her hand firmly clutching his bulkier one.

Kinsolving gulped as the starship dropped from hyperspace, the full array of sensory confusion assaulting him. He strained to hear the phantom music, but heard nothing this time. In its place, he tasted metallic bitterness on the sides of his tongue, and his feet froze as if he had thrust them into a bucket of icy water. Keeping him from complaining at the shift was the firm grip Lark kept on him the entire time. Knowing that someone shared all this with him eased the burden.

The vidscreen lit up with a display of approach numbers from the Paradise Port Authority and a small picture of the planet's surface. Kinsolving frowned. Such views normally came through the on-board cameras. They were still almost fifty AUs away, a distance making such detail impossible.

"They transmit a picture of what we're going to see," Lark supplied. "Isn't it wonderful!"

"Wonderful," Kinsolving agreed halfheartedly. He didn't like the idea of the Port Authority taking control of the vidscreen. The Lorr starship might be only seconds behind and he would be unable to detect it. Another shift might be necessary; he had to know if the aliens had followed. That new shift, if required, might destroy them. He would prefer to let the Paradise dry docks refit the yacht. Too many amber and red indicator lights popped up, showing how he had abused the vessel.

He toggled the ship-to-station communicator. "Earth ship *von Neumann* desiring repair facilities."

"Attention, *von Neumann,*" came the instant response. "We are sunward less than point one AU and read your problems. Are you able to reach Paradise orbit unassisted?"

Kinsolving poked at the vidscreen controls. The Paradise Port Authority had not released the vidscreen to allow him to pick up the other ship.

"We can attain orbit unassisted. Can you release remote override on my vidscreen?"

A tiny pop of static and a man so handsome that Kinsolving had to consider him beautiful appeared on the vidscreen. "Captain Luxor of the Paradise Assistance Fleet," he said by way of introduction. "Most of the ships coming to our planet like the view of the surface. I understand your problem, however."

"Oh, we're going to land on Paradise," cut in Lark. "I've enjoyed my other stays here."

"But we do have some on-board problems," Kinsolving finished.

"Do you have a Pleasure Code?" asked the captain of the other ship.

"It's the same as for Galaxy Pharmaceuticals and Medical Techtronics—GPMT."

Kinsolving stared at Lark. Was she lying? Then he realized that he knew little about her background. She never spoke of her family, of former lovers, of friends. Always Lark Versalles lived for the instant. Let it pass and it was as if she forgot.

"Lark Versalles," came Captain Luxor's reply, "welcome back to Paradise. We will happily escort you to Almost Paradise."

"Almost Paradise?" Kinsolving asked the woman.

"Their orbiting station. Paradise caters to all races. Almost Paradise allows time for quarantine, if necessary, acclimation, a chance to anticipate all that can come true on the surface."

"If they can repair the ship." Kinsolving went cold inside when Captain Luxor's image flickered on the screen, then firmed again. The captain had cut for transmission, probably to the main data banks on Paradise, and had not wanted Kinsolving to know.

"You are aboard a ship licensed to the sister of Aron duLong, chairman of Terra Computronics. Is Rani aboard?"

"She's just loaned us the ship," Kinsolving said quickly, turning even colder inside. Her body still rode in the main storage hold of the *von Neumann*, secure in a vacuum coffin.

Kinsolving did not want to consider a murder charge placed against him on yet another world.

"GPMT credit will suffice," said the captain. With those words, Kinsolving got a clearer picture of Paradise. If someone could pay, any trouble could be smoothed over.

"Should I dock or will you send out a grapple tug?" he asked of Luxor.

"We have already fastened lines to your hull plates."

Kinsolving tried to verify but found the sensors on the composite hull to be malfunctioning, like so much aboard the yacht. He had not heard or felt the vibrations from the magnetic grapples being attached to the special tug plates, but his Doppler radar showed a closing vector on Almost Paradise impossible without the lines.

The ship docked gently, barely jarring them. Lark shot out of her couch, her face radiant with every color of the rainbow. Not even trying to hide her excitement, Lark pulled on his arm and said, "Hurry, Bart, darling. There's *so* much to do aboard Almost Paradise. If it wasn't so much fun on-planet, I'd spend all my time on the station."

Kinsolving followed reluctantly. His bleak mood contrasted sharply with Lark's ebullience. So much needed to be done and he had no clear idea how to accomplish it. Cameron had killed the Lorr agent-captain; how could Kinsolving clear himself? IM had been prevented from burning out the brains of the aliens on Zeta Orgo; did they pursue their mad scheme on other worlds? Probably. He needed to find out for certain. The aliens might not know

of the danger posed by Interstellar Materials. They might
even deny any human capable of such intricate planning,
but Kinsolving knew. And he had to prevent Fremont and
the others from mass killing, whether the aliens appreciated his sacrifices or not.

The airlock cycled open. To his surprise, Kinsolving's
ears did not pop from poor pressure-matching between ship
and station. Someone had taken the trouble to mesh perfectly. A cool, scented breeze blew inward and peaceful
pale green lights shone on a tastefully decorated reception
area.

"Welcome, Lark," greeted a petite woman, hands held
out for Lark to grip. They kissed chastely. Something about
the small woman's attitude told Kinsolving that, for all the
overt friendliness, she was only an employee. Her smile
came too quickly. Every detail about her neat, conservative
dress spoke of carefully chosen effect. Kinsolving held
back asking her what she would have worn had she been
given a chance to choose her own clothing. He guessed
that her tastes paralleled Lark's. Something flashy, something skimpy, something scandalous.

But to dress like that in Lark's presence would have put
the woman in competition. Kinsolving had to wonder how
the greeting would have differed if he had arrived without
Lark.

"Welcome to you, too, sir," the woman said, her small
hand cool against his. She shook hands firmly, quickly,
then backed away without making eye contact. Her every
action was one of deference.

"Please accept my personal apologies about accommo-
dations aboard Almost Paradise. We cannot put you into
the Royal Suite because of a special conference on-planet."

"Conference?" Kinsolving asked.

"Terra Recreations operates Paradise as a restful envi-
ronment where any pleasure is available," she said, more
robotic than human as she slipped into her sales speech.
"From time to time we allow alien races the use of our
facilities for interspecies diplomatic conferences. Currently, we are honored with seven different species
on-planet while they conduct business with Earth

representatives on trade and other matters of mutual interest."

"But the Royal Suite." Lark pouted. "I had my heart set on staying there again."

"Oh, Lark," the small woman said, sounding genuinely sorry, "we just can't. The Trekan ambassador requires time to acclimate himself to Paradise's atmosphere. The Royal Suite is the only one suitable for complex gas exchange."

"It doesn't matter," said Kinsolving. "We're not going to demand anything that lavish." He glared at Lark when she started to protest his peasant attitudes.

"I'm so glad you understand, sir," said the woman. For the first time, her pale gray eyes locked with his dark ones. Kinsolving tried to read some message in that gaze and failed. He felt, however, that he had been thoroughly examined and found wanting.

"You do have *something* suitable, don't you?" asked Lark. "We've been cooped up in the ship for ever so long."

"Will the Xanadu Suite be adequate for your needs?" the woman asked. From the color shifts in Lark's cosmetic dyes, Kinsolving saw that the answer was a resounding yes.

"We'll need repairs done on the ship," said Kinsolving. "We have special cargo, though, and I'd appreciate it if the workmen didn't disturb anything in the hold."

"Sir, our workers, both robotic and human, are always discreet." She made it sound as if Kinsolving had mortally insulted her.

"Good." He did not trust himself to say anything more. This wasn't his world. Lark Versalles fit in perfectly and he stood out like a nova in the night. Kinsolving trailed along as the two women went down a long, curving corridor leading to the Xanadu Suite.

They entered an immense, lavishly furnished lounge area that seemed all the larger because it was deserted. A small noise alerted Kinsolving. He turned to his right in time to see a man duck from sight behind a long, imported Earth oakwood bar. Kinsolving started to go after the man but Lark called for him.

He looked back and failed to catch sight of the man again. Kinsolving tried to shrug it off. Another servant, perhaps. But the brief glimpse Kinsolving had got belied that.

Barton Kinsolving caught up with Lark and their servant-guide, even more uneasy than he had been before.

CHAPTER TWO

CAMERON'S PALE GRAY EYES flickered open and light painfully assaulted his optic nerves. The man lay still, not moving a muscle—unable to move. Panic welled up within him but Cameron fought it down. There had to be an explanation for his paralysis, for the light in his face, for the odd odors causing his nostrils to flare.

Smell—antiseptics. Light—disinfectant UV. Paralysis. —life-coma.

Memory flooded back now as the ocean of drugs in his body began to ebb. He had been injured on Zeta Orgo 4.

Damn Kinsolving!

A voice farther away than infinity said, "Response. The reading went off-scale."

"Must be a residual thought rising," said another voice.

Cameron concentrated. And remembered. He had been in the Interstellar Materials warehouse on ZOo and had laid a trap for the meddling former mining supervisor. Kinsolving had walked directly into the trap. But he had turned the brain burner against Cameron's robot. Short circuits. Power surges. Spikes strong enough to fry delicate artificial intelligence circuits. Cameron remembered the sight of his robots gyrating wildly and exploding. Some had crashed into walls while others had simply ceased functioning.

His heart pumped firmly now. Blood rushed through sleeping arteries. Oxygen burned in his lungs and he tried to cough, to choke, to breathe, to steal back life from the induced coma.

"More response. He's a strong one, coming out of the life-coma this fast."

"Son of a bitch hates harder than anyone I ever knew. That's what's bringing him around. Bet on it."

"You'd just be throwing your money down a black hole.

I know him. I had to repair him after his lab caught fire a couple years ago."

Cameron listened to the idle chatter. Memory returned fully now. He knew the two doctors who worked to pull him through from the other side of death. The life-coma had been necessary to return him to Gamma Tertius 4. The medical facilities on the arachnoids' planet had been unable to give him the treatment required to insure full recovery.

Cameron's lip twitched into a sneer. What did the damned Bizarres know of medicine, anyway? The Bizzies could never heal a human. Such art lay far beyond their abilities. He was better off back on GT4 in the hands—real hands!—of human and human-designed robotic doctors.

"Full response. He ought to be out of the life-coma now," came the disembodied voice, no longer distant.

"I am out of it, fool," Cameron protested. His voice came out as a weak mewling.

"He's vectored home to us," said the other, with some satisfaction. "Nothing more to do now but wait." Cameron felt a hand on his shoulder that was supposed to reassure him. "You'll be up and around in another week. Just rest now."

Cameron heard footsteps leaving. The brightness still hammered at the far side of his eyelids. He turned his head sideways, the effort sending pain shooting up and down his spine. He opened his eyes. At first he saw only white; he peered into a pillow. Cameron turned his head back in the direction of the light. The actinic glare dazzled him but he saw the room beyond.

Robotic equipment filled the tiny compartment. He had been given over to machines. Cameron relaxed. He understood robots. He trusted them. They were his faithful servants. His. Only his.

He slipped into a quiet, restful sleep.

"Chairman Fremont sent me," the bulky, powerful man said without preamble. Cameron forced himself to turn to face Metchnikoff. The IM director had not learned to temper his harsh voice with honeyed words to soothe and lull before betrayal. This was his only failing, as far as Cameron knew.

"I can report to you without fear of breaching security?" Cameron asked, his voice soft and polite.

"Dammit, of course you can. Fremont is in poor health. He requested a full report of how badly you botched the distribution of the brain burners."

"I carried out my orders to the letter," snapped Cameron, tiring of Metchnikoff. "If you truly represented Fremont, you would know that." The sight of the powerful man's eyes narrowing told Cameron that Metchnikoff had not been sent; he was seeking information for his own use.

"He wanted Humbolt dead," Metchnikoff said, more to himself than to Cameron.

"I had hoped you would bring word of my election to the board of directors to replace the unfortunate and inept Mr. Humbolt," said Cameron. A buzzing in his ears and recurring dizziness prevented him from sitting up in the automated bed. Dozens of threadlike tubes fed him, removed bodily wastes, kept his immune system at a peak for the operation scheduled later this day.

Metchnikoff sneered. "You? On the board? Never!"

"It would be such a fine token of esteem from Chairman Fremont. Recognition of my services on Bizzie worlds." Cameron's eyes flickered slightly. A gnat-sized aerial robot that had been resting on the ceiling activated and became airborne. A second blink would send this minute assassin into Metchnikoff's ear. The robot had been ordered to use a tiny laser to drill through the eardrum and find its way into its victim's brain. There, it would do as much damage as possible until its power source failed.

Cameron estimated that it would need only microseconds to destroy Metchnikoff's brain. How dare he insult the man who had Fremont's complete trust!

Unless . . .

Cameron stirred and tried to sit up. Political changes occurred constantly on Gamma Tertius 4. Had Fremont's health failed to the point that the drugs that kept him alert and alive no longer worked? Fremont was a frail old man, but Cameron had not expected any major power shifts in the few weeks he had been stranded on the Bizzie planet.

"You're being operated on this afternoon?" asked Metchnikoff.

"There is still pressure on points in my brain. Internal bruises. Subdermal hemostasia."

"You will become brain damaged—dead—without the operation," Metchnikoff said, again as if thinking out loud.

"Why did you come to visit? Not to cheer me with your presence," snapped Cameron. He almost started his robotic killer toward Metchnikoff's ear. Metchnikoff threatened him; he could justify the director's death later.

"You assume too much, Cameron. You are not a director. IM needs your services, but in a lesser capacity."

"Fremont needed me."

"As a trained killer only. Jump through the hoop like a trained beast. Sit up, roll over, kill." Metchnikoff saw the sudden flash of hatred boil in Cameron's eyes. "Don't think to use your pitiful little robot on me."

Cameron blinked.

The gnat glinted in the actinic glare of the UV disinfectant light as it arrowed for Metchnikoff. It emitted a tiny *pop!* before it found its target. Metchnikoff had surrounded himself with a damping field that prevented the small robot from reaching him.

"Anything larger I can destroy in other ways," Metchnikoff said, sneering. "For instance, an emotionless robot like you. All I need to do is reach over and squeeze." Metchnikoff's heavy fingers closed on Cameron's windpipe. He struggled to pull the choking hands away but his strength fled quickly. From the corner of his eye Cameron saw red warning lights begin to flash. His vital signs faded.

The intense pressure on his throat eased but the hands remained. Through the thunder of blood pounding in his own ears, Cameron heard Metchnikoff say, "We can aid one another. There is no need for trust, just respect. You are good at what you do, but you can never assume a directorship. I'll see to that. But you can gain more than you have now, if we work together."

"Stop," moaned Cameron.

"Ah, he speaks. But does he listen? I think so. You, Cameron, are an expert killer. But you are mortal and can become the victim of your own clever mechanisms." The fingers tightened slightly, then relaxed. "You might die now and no one would question the cause of your death."

"What do you want, Metchnikoff?"

"Your cooperation. Fremont is ill much of the time. I need support to gain control of IM. I am going to be the next chairman of the company." Metchnikoff removed his strangling fingers and stepped back. "You can stand behind and help me, or stand in front of me and be crushed under my heel. Which is it to be?"

The room spun in ever-widening circles. Deep inside his brain Cameron felt horrible, numbing pressure mounting. His nose began to bleed and a black curtain pulled across Metchnikoff's leering face. Before he sank into unconsciousness, Cameron heard the emergency alarms ringing —his secretly installed emergency alarms.

Metchnikoff had disconnected the hospital's.

"You're looking better, Cameron," the tall, dark woman said. She peered down at him with cold, flinty eyes. Maria Villalobos perched on the edge of his bed, reminding Cameron of a vulture waiting for its dinner to die.

"The operation went well," he said.

"I spoke with the doctors. One was very annoyed that you insisted on having . . . protection during the operation."

"My robots didn't bother the surgeons. They insured my survival." Cameron smiled wickedly. If any of the doctors had attempted to let him die while on the operating table, his assassin robots would have ended the doctor's career quickly. He had not been hesitant about letting the men and women know that, either.

"I would not have let Metchnikoff murder you." Villalobos reached out and touched icy fingers to his cheek. "I still need you."

"Am I nothing more than a replaceable part in your machine?" he asked. Metchnikoff irritated him; Maria Villalobos fascinated him. Cameron had to admit to lust for the woman. What would she be like in bed? Could any man fire her passions or did Villalobos concentrate solely on rising in Interstellar Materials' power structure?

"You are more," she assured him, a touch of irony in her tone. "You performed admirably on ZOo. Humbolt never knew that Fremont ordered you to kill him."

"I could have done more about the brain burners if I'd been in charge. The arachnoid Bizzies will never allow IM on-planet again. We had a good chance to remove an entire planet of them and Humbolt allowed it to slip away."

"Humbolt was a fool."

"Why wasn't I elected to replace him on the board of directors?" Cameron swung his legs over the side of the bed. Most of the medical support tubes had been removed, and he felt more alive than he had since arriving home."

"Director Liu and I discussed the matter," Villalobos said, her cold, dark eyes unwavering. Cameron knew she could lie and never show even a small muscular twitch to betray herself, but he sensed that she spoke the truth this time. "We did not have the support to elect you."

"Am I obligated to Liu for this?"

"You never cared for Liu, I know," she said. Villalobos shook out her long, lustrous black hair and let it fall in a cascade of raven softness. She smiled. Cameron kept his breathing under control. The look in her eyes, the way her tongue delicately touched and wetted her lips, the set of her body, all promised more than an IM directorship.

Why? What did Maria Villalobos want from him? And would he give it?

Cameron walked around the small cubicle on weak legs. Strength returned slowly, but he hid his weakness from the woman. Like the others in the company, like all those who believed implicitly in the Stellar Death Plan, weakness was always rewarded with death.

He wanted more from her than a new way to die.

Some ingenious use of technology allowed the woman to open the tight collar of her severe suit without touching it. Cameron found it impossible not to watch the slow parting of the fabric as it revealed Villalobos' swanlike neck, the warm flesh of her chest, the valley between her breasts, the firm swells of her breasts.

"We needed to maintain a position of strength for a new project. I felt that any . . . extraneous matters might jeopardize efforts to further the Plan."

"A new assault on the Bizzies with the brain burners?"

"Something more," she said. Villalobos leaned back on the bed. The suit parted further, revealing more of a breast until a dark aureole showed. Cameron found it difficult to keep his mind on the woman's words rather than her body. How many others had she lured into such a trap? Many, he decided.

"You need me to assist in the field?"

"Something like that," she said. "This is a joint effort between several companies. You know how touchy such matters can become. Each has its own method for advancing the Stellar Death Plan. We have decided to abandon the Bizzie brain burners in favor of a different approach, a biological approach."

"One initiated by GPMT?" Cameron guessed.

"GPMT is involved slightly. Our direct contact is with Terra Recreations, however."

Cameron frowned. He did not understand how an entertainment conglomerate entered the grand scheme for the elimination of all aliens and their humiliating treatment of humans.

"Three companies makes it too involved."

Villalobos dismissed his objection with the wave of her hand. "You failed on ZOo. We have to find something other than the brain burners."

"*I* failed!" cried Cameron. "It was Humbolt. All Fremont asked of me was to remove Humbolt, and I did."

"Then there's the matter of Barton Kinsolving," she went on, as if she hadn't heard.

"He's dead. He could not have escaped my robot sentries."

"No body was found."

"I've seen the repots. The damned Bizarres prevented examination of the warehouse after they found Humbolt dead. IM personnel were barred from the entire planet."

"That's not important at the moment. I just wanted you to realize that there were reasons for the opposition to your election to the board." Villalobos swung her long, sleek legs up and rested fully on the bed. "Fremont would look upon your promotion favorably if we succeed in this new venture."

"What is it?" He found himself intrigued by the way her hem hiked up to mid thigh. It was almost as if neckline and hem were in a race to touch at her waist and leave her vulnerable and exposed.

If Maria Villalobos could ever be described as vulnerable.

"A virus that attacks only Bizzies. Our mines on Askerath produce the only mineral that the virus will incubate in. Once released, it destroys aliens but allows humans to mingle with the infected at no risk. When the last Bizzie is dead, the plague dies out."

"We can take over entire planets."

"IM will profit," she agreed. "And so can I. So can we. We're of a kind, Cameron, you and I."

He looked at her and the wanton lust in her eyes. The suit parted completely and left her seductively naked to the waist. The skirt began opening. For him.

"Fremont won't live forever. IM needs new strength," she said. "Strengths that we can give it."

Cameron sat on the bed, then allowed her to pull him down. Even though the operation had enervated him, Cameron discovered the strengths within himself that Villalobos spoke of.

She was everything he had imagined—and more.

CHAPTER THREE

"ISN'T IT SIMPLY PHOTONIC!" squealed Lark. She spun around, arms outstretched as she took in the immense Xanadu Suite. Kinsolving wondered what the Royal Suite looked like if this was a "lesser quality" room. "Watch me. You'll love this, Bart, darling."

Lark took a deep breath, composed herself, then ran and jumped onto the immense bed dominating the center of the room. She landed feetfirst on the bed and sprang into the air. Kinsolving took an involuntary step forward to catch her as she somersaulted through the air toward a bulkhead. He need not have bothered. Hidden lenses picked up her action and robotic controls whirred into quick motion to lower a soft pad on the wall.

Lark hit, squealed again with joy and bounced back. She landed on her feet and stumbled into Kinsolving's outstretched arms.

"We're watched constantly?" he asked. Kinsolving tried to find the vidcams and failed. They were expertly hidden.

"Anything you want, just ask. They listen and they'll deliver." To demonstrate, Lark said, "Food: something gooey and tasting good, like vanilla or *denba* spice, perhaps. And hot. I want it heat hot but not spice hot. No need to worry about protein and those dreary things. What else?" She looked at Kinsolving, who frowned. She kissed him and then ordered, "I want the food delivered. Now."

Kinsolving jerked about, Lark still hanging around his neck, to see a small door opening in the far bulkhead. A metal tray laden with steaming, aromatic food hovered on a magnetic field.

"See?" she said. "Anything you want. Anything."

Lark kissed him. He started to pull back, the thought of spying eyes making him uneasy. Lark prevented any such precipitous move. For several seconds, they kissed. She finally broke it off and looked up into his dark eyes, smil-

ing broadly. "Let's eat!" Lithely, she spun from his arms
and went to the food tray, took it and placed it on a more
substantial table. Kinsolving joined her, his own enthusiasm for Almost Paradise not matching Lark's.

As he ate he carefully studied the sumptuous room. The
decks were covered with soft, springy green fabric that, on
first glance, looked like natural grass. No real growing
plant, however, had ever been manicured into such perfection of texture and eye-soothing color. The oyster-white
walls curved upward as if they sat within a real pleasure
dome. Kinsolving almost expected Coleridge to enter and
begin reciting his poem.

The furnishings were few but elegantly carved from natural woods. Some Kinsolving recognized. Others he
guessed to be from alien worlds. Impossible to ignore was
the circular bed with its twisted, white driftwood head-
board and elaborately turned bedposts. Nowhere did he see
a vidcamera or other electronics.

"I don't like the idea of someone spying on us all the
time," he said.

"Oh, Bart, darling, you're such a black hole when it
comes to these things. You can drain the good times away
so fast. Why do you think anyone *cares* what we do or
don't do? They are our servants, not our keepers."

Kinsolving did not dispute this, but other disquieting
thoughts fleetingly crossed his mind. Had the work crews
found Rani duLong's body in the vacuum coffin? The Lorr
had proven more tenacious in their attempts to return him
to the prison world than he'd have thought. He had injured
their pride in being the only escapee. Should he expect
them soon?

His mind took other turnings. Paradise catered to
humans and aliens. If he grounded, he might be able to
find an alien willing to argue his case with the Lorr. Cameron had killed the agent-captain. Kinsolving thought that
he might have gained easy acquittal if he had realized the
gravity of his position—and that Interstellar Materials
plotted against him because they needed a scapegoat.

Damn the Stellar Death Plan and all those working for
its brutal ends!

"Are we allowed to talk to the other guests?"

"Here in Almost Paradise?" asked Lark around a mouthful of food.

He nodded. "Or down on-planet."

"Anything that spins your rotor. Paradise is a *pleasure* planet. They cater to your every whim."

He smiled at her. How lovely she looked. The faint pinkish glow in her cheeks might come from the cosmetic dyes injected beneath her skin or from true excitement. He didn't care. Lark Versalles was exotic and innocent, sophisticated—a gorgeous package of contradictions.

"You're all the whim I need," he said.

"Why, thank you, Barton. No man has ever said anything quite that nice to me before." She smiled wickedly. "But then, you haven't been to Paradise yet. You might find amusements that make me pale in comparison."

"I doubt it."

"Wait," she said. "I never tire of the world. Anything you want, really want deep down inside, is yours. They always seem to know and give it to you."

Again Kinsolving twitched at the idea of being under constant surveillance. "Let's explore," he said, pushing away from the meal. Kinsolving had eaten little of the tasty food, yet found himself completely sated. Such a miracle product would have brought billions on the commercial market. Starships had little room for storage, yet often required vast quantities of food and water for the crews and passengers. Reducing the bulk of edibles might allow larger engines and faster travel times.

Kinsolving shook his head sadly. Even increasing the speed of a human starship by fifty percent would still make them seem like snails against the alien stargoing vessels. The aliens used a different drive mechanism, a different mathematics to thwart the speed limit of light—and they refused to share the secret with any human.

Sometimes, in the dim, distant recesses of his mind, Kinsolving wondered why he opposed IM and Chairman Fremont and the others. The aliens *did* treat Earth as a second-rate world. They *did* sneer at humans as being less than civilized.

But Kinsolving had seen the nobility among them. They did not deserve to be eradicated totally. No man, no company, no species should be allowed to obliterate entire worlds. The Stellar Death Plan evoked genocide, not cooperation. Those twisted minds conceiving of the Plan had refused to see that humanity was a recent addition to starfaring races. Hard work, winning confidence, improvement in all areas, those were the entry codes to the aliens' universe, not death and mass destruction. The one professor that had influenced him the most in college, Dr. Delgado, had been positive that mankind would one day be accepted as an equal.

Kinsolving believed that.

"You look distant, Bart. Are you feeling ill? Sometimes the air in Almost Paradise is changed to accommodate other races. Why, I can't say, but it is."

"I'm fine," he assured her. "Let's explore."

Lark grabbed his hand and pulled him behind her like a small child trailing his mother. "You'll *love* it. But don't get too attached. There's so much more to do on-planet. This is just the appetizer before the main course."

Kinsolving blinked as Lark led him along the curving corridors of the space station. He might have walked into a museum. Masterpieces from a score of worlds decorated the bulkheads. He could barely get Lark to pause and look at some. The old Earth polages done by an artist named Austine particularly impressed him.

"These are fabulous," he said. "I've seen similar work on Earth, but nothing this fine."

"Oh, Bart, darling, this is *nothing*. Come on!"

She tugged and he followed, his eyes lingering on the flowing, changing images and colors of the polarized montages. When they emerged into a large common room, he caught his breath and held it. Never had Kinsolving seen such grandeur. The ceiling had been removed—or so it seemed. The vast star-dotted Milky Way arced across the room, undimmed by atmosphere or light pollution. Just staring at the stars would have satisfied him, but the room held so much more.

"Anything you want, Barton, anything," Lark whispered. He shared her reverential attitude. It seemed a blasphemy to speak in normal tones in this room. The artwork dotting the room had come from myriad worlds. Even in the largest of Earth's museums he had never seen such artistry and genius.

"The finest creators in the galaxy have contributed to this display," came a soft voice at his elbow. Kinsolving jumped, startled from his rapt appreciation. The woman behind him took away speech. Lark Versalles was gorgeous. This woman was . . . more.

It took him several seconds to understand why. He turned wary when he decided where he had seen her before. She looked a great deal like Ala Markken, his lover, his betrayer. Ala had allowed Cameron to implicate him in the murder on Deepdig. Ala had tried to kill him in the mines. Ala had become a conspirator in the Stellar Death Plan.

Barton Kinsolving still loved her. And before him was a woman who touched him with the subtle but powerful similarity in their appearances.

Lark tugged at his arm and whispered, "Who is she supposed to be?"

"What?" he said, startled at the question.

"They've run a memory scan on you. She must mean something to you or they wouldn't have taken the trouble to—"

"She's been made up to look like Ala!" he exclaimed. "They made her up?"

"Ala," said Lark, as if the name burned her tongue. "Very common name." Lark turned and wandered off before Kinsolving could stop her.

"Who are you?" he demanded of the woman who looked subtly like Ala Markken.

"Whoever you want me to be. Call me Sheeda."

"Is that your name? Or did you adopt it like you did that face?" He spoke sharply and immediately regretted it.

"Don't be cruel to me," Sheeda said, tears forming at the corners of her soft brown eyes. "I meant no harm. They told me you would be pleased."

"They don't know me well enough." Kinsolving touched his forehead as if he expected to find electrodes attached.

"Almost Paradise tries to give the guest whatever he wants most. I've failed. They . . . they won't be pleased with me."

"Wait," Kinsolving said, stopping the woman as she turned to leave. "What will they do to you?"

"Nothing."

"You're lying." He lifted her firm chin and stared into the oddly tinted eyes. Something about them struck him as wild—and not quite human. For all the facial similarities to Ala, the differences overwhelmed them now that he looked closely. Soft waves of brunette hair fell away from Sheeda's face in the same style that Ala wore, but the texture lacked luster.

The human luster.

"No," Sheeda said softly. "I am not human."

"What!" Kinsolving started. He bit back the demeaning question and started over. "Which planet do you call home?"

"We're not supposed to speak of such matters. I am hired to be for you and nothing more. Many humans do not like the idea of . . ." Sheeda's voice trailed off.

"Of a chameleon alien assuming the shape of a loved one?" Kinsolving shared that distaste, but he could not fault Sheeda for what the owners of Paradise considered normal treatment of guests. She was as much a victim as he was of the cruel masquerade.

"I am from the world we call Onar."

"Never heard of it."

"Most humans haven't," Sheeda said. A sibilance in her words again shook Kinsolving. Ala never spoke this way. But Sheeda from Onar did.

"Are you a chameleon or did they perform surgery to . . . to achieve this face?"

"I have limited muscular control over my features. All Onarians do. It makes life interesting being with us. We can do things no other race can." Sheeda pressed close. He caught the faint, sweet, exciting scent she wore. Kinsolving took a half step back; he recognized the aphrodisiac and was unprepared to deal with the consequences.

"Are you sending me back?"

"You said they'd punish you."

"Demote me. Terra Recreations is not a cruel employer. I have worked hard to achieve the status of entertainer. I began work on Almost Paradise as a shipboard helper."

Kinsolving looked around the room, pulling his attention away from the starry rainbow above him and the eerie feeling that he stood exposed to the harsh infinity of space.

He caught sight of Lark with a pair of men across the room. She laughed and clung to one man, her cosmetic dyes flowing in patterns Kinsolving made out even at this distance. He had seen such complexity in her before. Lark Versalles had again found her element and enjoyed herself immensely.

"Do you know other aliens?" he asked. "Captain Luxor said that a conference was in progress on-planet."

"Do you . . . prefer aliens to those of your kind? You are not the first," Sheeda said, "but it is the first time I have ever heard a human so openly state this preference."

"Not sexually," Kinsolving said quickly. "I want to talk to them. I need to explain certain things to someone with influence."

"There are several ambassadors meeting."

"The Trekan ambassador is in the Royal Suite," Kinsolving said. "Tell me about him."

Sheeda shrugged. "I know little of Treka. My specialty is Earth. Few of your kind detect the differences so quickly. Few want to. It is better to relax and indulge your fantasies. I am expert at that." She drew long fingers along Kinsolving's cheek. Again he caught the aphrodisiac scent of her perfume. That chemical stimulus with the closeness to Ala's appearance should have been enough. Kinsolving thought for most men coming to Paradise that it would be.

Under other circumstances, it would have been true paradise for him, too. But not now. Time worked against him. He needed to warn others of the Stellar Death Plan. Only when the aliens truly believed that IM controlled resources capable of clandestinely destroying entire worlds would he be free of his burden.

Such an alliance might even be adequate to clear him of the Lorr murder conviction.

"How do I meet the Trekan ambassador?" he asked.

"He is undergoing acclimation therapy to prepare him for on-planet meetings," Sheeda said. "It might be an intrusion into his fantasy to introduce a human."

"But you'll do it?" He saw the flow of emotion across Sheeda's face as she wrestled with the moral dilemma.

"I am entrusted with pleasing you, but I cannot displease another in doing so."

"Show me to the Royal Suite. Nothing more. Let me

assume all responsibility." Kinsolving glanced back at Lark, who had forgotten him. She and the two men had sunk down to a soft couch. Kinsolving couldn't tell what they were doing, but a long, naked leg kicked lightly in the air—Lark's.

"If that is your wish, I will do it."

They walked along the art-strewn corridors until Kinsolving got lost in the complex maze. It seemed that every few meters a connecting shaft joined the main hall at a strange angle. The station's curvature also added a dimension to his confusion until he relied solely on Sheeda's homing instincts.

She stopped suddenly. A brief frown crossed her face. "There," she said. "The door with the engraved platinum studs. The Trekan ambassador is within."

"Thank you. There's no need to wait," he said, "unless you want to." Kinsolving was not sure if he wanted Sheeda waiting for him or not. A part of him begged for her to agree, to give even tacit support. Another part told him that she might find herself in deep trouble if his unannounced meeting did not fare well.

"I'd best leave," she said. In that moment she both looked and sounded exactly like Ala Markken. A lump formed in Kinsolving's throat. He nodded briskly, then left her in the center of the corridor.

He stood before the platinum-studded door, his hand almost touching the annunciator. Every second would count if the Trekan allowed him an interview. He had no idea how the alien would respond to his story—or if the ambassador would even listen. Kinsolving swallowed hard. He knew little about Treka and relied only on the being's position. Anyone sent as an ambassador had to have some standing in the alien community.

Kinsolving faced the prospect of the alien immediately summoning the Lorr to return him to the prison world.

He knew the risk and had to take it. Alerting the aliens to the potential evil of the Plan outweighed all personal considerations. He could not allow billions of intelligent beings to perish because of bigotry.

He touched the annunciator and heard a faint chiming deep within the suite. At the same instant he caught a reflection off the polished surface of a door stud.

Kinsolving spun and ducked—too late. A heavy blow struck him on the side of the head. He sank to his knees, turning enough to avoid a second blow. He lifted arms that had turned to lead. A kick landed squarely in his belly. As he doubled over a third blow crunched into the base of his skull. The universe again became populated with blazing stars.

Then all slipped into velvet blackness.

CHAPTER FOUR

BARTON KINSOLVING moaned and tried to roll onto his back to ease the pressure on his neck. He moved but the pain increased. He lifted his hand and banged it against a hard surface. Slowly forcing away the pain and trying not to panic, he opened his eyes. Dim light filtered through a vent set high on the bulkhead providing barely enough illumination to see. He reached out and ran his hands along the walls.

He found no opening. Stifling the waves of red pain washing through his head and body, he turned and sat with his back against one cool wall. He could not stretch out his legs in the cramped compartment. Forcing his feet out, he squirted himself up to a standing position. The chamber proved hardly wider than his shoulders but much higher than he could reach.

Kinsolving jumped, trying to grab the vent and pull himself up to peer out. He missed by centimeters. A second jump failed by even more. His strength faded fast. Panting, he bent forward, hands on knees. His head rested against the cool bulkhead.

"What is this place?" he wondered aloud. After he recovered, he tried once more. This time his stubby fingers found a grip on the vent grill. Kinsolving kicked and struggled and pulled himself up. He looked out into a larger compartment filled with heavy machinery. It took him several seconds to identify the waste disposal equipment.

His fingers began to throb with the pain of supporting his entire weight. Kinsolving gritted his teeth and shook the vent as hard as he could, trying to dislodge it. All he accomplished was losing his grip and tumbling back into the small chamber.

Kinsolving had been a mining engineer most of his adult life. The equipment outside he recognized as providing the gaseous and solid waste disposal for Almost Paradise. The function of the compartment he found himself trapped in proved too esoteric. He had no clue to its purpose, even after examining it carefully.

His fingers found a small elastomer air seal at the bottom of the chamber, and he thought he saw a similar seal around the ceiling but it was too high for him to be certain.

"Someone put me in here. No doors or other apparent openings except for the vent. That's got to be the way out." Kinsolving decided to worry about who had attacked him later. If he failed to escape, this tiny compartment might become his coffin. He had no food or water and, although the air coming through the vent seemed adequate, the seal at the bottom of the chamber worried him. Engineers never put in seals unless they were needed.

Jumping again gained him a view out into the equipment room. He shouted to attract attention. His cries were drowned by the bull-throated rumbles of the equipment as it worked. His fingers began to slip and cramp again. Kinsolving worked them deeper into the vent's mesh grill. He didn't want to injure those fingers; bloodied, they would turn slippery and prevent him from hanging on for more than a few seconds.

He pressed his face against the grill and tried to study the machinery closer to the bulkhead. He blanched when he saw the multiloader next to the vent. Kinsolving dropped back to the floor of his small chamber.

The loader filled his tiny prison with one of three kinds of waste: solid, liquid or gaseous. After spewing forth the waste, a special door sealed the loading vent—his only view to the exterior—and then? Almost Paradise evacuated its debris into space, probably toward the planet's atmosphere.

After the garbage jetted out it would enter the upper atmosphere and burn. Kinsolving had nothing to worry about on that score. He would die from lack of oxygen and the effects of hard vacuum before he incinerated.

He jumped up and began shouting again. "Let me out. Somebody, let me out!"

The hum of robot-controlled machinery rose until it became a scream over which he could never shout. To his horror he saw the protective grate pulling back. He leaped and caught the edge of the now-open vent—and got a smelly stream of semiliquid waste in the face for his effort.

Kinsolving grimly clung to the edge of the vent. He tried to pull himself up and force his body through the opening against the stream. He quickly found that the hose mechanism on the loader prevented this. His shoulders were too large to cram into the loader.

His fingers slipped and he dropped back into the tiny waste disposal chamber. But this time he did not reach the floor. Buoyed by the sewage, he floated a meter under the vent opening. Floundering about, he caught the edge of the opening again in time to see the grill descending. He kicked hard and screamed to give himself the extra strength.

His shoulders and upper body passed through the opening as the grill lowered. Kinsolving screamed in pain. The closing mechanism had not been set to react to blockage; it would mindlessly try to shut the grill no matter what it encountered.

His head had rammed deep into the noisome loader. He could go no further.

And in this Kinsolving found salvation. Small sensors ringed the loader hose to measure back pressure. He shoved his hand against a piezoelectric sensing crystal as hard as he could. Nothing. Kinsolving dragged his fingernail over the surface.

As he felt his grip slipping, his body sliding back into the sewage in the chamber, he heard a distant alarm ringing. It might bring a human to investigate. More likely, a repair robot would be dispatched to clear what it sensed as blockage.

Grimly, Kinsolving hung on. When the loader hose pulled back, he gasped. The edge of the vent caught him just under his arms and placed most of his weight on a sharp edge. He grabbed the loader hose and, as it retreated, let it pull him up and out of the disposal chamber.

He fell heavily to the floor. Kinsolving lay there gasping for breath and choking on the sewage. Alarms stopped ringing. The grill clanged shut. A pressure seal swung down and closed over it with a lewd sucking sound. He heard pumps start as the disposal chamber was highly pressurized. Getting up on shaky legs, he found that the floor was much higher on this side and that the grill was at eye level. Kinsolving pressed his face against the transparent pressure seal and watched.

He jumped away, startled, when the bottom of the chamber opened. Like a gas-powered rocket, the sewage shot from the chamber. The liquid boiled away almost instantly, freezing the sewage into a compact missile shape. Kinsolving saw the bottom of the chamber return and he lost sight of the sewage, now on its way to a fiery destruction in Paradise's atmosphere.

Turning, he slipped down the opposite side of the bulkhead from where he had been trapped and simply sat, numb and unable to think.

Death had been very close. But why? Who wanted to kill him like this? He saw how efficient the disposal of his corpse would have been. No trace would have remained.

"What the hell kind of pervo are you?" demanded a burly man in coveralls. He had come to check the waste loader. "I seen all kinds on this floating whorehouse but you're at the outer boundary. Wallowing in shit. Damnation!"

Kinsolving forced himself to stand. He shrugged his shoulders, winced at the pain, and said, "Don't complain until you try it."

"Damned Bizzies are easier to tolerate than the likes of you," the man said, eyes cold and face set in an unpleasant expression. "You damage my equipment?"

"Who else has access to this room?"

"Get the hell out of my sight!" the man roared. "I don't want you bringing pervo friends in here. Out!"

Kinsolving followed the direction the man pointed. Dripping sewage, he found a door leading to a gray-painted service corridor. He stopped to wipe off the worst of the sewage, but he knew he did a poor job. Walking through the elegant Almost Paradise would draw unwanted attention.

A small box mounted on the wall drew his attention. He opened it and heaved a sigh of relief. A com unit. Kinsolving pushed his thumb into the button and waited.

"How may we be of service, sir?" came a soft, sultry voice.

"Lark Versalles. I want to talk with her right away."

"I am sorry, sir, but Lark left orders that no one is to disturb her."

"I'm Barton—"

"Barton Kinsolving," the voice interrupted. "Yes, sir, we know." Kinsolving cursed under his breath. Of course they knew. Their damned vidcams were everywhere—except in the waste disposal compartment.

Or were they even there? Had he been watched? Thoughts of insane bets among the guests on Almost Paradise ran through his mind. Bets on whether he survived, whether he escaped within an allotted time, bets on how soon he turned to ash in the atmosphere after being ejected into space.

"Sheeda. Send Sheeda to me."

"Of course, sir."

Kinsolving lifted his thumb from the bottom and sagged against the wall. Anger burned bright at the center of his being and kept him from succumbing to the darkness trying to seize his mind.

"Barton?" came Sheeda's hesitant question. "Are you all right? What have you been doing?"

He looked around. The alien woman stared at him as if he had fallen into a barrel of shit. And he had.

"Get me back to my room without anyone else seeing me."

"Another guest?"

"Of course," he snapped. "Do you think I want to be seen like this?"

"There are many strange customs, even stranger pleasures. I have read about—"

"Sheeda," he interrupted, "my room. Now."

The alien woman motioned for him to follow. He saw her pert nose wrinkle at the odor and she danced away lightly as he reached to touch her arm.

In silence they went along sharply curving corridors. Kinsolving tried to imagine their route. His only guess was that they followed the outermost passages and avoided the central areas where the guests congregated. His relief was infinite when they came to the door of the Xanadu Suite.

"Do you want me to join you?" Sheeda asked, obviously hoping for a negative reply.

"I have some questions. Nothing more." Kinsolving

pushed into the room, stripping off his clothing as he went. Sheeda closed the door behind them and motioned. Obedient, silent ankle-high robots slipped from their stations along the walls and retrieved his clothing. Kinsolving didn't care where they took it. Let it be exhausted into space for all it mattered.

"Bath, on, maximum pleasure," Sheeda said. "For one."

Kinsolving stepped into the filling bath and discarded the last of his soiled clothes. Slipping down into the scented cleaning fluid gave a surge of pleasure that was almost sexual. He moved his hand over a nearby control. Tiny scrubbers began working on his body as the warm pink fluid continuously circulated.

"Sheeda, what happened when you left me at the door to the ambassador's suite?"

"I watched for a second, then went to report in person to my supervisor. I had displeased you in some way and needed further instructions."

"You didn't displease me," Kinsolving said. The soft scrubbing had stopped. New sensations replaced it. Tingling electric current flowed to relax his tensed muscles. Fresh fluids gushed into the tub. This time his scrapes and abrasions were treated by astringents. He relaxed even more, almost drifting off to sleep.

But he dared not relax too much. Not until he figured out what had happened when he had approached the Trekan ambassador.

"I'm glad," Sheeda said, sitting on the edge of the tub. Her fingers stroked his face.

"You didn't see who hit me?"

"What?" She jerked back, as if he had struck her. "No, I didn't know. Is *that* what happened to you?"

"Someone knocked me unconscious, then put me in a waste disposer."

"That's not possible."

"Every guest is watched closely. That means someone in your central control knows exactly what happened." Even as he spoke, he wondered if the person responsible for trying to kill him was listening . . . and plotting.

"That's not exactly true," Sheeda said. "Guests are not constantly monitored. If you speak certain words a com-

puter interprets it as a request and takes appropriate action.
There is no need to watch everyone. The robots and computers do much of the work. Mechanisms are not as likely
as humans to be inattentive."

"Then it's possible that no one saw my attacker."

"You are so suspicious, Barton. We on Almost Paradise
do not spy, we assist. Very seldom is there any violence.
Why bother, when anything you want is given freely?"

Kinsolving said nothing. He had known men and
women who thrived on violence. The act of hurting excited
them. As complete as Terra Recreations seemed, he did not
doubt that Paradise contained a special section for sadists.

His attacker, though, did not seem to be in that category
of guest. He had tried to remove all trace of Kinsolving's
body. Knowledge of the station's workings were needed.
Kinsolving could have hunted for a month without finding
the disposal equipment.

"Someone on the staff did it," he said, "not a guest."

"But why?"

Kinsolving did not answer the Onarian's simple question directly. He had not decided if he trusted her. Compli-
cating his decision was her uncanny resemblance to Ala
Markken. He had trusted Ala. Trusting another who looked
so much like her might have been logical but emotionally
presented huge barriers for him.

"None of the guests knew I was aboard the station. Only
the staff could have seen me."

"That doesn't answer the question of motive," she said.
"Did you book passage to Paradise so long ago that such a
plot could be woven against you?"

"No," he said slowly. His mind raced ahead, checking
possibilities and not liking them. "Someone acted on impulse. That means they recognized me."

"Are you such a desperate creature that our staff attacks
on sight?" The idea amused Sheeda. The corners of her
mouth turned up in a crinkly smile the same as Ala's.

He considered the elements of the attack. Someone
might have wanted to keep him from the Trekan ambassador. A guard? A more straightforward warning would have
sufficed. A Lorr police officer had no reason to stuff him
in the sewage. A prison world waited for him if the aliens
caught him. Had a repair crewman found Rani duLong's

body, recognized her—a former lover?—and vowed vengeance? That seemed too nebulous a reason.

Not many capable of such an attack remained except those involved with the Stellar Death Plan.

Not Cameron, he decided. The robot master had died or been so severely injured that he would never recover—Kinsolving hoped. If only he could have made sure of Cameron's condition!

Another in Interstellar Materials might have stumbled onto him. Director Liu had ample reason to attack him. Others working for IM and the Plan might also kill on sight—would kill, he amended. The method of attack, though, did not seem efficient enough.

"What about Lark?" he asked. "Where is she?"

"Enjoying herself. As you should do. This is Almost Paradise." Sheeda stroked his cheek, then pulled back damp fingers to begin unfastening her blouse.

"I want to go to Paradise," he said.

"Let me begin giving it to you here," Sheeda said, smiling broadly. She shucked off her blouse and began working on her slacks. As she stepped out of them, Kinsolving went pale.

"You," he sputtered. "You're—"

"I am Onarian," Sheeda said. "Does my sexual equipment not please you?"

"You're not a woman!"

"But I am," Sheeda said, chuckling at his confusion. "I am also a man. I am both. I can fulfill any need."

Kinsolving jerked away and grabbed a robe brought by a convenience robot. He stared at Sheeda. She is not human, he repeated over and over to himself. It did not help. Sheeda had both male and female genitalia. In a detached fashion, he saw how this made her a valuable asset to TR and the guests on Almost Paradise.

That did nothing to ease the discomfort he felt at being in her/his presence.

"I want to go to Paradise. When will I be able to leave?"

"Soon," Sheeda said. The Onarian quickly dressed and hurried to the door. Kinsolving saw the bright beads of tears in Sheeda's eyes caused by his rejection. "I will expedite your departure since there is nothing on Almost Paradise that pleases you."

Sheeda rushed from the room before he could explain. Kinsolving dropped to the bed and lay back, trying to pull all the jagged pieces of his life together. He finally gave up, realizing that he couldn't explain his reaction to Sheeda. He might not possess the xenophobia of those adhering to the Stellar Death Plan, but he was not a sophisticated traveller, either.

He was only a bumpkin from a backward Earth. Kinsolving vowed to apologize to Sheeda for his behavior, but he didn't have the slightest idea how he would do it.

CHAPTER FIVE

CAMERON SHIFTED his weight slowly. A small buzzing in his ears told him that he had not yet adjusted the automedic properly. His injuries were healed satisfactorily, but he took no chances with his health. The robotic guardian rested in the hollow under his left ear and monitored his brainwave patterns. Should any discrepancy between norm and observed frequency occur, it would alert him.

The human doctors on Gamma Tertius 4 had scoffed at him and his precautions. Although they had repaired him, he did not trust them. A part of him said that the doctors might have made major mistakes if he had not posted his robot killers in the operating room to oversee the delicate procedure. The doctors had taken over four hours to drill through his skull with a laser, find the clots threatening his life and remove them from his brain. At every stage his robot observers compared the results with optimum. Cameron had gone over their detailed reports; twice the doctors had deviated from the best possible course, only to be warned by the observant robots.

Cameron touched the automedic and worked at its minute controls until the buzzing vanished. He had worried needlessly about the device during the shift to Paradise. It had performed perfectly in hyperspace. Not even the increased atmospheric pressure and higher humidity aboard ship had affected the sensitive warning device.

"Mr. Cameron, a pleasure," greeted a Terra Recreations representative. The man had the look of a petty bureaucrat about him that immediately caused Cameron to dislike him. Maria Villalobos had sent him to this resort planet for a purpose. Filling out endless reports to be hidden away in obscure computer banks was not part of his mission.

"I'm to see Morgan Suarez," he said without responding to the man's outstretched hand.

"Dr. Suarez is, uh, in his lab." The man looked around, as if saying even this much in public might be a mistake.

"Then there is nothing for me to do but wait for him." Cameron smiled, his gray eyes as cold as polar ice. "I do not like to wait. I get nervous. When I get nervous, I kill things."

The TR agent had no doubt about what—whom—Cameron meant when he said "things."

"Dr. Suarez will be available in a few hours. Why, uh, don't you amuse yourself? Paradise is famous for its many diversions." The sweat beading on the man's forehead betrayed his discomfort at having to deal with Cameron. In a way, this pleased Cameron.

"At least you didn't force me to wait on the space station." He glanced up and saw a silvery dot in the azure sky. Cameron had been granted direct landing clearance, spending less than fifteen minutes aboard Almost Paradise before shuttling down. He wondered who among those on Paradise were adherents to the Stellar Death Plan. Most employees of Terra Recreations knew nothing, just as most of those working for Interstellar Materials had never even heard of the Plan. Companies had to make money to justify their existence. The Plan provided an added bonus for company and employee worthy of the knowledge.

Cameron could not hold back the involuntary shudder that shook him when he thought of the Bizarres and how they crushed mankind under their alien heel. He lacked altruistic purpose, but the end benefited humanity. Cameron could not bear the thought of being second-rate. Having Bizzies constantly tell him by word and deed of his human frailty and inferior intellect produced nothing but gut-churning need to excel.

"Are you all right, Mr. Cameron?"

"Not used to the planet yet," he lied. "I've been in space for some time."

"You were in TR's flagship," the man said, perplexed. "There's nothing faster out there, except for alien vessels, of course."

"Of course," Cameron said sarcastically. The TR ship had cut over a month of travel time off the GT4–Paradise route. A Bizzie ship—any Bizzie ship—shifted the same distance in one percent of the time. What humans measured in weeks and months, the damned Bizzies measured in minutes and hours.

"May I show you to your quarters?" the man asked. "We've followed your request and given you something out of the way, a small bungalow that isn't likely to be noticed."

"And the equipment?"

"It's already inside," the man said, motioning for Cameron to precede him along a small, winding, dirt path. Cameron strode off, confident that the man would not attempt to kill him. A dozen gnat-sized robots patrolled the path, each capable of stopping an assassin silently and quickly. All had been redesigned after his encounter with Metchnikoff to penetrate personal defensive screens, but to make certain of his own invincibility, Cameron carried four different devices, all programmed for self-defense and given autonomy to prevent any attack. The AI circuits had performed even better than Cameron had expected when he had tested them on GT4. Anything the robots could not kill outright they could outsmart.

"No insects," he observed. "Yet there are colored flowers. How do the plants reproduce?"

"All artificial, sir," the man said. "We've found that the buzzing of insects distracts many guests. Others fear insect bites."

"Fear? Isn't that a strong word to use for a minor annoyance?"

"No, sir," the guide said, warming to a safe topic. "Some arrive with immune system responses not geared to the native insects. Anaphylactic shock is certainly something to fear for many. On Paradise, our guests are shielded, and so there is nothing to fear. That makes it perfect for both human and nonhuman vacationers."

"Nonhuman," mused Cameron. "Are these Bizzies on Paradise now?"

"Usually, as much as fifteen percent of the total clientele is alien," the man said, obviously distressed at the pejorative term Cameron used.

"All planets? Lorr? Zeta Orgo 4?"

"We've never had any arachnoids. They stay close to Web. The Lorr are infrequent visitors. Currently, we have a large contingent of Trekans and six other species comprising the Lemma Cluster Confederation."

"A large Bizzie trade group," Cameron said, more to himself than to the guide.

"Yes, sir, one of the largest in all space. Here is your bungalow. If you should require anything larger, we can accommodate you." The man bustled about, pointing out the automated features. To Cameron they were almost laughably primitive. The simplest of his robots performed more tasks—and better. Quick hand gestures dispatched six of his aerial guardians to perform a complete scan of the small house. Before the TR guide had finished his sales talk, Cameron saw the flicker of a green light from the coordinator robot.

No hidden traps.

"You requested isolation mode," the man droned on. "If you require anything, you must toggle the com unit. Minimum response on Paradise is full verbal. We could then cater to your needs whenever you—"

"I need privacy, not instant service," Cameron said. He turned and moved the man toward the door. "Thank you for your time. Send a message when Suarez is available."

"Yes, sir. Would you prefer to see the resort director? Dr. Suarez might be some time. Supervisor Azmotega would be thrilled to meet someone of your obvious distinction."

"I have no need to see the director." Cameron shut the door and prevented any further blithering. He had arrived without notifying any but a handful of TR personnel. Although the arrival of TR's flagship would cause gossip, his quick transfer to the planet kept such talk to a minimum. Cameron wondered at TR's efficiency. His officious guide obviously knew certain elements of the Plan and Suarez's part in it, yet Cameron had been told that Supervisor Azmotega knew nothing—of the Plan, of Suarez's mission, of his own arrival.

He glanced around. The protective robots had positioned themselves in each of the room's four upper corners. Two others patrolled constantly. He went into the bedroom and found his requested equipment neatly packed in shipping crates. Cameron began unfastening the lids.

"This is more like it." The equipment set his heart

pounding a little faster. The automedic beeped a single warning, then realized that its human ward experienced only excitement, not distress. Cameron had been cooped up in the hospital for almost a week after the operation. The time spent in transit had worn on him, too, but he had not felt secure enough aboard the TR ship to work.

With tools such as the ones contained in the crates, he could again work robotic miracles of miniaturization. Cameron wasted no time setting up a worktable, the automated equipment carefully positioned around him. Within an hour he had fashioned a new and even more deadly aerial robot.

Back hurting, he leaned against the pneumatic chair support. Cameron stretched. Warm, syrupy gold sunlight slanted through the bedroom window. Cameron shook his head. He had been so intent on his work that he had forgotten to polarize the window to prevent unwanted spying.

"Getting careless," he said. He checked his patrolling sentries. They had not detected any spying activities, but optical observation from a distance was beyond their programming to notice. "Damned planet is too quiet. Lulls me."

Cameron did not want to admit that his head injuries might have affected him adversely. Better to claim a moment's inattention than to believe in a more permanent condition of sloppiness.

He carefully repacked the micromanipulators and made certain that anyone looking at the electronic remains on the worktable would be unable to determine the purpose of his project. Cameron held out his hand. Obediently, the aerial robot he had constructed whipped up and off the table and gently settled in his palm. He dropped a pair of magnifiers down over his eyes and examined the new creation critically.

Only when he was sure that it would do its task well did he remove the magnifiers. A slow smile crossed his lips. It had been some time since he had felt this good. Paradise was already working its subtle charm on him.

Cameron rose, checked his robotic sentries, then left the small house and walked briskly along the tiny dirt path. When he had gone fifty meters, he cut off the trail and plunged into the thicket. Cameron ignored the small cuts and scrapes he got from the tough vegetation. His course began to curve slightly. From a map he had seen and memorized he headed directly for an alien compound.

A sharp crack alerted him. A robot guard that patrolled ahead had found sensors. Approaching more deliberately, Cameron found what his robot had already discovered. He dropped to his knees and examined the sensor head carefully. It had IR and vid pickups, both temporarily scrambled by his robot's defensive EM field. Cameron might have sent his messenger of death on ahead and returned to his bungalow without dealing with the warning device himself.

He wanted to witness personally the death delivered by his new robot.

Agile fingers worked on the leads. In less than a minute Cameron had circumvented a sophisticated warning device. He connected a small box to the output wire. A few seconds later, the repeater had photographed the harmless vegetation and transmitted this false picture endlessly to anyone monitoring the sensor.

Confident, Cameron strode forward. From inside the Bizzie compound he heard snuffling and grunting.

"The Bizzies are feeding," he said softly to the small robot in his hand. "Help them diet—permanently."

Cameron put on a set of vid goggles. Through the clear part of the lenses he saw the alien compound. By slightly unfocusing his eyes, he got a view of the aerial robot's journey inward. It flew slowly, barely fast enough for its tiny ramjet to keep it aloft. Cameron began retreating. The robot worked well so far·in eluding the various detectors the Bizzies had placed for their safety.

Safety! With his skill, no Bizzie could ever be safe! Let them run, let them hide. He would ferret them out and destroy every last one of their kind!

Cameron watched his robot slide past the electrostatic shield intended to keep annoying insects away. As his robot encountered this electronic barrier, he frowned.

A blinding light blossomed in the vid goggles. It took Cameron several seconds to realize that the dazzling brilliance came from the robot's camera and not from a physical presence. He hastened back to the path and strolled along it until his vision cleared.

·He almost laughed out loud when he figured out what had happened. The tiny dot of artificial intelligence he had given the robot had saved it. It now hunted the alien occupant.

Cameron walked faster. It would not do if he were seen near the scene of an alien death. Terra Recreations would shield him to a point. Cameron had yet to learn who among the officials on Paradise knew of the Plan and would aid him. The planetary supervisor knew nothing but Morgan Suarez definitely did, if the man would ever deign to grant an audience. Cameron smiled crookedly. Let Suarez fiddle in his bio lab with weapons of subtle—and mass—destruction. Cameron fantasized billions of his little robots being loosed on a Bizzie world. No alien would survive. If the robots maintained a modicum of intelligence, they could outsmart any alien. He proved that.

His eyes had cleared completely and the robot sent him a picture that caused his heart to race. A loud buzz sounded in his ear. The automedic warned him of undue excitement. Cameron ignored it. This was the moment he sought so avidly.

Robot life against inhuman life.

Cameron could not keep the smile from spreading when he watched his minuscule machine center its sights on the alien. The Bizarre crouched, six-fingered hands outstretched, as if this would save it. The sudden change in perspective caused Cameron to wobble slightly and grab a tree trunk for support. The robot had lined up its target. Program conditions met, it expended all its propellant in a single strike. It arrowed directly into the Bizzie's chest.

Cameron knew the alien hardly felt the impact of the tiny laser drilling through arteries and organs once it penetrated the body cavity. All transmission from the robot ceased. Cameron took off the vid goggles and put them in his pocket. He knew that by now the robot had probably found the gut and raced along it, seeking out vital organs and burning through them with the minute laser. The power supply could last only a few seconds at this level of energy expenditure.

Losing the robot did not sadden Cameron. He rejoiced at the death of another hated alien.

"Mr. Cameron?" came a gravelly voice.

Cameron's fingers moved in an almost imperceptible pattern. A half dozen aerial robots prepared to defend him should it be necessary.

He studied the man who had spoken. Short, thick of body and mind, he did not impress Cameron unduly. Cameron decided before the man said another word that he was little more than an errand boy, a human messenger in a world where that function was better served by robots.

"What is it? Has Dr. Suarez come out of his hibernation?"

"Suarez?" The man frowned, as if the name meant nothing to him. Cameron watched as slow recognition came. "Oh, no. I don't work for him. I'm what you might call freelance."

"With an emphasis on free," Cameron said. Nothing about this man seemed professional. A report came from the aerial robot coordinating recon on the man. For all his blocky body and slow wits, he sported enough armament to fight a moderately sized war. Cameron noted with some satisfaction that the coordination robot had adequately evaluated the situation and had signalled for a dozen more mechanical killers.

"You are the Cameron from Gamma Tertius 4? You work for Interstellar Materials?"

"I'm on . . . vacation. Paradise is lovely."

"Yeah, well, I got some information you might want to look at."

The man held out a small photo of Barton Kinsolving. Cameron did his best to conceal his interest.

"What of him?" Cameron asked.

"I killed him."

Cameron did not know if he should rejoice or simply strangle the man for robbing him of his revenge.

CHAPTER SIX

"YOU LOOK LIKE DEATH just walked in and tapped you on the shoulder, Bart, darling." Lark Versalles stretched like an Earthly jungle cat and relaxed. She lay completely naked on the soft couch and knew the effect her movement had on him. More and more, she had begun teasing him, taunting him to provoke a response.

Kinsolving didn't like it. And he was beginning not to like Lark very much. They had been on-planet for over a week and all she wanted to do was explore the ever-changing array of perversions Paradise offered its guests. He had tried to convince her of the need to discover who had tried to kill him aboard Almost Paradise. She had been more than uninterested—she had been openly hostile. Lark had not called him a liar, but the word had all too often danced on her lips without actually being spoken.

"Enjoy all this. You're not paying for it. Daddy is, and he probably has no idea what it costs—or ever will." A hint of bitterness crept into her voice whenever Lark mentioned her parents.

"We've got to do more," protested Kinsolving. He paced as if he had been placed in a zoo cage. As he walked to and fro, he surveyed the "cage." Few animals had ever been given such noble treatment. On Earth he had seen pictures of the ultrarich's homes. This put all those to shame. Opulence on this scale had been reserved for only a privileged few in all history. And here he, a mining engineer and fugitive, was given the run of a modern castle.

All he needed to do was ask and an obedient servant would obey. Robots, humans, the entire mansion overflowed with them. Never did they intrude, but always they hovered just outside his line of sight.

"This is a nice place," Lark said, lolling back. Her legs drifted open slightly in invitation to him. The swirls of cosmetic dye on face and shoulders, however, told him that she was not interested in sex at the moment. He had no idea what did interest her.

"Nice?" he cried. "It's almost criminal to live like this."

"There's nothing criminal. GPMT is paying for it and the company earned the money honestly. Or as honestly as any company ever could. They sell drugs that heal and ease pain and make life longer and better. Why shouldn't we both enjoy the result of that?"

Kinsolving had no good answer for her. He had been unable to find who had tried to kill him. No way off Paradise existed until repairs were finished on the *von Neumann*. The damages had been more extensive than he had thought; the head of maintenance said it might be another week before the yacht was spaceworthy again. At first Kinsolving had thought this was only a ploy to entice Lark to spend more money—more of her father's money. Then he realized that the waiting list for even a day's stay on Paradise was impossibly long. They had no need to bilk GPMT or Lark or anyone.

Even more galling than his inability to board the starship and leave to seek out those who might help him fight the Stellar Death Plan was his repeated failure to see any of those aliens on Paradise gathered for their trade conference. The Trekan ambassador might as well have been the forty parsecs back on his home world. Sensors ringed his huge estate and prevented anyone from entering. Kinsolving had scouted the perimeter and had found how thorough those on Paradise were in granting a guest's wish for privacy.

The most humiliating part had been a TR agent taking him aside after being stopped from sneaking into the alien diplomat's compound and offering a mock infiltration. The agent had guaranteed that Kinsolving would not know the difference between an actor and the real ambassador, that the guards would be good—if this playacting happened to be Kinsolving's most heartfelt fantasy.

"Lark," he said earnestly, sitting on the edge of the sofa. Kinsolving tried to ignore the bare foot that the woman ran up and down his thigh. "The Stellar Death Plan has not been halted because we don't see any evidence of it. I need to tell someone else about it. The more who know, the less likely Hamilton Fremont and the others will be able to carry out their genocide."

The look of extreme boredom on her face carried over to the colors beneath the skin. The cosmetic dyes turned darker, more ominous. Kinsolving thought that storm clouds gathered around her finely boned, lovely face.

Then the sun came out from behind the clouds and Lark smiled brightly. But it was nothing he had done or said.

"Sheeda!" the woman cried. "Come on in. Where have you been, you naughty girl?"

Sheeda moved with catlike grace and slipped between Kinsolving and Lark on the sofa, her body pressing warmly against Kinsolving's. He tried to move away. A strong arm circled his shoulders and held him firmly. No matter how he tried, Kinsolving could not push away the revulsion he felt toward the Onarian. Sheeda looked and acted female, but the male genitalia shocked Kinsolving. And this made him even angrier at himself.

"I've been exploring. There are such nice caves not a kilometer away. Wondrous caves. We can explore, the three of us. Grottos opening onto the ocean, caverns with floors covered with moss softer than this carpet." Sheeda almost purred as she ran her bare feet over the luxurious pile rug. "Everywhere you look, a new and better spot for making love. Come, Lark, Barton, let's go now."

"Photonic!" cried Lark. "We can be there before sunset."

"You are such a poet, Lark," said Sheeda. "We can be making love as the sun vanishes into the ocean. Our bodies will turn all the colors of the sunset."

"Come on, Bart, darling," urged Lark. She tugged at his hand. He resisted. "Be like that. Sheeda and I will enjoy ourselves."

Sheeda rose lithely and paused for a moment on tiptoe, caught and frozen like a bug in amber. The look she gave him was one of sorrow. Kinsolving felt shock that Sheeda pitied him. The spell broke and Sheeda spun and dashed off with Lark. He started to call to them, to beg to be included. Kinsolving stopped himself and watched until they had vanished on their idyll.

He slumped back, eyes closed and mind spinning. No

matter how he tried to concentrate, Kinsolving got no-where.

"Might as well be sucked into a black hole for all the good I'm doing," he muttered to himself. A small sound caused him to jerk upright, ready for a fight. A human servant stood a meter away.

"Sir, you are unhappy. Your brainwaves show intense displeasure. If Lark and Sheeda do not interest you, may I suggest another form of amusement?"

"No."

"You have shown some desire to meet alien lifeforms."

"Sheeda's an Onarian," he pointed out.

The servant nodded. Kinsolving wondered how the small man kept his hair in such styled perfection. "That is true, sir," the servant said, "but it is in a sexual fashion that you have rejected her company. We might be able to arrange a social meeting with one of another species, if this is your wish."

Kinsolving shook his head. He knew what this offer meant. An actor, not an alien, would be introduced to him. He needed to forge a bond of trust with an alien in a position of power.

How else could he warn them of the Stellar Death Plan?

"I want to talk to someone in charge," he said.

"I am authorized to take care of any complaint. *Any* complaint," the servant said.

"Never mind." Kinsolving swung out of the room, wanting to run in frustration. But where would he run to? Paradise was a resort. For him, it had become a cell as confining as that of the Lorr prison world. The only difference lay in the quality of life.

Kinsolving slowed his gait and walked into a small commons area a half kilometer from his mansion. Few people sat in the carefully gardened area. Most who came to Paradise had specific ideas of enjoyment in mind—plea-sures unavailable anywhere else. Kinsolving had gotten a glimmering of some by watching Lark and Sheeda to-gether. On any other world, such coupling between species would have been considered perverted or a major crime. On Paradise, it was accepted as easily as breathing.

He walked aimlessly, trying to choose a definite course of action. The very luxury around him took some of the edge off his determination. Was mass species extinction so important? Let the aliens look after themselves. After all, much of what Fremont and the others said was true. The alien worlds locked together in an alliance against Earth.

Kinsolving heaved a deep sigh. The aliens did exclude humans in trade, in scientific exchange, in most fields. And it was for a good reason. Kinsolving knew humans. Pushy, aggressive to the point of recklessness, Earth had burst forth on the universe thinking to seize and conquer it as it already had a tiny solar system. The aliens had been starfaring for centuries or even millennia. No race welcomed competition, especially from those they considered immature. ·

He did not blame them. But they ought to be warned of the dangers facing them. Even a spoiled child can turn vicious and do great harm.

A buzzing caused Kinsolving to stop. He cocked his head to one side, listening intently. The sound was all too familiar. He tried to believe that none of IM's brain burners had found their way to Paradise, but he had to admit that such an addictive device would be popular here. Kinsolving followed the humming to a small niche carved in a head-high hedge awash in a tide of red and green blossoms.

He did not recognize the species of alien crouched in the small square formed by the hedge. Kinsolving did recognize the brain burner. The alien's eyes had glazed over and all rigidity had left his body. He slumped to one side, twitching feebly. Kinsolving dropped to his knees and tried to examine the creature.

The pebbly gray skin proved dry and warm. The irises had turned into ovals of gently changing color. Respiration was minimal. Kinsolving had no idea which, if any, of the conditions were abnormal.

"Medic!" he called. "Medical alert. Home in on my voice."

"Sir," came the almost immediate response from a small robot hovering at waist level. "This being is in no immediate danger of expiring."

"The brain burner. What condition is his mind?"

"Damaged."

"Do something. Help him."

"Sir, orders on this point are strict. He has requested no aid should he be found in this condition."

"Take me to your supervisor. Your *human* supervisor."

"At once." The robot's limited decision-making circuits had worked through the problems and chosen a course of least interference. Allowing Kinsolving to badger a human removed him as an annoyance and possible disruptive element in the alien's fantasy/addiction.

Kinsolving followed the robot along a crazy course through the commons area, down a small paved path, up steps and into a tiny garden that looked like something that had been transplanted from Earth. On Paradise, its simplicity was strikingly out of place.

"Who—" began Kinsolving. The robot guiding him had vanished.

He shrugged this off and touched the door panel. The annunciator chimed deep inside the house. Several minutes passed before a harassed looking woman came to the door. Seeing a human instead of a robot startled Kinsolving.

"I'm sorry. A robot brought me here. By mistake, it appears."

"You're Mr. Kinsolving."

"You know me?" He studied the woman more carefully. Ten centimeters shorter than his own one-eighty and considerably more fragile in appearance, she might have been just another guest except for a few details which did not fit. She was not dressed—or undressed—in the fashion of the guests on Paradise. The auburn-haired woman wore a simple dress out of fashion a dozen years ago on Earth.

The idea of this being some rich woman's fantasy vanished when he stared into her brown eyes. Kinsolving almost took a step back. Intensity and intelligence shone forth in an almost dazzling display.

"My name is Vandy Azmotega." She held out a thin hand for him to shake.

"I'm sorry. Am I supposed to know you?"

"Come in, Mr. Kinsolving, and let's talk for a few minutes." He did not miss the small eye motion toward an analog chronometer mounted on the wall. Vandy Azmotega's life ran according to a strict timetable and he had just been granted precious seconds of it.

The decor matched the exterior of the house. Simple, unpretentious, an oasis of taste in an overdecorated world.

"You seem to like my humble house," Vandy said, a small smile crinkling her lips.

"Better than most of the places you rent out." He sat down in a comfortable chair and for the first time in weeks managed to relax. The setting did not demand reaction from him, as did the spacious, awe-inspiring mansion he shared with Lark and Sheeda.

"The robot told me you had come upon . . . a guest."

"He was burning out his brain with a device manufactured by Interstellar Materials," Kinsolving said bluntly. "IM lets the aliens get addicted to lower power brain burners, then starts distributing high intensity units. By that time, the alien is so addicted to the private paradise granted by the device he is unable to stop. He ends up a drooling husk."

"You are quite frank, Mr. Kinsolving. This surprises me."

"That IM is doing it? They are doing it on many worlds. Zeta Orgo 4. Contact a law enforcement officer there named Quixx for full details."

Vandy perched on the edge of a chair, arms crossed on her chest, watching him like a hunting bird watches its prey. "Because of their capacity for inflicting permanent damage, I've tried to stem the tide of the devices—the brain burners, as you called them—and have failed. In a way, it is not my responsibility. TR makes it very clear that Paradise exists for *any* recreation." Vandy Azmotega made a wry face. "You would be startled at what passes for recreation among some species."

"I doubt it." Kinsolving paused, then asked, "You're the supervisor on Paradise, aren't you?"

"Although I don't advertise my position, neither do I make it a secret."

"I'm surprised that the supervisor of an entire planetary resort would choose such . . . plain quarters."

"What would your choice be, Mr. Kinsolving? This or where you and your companions are staying?"

"The point is well taken."

"Not many would agree with me, though," Vandy said. She slid back into the chair. She hiked her feet up onto a low wood table and leaned back farther. "Running Paradise is a full-time job," she said. "I like to be surrounded by familiar, comfortable things."

"You do a good job. I don't see anyone complaining."

"Except yourself, Mr. Kinsolving. What can TR do for you that it hasn't?"

Kinsolving liked Vandy Azmotega, but she was obviously highly placed in Terra Recreations' power structure. No one gained sole dominion over an entire world, especially one as profitable as Paradise, without being highly competent and even more highly thought of in corporate circles.

"You mentioned the influx of brain burners," he said, skirting the question. "You don't approve but TR does?"

"Something like that. There are other kinds of drugs and devices used that I am not pleased with allowing on-planet, but . . ." She shrugged her shoulders. "I am not appointed dictator of morality. All my company expects of me is that Paradise turn a profit and that the guests enjoy themselves. Why aren't you helping me do my job, Mr. Kinsolving?"

"Bart," he said. "Call me Bart."

"What does it matter? You're not going to enjoy yourself any more if I call you Barton or Mr. Kinsolving."

"Your records must be very good," he observed.

"The best."

"But not complete. I stopped IM on Zeta Orgo 4. When I saw the brain burner, I knew I had to stop them on Paradise."

"You oppose the use of such devices? That's charitable of you, Bart, but it is not your business. If you fancy yourself a savior, we can generate a small scenario for you. You can stop any kind of illicit activity you want. We do complete—"

"No!" he roared. "No fantasies. This is real." Kinsolving found himself telling Vandy of the Stellar Death Plan and how Fremont and the other IM directors wanted to destroy all aliens.

"I am torn between two courses of action," she said after he had finished.

"What?"

"I know you're telling the truth. The probes that have been focused on you show basal metabolic rates, galvanic skin responses, eye dilations, perspiration levels, a dozen other indicators. You are telling the truth as you know it."

"As I know it? It's true!"

"You *think* it's true. That can mean one of three things. You might be entirely crazy, in which case you would believe everything you say no matter how far out in orbit. Another possibility is that what you say is the truth, but that you are wrong. You might be the victim of some elaborate joke. Your co-workers, perhaps."

"That's ridiculous."

"I think so, too. The final possibility is that what you relate has actually happened."

"It comes down to answers one or three, is that it?"

"Crazy as a quark or the discoverer of a fiendish plot," she said, nodding.

Kinsolving calmed a little. "Which is it?"

Vandy did not answer. She continued to study him. But Kinsolving saw subtle changes in her expression.

"You believe me," he said. "Why?"

"I've reported incidents similar to the alien with the illegal brain burner to my superiors. They have done nothing. Recently, I have been ordered to accommodate certain researchers from the TR home office. I have not been allowed to examine the laboratories nor have I been told what research is being conducted. This is both unusual and offensive. I ought to be in complete charge of the planet. My immediate superior has refused to give a satisfactory explanation of the company's motives."

"You think it is something illegal?"

"More than that. Several alien guests have died. I cannot connect the arrival of Suarez—Morgan Suarez, the chief of research—but it is suspicious. Before his arrival, no deaths of any species. After he has been here a few months, four deaths."

"When was the last?"

"This afternoon," she said, frowning. "That one was a murder. A killer robot, is the best diagnosis from my med staff."

"A killer robot?" Kinsolving felt a chill of premonition pass along his spine. Cameron might not be dead, but how could the robot master ever have discovered him on Paradise? Kinsolving had not known his destination when leaving the Zeta Orgo system. He had taken the first alignment in an attempt to evade the Lorr.

"You make that sound as if you know more than I do," Vandy said.

"Has anyone named Cameron arrived? An IM official?"

"No to both questions."

"Sandy hair, steel gray eyes, medium height, stocky."

"Mr. Kinsolving—Barton—that might describe a hundred humans on Paradise. And more than a few aliens, too."

"I have no idea how far-reaching the Plan is among top level executives. It seems incredible to me that others beside Fremont might be involved, but it's possible."

"You aren't implying that Terra Recreations is involved in planetary genocide?"

"Perhaps not TR any more than the vast majority of IM. What of a few key officers?"

"Too far off orbit for my liking."

"What if only Suarez and his—your—superior are involved?" Kinsolving saw that the woman could accept this.

"Those two always were the little lost nebulas in TR," she said, thinking aloud. "They glowed and puffed and no one noticed them. With egos like theirs, that must be intolerable."

"Can we examine Suarez's lab? Without him knowing it?" He saw a peculiar expression on her face. "You've tried to get your surveillance vidcams in, haven't you?"

"I have," she admitted. "No use. I gave up. Running Paradise is a job requiring utmost attention to detail. Suarez is authorized to be here and to act independent of my staff." She shrugged, as if saying this ended her involvement. Kinsolving saw that her interest went much deeper.

"There are ways of observing without using robots," he said.

"Break into Suarez's lab? I cannot condone criminal activity on Paradise."

"It wouldn't be criminal if the planetary supervisor inspected equipment under her control, would it?"

"What are we looking for?" Vandy asked.

To that Kinsolving had no idea. But he had the gut level feeling that it might be more insidious than the brain burners. Even worse, he had the feeling that Cameron was involved.

Vandy Azmotega stood and gestured to Kinsolving. "Let's go do some burgling," she said. A slow smile crossed her face until she positively beamed. "What a fantasy this is! I've always wanted to be a desperate character, breaking into places and stealing things."

"Why didn't you arrange for a week or two of recreational fantasy?" Kinsolving asked.

"Wouldn't be the same. I'd know the difference. That's one of the penalties for spending all my time manufacturing fantasies for other people. You learn the difference. Reality can't be improved on, is my motto."

Kinsolving understood. And he would know the difference between a harmless experiment in Suarez's lab and one connected with the Stellar Death Plan.

CHAPTER SEVEN

CAMERON TOOK THE PHOTO from the man's hand and peered at it. "How did you kill him?" he asked in a mild voice that carried an edge of chilled steel.

"Shoved him down a waste disposal chute up on Almost Paradise."

"The space station," mused Cameron. His quick mind worked over possibilities and he did not like the answers he came to. The only reason Kinsolving would have chosen Paradise as a destination after fleeing Zeta Orgo was knowledge of the project Dr. Suarez undertook. How such information could have leaked out—and to Kinsolving, embroiled as he was with the unpleasantness with the arachnoid Bizzies on Web—eluded Cameron.

A significant security breach. Nothing else made sense. It lay beyond the realm of chance that Kinsolving had picked this planet at random when he fled.

Still, a muscle in Cameron's cheek twitched when he thought of Barton Kinsolving. Every trap he had laid for the former mining engineer had failed. Kinsolving had entered the secret offices IM used to carry out their part in the Plan—and had escaped. Kinsolving had escaped a phalanx of superbly wrought robots on Web. Had Kinsolving stumbled onto Suarez? Impossible, thought Cameron. Yet . . .

A tiny buzz from the automedic warned Cameron that his blood pressure was rising. He forced himself to relax.

"You know me?" he asked of the shorter man. "How do you know of my interest in this one?" He tapped Kinsolving's photo.

"You don't belong to TR," the man said. "I do. You and I are in the same line of work."

"That hardly seems likely."

"Name's Davi Jessarette." Cameron ignored the outthrust hand. Jessarette lowered it, a perplexed look on his face. "We got similar interests."

"In Kinsolving?"

"If that's his real name. I got this photo some time back from headquarters. Rumors came with it that you were hot to get rid of him. Everybody's heard of you, Cameron. Everybody."

Cameron seethed. This fool had no idea who he had tried to murder—to hear Jessarette tell it, *had* murdered. Cameron could not discount the chance that Jessarette had succeeded where he had failed so often, but nothing about the man inspired confidence.

"I want to examine the body," Cameron said.

Jessarette smiled. Two of his teeth had been broken and improperly fixed. Cameron edged away and unconsciously smoothed wrinkles from his own impeccably styled and fashionable clothing. The plum-colored doublet matched well with the burnt umber, skintight silk breeches with the silver conches. The flowing sleeves with their fluted ridges concealed enough electronics equipment to destroy half the planet; Cameron took pride in knowing that none of it showed.

Certainly not like this fool's heavy armaments. Not only did he have faulty teeth, his tailor had done nothing to insure that the lines of his clothing would remain unmarred by the sundry pistols and grenades he so obviously carried.

Cameron fleetingly considered bringing down a few robots and seeing how Jessarette handled them. If they killed him, no loss. If he lived, Cameron might better believe the tall tale of him slaying Kinsolving.

"No way," said Jessarette, grinning even wider. Cameron found himself unable to look away from the bad dental work. It repulsed him even as he stared at it. "I shoved his body into a disposal unit. It kicked him out of the station under pressure. His body burned up in Paradise's atmosphere. A clean kill."

"What were the events leading up to Kinsolving's . . . demise?"

"Saw him trying to talk to the Trekan ambassador. I got orders to let nobody near the Bizzie. I recognized him from the photo, slugged him and shoved his carcass into the disposal."

"Quaint."

"Effective," Jessarette said with some pride.

58 *Robert E. Vardeman*

"Why do you think that you and I share the same profession?"

"You're from Interstellar Materials' Security Directorate. I saw the records. You came to observe the test Suarez is going to run. The doc uses such weird metals in his lab, it makes sense that IM is supplying them."

"I know of no such 'weird metals,'" Cameron said truthfully. He had no interest in Morgan Suarez's work other than carrying out Villalobos' orders to observe. It came as no surprise, however, that IM supplied the scientist with rare metals, possibly some of the rare earths mined on Deepdig where Kinsolving had been supervisor.

Cameron seized on this thread. Had Kinsolving learned of this project some time ago? Now that he had ruined IM's planned distribution of brain burners on Zeta Orgo 4, did he turn his attention to other uncovered Plan projects?

Again the automedic warned him. He could not keep calm thinking of Kinsolving's interference in the Plan. Cameron reached up and toggled off the warning device.

"You on drugs?" asked Jessarette. "Never saw anyone wearing one of those who didn't get regular jolts."

"You learned of my presence from Suarez's records?"

"Space, don't get all nuked off over this. Suarez might not have known I was reading everything. He gets careless with records sometimes."

Cameron filed this away for future use. A researcher working for the Plan should never become careless. If an inept minor security officer like Jessarette could successfully spy, someone as clever as Kinsolving could learn everything about the project in a few minutes. Hadn't Kinsolving penetrated IM headquarters, found the secret offices used by Liu and the others and learned enough to prevent the deaths of more than four billion Bizarres?

Damn Kinsolving!

He took a deep breath. No matter what Jessarette said, Cameron did not believe Kinsolving had died. He had to proceed on the basis that the man still lived and still actively worked against the Plan.

"Perhaps we might exchange . . . techniques," Cameron said, hiding his loathing. "After all, as you said, we are in the same line of work."

"Photonic!" Jessarette exclaimed. "Want to go and split

a bottle? They got some good Earth whiskey at the employee commissary."

"Let's return to my bungalow. More private."

"Right. No snoops listening in. I heard how good you are with the robots." Davi Jessarette looked around, as if he might visually spot them. Cameron checked his small robot patrol. No one listened to their conversation or had them under electronic surveillance. He had no way to tell if someone at a distance watched them through an optical device, though this seemed a remote possibility. It never paid to take chances. He had been careless just once and Kinsolving had sent him to the hospital with serious brain injury.

The pair of assassins walked slowly back to Cameron's bungalow. Cameron silently motioned Jessarette to enter, noting that the man took no precautions. A trap might have been laid. He did nothing to check for even simple surveillance probes.

Cameron punched a drink order into the drink computer and waited for the glasses to rise from the countertop.

"How come you don't have full vocal command?" asked Jessarette.

Cameron shrugged to cover the shudder of disgust he felt for this ignorant fool. "A quirk. I prefer to do things myself."

"Weird," said Jessarette, taking the drink offered him by Cameron. "But the stories I heard about you say you're top of the line. None better."

"How did you get into this line of work? Are you employed by TR's home office or by the planetary supervisor?" Cameron settled into a straight-backed chair and waited for the drug he had placed in Jessarette's drink to take effect. A small robot hovering unnoticed a few centimeters behind Jessarette's head monitored the drug's progress through the man's bloodstream. When it winked green Cameron knew that the drug had effectively paralyzed this clumsy assassin.

"I got into it by accident," Jessarette said. The expression on his face told of the conflict raging within. He wanted to lie, to make his cold-blooded murdering seem more glamorous. Cameron cared little for this. He wanted information and complete obedience from Jessarette.

"Tell me about Kinsolving. Was there any reason other than the one you've mentioned for you to attempt to kill him?"

"No. I...I hadn't killed anyone in a long time. I needed the feel. The photo came through Bizzie channels with a flag on it from the home office about him."

Cameron closed his eyes and rubbed his forehead. He murdered without qualm. He had done so many times. The exact numbers dead because of his robotic assassins lay beyond reckoning, but never had he experienced a thrill from the act. He worked for Maria Villalobos, for Interstellar Materials, for his own ends. The Stellar Death Plan fit well into his personal view of the universe. The Bizzies had to be stopped and Earth governments were failing miserably in accomplishing that end.

But to kill for the stark enjoyment of it was as alien to him as any Bizarre. His opinion of Davi Jessarette dropped even lower.

"Do you know for a fact that Kinsolving's body was evacuated through the disposal? Did you watch?"

"No." The word twisted Jessarette's lips. He tried to lie and could not. Cameron's drug worked very well. He would have to thank his friend at Galaxy Pharmaceuticals and Medical Techtronics who had given him a few milliliters of the experimental potion.

"Tell me about Dr. Suarez's work."

"I'm not supposed to."

"You *want* to. More than anything else in the universe."

"It's a plague. He wants to test it on the Bizzies vacationing on Paradise."

"The nature of this plague?" Cameron did not expect an answer, nor did he get one. Such information lay beyond Jessarette's ability to comprehend. "Who knows of this trial?"

"Me. Suarez and his assistants. No one else."

"Not even the planetary supervisor?"

"No. Vandy Azmotega doesn't know about the Plan."

"Stand," ordered Cameron. "Put down your drink. You will show me Suarez's labs. There is no need to inform the doctor of our visit. We will explore secretly, without allowing anyone to see us, until I say otherwise. Do you understand?"

"Yes." Sweat broke out on Jessarette's forehead as he fought the orders. Cameron noted that the battle did not last long. Jessarette's will was far weaker than the mind-controlling drug.

Cameron followed a half dozen paces behind Jessarette. If the man made a mistake and blundered into a defensive system, Cameron wanted him to expire first. A quick glance showed more than a dozen robots floating at different levels, some barely above the ground, others as high as ten meters. Cameron felt secure behind such a formidable defensive screen of robot killers.

"The lab," called Jessarette after they had followed a small gravel path for almost a kilometer.

Cameron motioned. An aerial robot shot forward and returned almost instantly. He inserted a decoder into his ear to receive the robot's encoded surveillance report. A short burst carried full information about the laboratory. Only a few inconsequential sensors dotted the area. Cameron saw why Jessarette had been able to enter and spy so easily. Suarez desperately needed a competent security agent to protect this project.

"Disable the sensors," Cameron ordered two robots. Less than a minute passed before he received microburst assurance from the robots that the task had been satisfactorily completed.

How efficient they were compared to the doltish Jessarette!

"Inside," Cameron ordered his drugged guide. "Show me the records office where you learned so much about the Plan."

Jessarette entered the door. Cameron cast a quick look around, not really expecting to see anyone. The robots had given the clear signal on the corridors and office. He followed Jessarette into the small office and pushed the man aside. Sitting in front of the computer console, Cameron began work.

He did not like what he saw. Too much sensitive material had been entered into the computer data banks without adequate protection. It had taken him only a few tries to find the key. Even with his expertise, he should have needed a day or longer to break the codes. What bothered him the most was the easy availability to anyone simply

blundering into the office. They need not be looking specifically for information. All they needed to do was glance
at the unprotected screen and learn more than had been
revealed by all the other adherents to the Plan since its
inception four years earlier.

Cameron watched the slow march of information about
Project Unravel. He speeded up the readout and let a robot
record the full information. He could study it in detail later.
When information about the security measures and personnel came on-screen, his full attention returned.

Complete personnel dossiers on the project scientists
amplified what he had been told by Villalobos. Very little
about Jessarette showed. A few entries about Vandy Azmotega confirmed Jessarette's appraisal that she knew
nothing about the Plan.

"Enough," Cameron said, leaning back in the chair. "I
know enough about Project Unravel to take command."

"Command? But Dr. Suarez has full authority from TR
headquarters. He reports directly to the director of off-
planet operations," said Jessarette.

"It is interesting to note that the chairman of TR's board
is not involved in the Plan," said Cameron, more to himself than to Jessarette.

"Dr. Suarez is in charge."

"No," Cameron said in a velvet voice. "I am the new
leader of the project. You will obey me in all matters. Your
superiors want this. Do you understand?"

Jessarette's willpower had faded to nothing under the
drug's influence. He nodded eagerly.

"Take me to Morgan Suarez. We have much to discuss,
the doctor and I." Cameron followed his drugged cohort
from the office, more confident than he had been since
leaving the hospital on Gamma Tertius 4. Under his guidance, Project Unravel could kill billions of Bizzies.

The Stellar Death Plan would be served. And Cameron
would seize the IM directorship that should have been his!

CHAPTER EIGHT

"THIS DOESN'T LOOK like much," Barton Kinsolving said. He peered around a large-boled tree at the research facility. The small building stood a mere one story tall and could not contain more than five moderately sized rooms. "Suarez must not have much equipment."

"He has almost four metric tons," came Vandy Azmotega's answer. She pressed close to Kinsolving, spying on the lab as if she had never seen it before. Kinsolving understood her excitement. The woman supervised the fantasies of others and never indulged herself. This small personal surveillance excursion gave her the opportunity to sample what the guests accepted as their due.

Kinsolving had worried about trusting Vandy until he saw the sparkle in her eyes as they skirted the perimeter of Suarez's laboratory. She would not have been so excited if she had known what went on inside. Kinsolving had given her an excuse to find out, and Vandy Azmotega was stimulated by it. Only a superb actress could fake her reaction.

"He must be crowded—or it must be as massive as neutronium."

"A large portion of this complex is underground. We used it as storage before Dr. Suarez arrived. There are service tunnels leading to some of the rooms."

"Never show the guest how the magic is performed, is that it?" he asked.

"Exactly. No one wants a vacation spoiled by listening to loader robots clanking around above ground."

"Sensors?"

"Only a couple warning devices put there to keep away curious guests. I don't know if Suarez has added more. I haven't checked on him. Being ordered to leave him alone helped, too. There's too much to attend to on Paradise without adding a researcher."

Kinsolving dropped to the ground and wriggled forward

63

on his belly. The first sensor he found had been deactivated. He examined it carefully and saw the pockmarks of small laser burns on its case. Someone had already entered —and had not wanted to announce himself.

"Burned out," he said. "Unless I miss my guess, all the sensors are burned out."

"I'll have to alert the repair crews. They don't usually slack off like this."

Kinsolving swallowed hard. He knew that telepathic powers were a fantasy, that action at a distance was not possible. But he had the crawling sensation up and down his spine that he knew who had preceded them. For several days he had the hunch—the precognition—that Cameron was here. Such sensor destruction, done with efficiency and skill, carried Cameron's trademark.

"What's wrong, Bart?" asked Vandy. "You look as if you stabbed yourself."

"Your repair crews aren't falling behind in their work. The sensors aren't even putting out 'damaged' signals."

"But they..."

"Cameron's work. I'm sure of it."

"The man you asked about?"

"He must be here. I'd hoped he had died on Zeta Orgo, but I didn't know for sure."

"He followed you?"

To that Kinsolving had no answer. It sounded paranoid for him to agree, yet it seemed too much of a coincidence for Cameron to come to Paradise to take part in Suarez's project. From what Vandy had said, Suarez was a biologist, not a roboticist. Did the experiment, whatever it was, require Cameron's expertise? Kinsolving knew that there was only one way to find out.

"Let's see what is going on inside. Will the researchers be in the underground section?"

Vandy shrugged. "Probably. Dr. Suarez hasn't seen fit to confide in me." Something in her tone alerted Kinsolving.

"Is that unusual?"

"Not really. We have HPGs—highly placed guests—on Paradise all the time, usually top officials from Terra Recreations. Some are secretive, but not like Suarez. With him, everything came as an order from the vice president in charge of off-world resorts—my boss."

"And?" Kinsolving urged. "What else is bothering you? The aliens' deaths?"

"More than the deaths. Although it's difficult to say, I think that as many as four more aliens are missing."

"Why don't you know? I thought you kept track of all your guests."

"Some want privacy. I've been told that on some alien worlds, especially those with hivelike societies, it's a perversion to want to be alone."

"You get those aliens."

"On Paradise it isn't a perversion," Vandy said indignantly. In a lower voice, she added, "Even some of the acts human society has ruled to be pervo are done here. No harm to others, maximum pleasure to our guests. That's our motto."

"Nothing wrong in that," said Kinsolving. But his mind soared ahead. He cared little what happened on Paradise—unless it meant a new plot in the Stellar Death Plan being started. If Cameron had come to Paradise, and if Morgan Suarez was working on a secret project, Kinsolving could only conclude that a new method of genocide was being researched. Luck had come his way in finding a highly placed official of TR not involved with the Plan and concerned with the deaths in her jurisdiction.

He touched Vandy's arm and motioned for her to enter the small building. She started off, walking carefully. Once, she bent over to examine a damaged sensor. Other than this, she made no suspicious movements. Kinsolving's confidence in her grew.

Standing in the doorway, she turned and said, "Empty. They must be at the lower levels."

A tiny flash of light caught Kinsolving's attention. He yelled and dived forward, arms circling Vandy's waist. She cried out in surprise as his weight carried her into the building. His tackle had been perfectly timed; the aerial killer robot flashed by on its deadly trajectory, missing her by millimeters.

"Robot," he panted out in explanation, rolling over and trying to get free. He yelped in pain as the robot spun on its axis and fired a small laser. The beam burned away part of his sleeve and bit deeply into his triceps.

"It fired a laser!" Vandy Azmotega sounded stunned that such a minuscule aerial device could carry a deadly weapon.

"Get out of here," Kinsolving ordered. He jerked her hard against a wall. The laser cut a deep groove in the hardwood floor, leaving behind a smoldering cut almost a centimeter deep. "It might not follow you."

Vandy scrambled to her feet and ducked outside the building. Kinsolving had ripped off his shirt by this time. He jumped to one side, avoiding the deadly lance of coherent light. In the same motion, he cast his shirt like a net.

The robot burned a hole through it with a single microsecond burst. But Kinsolving had achieved his purpose. The visual sensors on the sides of the slender robot were momentarily blocked. He grabbed for it and jerked around, smashing it to the floor. Kinsolving felt metal and boron composite yield. He also felt a new explosion of pain in his hand and leg. The laser beam had shot through his calf and left palm.

Beyond conscious thought, he stamped hard on the crippled robot. A new pain, this time in his heel. Then came the satisfying crunch of metal. He had crushed the killer robot.

"Barton, you're hurt. All over!"

"I'll be fine. It's dead."

"Deactivated," she corrected. "Robots aren't alive."

"This one might as well have been. Clever, quick, tiny, smarter than most human assassins."

"So small," she agreed. "Hardly longer than my little finger. How could it carry such a powerful weapon?"

"This is Cameron's handiwork. I'm sure of it." He pulled Vandy from the building. "He set the robot to protect his back. It probably signalled intrusion the instant it fired the first laser bolt."

"You make it sound intelligent. There's no way to put even the most rudimentary intelligence into such a small machine."

"Cameron does it all the time. The man's a robotics genius." He kept pulling her along until they had gone several hundred meters into a thicket. Kinsolving didn't know if this would be far enough to discourage pursuit by other robot sentries. He hoped so. They showed true intelligence and might reason that following Kinsolving could be a diversion. Kinsolving waited several minutes, every sense alert, but no new robots appeared.

"That wasn't one of the approved TR sensors," Vandy said. She looked at him, brown eyes wide. "This mythical Cameron," she said. "He works for IM?"

Kinsolving nodded. He tore away the burned cloth around his leg wounds. The searing beam had cauterized as it passed through. The burn on his left palm proved more painful than disabling. Even the one through his heel did not slow him—much. He slipped back into his shirt. The beam had burned through a spot directly over his heart; he was glad he had not been wearing it when the robot killer had fired.

"We've got to see what they're doing," Vandy said with real determination. "I refuse to allow this to go on in Paradise. Dammit, this is *my* world, my responsibility." Cameron stopped her before she could storm off.

"Where do you think you're going?"

"To alert security."

"How loyal are they—to you personally?"

"No," she said, shocked at what he implied. Vandy Azmotega was even more shocked when he told her in detail what had happened to him aboard Almost Paradise.

"It might have been a TR security officer," Kinsolving finished.

She shook her head but no words formed. He let her consider the possibility that she no longer controlled Paradise, then asked, "Where are the entrances to the underground service tunnels? We can enter the lab that way."

"There's an entrance over there somewhere." She pointed to a camouflaged grate set flush with the ground. Kinsolving brushed dirt and leaves away from the lock. Vandy reached past, using a card key to open the grate. It slid silently into its frame, a small light coming on to light a metal rung ladder.

"Go back to your office and get guards you can trust," he said, swinging down to get his feet on the ladder. "And don't include the ones who were on Almost Paradise—especially any guarding the Trekan ambassador."

"Brake back," she snapped. "You're missing orbit by a solar system. I'm not letting you go down there alone. I know the tunnels and you don't." She looked at him sheepishly. "And I don't think I can trust *any* of my security personnel. Not after what you just told me."

Kinsolving said nothing. Vandy seemed open and honest; her response was what he would expect from someone who doubted—just a little—not only his story but also her own personnel. From much of what she had hinted at, Paradise had become something less in the past few months and this worried her greatly.

"It might be dangerous down there," she said, eyeing the lighted opening with no enthusiasm. "I might be able to come back with a few robot workers. We could send them ahead to see if it's safe."

"No," Kinsolving said. "That would only warn Suarez and Cameron, unless your robots usually patrol the tunnels."

"Not here," she said, shaking her head. Her auburn hair had become slightly matted with sweat. Kinsolving saw the strain working on the woman. She had been entrusted with the safety and security of guests on Paradise. All that had slipped away gradually. Confronting the source of her problem lay beyond her training. Even though Kinsolving had no reason to believe it, he doubted if she had experienced anything more deadly than not having enough intoxicants for her customers.

Kinsolving took a deep breath, then swung around and started down the ladder. The rungs cut at his hands; it had been many months since any human had ventured here. At the bottom he peered along a tunnel so dark that he would have to feel his way. For him, it was almost like coming home. He missed the mine shafts. Being an engineer had taken him deep beneath planetary surfaces enough to enjoy it—or had he always liked the closed-in feeling that drove some people phobic?

"To the left," he said, a sureness in his voice that he did not feel inside.

"That's the way to the lower level in the lab," Vandy said, a tone of surprise in her voice. "You haven't been here before, have you?"

"No." As they walked along the dark tunnel, Kinsolving gingerly feeling his way, he told her of his job and life in the mines. Part of him enjoyed holding the woman's hand and talking with her, but another part screamed *danger!* Darkness masked much. Cameron's killer robots could work easily with IR or radar. And there would be no place to fight or run in such a small tunnel. Less than a dozen paces into the tunnel, the lights slowly rose to a level where he could see.

He glanced at Vandy. "Automatic," she said. "Humans trigger the sensors; robots don't."

Kinsolving doubted they would face another human. He worried about Cameron's robots on guard. Even though he watched carefully, he found no sensors, no traps, nothing. This was nothing more than what Vandy claimed: a service tunnel.

"There," she said, seeing the recessed door a few seconds before he did. "That leads into Suarez's lab. I . . . I don't know if he even uses this part of the basement. All I ever used it for was a storeroom."

Kinsolving ran his fingers around the seal on the door. Parts of the silicon rubber seal had dried over the years. He found no indication of tampering for a long, long time. But what really lay on the other side?

He tugged at the door, then had to put a foot against the wall and pull with all his might. When the door yielded, it sent him stumbling back into Vandy. Her arms circled him and they went down in a heap.

"There are easier ways of getting together," she said, laughing. "Not that I mind, but this is hardly the time or place."

"Later?" he asked. For a few brief seconds something other than the Stellar Death Plan and Cameron's mechanical minions entered his mind.

"If there is a later," Vandy said, struggling to get out from under him. Kinsolving got to his feet and helped her up. They peered through the door. Kinsolving had not expected to find anyone—or anything—waiting. The commotion getting the portal open would have drawn instant fire if guards had been posted. A heavy blanket of dust lay over the few crates strewn around. He doubted anyone had been inside this room in more than a year.

He made his way to an inner door. This one he did not immediately open. Sounds from the other side caused him to motion Vandy to silence. She pressed her ear beside his against the plastic panel. Their faces were just a few centimeters apart.

". . . release soon for a field test."

"The lab results do look promising, Dr. Suarez," came another voice.

"Suarez and his assistant," Vandy whispered.

Kinsolving opened the door enough to peer around the edge. The bright light momentarily blinded him and the sharp, astringent smell of a bio lab caused his nose to wrinkle and eyes to water. He waited impatiently and caught a glimpse of Morgan Suarez. The man was small, darkly complected and had jet black hair swept straight back in a severe style that gave him a fanatical aspect.

When Suarez spun suddenly, his hand reaching inside his white lab coat, Kinsolving's heart jumped into his throat. He thought he had been seen. When Suarez drew out a tiny laser, Kinsolving knew the scientist had discovered him.

But Suarez faced off at an angle, his right shoulder to the door. Kinsolving tried to hold Vandy back but the woman pushed around to a spot under him to watch, too.

"What in the empty hell are you doing here?" Suarez demanded. Kinsolving could not see the intruder who upset the biologist but the answering voice was all too familiar.

"You neglect me terribly, doctor," came Cameron's voice. "I do not like to be ignored."

"You overstep your bounds, Cameron. And you, Jessarette, you shouldn't have brought him down here. It's dangerous."

"Jessarette?" Vandy stirred. "He's on the staff as a security specialist. I had him guarding the Trekan ambassador on Almost Paradise. He's supposed to be overseeing security for their conference, not—"

Kinsolving clamped his hand over the woman's mouth. A gaudily dressed man swaggered into view. The bright colors and the soft rustle of natural silks betrayed Cameron as surely as the glints off his guardian robots hovering high in the room. Kinsolving dared not close the door. Such a slight move would alert the robotic killers.

"Mr. Jessarette did not lead me here of his own free will. Let us say that I persuaded him."

Suarez examined Jessarette, who stood docilely. "Drugged," the researcher said. "It might be a derivative from the Astkonian night juggler flower."

"A synthetic," Cameron said, smiling. "You are very knowledgeable. Not many have heard of the night juggler's lovely black flower."

"It only blooms every four planetary rotations—a dozen standard years," snapped Suarez. "What is it you want, Cameron? To discuss botany?"

"To discuss your project. Director Villalobos sent me to oversee progress. You have refused to see me. That is a clear violation of the agreement of friendly cooperation between our superiors."

Vandy Azmotega tried to speak again. Kinsolving tightened his grip. He dared not even hiss at her to be silent. A patrolling robot slowly floated by a meter away. The slender twenty-centimeter-long robot carried enough armament to burn its way clear of a steel-walled vault. Against an unprotected human, it might take only microseconds for a quick kill.

"Project Unravel proceeds well," Suarez said. He moved and returned the impact laser to its hidden holster. Kinsolving did not relax; the robots might be more attentive to other threats.

"Ah, yes, the project. Jessarette has told me something of it. Director Villalobos has gone a bit further. But I need more details, Dr. Suarez. Ones that only you can provide."

"This is a busy time, Cameron." Suarez spun and started off. He stopped and stared. Kinsolving could not see what had halted the scientist, but he thought he knew. In a few seconds a killer robot rose to shoulder level.

"My friends are not likely to allow human emotion to get in the way of a detailed report," Cameron said, obviously enjoying Suarez's discomfort at being confronted with a deadly robot. "A short report, doctor. That is all I ask. At this time."

Cameron moved around. Kinsolving thought the robotics genius lacked some of the swagger he once had in his walk. A hesitancy? Or an injury? Cameron's head wound might have been worse than it appeared. Kinsolving cursed the bad luck that Cameron had not been permanently disabled.

And Kinsolving still wished he had been able to kill Cameron.

"The bioweapon will be introduced soon. The Bizzie conference is a perfect place. There are seven different species attending. Over fourteen hundred aliens total are on-planet, adding a few more species to the count. We shall be able to judge the efficacy of the project by the number who die within a week."

"It unravels their DNA?" asked Cameron.

"Did Jessarette tell you that?" Suarez looked at Davi Jessarette. The look was one of pure contempt.

"I doubt he understands such matters. No, doctor, I unraveled it on my own." Cameron chuckled at the wordplay. "Not everyone you deal with is incompetent—or stupid. Can you imagine, he tried to kill an adversary of mine. I doubt he succeeded. But this is of little consequence. Tell me of Project Unravel."

"You are correct in your appraisal. I have spent almost two years developing a strain of virus that works solely on Bizzie DNA. To humans it is completely harmless."

Vandy stirred again. Kinsolving released his grip but silently cautioned her to remain quiet. She moved back from the door and stood behind him, peering over his shoulder.

"An interesting plague," mused Cameron. "A plague in Paradise."

"I am very busy, Cameron. Get your damned robots out of here and let me work. I'll give you a complete report after the bioweapon is released and analysis is completed."

"No, Dr. Suarez, you'll give it to me now. That was the agreement made by our superiors. Who are we to go against their wishes?"

Suarez made an impatient gesture, then edged around the robot blocking his way. Cameron laughed and followed. Behind him Jessarette walked as if his mind had been burned out. His mouth hung slack and his eyes were dull and unfocused.

"We can't let them do this!" exclaimed Vandy.

Kinsolving started to caution her to silence, then saw it was too late. The robot hovering in the center of the laboratory began to swing about, sensors at full. He closed the door and pushed her across the storeroom to the tunnel beyond.

"Run like the sun's going nova," he told her. "We triggered a guard robot's pursuit sensors."

"But—"

Kinsolving shoved her into the tunnel; she stumbled in the wrong direction. He started to reverse course to head back for the ladder leading to the surface. In the storeroom behind, he heard a sharp hiss. The smell of burned plastic reached his nose. The robot had blasted its way through the door. He closed the door leading from the room into the tunnel, hoping that the robot would scan the entire storeroom before finding it.

He might as well have wished for the device to fuse its own circuits.

Kinsolving pushed hard against Vandy, giving up his hope of reaching the ladder to the surface. "Keep going. It'll be on us in a few seconds. Down there." He jerked her around and sent her reeling down a branching tunnel.

"No, not this way!"

Kinsolving wasn't listening. He herded her in front of him. They ran hard down the long, dimly illuminated corridor. He frantically sought a door, another branching tunnel.

"Barton, no, not that door," she begged. He worked feverishly to pull back locking bars. Kinsolving glanced back down the tunnel. The robot had found their trail. Scent, sound, visual, it no longer mattered how this killer tracked. It had locked onto its target. And it would never stop until they were dead, dead, dead.

Kinsolving ripped open the door and screamed. Rising in front of him was an oyster-white creature fully two meters tall, with enormously powerful arms and savage talons that raked at his face. He ducked and narrowly avoiding having his eyes gouged out. The stench from the beast overwhelmed him. He gagged and dropped to one knee, hands trying vainly to stop the odor.

The furred behemoth turned sluggishly and came for him. Kinsolving sagged back against a wall, all strength gone from his arms and legs. He could only watch as the beast came for its prey—him.

CHAPTER NINE

CAMERON TURNED and frowned when a tiny flash caught his attention. The guard robot he had posted in the corridor had sighted a target and gone after it. The man quickly checked the remaining robots and decided they were adequate to any threat posed by Morgan Suarez and his assistant. He did not bother considering Davi Jessarette in the equation. The night juggler drug still held the clumsy assassin in its thrall.

Suarez saw his sudden inattention and asked, "What's wrong? Did you hear something?"

"Your sensors are inadequate for protecting such a valuable part of the Plan," Cameron said lightly. He wanted to check the prey his robot had locked on but did not want to reveal the full capacity of his defenses to Suarez. Cameron saw that Villalobos had done well to send someone of his ability to oversee the scientist. Although Suarez had the proper instincts for mass destruction and death, he lacked discipline and attention to details. The researcher would be expendable should it become necessary.

Cameron hoped that it would. He needed to hone his talents and test another of his metallic murderers.

"Leave us," Suarez said, making brushing motions with his hands, as if this would hasten Cameron on his way. Cameron straightened his silk doublet and locked his cold gray eyes directly with Suarez's. The scientist was the first to break away. Content in his belief that Suarez knew who was really in charge of Project Unravel, no matter what their official status, Cameron spun and walked off. He left Jessarette standing dumbly. Suarez could deal with him or not. To Cameron it made no difference now.

He had established contact in a satisfactory way. His robots had prowled this small research facility. Locked away within their incredible brains lay the full details of Suarez's DNA project. Even more important, Cameron had shown this upstart from Terra Recreations that he would not be able to operate without full consent from IM's representative.

Cameron did not know if Villalobos had intended it to be this way, but he thought so. He smiled as he walked into the bright sunlight. The gentle scent of flowers dilated his nostrils. The designers of Paradise had thought of everything. Flowers with properly pleasing scents but no insects buzzing about to annoy. Warm sunlight interspersed with gentle rains to moderate the heat gave a sense of tranquility. Everything was perfect on Paradise.

In a day or less the bioengineered virus would be loosed and alien DNA helices would begin unwrapping. Cell reproduction would cease—or even better, to Cameron's way of thinking, cell reproduction would go berserk. Blood cells would not carry oxygen. Cancers would sprout up throughout the infected's body. Metabolism would go awry. No single medicine could stop it. Viruses were notoriously difficult to isolate and destroy. The wide range of symptoms would mask the true danger since only a few cells in the alien's body would be infected.

What pleased Cameron most was the notion of killing thousands of the Bizzies. He found himself tense and shaking at the prospect. He forced himself to relax, to open his fists and flex his fingers. Killing the aliens was more than a part of the Stellar Death Plan for him. It was even more than an exercise in destruction for his prized robot hunters. Life had not been easy for him on Earth.

The damned Bizzies had made it even worse.

Cameron seethed at the ancient memories rising once more, memories he tried to keep buried. His parents, two sisters and a brother dead because an alien cargo ship refused to answer an emergency beacon when they learned it had been activated by humans. His own career stifled and almost aborted because of restrictions the aliens placed on robotic devices imported into their cultures. Most alien worlds refused to consider for purchase any product manufactured on Earth worlds. They went further. They stopped commerce in all finished goods originating on Earth, allowing only raw materials to be shipped.

The technology freeze made Cameron even angrier. The Bizzie starships were dozens, perhaps hundreds, of times faster than equivalent Earth vessels. And they refused to share the secret of their superdrive.

The alien worlds had banned together, perhaps informally, perhaps in some secret treaty, to hold back humanity.

Cameron swelled with pride knowing he helped turn the knife in a wound not yet felt by the aliens. Interstellar Materials had failed with the brain burners on Zeta Orgo, but TR's bioweapon carried with it the feel of sweet success. Cameron's only regret was that another would release it and have the satisfaction of killing untold billions of Bizarres.

As he strolled along the path, he motioned. An attentive patrolling robot surged down and hovered beside his left ear. "Where is the hunter-killer that vanished from the laboratory?" he asked. The robot had a laser trained on his lips. It was far too small to use a mechanical microphone and relied on oscillations in a different part of the EM spectrum for input.

Cameron watched from the corner of his eye as the robot emitted a coded signal only he could read. The other robot had not returned. Cameron felt no uneasiness at this. The device was one of the most intelligent robots he had fashioned. Its decision-making abilities far outstripped most humans'. He had supreme confidence that it would return when it had satisfied its urges.

His footsteps turned toward the immaculate, deserted beach stretching for kilometers along the shoreline. The brisk wind whipping off the ocean and pulling up white-caps on the surface gave him a sense of well-being. Cameron relaxed. He had been through much and only slowly healed from the operations that had saved his life.

His hand touched the minute scars under his hairline where the surgeons had invaded his skull to relieve the pressure on his brain. Damn Kinsolving!

Even as the name crossed his mind, he reached into a pocket and pulled out the photo taken from Jessarette.

"No," Cameron said slowly as he gazed at Kinsolving's image, "you aren't dead. That fool could never kill you. Where's the proof? You are too good for him, far too clever. You will be mine one day. Oh, yes, all mine."

A worthy opponent added spring to Cameron's step, but

the sudden explosion of sea birds from behind a rock
stopped him in his tracks. He looked around. His robot
guards had drifted away to give him a sense of isolation—
and to better survey the countryside for possible danger.
Ahead he saw a tiny winking green light.

Instantly, two robot sentries moved in and hovered near
him.

"What's happened?" The answer came quickly. He went
to investigate personally. Dropping to the surface of a huge
rock, he crawled lizardlike to the top. Pressed flat, he spied
on the dozen people enjoying a small party on the other
side. They danced and paired off, talking intimately, only
to reform into different groupings.

Cameron almost envied them their ability to mingle so
easily. But this was not his world. Any one of those cheerful people might be a killer laying a clever trap.

Even as the thought crossed his mind, he stiffened. One
red-haired woman caught his attention. It took several seconds for him to recognize her as a secretary in Metchnikoff's office. Even then, he was not absolutely certain of
the identification. He ordered a robot to ID her. It drifted
away, then shot from sight, going straight up to form a
line-of-sight computer link. It might take several minutes
for the report. Cameron could wait.

"Hey, come on down and join us!" the redhead shouted,
waving at him. Cameron had been seen. A moment's hesitation gripped him. If another director of Interstellar Materials had sent an aide to Paradise, that meant power
struggles. Cameron could not forget the threats Metchnikoff had made at his bedside in the hospital. The director
had prevented him from being appointed to IM's board.

What else did Metchnikoff have in mind? Did he hate
Cameron enough to send a spy? An assassin? Cameron
could not for a microsecond believe that a mere secretary,
even one for a director with aspirations to be chairman, just
happened to come to Paradise for a vacation at this precise
instant. The expense for even a day at this planetary resort
was staggering and beyond most lifetime incomes.

"Come on down. Don't be shy!" the woman called.
Cameron put his robots on guard. He had to deal with this
directly. He slipped over the top of the rock and landed
lightly in the sand not a dozen paces from the woman.

"Thanks," he said.

"There's no need to hide when we're having such a good time. Join us," the small, frail-appearing woman invited. She cocked her head to one side, then smiled, as if suddenly remembering something pleasurable. "I know you. You work at IM, too! I've seen you around headquarters on GT."

"This is a coincidence, isn't it?" he said. "How long have you been on-planet?"

"Just arrived not two hours ago. Come on, let's dance." Cameron let her take his hand and pull him nearer to the music cube. It took him a few seconds to study the others and see how they moved. He did not enjoy dancing usually, but his superb coordination allowed him to blend in well. He found himself liking, if not actually enjoying, the sensation of his body moving smoothly once more.

"You do that well. And those are photonic clothes you've got on! Pick them up in a shop here?" she asked.

The woman's own apparel consisted mostly of a tiny gold metallic patch dangling between her legs. Cameron was not interested in her body but in whether she carried any weapons. It seemed unlikely, but his own armament required little in the way of concealment because of its smallness.

As they danced, Cameron saw tiny veins just under the skin on the woman's legs. He heaved a sigh. She had been expertly wired. The pressure of blood rushing through her blood vessels powered the transmitter. Who received the transmission? He had no idea. Metchnikoff might have sent an entire team to spy on him. Cameron wondered what the director knew about Project Unravel.

Cameron hoped that he knew nothing. Allying himself with Maria Villalobos had been dangerous. For a moment, pleasurable, but in the long run a deadly gamble on his part. The less Metchnikoff knew, the better able Cameron was to turn the project to his own ends and possibly recapture a chance at the IM directorship.

"Let's go somewhere more private," he suggested to Metchnikoff's spy.

"Private?" The woman's red hair seemed to be on fire in the intense sunlight. "All right. Where?"

"Let's just take a short walk." Cameron made a vague

gesture inland toward a small stand of trees. Hand in hand they left the others. Cameron made certain that no one took special note. Anyone in the party might be in league with the woman and Metchnikoff. That was a chance he would have to take.

"Here?" she asked, stretching out on a soft, mossy patch that seemed to have been designed for lovemaking. She propped herself up on her elbows and grinned.

Cameron walked around, eyes alert. He sent two hovering robots to patrol the area. Another monitored the output from the woman's in-body com unit. He worried at the content of the signals. She might not even know the sophisticated device had been implanted. He doubted that, but it was possible. Metchnikoff was a cunning son of a bitch. Such deception was not beyond his capacity.

"Are you going to walk in circles or are you going to ...join me?" the woman asked. Even the tiny gold patch had twisted to one side. She seemed more naked than ever. And the wanton invitation was not one Cameron dared refuse unless he wanted to arouse her suspicions.

"What do you want from me?" he asked.

"I think that's obvious," the redhead told him, rising up and gripping his wrist. She pulled him down. Their lips met.

Cameron recoiled instantly. He had been drugged just as he had trapped Davi Jessarette! The faint taste of the woman's lip gloss lingered. He tried to rub it off.

She laughed. "That won't be good enough, Cameron. They told me the drug is efficient—and fast acting."

"But you're wearing it!"

"Special polymer between my lips and the drug. It is damned hard not to lick my lips."

Cameron's knees turned to jelly. He sank down. The woman swarmed up and on top of him. "A wonderful drug, they tell me. You can still respond. In some ways." She pulled expertly at his brightly colored clothing. "You are a handsome one. Too good for the likes of me usually. Not now."

Cameron felt himself responding to all the woman did to him. Even worse, inhibitions slipped away. The drug worked to rob him of his volition. He moaned softly as she slipped up and down his body. Another kiss insured his cooperation.

"Such a *wonderful* drug," she cooed. "Metchnikoff has never let me use it before. I promised him that this was a special case."

What the red-haired woman did to him was pleasant, but Cameron preferred having some choice. She moved faster, her fingers gripping at his sides, his shoulders. She moaned, stiffened, then relaxed, sweat dripping from her body onto his.

"That's probably the best you've ever received."

"Maria Villalobos was better," he said. "More energy. Greater expertise."

"You lying—"

"With her, I wanted it."

The woman glared at him, hatred flaring. "You can't lie, can you? No, you can't. It's impossible because of the drug. But you'd say those things just to annoy me. That's the kind of space-sucking bastard you are."

She pushed off him and towered above his supine body. "Metchnikoff wants full disclosure of Villalobos' scheme. What is happening on Paradise that requires your presence?"

Cameron thrilled at this. Metchnikoff did not know anything about Project Unravel. Some advantage might still be gained. But he felt the details rising to his lips, pulled from the most protected recesses of his mind by the insidious drug.

"Yes, my dear Cameron, tell me everything," the redhead cooed. "Then I'll have everything I need from you."

"The Plan," he gasped.

"Yes, what of it?"

His eyes blinked rapidly. The woman's face showed intense surprise. Then she toppled forward onto him. He tried to roll to one side but could not move. A tiny whir and a breath of air brought one sentry robot level with his eyes. Rapid eye blinking sent it away. Within minutes, it returned with larger, more powerful machines.

The pressure of the woman's dead body left his. Cameron watched in fascination as his robots systematically lasered the corpse into cinders, then buried the ash. He had not ordered them to do this specifically. His command had been more general: hide the body so that it cannot be found. The robots showed more initiative and inventiveness than even he, their creator, had thought possible.

A sharp pain on his thigh brought him upright. Heat sprang from the point of injection until his entire body blazed with the neutralizing drug.

Legs still shaky, he made his way through the tiny forest and returned to his distant bungalow. As he walked, strength flowed through him. With it came determination to turn this to his advantage. Metchnikoff might have several other agents on-planet. They mattered little to him now that he knew they existed.

Metchnikoff. Kinsolving. Project Unravel. It came together in a neat framework in his head. All that remained was for the touch of genius only he could bring to the situation. Before the plague ran its course, he would have a directorship in Interstellar Materials.

CHAPTER TEN

BARTON KINSOLVING fought desperately to move his arms and legs. The stench from the monster towering over him robbed him of air and took away his strength. Kinsolving held his breath, then exhaled as forcefully as he could. A small surge of power coursed through him. As the creature swiped at him with a wickedly taloned paw, he jerked to the side and rolled. He felt flesh being stripped from his back but no pain blasted into him. Kinsolving kept rolling. He heard Vandy Azmotega shouting, but her voice sounded a parsec away.

His vision narrowed until he thought he peered along a dark tunnel. Kinsolving's lungs approached the point of rupturing, but he grimly held his breath. Something about the creature's odor paralyzed. He might be robbing himself of oxygen but he also robbed the ponderous monster of a potent weapon against him.

As if the world had collapsed to a small, bright spot, Kinsolving stared up and tried to figure out what he saw. The creature bellowed and roared to one side of the small room—this was a new danger. Through his confusion and mounting agony Kinsolving recognized the flitting silver speck as the killer robot that had chased them into this room.

He could not stand but he waved his arms weakly and attracted the robot's attention. With it came the monster.

Kinsolving's strength faded too rapidly to move farther than the corner of the room. Half propped against the wall, half sprawled on the grimy floor, he watched the battle through a gathering veil of inky darkness.

Hands shook him. He tried not to breathe but his body demanded oxygen. He panted harshly and life-giving gases flowed once more into his body.

"Bart, wake up. Are you hurt?"

His eyes flickered open and focused on Vandy's face.

"We're alive?" From all he remembered, this seemed unbelievable. The monster was too big, too powerful to fight. And the stench! It had paralyzed him.

"The robot and the *friz* collided. The robot destroyed it by drilling into the creature's belly and exploding."

Kinsolving sat up and winced. His back had turned into a field of molten pain. He looked around and saw bits of dirty white and cream-colored fur, burned meat and blood spattered on walls and ceiling. The monster's carcass had been blown backward into the far wall.

"Friz?" He couldn't get his mind to work properly. He caught on the strange word and held to it, more to assure himself that he wasn't dead than to maintain a semblance of intelligence.

"The Trekans bring them along. Pets, they call them. I don't really know what they use them for. Not pets." Vandy shuddered. Bits of the creature's blood dribbled down her face. Kinsolving reached up and brushed it away; all he succeeded in doing was smearing it.

"Some pet."

"They wanted to let them run free. I stopped that when a *friz* attacked two of my staff. The Trekan who had brought it thought it was cute."

"That it hunted humans?"

Vandy only nodded. From the tight line of her lips Kinsolving knew this was still a sore point with her. Not for the first time he wondered if Cameron and the others might not be doing the right thing with their Stellar Death Plan. The aliens *did* treat humanity with contempt.

He came fully to his senses. No, the Plan was wrong. Genocide was not the answer. Earning respect in spite of the alien opposition was. Prove to them that humans were their equals. Just as there were evil humans—Kinsolving had to put Cameron and Hamilton Fremont and the others involved with the Plan in this group—so there were evil aliens. He had met those who just did their job, who were pleasant and even kind. The Zeta Orgo policeman, Quixx, was one with whom he had developed some rapport. Kinsolving wished their meeting had come under other circumstances. He felt that they might call each other friend.

Vandy helped Kinsolving to his feet. He wobbled. She

put her arm around his waist gingerly and guided him to the tunnel.

"You need an automedic. The *friz* raked your back. The wounds are shallow but the dirty claws might give you an infection."

"I couldn't move," Kinsolving said, strength returning faster now that he got out of the creature's den. "I took one breath and it reduced me to a quivering blob."

"They hunt using an airborne protein that stuns its prey. It's also part of their mating."

"Photonic," Kinsolving said sarcastically. "I don't know if it meant to eat me or mate with me."

"From all I've seen of *friz* behavior, there's not much difference. Come on, up you go." Vandy pushed him up a ladder. Kinsolving clung on and managed to emerge in the brightness of Paradise's sun. With the woman's help, he got back to her small bungalow.

"Just sit there," she said, "and I'll get the automedic over here."

"I'm doing better," Kinsolving said. He did not sit; he flopped facedown on the floor. This relieved the pressure on his wounds. He slipped off to sleep and awakened only when the buzzing robot doctor began its work.

"This will be reported," the automedic said. "Such wounds are of class three severity."

"Report them. Mark them for the same file as Steev and Gonzales."

"*Friz* wounds," the automedic agreed. With that, it spun on its axis and left.

"I won't let your name be publicly mentioned," Vandy said, "but the report to the home office has to mention you."

"Is that a smart thing to do?" asked Kinsolving. He moved his arms carefully, waiting for pain. It never came. The automedic had done its job expertly. If he hadn't experienced some stiffness, he wouldn't have known he'd been injured by the beast.

"It's part of my job. We are very careful about keeping records on such accidents. Paradise caters to a wide variety of species. Keeping one race's fun from injuring another is difficult."

"That's not what I meant. Who can you trust at Terra Recreations?"

Vandy Azmotega settled back in a padded chair and simply stared at him. She had cleaned off the *friz's* gore, changed clothes and seemed better able to concentrate on important matters. He saw the woman's face alter slightly when she realized the implications of his words.

"I resented Suarez being here, but he carried orders from my boss back on Earth. Overhearing what he plans . . ." Her words trailed off.

"Your boss might not know. And *his* might not. But someone at Terra Recreations authorized Suarez's work and wants him to kill all the aliens on Paradise with his bio-plague. There's no way to know who sent him."

"I have nothing to do with it!" The sharp tone told of her concern and anger. Vandy had been in complete charge of the resort world until Suarez came. His Project Unravel would turn Paradise into a death planet—and this was just a minor field test. If the virus worked to expectations, it would be dumped into the atmospheres of hundreds— thousands!—of alien worlds, killing trillions of living, thinking beings.

"Never thought that you did," said Kinsolving. "But someone is responsible. Cameron was sent by a director of Interstellar Materials to observe. Knowing him, he'll end up running the project."

"Suarez is a capable man."

"He might be the best researcher in the galaxy, but Cameron is a killer. When it comes to fashioning new and more deadly robots, he is second to none."

Vandy shuddered. "We were lucky to get away from the robot in the tunnel."

"It saved me. If the *friz* hadn't attacked it, I might have been split between the two." The vision of being lasered while the *friz* ripped the flesh from his bones did not appeal to Kinsolving.

"When it doesn't return, this Cameron will be suspicious."

"Count on it," Kinsolving said. "Can you check guests to find out if anyone came with Cameron?"

Vandy reached down beside her and drew out a light wand. She aimed it at the far wall, which turned from a quaint Earth setting to a full-sized vidscreen. She worked on the light wand controls. An array of information popped onto the screen.

"See for yourself. He came alone from Gamma Tertius 4."

"Others arrived later," Kinsolving pointed out. "Two others."

Vandy worked for a few seconds, then frowned. "We can trace anyone on Paradise. Some of the pursuits requested are extremely hazardous. Mostly, the guests just want instant service."

Kinsolving said nothing. This continual spying might have reasons which satisfied most patrons, but it seemed to be unnecessary surveillance to him.

"We've lost track of Rossa Dantelli. Probes can't find her anywhere. Last tick on her was on the beach when she requested a music cube for a party."

"Who was with her then?"

"A dozen others. All human. From a variety of worlds. Her companion, Gerta Urquhart, is, uh, engaged at the moment. And was when Dantelli vanished."

"Can you track Cameron?"

"He apparently requested no service. We have honored it. But look at this." The picture dissolved and reformed. Cameron and the missing woman were together on the beach. "This was the last picture of Dantelli we recorded."

"Cameron killed her. Why?"

"Records show she is a secretary at IM headquarters."

"How does a secretary pay for such a lavish vacation?" Kinsolving wondered out loud.

"Paid for through IM accounts. Going back along the audit trails, back, back, there. Paid for from the special fund, Vladimir Metchnikoff, director."

"An internal power struggle," said Kinsolving. "That must be the reason Cameron killed her."

"We don't know he did anything to her," protested Vandy. She did not want more deaths logged as having occurred on Paradise.

"Cameron eliminates any threat. He is very efficient at his job, and his job now is Project Unravel."

Vandy said nothing, but Kinsolving knew the dilemma she faced. If she acted against Cameron and Suarez, she took the chance of losing not only her job but her life. Someone superior to her had authorized Project Unravel. Who? She had no way of knowing.

"This," she said, "might not go all the way to TR's board. Some junior officers might have given Suarez the funds. Who knows how much is in slush funds that are never directly accounted for."

"It infects IM's board," Kinsolving said, trying to show her the full extent of the Plan. "Fremont is the leading proponent of alien genocide there. The Plan is a secret to most employees, but not to IM's board. I'm wondering if the same is true for Terra Recreations."

"No," Vandy said. "I can't believe that. Our chairman has always sought out alien contacts. He opened Paradise to other species over a split vote. They had to go to a shareholders' meeting for final approval."

"We might identify some of the conspirators in the Stellar Death Plan by looking at that vote," said Kinsolving.

Vandy turned paler. "The director of my section voted against an open-species policy, but that doesn't mean he is part of any plot to murder entire planets!"

"No," agreed Kinsolving. "It doesn't. It just makes it more difficult knowing who to trust. Anyone might—or might not—be involved. Can you contact the chairman directly?"

"I can try. I'll send a special courier right away." Vandy paused, shaking her head. "What do I say? That another Earth company has assassins on Paradise killing each other and they're waiting for one of our scientists to slaughter almost fourteen hundred aliens with a bioengineered virus? He'd suspend me for indulging in some of our more mind-bending diversions."

"Send a courier you can trust with the message," said Kinsolving. That would not be enough. It might take weeks for the warning to be delivered and even more weeks for a positive response. Even worse, there might be no response at all—or Vandy might discover everyone at TR was implicated in the Plan. Whatever had to be done to save the aliens on Paradise had to be done soon.

Barton Kinsolving would have to do it. But what?

CHAPTER ELEVEN

CAMERON STARED at the spot in the small forest where Metchnikoff's assassin had been buried by the robots. He worried over the information lost by the woman's abrupt death, but he remembered the faint drug tingle on his lips. He had been given no opportunity to question her. Cameron hadn't even learned her name, as if that were important. Killing those who tried to kill him carried with it some small pleasure. He had triumphed, she had died. Simple.

But he needed information. Suarez would prove reluctant, Cameron knew, to obey. Suarez thought he worked for others in the TR hierarchy. That had ended when Villalobos sent Cameron to Paradise. Cameron would take charge of this ingenious weapon, whether anyone working for Terra Recreations wanted it that way or not.

"What others might Metchnikoff have sent?" he asked aloud. A thick aerial robot whizzed up and came to a halt in front of him. On a small one-line screen mounted in its side, the robot disgorged information almost faster than Cameron could read it.

"Gerta Urquhart," he mused. "Metchnikoff's other spy. Should I remove her immediately? No, I should save her. Let her wonder what happened to her friend." Cameron smiled broadly. He liked the idea of making Metchnikoff's spies suffer. Rubbing his lips, Cameron started away from the unmarked grave and walked toward the beach. Halfway to the water he stopped, turned and blew a soft kiss to his fallen opponent. She had not been very good, either as a spy or as a lover, but she had worked for IM. She deserved that much.

Cameron motioned and the information-carrying robot moved to a position where he could more easily read the rest of the report. The infobot had accomplished its task—partially. The part he needed most was missing.

"Nothing on Kinsolving's whereabouts, eh? But we have enough to find Lark Versalles. Where?" He studied the single line as it flashed the answer. Cameron continued walking along the beach, enjoying the soft sea breeze and the sharp tang of salt in the air, then abruptly turned and went inland.

He felt the pressure of time mounting. He had so much to do and so little time. The narrow pathway he found led him to a grassy meadow dotted with billowing particolored silk tents. It might have been a scene out of some medieval adventure except for the omnipresent metallic servants hovering nearby to cater to the guests' every whim.

Cameron allowed his own robotic guardians to drift further away in their patrols. He halted and studied the people gathered in the middle of the meadow. He had no trouble picking out Lark Versalles in the crowd. Her cosmetic dyes reflected ever-shifting patterns of silvers and gold in the noonday sun. Cameron skirted the group, approaching Lark from behind. She had her arm around another woman as they watched a group of gaily painted dancers performing acrobatic feats that defied both gravity and anatomy.

He had hoped to find Kinsolving with Lark. That the cause of Cameron's problems was not present did not bother him unduly. The hunt was always the sweeter when the prey proved exceptionally astute.

". . . so good!" squealed Lark. She turned and kissed her companion full on the lips.

Cameron frowned. Lark's companion appeared to be a human female but subtle indications to the contrary worked at the corners of his mind.

"Report," he said. The infobot flashed a single name: Onar.

Cameron went cold inside. Lark had taken a Bizzie lover. Lark Versalles was stunningly beautiful, but with that beauty went a decadence that sickened Cameron. How could she make love to a creature as much male as it was female? This miscegenation only fueled Cameron's hatred. People like Lark Versalles had to be saved from their own base instincts. Dealing with the aliens because of business pressure was one thing. Having social—sexual—relations transcended necessity.

He would be interested in seeing how effective Dr.

Suarez's virus was against Onarians. If it proved ineffectual, Cameron vowed to remove the Bizzie himself. Lark was too fine a woman to waste on aliens.

What would her family say?

Cameron pulled his attention from the pair and scanned the crowd. He did not find Kinsolving, either in disguise or hiding in some other fashion. But then he had not expected to. His robot had already scanned the crowd and identified them. Most were from Earth, children of rich parents out for a few brief and diverting days of vacation. Others bought their way to Paradise with more illicit funds. Cameron recognized two assassins working for other companies and a freelance killer whose reputation exceeded her ability. Of Gerta Urquhart he saw no sign.

A tiny flash from a robot alerted him. He said softly into a pickup mike under his lapel, "I will be there within five minutes." Cameron turned and walked away from the dance troupe. For such frivolous art he had no time. His art matched his craft; well-designed circuits, innovative AI contrivances, robots undreamed of by others. And smaller. Always smaller by half.

The brisk walk upslope took him to another path. He maintained his steady progress until he came to the small building housing Suarez's underground laboratory. Davi Jessarette stood guard outside, arms crossed and a sullen expression clouding his ugly face.

Cameron had expected him. Two patrolling survey robots had already reported the assassin's presence before he had come into view.

"Suarez is waiting for you," Jessarette said. The sour expression and his tone showed that he felt betrayed. He had trusted Cameron and been turned into a robot to be ordered around. Cameron wondered if Suarez had neutralized the night juggler drug or if he had allowed it to wear off. If the latter, Jessarette would have experienced severe spasms and stomach cramps.

"I'm aware of that. He signalled me directly."

Cameron moved quickly as Jessarette opened the door. A slight shift in weight and Cameron slipped past Jessarette, making it seem as if the other killer had been reduced to opening doors. Cameron donned his vid goggles and touched one temple. A view of all that happened behind him flashed across the special lenses without impairing his forward vision. He saw Jessarette reach for his weapon, then reconsider.

Cameron's back presented a good target. Too good. Jessarette looked around and saw no fewer than ten robots trailing behind their master. The man relaxed and moved his hand away from his weapon.

Cameron tried not to laugh out loud. None of the ten robots would have fired. Not when one had attached itself to Jessarette's collar. The slightest muscular tension signalling real danger would be acted upon by that robot. The small explosive charge would blow off Jessarette's head before the signal to squeeze a trigger could be sent from brain to finger.

Cameron considered ordering his killer robot to detonate and put Jessarette out of his misery. The man suffered and did not know the reason. Cameron decided to allow the pathetic man to live for a little longer. Jessarette's death should serve a purpose other than simple whim gratification.

"Doctor," Cameron called out, "when will you release the virus?"

"I wanted to give a brief report, Cameron," Morgan Suarez said, "because it seems to be expected in higher circles. You are not in charge of this project."

"Report," Cameron said crisply. He saw Jessarette stiffen but the muscles along the man's shoulders did not tighten in the way indicating that he would draw his weapon.

Suarez's dark eyes burned with anger. "I have completed the preliminary production. We have enough virus to infect the fourteen hundred plus Bizzies currently on Paradise."

"Then release the virus. Why delay?"

"The delivery mechanism must be precise. We need complete and accurate information at every stage of the infection. I will release it slowly, in specific populations of aliens. We are not equipped to study more than two or three at a time."

"You have fourteen hundred Bizzies from a dozen or more species as your test subject and you're only going to use it on two or three?" Cameron shook his head in disapproval.

"This is not an actual attack, Cameron. It is a field test —nothing more."

"Then, by all means, let us *test*."

Suarez's assistant shouted and dived for the table containing the vials of bioengineered death. A second shout terminated suddenly as a laser beam drilled through the side of the man's head. He fell facedown on the floor, fingers fastened on the edge of the table.

"This is an outrage!" cried Suarez.

"He tried to prevent my robot from . . . appropriating your virus."

"What are you doing? Stop it!"

"Really, doctor, I am only doing what you said you'd do if you had the equipment. My robot has an aerosol spray attachment. It is loaded with eighty milliliters of distilled water now infected with your virus. The remaining twenty milliliters from the vial is untouched."

"You don't know what you're doing. We need to study." Morgan Suarez took a step toward Cameron. An angry buzzing from a guard robot froze the scientist. "You dare to threaten me!"

"I, sir? Not at all. I am merely doing as Director Villalobos instructed. I am here to make sure that the proper tests are conducted. You worry needlessly. We are not adversaries. Rather, we are on the same side."

Cameron wondered if that were true of Davi Jessarette but did not include him in company of those adhering to the Stellar Death Plan.

"Where is it going?" demanded Suarez when he saw the thick cylinder of the robot floating out of the room. To Jessarette he shouted, "Stop it! This fool will ruin the test!"

"Davi," Cameron said in a soft voice. "You will die if you try to obey him. He seems to have forgotten why we are all here."

"But the vice president in charge of Paradise told me to do whatever Dr. Suarez said," the man protested.

Cameron filed away the information. He had no inkling of those involved with the Plan in other companies. Even within the IM ranks, he knew of only a few.

"You will be carrying out the vice president's wishes

more fully by doing nothing." In a voice even softer and infinitely more deadly, he added, "That is because you will still be alive."

"Jessarette," hissed Suarez.

"Enough." Cameron moved to the monitoring panel Suarez had set up for the test. Two small vidscreens showed inside a Bizzie compound. The lizardlike aliens lounged at the edge of a boiling hot pool of mud. He studied the scene and decided that Suarez had smuggled in two rice-grain cameras for the surveillance. He did not quite sneer at such primitive equipment but his opinion of the researcher dropped several degrees. Morgan Suarez might be a genius with recombinant bioweapons but his electronic expertise was positively twentieth century.

"I have positioned more than twenty aerial cameras at altitudes ranging from one kilometer up to fifty kilometers above the planet," he told Suarez. "These will provide continuous viewing and give the most minute details possible of the infectious process."

"Impossible. I need sharp definition. I need..." Suarez's voice trailed off when he saw the vidscreen. The picture showed a lounging reptile so distinct that he might have been looking through a visual microscope.

"Closer?" Cameron gestured. The texture of the rough alien skin turned into mountains and valleys more appropriate on the surface of a planet. "More?" The very pores in the skin opened. "This is taken with an electronic camera two kilometers overhead. I can bring in a close-up. It's not quite as good as a scanning electron microscope at that range, but it is good."

"This is incredible. I never knew it was possible."

"This is adequate? I can monitor forty channels simultaneously. It is all being fed into your computer for analysis."

Suarez looked at Cameron. "And is being recorded for your own use?"

"Mine? I have no use for this. The Plan must be served, and Interstellar Materials is intimately involved with the Plan."

"How are you proposing to release the virus? It must be done slowly, and in precise amounts."

"Down to a microliter? My robot sprayer can oblige."

"Do it. On this compound, four microliters at an altitude of ten meters."

"Done," said Cameron. He pointed to the controls for the spraying robot and let Suarez work on his own.

Within an hour the entire load of deadly virus had been precisely delivered to the most opportune targets. All that remained was data collection—and alien death.

CHAPTER TWELVE

"NO," VANDY AZMOTEGA SAID, shaking her head vigorously. "It matches everything I've seen and heard, but it is too fantastic."

"You were the one who said that alien guests were dying. Is that the reputation you want for your resort?" Kinsolving knew the battle Vandy was fighting inside. She had to be convinced that Terra Recreations had authorized murder to test a bioweapon. He guessed that her association with TR had been nothing but pleasant until this moment.

"Cameron. Maybe he has corrupted Suarez."

"You heard them. Who came to Paradise to observe? Suarez had his project well under way before Cameron arrived." Kinsolving lounged back, wincing slightly. The numbing anesthetic had begun to wear off; his back burned as though someone had run a laser over it burning in parallel grooves.

"Why should I trust you?"

Kinsolving heaved a deep breath. "You probably shouldn't. This might prejudice you against me, but you deserve the full truth. I was supervisor on Deepdig, a planet IM leased from the Lorr. I discovered massive losses in the rare earth ores. Tracing them, my . . . I found that my assistant was responsible."

"Your assistant?" probed Vandy. Her eyes burned.

"My lover, too. Ala Markken. At least I have reason to believe she was responsible for the thefts and that she tried to kill me. And that she knows about the Plan."

Vandy studied him critically. Kinsolving shoved to his feet and walked to the window. For a moment he swayed, off balance. The small house seemed out of place in a world of opulence, but Vandy allowed herself some luxuries. The view was not of Paradise but an Earth ocean smashing against a rocky cliff. He had not expected the appearance of a sheer drop just centimeters away.

"The rare earths were siphoned off and used in the brain burners. A single crystal of cerium oscillating at the appropriate frequency acts like a drug for some alien species." Kinsolving turned from the window and faced Vandy. "There is more."

"It has something to do with Lark Versalles?"

"No," he said impatiently. "More. Cameron made it appear that I had murdered a Lorr official. He did it, but I was sentenced to exile. Lark happened along and rescued me. A chance in a million. The Lorr are looking for me as an escaped murderer. Cameron wants me for the sheer joy of killing me. Anyone having to do with the Stellar Death Plan would cheerfully kill me, too."

"That's all I needed to know."

"What?"

"I intercepted a message packet routed through IM channels. You carry a hefty reward on your head. And a few months ago the Lorr left a photo facsimile of you. I routinely circulated it among the security staff. The Lorr are hunting you, Bart. Actively. You seem to have stung their pride."

"A mere human escaping a prison world where no one has ever escaped? I should think that would do it."

"You could kill," Vandy said.

"I have. But I didn't kill the Lorr."

Kinsolving saw that the woman had decided. She had accumulated enough facts, sifted through them, mixed in her own feelings and come to a conclusion. Running a resort planet like Paradise did not permit the luxury of protracted decision making.

"We've got to find Cameron and stop him," she said. "My security force is not up to the task. Not since any of them might be working with Suarez." She swallowed hard. "It's obvious to me that Jessarette saw your photo and tried to kill you on Almost Paradise. He might have heard something about you and Cameron. He's always shown good intelligence-gathering skills."

"Cameron would be far harder to capture—or kill—than Suarez," said Kinsolving, going to the heart of the real problem facing them. "We should find the virus and destroy it. But there will be some problems."

"Death, for one," said Vandy. "You don't have to convince me how dangerous this is. But there's one factor in our favor: I'm still in charge of Paradise, and I command all its resources. An entire planet is a powerful force."

Kinsolving did not want to discourage her. They both needed confidence that they might succeed, but he had the gut level feeling that Cameron's cleverness had already undercut much of Vandy's power.

"Try the computer banks," he requested. "Track Suarez and see if you can even locate Cameron."

She lifted the light wand and pointed it at a few key toggles on the wall vidscreen. A flash and then . . . nothing.

Vandy frowned. "Hard to believe it's out of order. I just had the entire system maintenanced a month ago."

"See if you can locate Jessarette. I can't believe Cameron held him in too high a regard. He seemed to be drugged in the lab."

"Davi Jessarette's not too bright but he has his uses. Some guests become rowdy and require a human touch. Not everything can be done using robots."

"There," Kinsolving cried when an aerial scan of a crowd panned past Jessarette. "And that's Suarez with him."

"I still can't lock on Suarez. It's as if the computer refuses to acknowledge his existence, yet we can see him."

"Do another check. Cameron has been tinkering with your computer banks." Kinsolving moved closer to the vidscreen and peered at the two men. The researcher used a small, hand-held device to sample the air.

"Bart, he might be releasing the virus!"

Kinsolving experienced a moment's nausea. "No," he said. "They've already released it. He's sampling the air to see how effective the virus is."

"Let's go find out for ourselves," Vandy said. She reached into a cabinet and pulled out an impact laser. "Can you use this thing? I've had it for years and never even fired it."

"I learn quick," Kinsolving said. He checked the charge levels. The small laser locked onto target, then fired, rapidly varying the lasing frequency. No energy weapon had stopping power, but the impact laser came close as it produced a differential heating zone in its target. With luck, it would duplicate the impact of a small explosive projectile. At worst, it burned the hell out of its target.

"Down on the sward. We were duplicating a medieval fair. The aliens tend to like it more than our Earth guests. Shows how primitive we really are."

Kinsolving and Vandy hurried along the deserted paths, taking one that only service personnel used. "There," Vandy said. "A cab. One of ten we keep nearby for getting around when we need to. Otherwise, we walk or let the robots carry our supplies."

Kinsolving jumped into the small cab and pulled the plastic air shield down. Vandy slipped into the seat beside him and pressed her key card into the ignition. For a moment, Kinsolving tried to figure out what was bothering him. Dozens of observations came crashing together in his mind and formed a deadly picture. He yanked out the impact laser and used it on the air shield. It exploded in a molten burst. Vandy protested but he cut her short, grabbing her arm and pulling her through the fiery-rimmed hole he had just burned.

The cab erupted in a sheet of searing orange flame seconds after they had exited. A powerful hand plucked at his body, lifting, tearing, turning. Kinsolving landed heavily, moaning because he had opened the wounds on his back by sliding along the ground.

"What happened? I never saw anything like that before."

Kinsolving levered himself to a sitting position. "Cameron is efficient. When I locked the air shield down, I noticed two newly installed block circuit connections. The one circuit hummed when you used your key card. Anyone else could use the cab with no trouble. Your identicard triggered the bomb."

"Cameron knows?"

"He must. His robots are everywhere."

"Why wouldn't he simply kill me? If the robot killers are as good as you say, why not just use them?"

"How can you explain a cat playing with a mouse? He thinks he is in control." Kinsolving sat and thought hard. "It might be something else, though. I've kept a low profile since Jessarette tried to kill me on Almost Paradise. This might be his doing. Cameron wants me, and Jessarette thinks using you as bait is the way to finish what he started and show Cameron up at the same time."

"He came damned close," Vandy said. She brushed smoldering plastic from her hair, then checked to be sure she hadn't missed any. "If we split forces, though, we weaken our position. I have access to anywhere on-planet. And you know more about Cameron than I could learn in a few minutes."

"Let's walk. If we can get to Suarez, we might find out something about stopping the virus."

Kinsolving doubted it but they had to do something. If Suarez had released the recombinant DNA airborne weapon there might be nothing that anyone could do until it had run its course—killing untold numbers of aliens on Paradise.

Panting, sweat running in salty rivers down his back and burning his wounds, Kinsolving found himself hard-pressed to keep up with Vandy as they ran through the sylvan glades and thick, well-tended forests. He about doubled over from exhaustion when they emerged from a copse and looked down the grassy slope to where Suarez and Jessarette still stood.

"What now?" asked Vandy. "Shoot them with the laser?"

"They deserve it, but we need information, not retribution. Even if they've released it, there might be an antidote or something that will kill the virus before it can work."

"Bart, Jessarette has spotted us!"

He saw that Vandy was right. Davi Jessarette tugged at Suarez's arm and pointed upslope in their direction.

"We can't reach them before they melt into the crowd," said Vandy, her sharp eyes judging distances and speeds.

"Let's see if I can herd them away," said Kinsolving. He pulled out the impact laser and sent the faint red sighting beam out to a spot halfway between the men and the bulk of the crowd gathered for the medieval exhibition. He triggered the laser. A rock exploded at Jessarette's feet, sending the man stumbling back.

"You missed!" cried Vandy.

"All I want to do is keep them away from the others."

Kinsolving fired again. Jessarette had drawn a weapon of his own. Suarez yelled something that turned into a muffled shout of anger by the time it reached Kinsolving, but the intent was crystalline. He wanted Jessarette to remove the danger.

Kinsolving tried to hit Jessarette's legs and missed. Jessarette moved quickly and well to avoid becoming a good target. Kinsolving's experience with combat weapons was limited. Jessarette did far better with his own weapon.

A sudden glint as Jessarette fired it gave Kinsolving all the warning he was likely to receive.

"Vandy, into the forest. Hurry. *Now!*" He had thought to drive Suarez and Jessarette away from sanctuary in the crowd gathered for the medieval spectacle. A single shot had turned his strategy against them. They were now the pursued instead of the pursuers.

"What's wrong?" she demanded. "What happened?"

Kinsolving glanced over his shoulder and caught a second glimpse of sunlight reflected off a long, slender projectile.

"One of Cameron's toys," he panted. Already he was short of breath. He had come too far too fast to be in good shape. Kinsolving jerked Vandy to the left, ducked, turned and tried to run at an angle. A snapping sound came from behind. An overhanging branch limb burst into flame. The pursuing robot's laser had ignited the dried wood.

Kinsolving sensed rather than saw the danger. He shoved Vandy sprawling as he whipped around, his own laser up and struggling to find a target. The tiny robot proved too elusive a target. He fired and missed. The robot fired—and struck.

Kinsolving yelled in pain. His hand trembled too much for him to properly aim with the impact laser's sighting beam. The pursuing robot whirred around in an orbit so fast that Kinsolving knew he was doomed.

"Bart!" Vandy Azmotega stood and took a step toward him.

"Keep down!" he shouted, but it was too late. The robot spun on its axis and aimed its deadly laser directly for Vandy's head.

CHAPTER THIRTEEN

KINSOLVING WAS NOT even aware of acting. He pointed the impact laser in the general direction of the robot and fired repeatedly. One shot might have struck it; the ionization cloud from the laser discharge might have disrupted vital circuits; the robot might have damaged itself in its flight through the forest. Whatever the cause, the robot exploded, showering Vandy and Kinsolving with a molten rain of sundered parts.

He lay back on the ground, stunned. Shaking off the effects, he rolled and came to his feet. Vandy Azmotega struggled to stand. She, too, had been dazed by the blast.

"You're either a damned good shot or luckier than you have any right to be," she said. "Help me up."

He gave her a hand and said, "I don't know much about assassin projectiles. This might be a standard issue, but I don't think so. If it is one of Cameron's, he already knows it failed."

"You think he'll send another?"

"He might send a thousand." Kinsolving looked up through the green leaves to the azure sky. He had no way of knowing what Cameron would do. The man had been on Paradise long enough to have a million self-contained, deadly, thinking robots everywhere.

"We can't let this stop us," Vandy said. "Paradise's reputation is at stake. Suarez can't be allowed to kill guests." She sounded more aggrieved about the pleasure planet's reputation than the lives of her guests, but Kinsolving understood her sentiments.

"Jessarette and Suarez will be long gone," he said. "Where is the nearest enclave of aliens? You said Jessarette had been guarding the ambassador. They might have used Jessarette to get past the Trekans' own security system."

"This way." Vandy wobbled a little, then walked with her usual firm, brisk stride through the forest. Kinsolving held back, letting her go first. His dark eyes scanned the branches and open spaces for the slightest hint of another laser-equipped robot.

He saw nothing, and this worried him more than finding an entire flock of metallic killers. Was Cameron toying with him or was this part of some grander, more devious scheme? Cameron could not have known he would come across Kinsolving on Paradise. Kinsolving had not known where he shifted when he fled Zeta Orgo 4.

Coincidence? Or destiny? Kinsolving tried not to believe in destiny or luck, yet his continued existence worked to erode his disbelief. Escaping the Lorr prison had been luck. The only parts that had been skill lay in keeping alive. Even discovering the details of the Plan had been accidental.

If accident had put him on this strange and dangerous path, only clever planning and ability would keep him alive.

"They had sensors placed around their compound to keep out casual interlopers," Vandy said. "I know where they are and how they work. I insisted on knowing. This way."

She traced a complicated path across an innocuous-appearing lawn until Kinsolving called to her to stop. "Show me one of the sensors."

Vandy silently pointed to a small mound in the grass. Kinsolving knelt and brushed the mosslike grass back, exposing the dirt. Careful prying lifted the device.

"Their guards will be all over us," she said tiredly. "We should have announced our arrival. Maybe I can tell the ambassador that you're a tech doing some repair work."

"No need. A new circuit has been built into the sensor, circumventing its function."

"Cameron?"

"I don't think so. This is sloppy work. I saw it instantly; anyone would. Someone else has been plying their trade, and not doing it nearly as well as Cameron."

"You found Cameron's booby trap in the cab."

"That was substandard work, too. Better than this, but not up to his exacting detail. Is Jessarette capable of such work?" He held up the sensor for her inspection. Vandy shrugged.

"He might be. I never got good work from him, but he never really failed, either. His profile shows that he has a higher opinion of his abilities than reality warrants." She gave a strange little laugh. "That's nothing. Most of us on Paradise have the same notation on our psych profiles. Goes with the work of satisfying other people's fantasies."

Kinsolving dropped the gimmicked sensor. Jessarette had a hand in much of what had happened. He had guarded Morgan Suarez and had been in charge of the Trekan ambassador. Kinsolving felt a tightening in his belly. Jessarette might be the stumbling block more than Cameron. If so, they had a chance. Cameron made few mistakes—and those had already been committed. The foppish assassin never made the same mistake twice.

"No guards along the walls?" Kinsolving strained to see the top of the shoulder-high rock wall. "Not even any vidcameras?"

"Full array. Hidden to keep the guests from feeling imprisoned," answered Vandy, but the tone she used showed worry. She walked along the wall and opened a hidden junction box.

"Let me guess," said Kinsolving. "All the circuits are gimmicked."

"A relay transmitter, too. Whatever is seen is broadcast to an unauthorized location. We use fiber optic cables to prevent eavesdropping. This is all added."

Kinsolving wiggled to the top of the wall and then dropped over, expecting fiery beams to cross in the center of his chest. Nothing. Vandy followed him over rather than going the hundred meters along the wall to the front gate.

"Fancy building," Kinsolving said. He had worked in the mines most of his life and was unused to luxury in any form. Even these alien palaces struck him as extraordinary.

"We try to please," Vandy said. She grabbed his arm and stopped him, head canted to one side and a look of extreme concern on her face.

For a few seconds Kinsolving wondered what troubled her. Then he heard it, too. At first, it was faint, almost too vague to hear. Then it came in a roar that equalled any physical blow he had ever received. If an entire zoo had been turned loose, the cacophony of barks and whistles and howls of rage and pain could not have matched it.

"The ambassador," Vandy said in a weak voice.

Kinsolving would not have recognized the creature that burst from the mansion doors as sentient if she had not warned him. Fiery red eyes blazed as the beast rushed across the lawn toward them. Fingers hooked like talons raked the air. Worst of all was the demented shrieking.

"The laser, Bart. Use the laser!" Vandy cried, when it became obvious that they were the rampaging Trekan's target.

Kinsolving reacted too slowly. Shock at seeing such a wild being prevented him from responding with the deadly bolt that would have snuffed out a life. By the time he recovered, it was too late to use the laser. The ambassador from a civilized and sophisticated world ripped and tore at him like a rabid dog.

Kinsolving and the alien tumbled to the ground and rolled, the laser falling from Kinsolving's grip. Kinsolving came out on top and used his superior weight to hold the ambassador's shoulders down. His face pressed close to the Trekan's. Kinsolving wished he dared release the alien. The Trekan's face looked more like a pale green dog's than a human's. The long snout protruded only half as long as an Earth canine's, but the teeth were definitely a carnivore's. Above the lips, pulled back in a feral snarl, were tiny pockets of what appeared to be pus. One sac burst and yellow ichor dribbled down the ambassador's cheek. Wherever the liquid touched it burned.

"Easy, keep calm," Kinsolving urged. The Trekan was beyond reason. Froth speckled his lips. He surged again and sent Kinsolving flying. Seldom had Kinsolving felt such berserk power—and never directed against him by such a small being.

The Trekan dropped to all fours as if denying ten million years of evolution. Eyes turned to slits, the alien shuffled forward. Kinsolving had no strength left. He had fought too many battles.

The ambassador gasped, let out an all too human sigh, then sagged to one side.

"What happened?" asked Vandy. She had picked up Kinsolving's fallen impact laser. "I started to fire, but he keeled over before I did."

"He's dead." Kinsolving carefully avoided contact with the ichorous sores.

"The virus?" Vandy's words were muffled by a gentle breeze blowing from the direction of the mansion.

"I'm afraid so." Kinsolving sniffed and detected an odor that gagged him. It took incredible determination but he walked slowly to the mansion door through which the ambassador had come and peered inside.

His reflexes saved him. He had the impact laser up and firing before he realized what he was doing. Two Trekans exploded as if miniature suns had blossomed in their chests. Kinsolving recoiled and ran into Vandy, who stood and stared, openmouthed.

"I've never seen anything like this. I thought I had seen it all, but this!" She shook her head, sending a soft auburn cascade down around her shoulders. Kinsolving fixed his gaze on her hair—human hair, normal, natural, something to stroke and enjoy and normal, normal, not like the hideous scene within.

"They're all dead. The virus is doing this to them. Turning them insane. It must affect the neurochemicals in their brains."

· "The limbic system. It's taken over conscious thought. Their physiology is similiar to ours," said Vandy. "I have complete workups on them. On all the aliens." She swallowed hard. The paleness of her face made Kinsolving wonder if she was about to faint.

The dizziness he felt made him wonder if *he* was about to faint.

"The neurotransmitters are failing," she said. "The chemicals that allow the Trekans to think like civilized people aren't being reproduced. That must be it."

"But the sores. Those can't be natural."

Vandy shook her head. "Who knows what Suarez has loosed on my planet. Damn him! I'll stuff him down a black hole when I find him!"

"Is there another compound nearby? Other aliens?" Kinsolving was afraid of what they might find, but he had to look. There might be a small chance of saving some of the fourteen hundred aliens on Paradise.

He did not really think it was possible, though, not after seeing what the Trekans had become.

Vandy Azmotega led the way across the field and to another dazzling white marble palace set high atop a hill. From the side Kinsolving saw the ocean's waves crashing into the sandy shoreline. This was an idyllic place to sit and relax, but he got no sense of serenity. The mansion was preternaturally quiet. The Treka household had been noisy as the beasts within each civilized creature had been set free to roam. He heard no sound here other than the wind and water.

"How awful," gasped Vandy.

Kinsolving had steeled himself for what they might find. This exceeded his worst expectations. He could not even identify the species of alien. Each had died in horrible pain.

"They broke every bone in their bodies trying to—what?" asked Vandy.

"Hallucinations? Pain? Who knows what Project Unravel did to them," Kinsolving said bitterly. "This is the legacy the Stellar Death Plan will give the universe."

"How can they?" moaned Vandy. "If they see how hideous this is, they'll stop. They have to!"

"They won't," Kinsolving said. "I doubt this affects Suarez at all. Maybe he's happy at the efficient way of killing he's found. He might be displeased if it didn't work fast enough or on every alien."

Vandy turned and ran from the mansion. Kinsolving held his gorge down as he followed behind her. Putrescence would soon set in, turning these fabulous houses into charnel pits.

He could not allow anyone advocating annihilation of all aliens to continue along this path. He had to stop those behind the Plan.

Barton Kinsolving stopped a few paces from where Vandy Azmotega hunched over, trying vainly to regain her composure. He looked up and saw a flash of light against the bright blue sky. Kinsolving lifted the impact laser and carefully aimed. He had to take a dozen shots before he hit the weaving, dodging robot.

It crashed to the ground a few meters distant.

"That's it," he told Vandy. "They used robots—probably that very one—to spray the virus into the air where the aliens inhaled it." He directed the aiming beam to the center of the partially destroyed machine. A final laser blast completely destroyed the aerosol spraying robot.

The booby traps might have been Jessarette's work. Kinsolving recognized a master's design in this machine.

Cameron had just delivered the virus that destroyed fourteen hundred living, breathing, thinking beings.

CHAPTER FOURTEEN

KINSOLVING STARED at the vidscreen, not seeing the three-dimensional parade of faces and figures. Vandy Azmotega muttered constantly to herself and she worked to bring her computer banks under full control again. The harder she worked, the more she failed.

"I give up. I thought I knew the system, but there's no way I can get the scanners to pick up Suarez. As for Cameron, the vidcams won't even register his bungalow, much less him. Imagine that!"

"He's good," Kinsolving said, still distracted. Too much had happened. The virus had worked rapidly and with a vicious effectiveness. He hoped that Vandy would not do another quick-scan of the alien quarters. The crews she had dispatched worked with remotes to prevent further contamination, but Kinsolving knew that no human could catch the plague that had destroyed so many others.

It had been specifically designed to kill only Bizarres.

"I even did a complete program wipe and reinstalled. Nothing works as it should," complained Vandy. "It's almost as if he had access to system level."

"Considering how expert Cameron is, he might have designed the system you use." Kinsolving sat upright, ignoring the momentary pain in his back. He made a mental note to have the automedic take another look at his injuries. They should have completely healed by now. But a disturbing thought intruded.

"Can you punch up every other guest on Paradise?" he asked. "Locate Lark Versalles for me."

"Lark?" Vandy's tone indicated what she thought of the other woman. She pointed her light wand at the vidscreen and a kaleidoscopic twisting brought Lark's face into sharp focus. The cosmetic dyes appeared muted and even somber in their olive drabs and beiges. Kinsolving hardly recognized her because of that.

"Can you contact her and have her come here?"

Vandy tapped in a new command to the light wand. Lark's image jumped. Vandy had not brought up the sound but Kinsolving saw from Lark's frightened expression that a voice spoke from thin air. This could not be the source of Lark's discomfort.

"Pan," he ordered. "Stop! There. Look at her. Sheeda. I had forgotten about her. She's an alien. An Onarian."

"She's not dead, though," Vandy said, more curious than irritated now. She used the light wand to issue new commands. On-screen Kinsolving saw a contamination-suited staff worker enter and place Sheeda on a mobile stretcher. Lark followed behind the floating stretcher, wringing her hands and looking increasingly miserable.

Within ten minutes the door chimes sounded. Kinsolving let the trio in. "Put her over there," he told the suited man, indicating a spot for Sheeda's stretcher.

"Bart, darling!" cried Lark when she saw him. She threw her arms around his neck and buried her face in his shoulder. Hot tears burned through his shirt. "Something happened to Sheeda. No one will get her a doctor. She's dying, Bart!"

"I'm afraid so," he said gently. He stroked her fine hair. She had changed its color since he had seen her last. Stripes of verdant green and fuchsia turned her into something both clownish and exotic. "This is Cameron's doing."

"Barton, no! He wouldn't . . ." Lark's voice trailed off. She knew differently. "That son of a bitch. I'll shove him feet-first into a plasma torch!"

"This isn't the first time he's killed your friends," he said. "Remember back on Gamma Tertius 4? Dinky and the others? And how his robots killed Randi duLong aboard ship? This time he's released a plague killing only aliens."

"But Sheeda hasn't done anything to him. Why does he want to hurt her?"

"Prejudice isn't rational," he said, knowing this was not what Lark wanted to hear. But Kinsolving had no words to comfort her. For all the uneasiness he felt in Sheeda's presence, he wished the dual-sexed Onarian no harm.

Vandy had started her automedic working on Sheeda. The alien lay on the stretcher, as pale as death and in a light coma. Occasionally her eyes opened but no intelligence shone forth. The glaze made Kinsolving think that the woman/man endured a fever of incredible proportions, even though the automedic recorded normal temperature levels.

"The robot's doing a full workup now," said Vandy. "Sheeda might be the only alien left on Paradise. I've scanned all the guests and haven't found any others alive."

"No one knew about this," said Lark, still in shock. "The others. The humans. They . . . they didn't say a word."

"As far as our Earth guests are concerned, nothing *has* happened," answered Vandy. "We'd like to keep it that way. But I've had to shift out message packets to the aliens' home worlds. It will be a few weeks before answers come back—probably as indignant delegations wanting to sever diplomatic ties with Earth for such an atrocity."

"A few weeks," mused Kinsolving. "By then IM will know of the success. Cameron will have sent back a message packet to GT4."

"I've interdicted all messages except for those I approve," said Vandy, as if she thought Kinsolving were a fool for not believing her capable of doing her job. Then his meaning struck her as hard as a blow to the jaw. "Cameron can send whatever he wants. He has control of my computer."

"And anything else he wants on Paradise. But he might not trust his report to a packet. This news is something he might want to deliver in person."

"The automedic's finished," cut in Lark. "What does it say? Is Sheeda all right?"

Kinsolving scanned the report. He had been trained to work with field automedic units on Deepdig. Interpreting the robotic results had been part of that training. He shook his head. "This only shows a chemical imbalance in her system. The automedic isn't equipped for full alien biochemistry workups. But I think we can keep her alive. Not repair the damage done, perhaps, but keep her alive until we can ship her back to Onar for proper medical help from her own doctors."

Lark sank to her knees beside the feverish Sheeda. "There, there, it'll be all right. Barton says so. He wouldn't lie to you. Never. Oh, darling Sheeda, why did this have to happen?"

Kinsolving drew Vandy aside. "Check the scanners and locate Davi Jessarette."

"If Cameron has blanked out himself and Suarez, why not cancel Jessarette from the computer banks, too?"

"Cameron must have a reason, if we can find Jessarette. Whatever it is, you can bet that it's part of a bigger scheme." It did not surprise him when the stocky security agent popped onto the vidscreen.

"That's in an area we're repairing," Vandy said, studying the surroundings. "Every few months we renovate. Suarez might have moved from the underground lab to one of those buildings. Nothing but robot workers would be around. They wouldn't report back unless someone tried to stop them while they worked. Only the supervisor robots have the capability of evaluating if something is amiss outside their programmed area of responsibility."

"Cameron could circumvent them easily enough," said Kinsolving. He worried at the ease in finding Jessarette. What did Cameron have in mind? Did he use Jessarette as bait for a trap? If so, the prey was about to step boldly into the jaws of the trap.

"Bart," spoke up Vandy, "there's something wrong with this. Let me send in a security squad."

He shook his head. "He might not allow it. If Cameron wants me there, then I'll go. But I've got to have an edge, something to insure that he doesn't simply walk away after killing me."

"What is that?" asked Vandy.

Kinsolving had no answer.

"I don't want you coming with me," said Kinsolving. "It's too dangerous."

"Just being supervisor of Paradise has become 'too dangerous,'" said Vandy Azmotega. "Fourteen hundred of my guests are dead and there'll be hell to pay when the news arrives on their respective planets. On the entire planet, only Sheeda and one other Onarian are still alive. Both are closer to dead than alive, too."

Kinsolving pushed that from his mind and tried not to panic. The large villa where Jessarette hid might have been designed for use as a fortress—or a prison. Once inside, there would be no easy escape. Cameron had lured him here. He had to find out why.

"I know the place better than anyone else," she said. "Even if Cameron has complete access to my computer, I know this place better than he ever could. This project has been partly rebuilt according to my verbal orders. No computer-recorded plans."

Kinsolving thought she was lying just to join him. He decided that this was her planet, her responsibility, her need to see justice done.

"How do we get inside without triggering all the alarms?" he asked.

Vandy smiled. "This way. A hole in the wall."

They crawled on their bellies through a low ravine and under a rock fence. Inside Vandy explained, "I was going to divert a stream here, then changed my mind."

Kinsolving caught her arm and squeezed, silently cautioning her against speaking. A shadow passed across a wall. He drew the impact laser and felt naked, even with it in hand. Cameron was expert at hunting and killing. And his robots were even better. What chance did anyone really have against a trained assassin?

Kinsolving saw no other choice. Vandy Azmotega had lost control of Paradise because of Cameron's expertise with computer systems. She could do only those chores he allowed. Communication to the alien worlds had been allowed: Cameron wanted fear to spread. Kinsolving wondered if the Plan depended on the arrival of alien vessels to investigate.

He doubted it. As paranoid as those adherents of the Stellar Death Plan were, they would expect the aliens to nuke the planet. Another way of infecting the alien worlds had already been chosen. Of that Kinsolving was certain.

But Cameron might want to play out his hunter-prey games, with nothing more to be gained than satisfaction from killing Kinsolving. That did not ring true, either. Cameron was efficient and would relish Kinsolving's death, but the Plan came first.

"Barton, look," Vandy whispered urgently. She held another impact laser, clumsily pointing it in the direction of the moving shadow.

"Don't fire yet," said Kinsolving. "There's more to do first. Be sure of your target." He made certain she understood.

He had not counted on a voice pickup microphone being trained on him. His words boomed across the large walled estate. The shadow vanished instantly. Kinsolving swore under his breath. Even these words were picked up and clearly broadcast. He bit his lip and looked around, scanning not only the sky but the ground at his feet. A small lump looked suspicious in the perfectly tended lawn. He fired the impact laser. The greater-than-expected explosion told him he had destroyed the remote sensor that had betrayed him.

The satisfaction he felt at finding Cameron's relay robot was instantly blotted out by a high-energy laser bolt ripping through the air and destroying a portion of the wall behind him. The purple haze from the ionization trail snaked back in the direction of the main house. Whoever had cast the shadow had armed himself with a powerful combat laserifle.

The impact laser in his hand made him feel even more helpless. A tiny pistol against such armament spelled suicide. Kinsolving did the only thing he could do. He attacked.

"Cover me!" he yelled over his shoulder at Vandy. She gasped, then settled down and began firing. The pathetic little bolts nipped at the corner of the house. Kinsolving wanted to guide her firing but could not take the time. He kept his head down and charged. Another bolt turned the dirt at his feet into plasma.

He stumbled and rolled and came to his feet in time to tuck his head between outstretched arms. He crashed through an ornate, decorative window. Amid a shower of stained glass he landed facedown inside the mansion. A silent prayer went out. If Vandy had opted for the more usual plastic panes instead of the colorful and archaic stained glass he would have knocked himself out.

Echoes betrayed the rifle wielder. Kinsolving followed the shadows dancing inside the empty house and waited, holding his breath, hand uncommonly steady. The muzzle of the high-energy laserifle poked around the corner of the door. Kinsolving waited, thumb poised to send out the aiming beam. He hardly knew he exhaled slowly when more of the rifle came around. A hand. A wrist. An arm and shoulder.

His thumb touched the toggle. A cherry red aiming beam found a spot on the rifleman's chest. With the sudden understanding of perfect alignment, Kinsolving pressed the trigger. The variable frequency impact laser fired, working its deadly magic on the victim's torso.

A shrill scream split the silence inside the house. Echoes vanished down long corridors. The heavy laser fell from lifeless fingers as the body toppled forward into full view.

Several seconds passed before Kinsolving moved. He had expected to see Jessarette's blasted body. Or, as a distant hope, to find Cameron's corpse. A woman stretched out prone on the floor. He advanced cautiously and pulled the laserifle away. It still carried a full charge. He hefted it, trying to decide which weapon suited him best. Opting for the laserifle's power, he thrust the impact laser into a pocket.

"Barton," came Vandy's breathless voice from the door, "what happened?"

"I thought I'd shot you by mistake," he said, "but I've never seen this woman before. Is she on Suarez's research team?"

"No, he only had the one assistant." Vandy knelt and lifted the fallen woman's head to study the face. "Familiar. Wait a second." Taking her light wand out, she scanned the slack face. Identification came back instantly. "She's a guest. Gerta Urquhart. From Gamma Tertius 4."

"Let me guess," Kinsolving said in disgust. "She's the other guest who arrived after Cameron did. And her friend is already dead."

"And I thought telepathy was impossible." A faint smile wrinkled the corners of Vandy's lips. "Any other lucky guesses?"

Kinsolving could not make sense of it. He had expected Cameron or Suarez and had run afoul of another IM director's employees.

A sudden sharp sound from upstairs alerted him. He motioned Vandy behind him, then started up the broad, winding marble staircase. The lack of furnishings allowed echoes to race unhindered from one end of the mansion to another and made it difficult to determine the exact source of the sound, but he thought it came from the second floor.

He hoped so. He presented a good target should Cameron decide to use him for target practice. But Kinsolving wondered if the robotics master had such a crass end in store for him. Any of a dozen times would have sufficed to send a single killer robot after him. Cameron seemed content to let this strange play unravel, just as the DNA helices in the aliens had already unraveled.

Shards of broken glass on the hall floor told of recent use of the room beyond. Kinsolving pushed the glossy wood door open with the muzzle of the laserifle and looked inside. A makeshift workbench stretched along the far wall. Strewn around were broken glass test tubes and carrying cases for biologic specimens.

Kinsolving opened the door further. He saw a man hunched over, working frantically at a remote console.

It took all his willpower to keep from pressing the firing toggle on the laserifle. Instead, Kinsolving said, "Move away from the computer, Dr. Suarez. We have much to discuss."

Morgan Suarez spun, a startled look on his face. His mouth opened but no words came out. As if he were a marionette and someone had cut his strings, he simply sat down on the floor, eyes glassy and body slack.

CHAPTER FIFTEEN

"HE'S TRYING TO KILL ME," sobbed Morgan Suarez.

For a few seconds Kinsolving thought the man meant him. Kinsolving's finger tensed on the laserifle's firing toggle, then relaxed only through immense force of will.

"He's trying to steal everything I've done. I hate him!"

"Cameron?" Kinsolving moved into the room and quickly glanced around. The worktables were strewn with broken glassware, as though someone had taken a club to the fragile test tubes and complex test equipment. "Do you mean Cameron's trying to kill you?"

"He wants my discovery. No one else has ever done such fine work on Bizzie physiology. No one else has ever unlocked the secrets of their genetic structure—and he wants it for himself!"

"And all you wanted was to kill a few trillion intelligent beings," raged Kinsolving. He had no sympathy for Suarez.

"You're not with him. You're working for them, for the Bizzies, for the enemy!"

Kinsolving felt Vandy Azmotega move up behind him, her hand resting lightly on his shoulder. "He's crazy," she whispered. "Listen to him. He's turned to vacuum between his ears."

"He was crazy long before Cameron arrived," said Kinsolving.

"He stole it all, and I can't get it back. He's got the process."

Kinsolving stared at the scientist huddling in the corner of the room. Not a flicker of pity went out to the man. Suarez had personally murdered fourteen hundred aliens on Paradise. Anything that happened to him was only justice. But Kinsolving could not imagine insanity as fitting punishment for what this man had unleashed. Suarez hardly knew where he was. Kinsolving wanted him to suffer, to regret every day of continued life, to share in the pain he had created.

"Where is Cameron?" he demanded.

"He took it. He got into my work computer and stole the process information. He knows it all!"

"Here," Kinsolving said, handing the laserifle to Vandy. "Be careful. I want to see if I can't help him remember better." Kinsolving walked in a wide berth away from any potential firing line. Suarez stared at him with fright-widened eyes. No intelligence shone forth from those dark eyes that had once flashed with hate. Kinsolving grabbed Suarez and jerked him to his feet.

"Please, stop him. He's got it all."

"What's Cameron going to do with it?"

"He stole it. They—they're trying to take over. They're trying to keep TR from taking part in the Plan."

"Do you mean Interstellar Materials?"

"Yes, them! Fremont and Villalobos and Cameron. That son of a bitch!" wailed Suarez. "Cameron stole it for them. They want to prevent anyone else from taking part in the Plan. They want it all for themselves!"

"The Stellar Death Plan?"

"The universe! With my discovery, they can have it all. Get it back for me." A cunning look came into the demented, haunted eyes. "Steal it back and I'll reward you generously. Anything you want. Just get back the process files!"

"Where is Cameron?" asked Kinsolving, shoving Suarez back against the wall. "I can't do anything for you unless you tell me."

"He's clever, but I'm a genius. *I* invented the process that unravels their DNA," gibbered Suarez.

Kinsolving slammed Suarez hard against the wall. "Where is he? Tell me."

"Cameron? He took it and is smuggling it off-planet. He wants to get it back to IM on Gamma Tertius 4. He told me, the son of a bitch. He's evil. He took it and went back to—"

Suarez's words were abruptly silenced by the roar of an energy weapon. Kinsolving jerked to one side, his sleeve aflame. He spun around to face Vandy, to shout at her for killing Suarez before he had gotten the information he needed. But Vandy was not in the doorway. He saw her feet through the door—and then nothing but the ugly muzzle of the laserifle filled his sight.

"Good riddance," came Jessarette's shrill, cracked voice. He sounded as crazed as Suarez. "I should have killed you on Almost Paradise. Don't know how you got away then, don't know how you got away from my seeker-killer in the meadow, but you won't get away now!"

Kinsolving dived behind a worktable in time to avoid the laserifle's deadly lance of coherent light. Kinsolving felt the beam slicing through plastic and wood just above him. He wiggled on his belly and came to a kneeling position behind an overturned chair. Fumbling for the impact laser in his pocket, Kinsolving waited for Jessarette to move into the room for the kill.

A heartbeat. Two. A dozen. Davi Jessarette did not appear. Kinsolving wondered if the assassin played a waiting game intended to lure him from behind his pitiful barricade.

"Vandy!" he called. "Are you all right?" No answer. Kinsolving gripped the handle of his weapon so tightly he felt the circulation leaving his fingers. Cold hand on the impact laser, he spun around, put his back to the wall and edged along until he got behind the door. Peering through the crack between door and frame, he saw ony Vandy lying facedown in the hall. Kinsolving listened intently. He heard nothing but the subtle sounds of the mansion: air moving through halls, settling noises, occasional pops and whines from plumbing being reworked.

Barton Kinsolving leaped out from behind the door, legs bent and weight forward. His finger almost depressed the trigger of his impact laser. But he had no target. Jessarette had gone. Kinsolving checked in both directions along the hallway before dropping down beside Vandy. He rolled her onto her back and pressed his fingers into her throat, checking for a pulse. He almost cried with relief when he felt a slow, firm beat in the carotid artery.

Her eyes flickered. She opened her brown eyes. For an instant she looked confused. Then memory rushed back. "Someone hit me!" she cried, trying to sit up. Kinsolving held her down.

"It was Jessarette. He's gone."

"What about Suarez?"

"Jessarette used the laserifle he took from you. He killed him." Kinsolving could not keep the bitterness from his voice. "He killed Suarez before he told me where Cameron had taken the information he stole."

"Cameron's got it?"

"Suarez wasn't too clear but I got the impression that IM sees this as their chance to be number one in everything. They want to kill the aliens and take over their worlds. They also want to prevent others involved in the Plan from gaining."

"A falling out among thieves and murderers. Seems like justice," said Vandy. Kinsolving let her sit up slowly now. The woman's eyes had lost their shocky glaze and she seemed none the worse for the blow to the back of her head. A small spot there still sluggishly oozed blood, but it did not appear to be a serious wound.

"The sides are lining up wrong, though," observed Kinsolving.

"What do you mean?"

"Why would Jessarette kill Suarez? They both worked for TR. It looks as though Jessarette is in league with Cameron." Kinsolving frowned even as he spoke. He had seen the drugged look on Jessarette's face when he had seen the trio together in the underground lab. Jessarette had been under Cameron's control. Later, however, Jessarette seemed free of the robot master's influence. Why should Jessarette want to kill Suarez unless he had gone insane, too?

"Do you think the virus affected them?" asked Vandy, as if reading his mind.

"Possible, but I doubt it. Everything you said about Suarez makes me think he was a meticulous researcher. He would have tried out the unraveling virus on humans before pronouncing it 'safe.'"

"Safe," she scoffed. "He might have created a time bomb for humans. Aliens it kills immediately. Humans might take longer. Days or weeks or even years."

Kinsolving did not think this was true. "A better explanation is that Jessarette wants it all for himself. With Suarez dead, he might think he can recover the details of the process from Cameron and then turn it over to his boss at Terra Recreations."

"Jessarette doesn't have the ability to get it back from Cameron," Vandy said. Together, they wobbled and teetered out the mansion's front way. The grassy lawns surrounding the estate were empty of all human life.

"You're right about that. Where would Cameron go? How would he try to get the data back to Fremont on Gamma Tertius 4?"

"Message packet," answered Vandy.

"Chancy," said Kinsolving. "Cameron would want to take it himself. He would know it arrived, carrying it himself. He'd want to gloat when he turned it over to Chairman Fremont."

"There'd be a promotion in it for him. That might be his way of insuring he gets credit."

Kinsolving thought Vandy had struck on a plausible reason for Cameron taking the information back personally. It fit with everything he knew of the robot master. Cameron was only hired help at IM. Kinsolving wondered if Cameron's ambitions did not soar to greater heights—such as the chairmanship of the company. Such power would give him a base for even greater conquests.

Did Cameron want to rule human-occupied space by economic power and alien space through stark destructive power? Those involved with the Stellar Death Plan thought in those terms. And of them, Cameron was the most ambitious Kinsolving had encountered.

"How often does a shuttle go up to Almost Paradise?" he asked Vandy.

"Whenever anyone wants to leave. We never keep schedules. Our guests dictate policy in the broadest sense. We want only to please."

"He might be gone, then." The emotional letdown Kinsolving felt at this made him sag visibly.

"Not yet. The shuttle had left for the station to pick up a pair of incoming guests. It can't make the return for at least an hour. Possibly longer."

"How can you stop it?"

"Let's get back to my house. All it takes is one simple order. I am, after all, the supervisor on Paradise."

To this, Kinsolving said nothing. After Cameron had

finished reprogramming the Paradise computer, he wondered whether anyone—other than Cameron—would ever be in charge of the resort planet again.

They hurried back, Kinsolving nervously waiting for Jessarette's laserifle blast to cut him in half. Of the TR security man he saw no trace. Kinsolving insisted on entering Vandy's quarters first to check for traps. He found no sign of Jessarette or Cameron's insidious robots.

That worried him more than if the house had been filled with automated booby traps.

"Punch up the schedule on the shuttle. There. Just as I thought." Vandy settled into her chair, light wand in hand. "Three passengers coming in from Almost Paradise instead of two." She frowned and worked through a passenger profile as Kinsolving waited.

"What's wrong?" He saw the expression on her face turn even darker as a swift parade of data marched past on the vidscreen.

"Two people from IM, one from TR. That's the vice president in charge of off-world resorts on the shuttle. My immediate superior. Ivan Denho." She leaned back in the chair, her face bleak. "The only reason he would be here now is that he knows about Suarez."

"You mean, he sent Suarez here." Kinsolving said the words flatly, as a statement of fact and not a question.

"That's the only possible conclusion. I sent a message packet explaining the plague to the chairman, not Denho. It could not have possibly arrived. Won't for weeks. Denho was already in transit."

Kinsolving sighed. Another supporter of the Plan. Another human who wanted all the aliens in the universe slaughtered.

"The shuttle arrives in thirty minutes. I've put a hold on immediate return to orbit. We should meet it when it arrives."

"And?" he asked.

"Denho is here to see the results of Suarez's field test. I want to show him personally. The automedics had put some of the aliens into a freezer. I want to be sure he sees firsthand what he has released."

"That might not shock sense into him," said Kinsolving.

He knew that the men and women involved in the Plan were ruthless in business. For conquest of the galaxy, they could be even more treacherous and unfeeling.

"It's a start. If that doesn't do it, well, I'll think of something." Kinsolving saw the woman touch the impact laser she had tucked into her pocket.

He started to leave for the shuttle port, then stopped. Something gnawed at the fringes of his mind. It finally came into focus. "See if you can find Cameron with your security system." Vandy tried and failed. Kinsolving had not thought she'd succeed. "Try Jessarette."

"He's already at the shuttle port," she said in surprise. "The system still picks him up."

"Cameron wants us to know where he is. Don't ask why. I have no idea."

"Jessarette is hiding at the north end of the landing port. We can get near him by taking an underground service tunnel that goes to the liquid metals supply building."

Kinsolving stared at the vivid, three-dimensional image of Jessarette on the vidscreen, then shook his head. Cameron was luring them into a trap. Or was Jessarette more than bait?

Vandy and Kinsolving hurried to an underground access point, went down and ran along the tunnel, choosing not to take any of the conveyances they found. Neither had any desire to repeat the experience with the bomb aboard the travel cab. Kinsolving thought that Jessarette had been responsible for that clumsy attempt on their lives, but he could never know for certain. Better to travel on foot than to risk Cameron's more subtle destructive skills.

"How much farther?" Kinsolving gasped. While working as a mining engineer on Deepdig, he had stayed in peak physical condition. Since he had arrived on Paradise, he had accumulated injuries to the point where he was one step away from collapse: his back hurt; the burn on his arm from Jessarette's near miss had not been tended and only now began to annoy him. And rest? He could not remember when he had last gotten a good night's sleep or a square meal. For most, this was a pleasure resort. For him it had become an endurance contest.

It was a contest he was losing slowly.

"Here we are," said Vandy. Sweat ran down her face in

salty trails. She did not look in any better shape than he felt. "What's the plan?"

"Cameron seems to want us to stop Jessarette. Why else leave his recognition symbols in the security system? Since we have nothing better to do, we go after Jessarette."

"Cameron wants us to stop Jessarette so he won't have to. Jessarette knows Cameron stole the process to create the unraveling virus. That's got to be it." Vandy sounded satisfied with this reasoning. Kinsolving didn't bother to tell her that Cameron could remove Jessarette easily whenever he wanted. The man was playing a game with them. Cameron could as easily order his armada of robot killers after them. There would be no place in Paradise to hide if he decided on their deaths.

"This comes out behind Jessarette?" he asked.

Vandy nodded. She stared at him for a moment, then impulsively stepped forward and kissed him. "For luck," she said.

Before Kinsolving could speak, the supervisor of Paradise scampered up the ladder and irised open the door leading to the shuttle port. Warm sunlight flooded down the shaft and softly caressed his face. He could almost believe in peace and relaxation and taking a vacation on this serene planet. Almost.

He followed, impact laser in hand. Kinsolving sidled past Vandy and onto the tarmac. One story warehouses dotted the area. Davi Jessarette could be anywhere, waiting.

"What's he waiting for?" Kinsolving asked aloud. "Is he really waiting to kill Cameron or is he waiting for Denho?"

"I didn't know the vice president was coming. How could Jessarette?" Vandy put a hand over her mouth as she spoke. "Oh. He might have known. Denho might have told him that he'd be out to see the field test of the virus."

"Paradise," said Kinsolving, shaking his head. "The planet is more like a hunting preserve. And we have to guess who's being hunted and why and where we can hide to keep from being killed."

"Sounds like an interesting game. And it would be," said Vandy, "if our lives didn't depend on it."

Kinsolving decided on one warehouse as the best observation point. He motioned to Vandy to stay where she was in the safety of the service tunnel entrance.

"Wait, Bart. I've got an idea. What if Cameron isn't the one with the process information?"

"What?" Kinsolving tried to pull his mind from attack-mode and into thinking about what she said. It proved too difficult. "I don't understand what you mean."

"What if Jessarette is the one with the information and Cameron wants us to get it for him?"

"No," he said without conviction. Jessarette might have Suarez's records, but Cameron could get them too easily. Why use Kinsolving and Vandy to kill Jessarette? Unless it amused him?

"He might. This has to be it. Jessarette has Suarez's process and is going to turn it over to Denho when he arrives. Cameron wants it and is going to let us kill Jessarette, then will kill us to get it. He wants us to risk our necks rather than do it himself!"

A tiny movement in a warehouse doorway alerted Kinsolving to the danger ahead. He grabbed Vandy and pulled her along, hoping that Jessarette had not seen them. The deadly lightning bolt from the laserifle that gouged a huge smoking rut in the tarmac convinced him that they had been seen.

"Circle the building," Kinsolving said. "If Jessarette is alone, one of us will be able to get a shot at his back. Don't try for heroics. It's too dangerous. Go on. Do it!" He shoved Vandy around the side of the building, knowing it would take her several minutes to get into position. By then, the fight would be over.

Either he or Davi Jessarette would be dead.

Kinsolving swung around the corner of the building, ready to fight.

CHAPTER SIXTEEN

BARTON KINSOLVING paused for an instant, then entered the warehouse. Hellacious heat boiled in front of him as the door melted. Jessarette's laserifle reduced the metal-clad door to a puddle. Kinsolving brushed off the bits of metal stinging his cheeks and dived forward onto his belly. He landed hard and skidded, impact laser ready.

Wherever Jessarette hid, he gave Kinsolving no target. Kinsolving scrambled to get his feet under him. Another lance of coherent light took the flesh off his back. Kinsolving almost fainted from the agony that lanced into him. Every injury he sustained seemed to be to his back. He collapsed onto his face, grimly hanging on to consciousness.

He watched the red sighting beam bob and bounce closer and closer. At the last instant he heaved himself to one side. The tiny red bead held steady on the spot he had vacated. Concrete exploded when Jessarette triggered the laserifle again.

Kinsolving had no idea how many times Jessarette's power laser weapon could be fired before it needed recharging. The way he felt, it might not need recharging. A simple ion arc might be enough to knock him over. Wincing with the pain, he duck-walked around the perimeter of the warehouse. Automated equipment went about its business, moving crates in and out, finding the provisions asked for by those who ran Paradise and delivering them.

Ignoring the robot workers wasn't as easy as Kinsolving hoped. They worked in every section of the large warehouse, and he jumped in reaction every time one came near.

"You won't be able to get away with this, Jessarette," he called, hoping the man would betray his position. Jessarette did not respond. Kinsolving dropped to his knees and leaned his forehead against a crate, sweat and blood trickling down. He touched the bloody scratch. He had no idea when he had done this—or how. Pain from his back overrode any other sensory message his body sent his brain.

Through it all came the thought that Jessarette had not answered. This was unlike the killer. Jessarette was a braggart, a man who boasted to increase his own minuscule self-esteem.

Kinsolving used the pain as a goad to get himself moving. He burst forward, smashed into the side of the crate and sent a robohandler bleeping in distress. But the sudden exposure did not bring instant death from the laserifle.

Kinsolving cursed. Jessarette had left the warehouse after the last attack. Where had he gone? Kinsolving looked around frantically and finally saw a small inspection window whose frame had been twisted. He ran to it and peered outside.

He went cold inside when he saw Vandy sneaking around the corner.

"Get down!" he shouted. "Jessarette's outside. He—" The rest of his words were drowned out in the sizzling roar of the laserifle firing. He watched Vandy straighten, look down at the fist-sized hole in her chest, then slowly twist to one side. She fell to the tarmac and lay there, not moving.

Kinsolving's gaze traced back along the purpled ionization trail left by the laser beam. He saw the stack of crates being tended by the robohandlers. One side of a plastic crate had bubbled and flowed. Jessarette had rested the heavy laserifle barrel against the crate to steady his aim. The slight dispersion in the barrel had caused the damage.

When a shadow appeared on the ground, Kinsolving raised his impact laser. He had passed emotion. He had become a hollow shell driven only by instinct. Killing Jessarette would not be revenge; it would not be pleasure; it would be a simple act like breathing.

Jessarette poked his head out around the crate. Kinsolving's finger squeezed down on the impact laser's trigger. The high frequency whine had barely died when Kinsolving realized that he had missed. The aiming laser on his weapon had been knocked off target. Even though he had pinpointed Jessarette's temple, the variable-frequency beam had ripped apart the crate beside him.

"Come back here!" Kinsolving screamed. All the emotion he had pushed aside came rushing back. He trembled so hard that he was unable to properly aim the laser using both hands. He fired repeatedly, the shots going wild. One struck a robot cargo handler. Its silvered carapace exploded and sent a rain of molten metal down over the shuttle port. Another blast melted through a cargo case and set fire to the material inside. Huge plumes of heavy black smoke billowed from within. Kinsolving heard alarms sounding in the distance.

Pain wracking his every move, he tumbled through the small window and fell to the tarmac. He got to hands and knees, then struggled to his feet. As if his boots had been dipped in lead, he moved with agonizing slowness toward Vandy Azmotega. She lay on her side. He turned her over and saw the surprised expression on her face. Death had come too quickly for her to appreciate it. For that small boon, Kinsolving was glad.

"You'll die for this, Jessarette," he vowed. "And you, too, Cameron. You, too!" Kinsolving spun and fired his impact laser from the hip. The beam caught an aerial robot and blew it apart so thoroughly that nothing fell to the ground. The robot spy had been reporting back to Cameron, he knew. Kinsolving reached out and braced himself against the building as he scanned the azure sky for sign of other aerial robots.

They were probably somewhere, but he failed to locate them. Sirens came closer. He guessed that it was the fire-fighting robots racing to extinguish the blaze in the pile of crates. Whatever had been in the crate he had hit ignited the cargo on either side. A minor fire had become major.

Kinsolving slid the impact laser into his pocket, reached down and took Vandy's weapon, then staggered off across the tarmac. The shuttle would not land for a few minutes. He had time. He had to find Jessarette and kill him. Nothing else was in his mind.

He had no idea where he was going. He tried to walk in a straight line in the direction he thought Jessarette had taken, but he came to the shuttle waiting room. Shaken, weak and almost beyond the limits of his endurance, Kinsolving leaned against the building, its cool plastic wall soothing him.

"Barton?" came a tremulous voice. "Is that you? You're a fright!"

"Lark, help me," he said, tumbling into her arms.

Kinsolving never—quite—lost consciousness. He knew she had summoned an automedic and that the diligent robot doctor worked on him for more than ten minutes. And he silently thanked Lark Versalles when she argued with the machine about putting him into a life-coma. It would be the safe course; every bit of programming in the automedic would dictate it.

Lark convinced the machine to wait.

"How are you feeling? You look positively nuked out!"

"You know how to cheer up a patient, don't you?" he said, trying to smile. He managed only a weak grimace. "Why are you here? At the shuttle port?"

"I've got Sheeda's remains," Lark said, her expression turning even more forlorn. "I'm sending it—her—back to Onar. I never heard what their burial customs are. I . . . I didn't have the heart to find out." Tears rolled down Lark's cheeks. For several seconds Kinsolving tried to figure out what was wrong. It finally came to him. Lark's cosmetic dyes had been neutralized. He stared at unaugmented, naturally colored skin.

"You've got to help me," he said. "More than you have already. Jessarette did this. And Cameron has the full process information on how the virus that killed Sheeda was incubated. Cameron will use it on thousands of alien worlds unless we prevent him from getting it back to Gamma Tertius."

"Your back is burned. The automedic said it was a laserifle."

"Jessarette," he gasped out. "Jessarette did this. And he killed Vandy Azmotega."

"Who?"

"The planetary supervisor. We tried to stop Suarez. Jessarette killed him. And he's hunting for Cameron. Only—"

"Barton, darling, please." She pressed a cool finger to his lips. "You're babbling. I don't understand a word of this. If you keep on, nothing I say will stop the automedic from putting you into a life-coma until a hospital automedic can analyze you."

Kinsolving rolled to one elbow and lifted his impact

laser. The automedic moved fast; Kinsolving reacted faster. The laser bolt blew the compact robot apart.

"Why'd you do that?"

"It won't try to put me into a life-coma now. Help me stand up." Lark's arm provided support but no strength. He had to rely on his own inner resources for that. To his surprise, he found it easy to stand without her assistance.

"Paradise is misnamed," said Lark. "Hell is closer."

"When did Sheeda die?"

"An hour ago. She faded more and more and . . . never regained consciousness. The automedic said that her body chemistry had failed. Enzyme levels or something. I didn't understand."

"The plague works on alien DNA. Cameron knows how to duplicate the virus. Because of the Plan, he'll destroy every alien in the galaxy."

"I don't want any part of this, Bart. Please. Try to understand." Lark cried openly. "Sheeda was more than a friend. I . . . I loved her. We had only known each other for a short time, but it was real, Barton. It was *real*."

He hugged her close and let her cry. The hollow feeling had passed entirely. Replacing it was a burning emotion that threatened to consume him even as it gave him strength.

"There'll be others like Sheeda to die," he said. "Cameron murdered fourteen hundred aliens on Paradise—and it was only a test. He must not be allowed to use the virus on other worlds. Billions more will die. Help me to stop him, Lark. I need you." He held her even closer.

"All right, Barton. But how? What can we do? He has robots that came out of nowhere. You know how lucky we were on GT4 to escape him."

"I know. But we've got to keep trying. He won't give up. We can't do any less."

Kinsolving's mind slipped into a strange state. Solutions rose and died with increasing speed. Only one came with lucid conviction. "Cameron is playing with me. He wants me to kill Jessarette for his amusement. I'll kill him, but it won't be for Cameron. It's going to be for *me*."

And for Vandy, he silently added. She deserved better than a laserifle blast.

"Who is this Jessarette?" asked Lark. Kinsolving quick-

ly explained all that had happened starting with their brief
stay on Almost Paradise. Lark fought to believe him. Kinsolving didn't care whether she believed him or not. All
that counted was her helping him.

"I think Jessarette is a creature of habit. He isn't clever
enough to change his pattern. After killing Vandy he'll
look for a place where he feels safe."

"Where's that?"

"We can find out where his quarters are." Kinsolving
and Lark left the shuttle port waiting room, Lark glancing
back at the small shipping coffin containing Sheeda's cre-
mated remains. Then her attention was fully on the task.

She brightened and said, "I never knew how dull life
was before you came along, Bart, darling. There's a
certain . . . thrill . . . to all this, isn't there?"

He had to admit that she was right. On Deepdig he had
done his job well, had loved Ala Markken and had been in
a rut without knowing it. Nothing new happened. He had
no future except more mining projects. Now he had a mission, a purpose transcending all others. With or without
their help, he had to save most of the intelligent beings in
the known galaxy. The impossibility of the project forced
him to rise above his personal limitations.

And in so rising, he triumphed where he should have
failed.

"There," he said, walking even more briskly. "That's
Vandy's house."

"A supervisor on Paradise lives in a hovel?" Lark's
shock matched his own surprise when he had seen the simple quarters. He pushed inside and found the light wand
Vandy had discarded. He aimed it at the vidscreen and
began working through the data he ordered using her executive computer authorizations.

"There's Jessarette's house. Down by the shore."

"That's not five hundred meters from here," said Lark.
"Are you sure you want to do this?"

Kinsolving was already out the door, forcing Lark to
make a dash to catch up with him. "I want him. He's part
of everything that's ugly on Paradise. Jessarette's only a
henchman, but he's responsible."

"Barton, wait, please," gasped out Lark. "A question

first. Why don't we use a cab to go there? He wouldn't know it was us. My feet are tired!"

He explained the problems he had experienced with the local transportation. Even as he spoke, Kinsolving looked up into the blue, blue sky for some sign that the shuttle from Almost Paradise was coming in for a landing. He saw nothing, but he picked up the pace until Lark ran to keep even with him. He had to finish dealing with Davi Jessarette in time to meet the shuttle.

Another adherent to the Stellar Death Plan would be aboard: Ivan Denho, vice president of Terra Recreations and as cold-blooded a murderer as any on Paradise.

"It looks so peaceful," Lark said, stopping on a cliff overlooking the ocean. Whitecaps crested on the gentle surf as the water lapped against the pure sand of the beach. "I can't believe such venom has come from this world."

Kinsolving grabbed her in his arms and knocked Lark flat in time to prevent a half dozen laser beams from slicing her into bloody pieces.

"Automatic weapons," he whispered. "Jessarette won't be content to rely on them. He'll have to come out to check." Kinsolving rolled onto his back and experienced a small twinge. The automedic had deadened the pain well this time.

He used his impact laser on rock outcroppings. Repeatedly firing, he exposed the sensors Jessarette had planted to monitor anyone approaching his secluded dwelling. Then Kinsolving began work on the laser traps themselves. In less than five minutes he had produced a dozen minor explosions.

"That ought to take care of Jessarette's defenses," he said smugly.

"What now?" asked Lark.

"We wait for him to get nervous." But it was Kinsolving who got tired of waiting. He did not want Jessarette slipping out by a hidden escape route.

Kinsolving motioned for Lark to be silent, then moaned in mock agony. Louder, he called out, "Damn you, Jessarette. Those lasers of yours cut off my legs. The shock's wearing off. The pain's too much! I'm going to die!"

Kinsolving gripped his impact laser so tightly he felt the

tingling of lost circulation. He relaxed. He had to be precise. There might be only one shot at Jessarette when he came to personally kill his victim.

Kinsolving waited—and grew more impatient. Jessarette did not rise to the bait.

Lark Versalles moved so unexpectedly that Kinsolving could do nothing to stop her. The woman stood upright, blond hair gleaming like gold in the sun, the other colors in her hair making her stand out even more. She cried, "Barton, darling, don't die! I'll help you!"

A dislodged rock warned Kinsolving in time. He had been watching the front entrance to Jessarette's house. A portion of a boulder ten meters to the side swung open to reveal a passage drilled through solid rock. Jessarette had stepped out and turned his ankle on a loose stone. This noise brought Kinsolving's impact laser about.

He fired and missed.

Jessarette yelped in surprise and tried to retreat. Kinsolving held the trigger of his laser down discharging it completely. The vibratory beam struck the rock in front of Jessarette and blew the boulder apart, cutting off his passage. The killer spun, heavy laserifle in his hand. His lips pulled back in a snarl. "I got you now, Kinsolving. That drained your laser."

Kinsolving reached into his pocket and withdrew the laser he had used in the warehouse. He silently reminded himself that the aiming beam was off. He corrected for this. Then he stood.

"Bart," gasped Lark. "He's got a *rifle!*"

Davi Jessarette's face lit with triumph. He had a laserifle. But Barton Kinsolving had justice on his side. The bolt from the impact laser removed Jessarette's head from his shoulders.

Kinsolving stared at the headless corpse and said, "You should have suffered more."

The thunderclap rolling across the ocean drew his attention skyward. The shuttle glowed a cherry red as it slipped through the heavy atmosphere of Paradise on its way to a landing at the port.

"Come on, Lark," he said. "We've got more to do.

We've got to stop Cameron from leaving with the information on the virus."

Kinsolving slowed only long enough to scoop up the fallen laserifle. He knew he would need it later.

CHAPTER SEVENTEEN

BARTON KINSOLVING reached the shuttle port in no condition to do anything more strenuous than sit on the ground and gasp for breath. Lark Versalles stood over him, glowering. "You should have let me pick out a cab. We could have been here in half the time with no effort. Sometimes I wonder about you, Bart."

·"The bomb," he said, knowing how silly this sounded now. Davi Jessarette was dead. The other woman sent by Interstellar Materials was dead. Only Cameron remained —and why would the robot master choose a crude bomb when his sophisticated, almost undetectable robot killers would be more suitable? Kinsolving cursed his stubbornness. He and Vandy had almost been blown up. The thought stuck in his mind and refused to go away.

For all the good saving her had done, he thought with real bitterness. He tried to come up with substantive accomplishments and failed. Sheeda was dead, along with fourteen hundred aliens. The test for the Stellar Death Plan had been successful. Cameron had stolen the genetic blueprint for the engineered virus and had seen to removing Morgan Suarez. As surely as if he had lasered the scientist, Cameron had killed him, Kinsolving knew. Davi Jessarette had been a pawn and nothing more.

"The shuttle's down," said Lark. "Who is it you want to stop?"

"Ivan Denho, a vice president for TR. And I think he's here to carry the genetic map for the virus back with him to Earth."

"Why?" asked Lark.

"What? So he can finish what they've started. Mass produce the virus, release it, kill the aliens. You know that."

Lark shook her head and sent a soft cascade of hair falling into her eyes. She brushed it away with an impatient gesture. "You said Cameron wanted it for himself. Why turn it over to TR? They probably think it's theirs since Dr. Suarez was their researcher, but why would Cameron suddenly cooperate?"

"He has to get it off planet and knows we're waiting," Kinsolving said, more to himself than to Lark. Everything the woman said made sense. Cameron had put himself into competition with TR. Denho arrived, knowing nothing of the power play being acted out. Kinsolving's mind worked through what it would be like when Cameron met Denho.

"Cameron goes up the corporate ladder if IM controls the plague, not TR," he said.

In a way he and Denho were working for the same goal: to prevent Cameron from getting the information off-planet. The difference lay in what would be done with the information should either get it.

Denho would use it. Kinsolving would destroy it.

"Destroy it," he said aloud. "We've got to get the information away from Cameron and destroy it."

Lark looked at him, annoyance written on her face. "Barton, darling, are you all right? That's *silly*. Really a vacuum thing to say. Nature is a blabbermouth. What Dr. Suarez discovered, someone else can duplicate. You can't think that TR doesn't have others who know what he was trying to do."

Kinsolving sat and shook all over. His body hurt, his temples throbbed with the beginning of a massive headache, and he found it harder to keep a logical train of thought moving along. Lark was right. Simply destroying the information would do nothing to prevent others from working on it.

"What else can we do?" he said numbly.

"Get the bioweapon from Cameron and turn it over to the aliens. Let them see what's been done. They've got labs of their own, I suppose. They can develop a vaccine for it."

"That's a good idea, Lark." Kinsolving painfully worked to his feet and leaned against her. "I'm glad you're helping me. I really am."

"You look worse than ever," she said, eyeing him critically. "Pale. Your hands shake. You can barely walk. What good are you going to be against this Denho—or Cameron?"

Kinsolving did not answer. His mind slipped into its more usual channels of clarity. "What do we need Denho for?" he asked. "Cameron isn't going to give him the bioweapon. Denho is here thinking he'll meet Suarez."

Lark and Kinsolving exchanged glances. They both smiled broadly. "So we tell him all about Cameron," they said in unison.

Excited now, Kinsolving went on. "Let Denho do the work for us. Let him track down Cameron and get the information. Then we take it from *him*."

"We're making a big assumption," said Lark. "How good is this Denho? Good enough to best Cameron?"

Kinsolving shrugged. They could only hope that Terra Recreations did not promote idiots to the rank of vice president.

"Here," said Lark. She had motioned over a small flatbed cargo loader. "We ride out to the shuttle. No more walking. I'm tired; you're *exhausted*."

Kinsolving climbed onto the cargo platform. Everything Lark said was true.

He pointed when he saw a low-slung cab leaving the shuttle. "Are we too late? There're two people inside."

"There's a guy leaving the shuttle who looks like his name ought to be Ivan Denho." Lark gave an involuntary shiver and snuggled closer, her arm circling Kinsolving's waist.

The man waiting impatiently on the tarmac did look as though his name would be Ivan Denho. Shaped like a fleshy bullet, his shaved head gleamed in the bright sunlight. Thick arms threatened to split the sleeves of a conservative royal purple and pastel pink business suit. His bulk made him appear fat; Kinsolving saw no evidence of that in the man's quick, precise movements. Strength and a quick reaction time lay under that brutish exterior.

"Someone broke his nose," Lark said with some distaste. "Why didn't he get it fixed? And made smaller—it looks like a fat potato all mashed over his face."

"Our Mr. Denho is obviously a man who cares little for appearance." Kinsolving had seen this type of executive before. All that mattered was action, accomplishment, results.

Kinsolving thought that Denho might stand a chance against Cameron. He had feared that TR's vice president might be some office-bred bureaucratic lackey who had advanced by saying "yes" to the right people often enough. If anything, Ivan Denho had fought his way to his present position.

"What should we do?" asked Lark. "We've got to think of something. We're almost there."

Kinsolving tried to formulate a clever plan that would give him exactly what he wanted, but exhaustion again claimed him. His thoughts jumbled and he failed to decide anything workable.

Denho settled the matter for him. The man shouted and waved a pudgy hand, summoning them over. Lark ordered the cargo transport to the shuttle.

"You two, I need immediate transportation to Supervisor Azmotega's office."

"Climb aboard, sir," said Kinsolving. "Nothing fancy, but it'll get us there."

Denho hopped onto the platform and sat down, not caring that he dirtied his expensive suit. The man's dark eyes peered from under heavy bony ridges. Nothing moving across the tarmac escaped his notice. "What the hell's wrong with this place?" he asked. "Supervisor Azmotega is more capable than this operation appears." Denho turned and scowled at Kinsolving.

"Nothing's been right lately, sir," said Kinsolving. "Plague. Killed all the aliens on Paradise."

Denho jerked as if Kinsolving had touched him with an electric wire. "How do you know that?"

"Hard to stack that many bodies without someone noticing and commenting."

"Do the human guests know?"

Denho had mistaken Kinsolving for a common worker. Kinsolving hoped that the man did not look too closely at Lark. Even without her expensive cosmetic dyes activated, it would be difficult to believe that she was anything but a customer on Paradise.

"No," answered Kinsolving. "But there's more than a few thousand deaths on Paradise," he said. "The supervisor is dead. She was killed when a . . . security agent went crazy. Must have been from the plague." Kinsolving saw no reason not to sow the seeds of uneasiness concerning the plague in Denho's mind.

"What are you saying?" the man demanded. His attention focused fully on Kinsolving. Kinsolving felt as if he had become a specimen under an electron microscope. The only relief he felt from this was that Denho completely ignored Lark.

"Davi Jessarette," explained Kinsolving. "He murdered her."

"Jessarette?"

"None other," said Kinsolving. "Rumor has it that he and an Interstellar Materials employee named Cameron did it. Some dispute over money, maybe."

Denho's face lost all expression, but Kinsolving saw the new hardness come into the man's already flinty eyes. He did not need to tell the TR vice president anything more about the deaths. Denho had figured it all out in a flash.

"Take me to this Cameron," Denho ordered.

Kinsolving shook his head. "Can't. Don't know where he is. Supervisor's dead. Only she had access to the computers. You know any way of finding him?" Kinsolving did not want to appear too knowledgeable by telling Denho of the planetary computer's malfunction—of Cameron's reprogramming.

"Take me to Supervisor Azmotega's office."

Kinsolving motioned. Lark altered the direction of travel slightly. They cruised back to Vandy's house in a fraction of the time they'd taken getting to the shuttle port. When they arrived Denho slipped off and stalked into the house without uttering a word.

Lark watched his broad back vanish inside. Only then did she speak. "Should we spy on him?"

"Why not?" Kinsolving and Lark went to the still open door and peered inside. Denho reached into his pocket and drew out a light wand similar to Vandy's. To Kinsolving's surprise, Denho was successful in using it to locate Cameron.

"It worked," he muttered to Lark. "That means either Denho had access to a deeper level in the computer than Vandy or that Cameron wants him to find him."

"You two, take me to these coordinates." Denho barked the numbers. Kinsolving had no idea where it was. Lark punched the numbers into the cargo loader's navigation computer and they started off. Kinsolving started to ask Denho more about locating Cameron, then subsided. Denho sat, powerful arms crossed, his face a mask. He radiated the message: Leave me alone.

To Kinsolving's surprise, the coordinates turned out to be the mansion being renovated where Suarez had been killed. The loader platform came to a halt at the foot of a path. Denho hopped off. He made a brusque motion of dismissal. "That'll be all."

"You need a security team, sir?" asked Kinsolving.

His only answer was a grunt and watching Denho's broad shoulders vanish through the door. Ivan Denho was a man of few words.

"What now?" asked Lark.

"We've been dismissed. I suppose we can take a break." Kinsolving reached under the pile of rags in the cargo bed and drew out the laserifle he had taken from Jessarette.

"Inside?"

"Where else," he said, smiling. He had been able to rest enough to regain strength. With Lark a step behind him, Kinsolving went to a window and peered inside the abandoned mansion. Since he had been here a few hours earlier, robot workers had stripped the walls and had begun to install new electronics equipment. Kinsolving couldn't begin to understand what this room would be used for when they finished.

His only interest lay in Denho. The squat, bald man stood stolidly in the center of the room, studying his wrist chronometer. From the faint blue glow, Kinsolving guessed that it told more than the local time. Denho moved slowly in a circle until he was satisfied with the readings given by his sensors.

He walked to the stairs leading to the room where Suarez had died. Denho paused, drew out a weapon unfamiliar to Kinsolving, then started up.

"What do we do now? Wait?" asked Lark.

"There's nothing upstairs. I looked through the room where Suarez had his lab. He was trying to get the data he needed from his computer, but Cameron had already erased

it." Kinsolving glanced back over his shoulder, an eerie
sense of being watched making him increasingly uneasy.
He saw nothing, but Cameron's robots could be anywhere.
Although he did not know, he thought they might even be
high in the air looking down. Their size made them impossible to see if they were more than a few hundred meters
above.

"Here's a door into the lower levels," said Lark, peering
into the darkened stairway leading down.

"Cameron's down there," Kinsolving said with sudden
conviction. "Don't ask me how I know. It just feels right."

He hurried down the stairs and found the door securely
locked. He used the laserifle on it, sending molten fragments back into his face and across his chest.

"Barton, be careful," chided Lark. "You'll set us both
on fire, doing things like that."

Kinsolving ignored her protest. He hurried inside,
knowing that the roar of the rifle would have alerted
Denho. Kinsolving stopped and lifted the laserifle, triggering it repeatedly when he saw small movements at the
edges of his field of vision. Tiny explosions marked each
robot he destroyed.

"The robots!" cried Lark. "Cameron *is* here!"

Kinsolving rushed forward, laserifle swinging to and
fro, ready for instant use. He had to use it on several larger
robots.

Then he met one machine too heavily armored to be
stopped by the potent energies released by the weapon he
carried.

"It's like a tiny war tank!" warned Lark. She huddled
down behind Kinsolving.

He motioned her back. "Cameron's still here. Denho
found him—or Cameron wanted Denho to find him." His
next words were drowned out by the throaty roar from the
robot's laser cannon. The entire corridor exploded in
flame. Kinsolving was protected by a shallow doorway but
quickly found this was not enough. The superheated air
rushed out the open doorway—and along with it went his
breath.

Gasping for air in the vacuum caused by the miniature
firestorm, Kinsolving fell to his knees.

More from reaction than thought, he fired his laserifle.

It blew a deep hole in the floor in front of the robot tank. For a split second, the tank rumbled forward and fell laser muzzle first into the hole. Kinsolving aimed this time and raked the laserifle's beam of coherent light over the top of the robot.

"You killed it," marvelled Lark, when she saw the machine struggled to right itself and failed. "It can't get out."

"I just wounded it," said Kinsolving, thinking of the robot as a living creature, too. "But now it dies." He had damaged the right track system. He melted it off with a dozen more bolts. Then he began blasting at the left side. Even after absorbing enough energy to kill a thousand men, the robot struggled to come after him.

It proved a futile effort on the machine's part. It only succeeded in burrowing deeper into the glassy grave Kinsolving had blasted for it in the floor.

Kinsolving motioned for Lark to edge past the still fighting robot. He spun and burst into a room. Empty. The next proved equally as deserted. The third, however, had a stairway leading upward. He caught a momentary flash of flame-orange and gray fabric.

"Cameron!" he shouted. "Get back here and fight!"

He lasered four robots who answered his challenge. But their master had vanished up the stairs.

"Barton, whatever was here is gone," said Lark. She pointed to a small computer. Its block memory had been removed. "Cameron took the permanent memory with him."

Kinsolving turned to follow Cameron, then stopped. He went across the littered floor to the small computer unit and stared at it. "Find me another block circuit. There must be one around somewhere."

"Here," Lark said. "But it's empty. Blank. Cameron's got the one with Dr. Suarez's bioweapon plans on it."

"You're right when you said that Cameron took the permanent memory. But the computer is still on. The transient memory might still contain the information we want if Cameron was examining it when we burst in on him."

"What good does that—oh!" she exclaimed. "If it's still in transient, you can read it off to a permanent block as long as the power hasn't been turned off!"

"It's worth a try." Kinsolving inserted the blank circuit,

then began to work on the console. A broad smile grew until it was almost painful. Complex diagrams of DNA helices began to appear on screen. Following this came a detailed description of how to incubate the genetically engineered virus.

"Are you recording it?" Lark asked anxiously.

"All of it. There!" Kinsolving snatched the block circuit from the computer and tucked the slim ceramic cartridge into his pocket. "Now we can find Cameron."

He started up the stairs slowly, laserifle ready for anything. Kinsolving would not let Cameron escape. He wouldn't!

CHAPTER EIGHTEEN

BARTON KINSOLVING fired at the robots moving toward him, even though they did not seem menacing. He had seen Cameron's craft too often to take chances. The robots *popped!* out of existence. He peered cautiously into the room at the head of the spiral staircase from the cellar. Work robots labored to renovate the mansion. He saw the eye-dazzling combinations, the optical effects that turned the room into one a thousand times bigger, the tricks and decorations and programming of robots paramount.

Of Cameron he saw nothing.

"What's happening, Barton?" whispered Lark.

"He's vanished. I don't see him anywhere."

"Did you hear a door closing?"

"No," Kinsolving said. "But that doesn't mean he's still inside. There are other ways outside. A window might have been open—the work robots are tearing out walls everywhere."

"He's still inside," Lark said firmly. "I feel it."

Kinsolving did, too. Cameron had a chance to flee and had not taken it. Why? A trap? Possibly. Kinsolving had a gut level feeling that it was more. Cameron had been surprised in the cellar. The residual memory in the computer proved that. Cameron's usual thoroughness would have made him erase the transient memory if he had not been interrupted.

A pair of scintillant points came wobbling into the room, orbiting around one another. Bright blue sparks shot from the tiny points of pure energy, setting fires wherever they touched. Two safety robots trailed behind, putting out the incipient blazes.

"What are those?" Kinsolving wondered aloud. He raised his laserifle but did not fire.

"I've never seen anything like them," said Lark, standing on tiptoe and peering over his shoulder. "They don't look friendly."

"They don't look like robots," Kinsolving said.

"That doesn't mean Cameron didn't send them after us."

Even as the woman spoke, the brilliant specks revolved around and aligned in such a fashion that one was hidden behind the other during part of the orbit.

Kinsolving fired at the same instant that the hidden speck blossomed and grew into a blinding flower of light. The shock wave knocked him back into Lark. Her arms wrapped around Kinsolving's body for support, the pair tumbled back down the spiral staircase to the cellar.

"Are you all right, Bart, darling?"

"Blinded. No, just temporarily blinded. All I can see are blue and yellow dots." He closed his eyes and when he opened them in a few seconds, vision had returned. Tears streamed down his cheeks and small blisters popped up on his face.

Lark took the laserifle from his hands and pointed it upward. He started to tell her that she didn't have her finger on the firing toggle when the remaining spark appeared at the top of the stairs. As though blind and cautiously descending, the dancing spirits came downward, following the stairs rather than floating directly into the cellar.

"Don't shoot," Kinsolving said. "I think that's what blinded me."

"I don't want it touching me," Lark said in distress. She cowered from the bobbing mote of pure energy. It followed her movement.

"It's tracking you," Kinsolving said. "Don't move. Let it come closer. It's some type of free-floating plasma."

"It's getting closer!" she shrieked. "Don't let it hurt me, Barton!"

Kinsolving waved his arms. The speck stopped in its inexorable pursuit of Lark and seemed to home in on him.

"It's not motion sensitive. I think it follows air movement. Maybe we generate positive ions when we move. It acts as though it is being drawn electrically." Kinsolving moved his right hand to the side. The speck curved in its path to mimic his every movement.

"Do something!"

Kinsolving acted without thinking. He sprinted for the far side of the cellar. As if imbuing new life into the scintillant spark, this sudden movement brought it after him almost faster than vision could track. Kinsolving dived behind Cameron's discarded computer console.

The explosion just centimeters above him blew him facedown into the floor. He shook off bits of burning plastic and cracked ceramic vidscreen from his back and stood.

"It destroyed the computer," Lark said in a low monotone, as if in shock.

"It came after me but it couldn't change direction fast enough to avoid hitting the computer. Everything shorted out. The drop of ball lightning discharged itself along the computer's ground wires."

"How did Cameron . . ."

"Not Cameron's," Kinsolving said with conviction. "This must be something put into the fight by Denho." He remembered the man's confidence in confronting Cameron. Even if he did not know of Cameron's expertise with robots, Denho had to guess that he faced a trained killer possibly responsible for Vandy Azmotega's death. Ivan Denho had not hesitated. To Kinsolving this meant that the TR executive carried enough weaponry to win any battle.

Kinsolving motioned for Lark to go back through the cellar and outside. Going back up the stairs to the rooms above only gave Cameron and Denho a second chance to waylay them. Exiting onto the broad, grassy lawn beside the mansion, Kinsolving exercised caution.

"There!" cried Lark. "Going into the woods. Two men."

Kinsolving had seen the bright splash of Cameron's jacket. Of Denho he had seen nothing, but he did not dispute Lark's word. She had been looking directly into the small stand of low-limbed trees while he checked the front of the mansion.

He tried to decide between pursuing the pair and just letting them kill each other. Kinsolving's mind raced. He came to a decision. It seemed more like justice if Denho and Cameron died by his hand. Kinsolving started after them.

"Barton, wait," called Lark. She hung back. "Don't.

Let them go. You have the block circuit with the information about the plague. All you have to do is get it to an alien official."

"I can't give up on Cameron. I just can't." He tried to make her understand, but he wasn't sure that he understood his own motivations. Cameron and the others had used him as a pawn in their treacherous schemes. He had it within his power to fight back, and he was going to do it.

He had to!

Kinsolving heard a distant roar and looked up into the sky. A pinpoint of orange and blue appeared, grew larger, more distinct. The form of a ship all too familiar shone in the bright Paradise sun.

"What is it, Bart?" asked Lark, following his upward gaze.

"A ship landing. From the silhouette, it looks like a Lorr ship."

"They couldn't be after you. They don't know you're here. They can't! We lost them in the Zeta Orgo system."

Kinsolving wondered if Cameron had access to a message packet. Vandy had claimed that she held the reins of power on Paradise, but she had died. Cameron might have sent for the Lorr.

The aliens' presence made it all the more imperative for him to kill Cameron. He might not have another chance.

"Here," he said, thrusting the computer memory block at Lark. "Make sure that this is given to the Lorr. Tell them it's an analysis done by Suarez, that he tried to stop the plague. Lie."

"But, Barton . . ."

"I've seen firsthand that the aliens won't believe that any human is capable of formulating anything as diabolical—and successful—as the Stellar Death Plan. Try to convince them of the danger facing them, but don't strain their credulity." Kinsolving paused, stared deeply into Lark's fathomless eyes, bent and kissed her, then went hunting for Cameron and Denho.

He didn't care for trophies, but he wanted proof that they would never again menace any living being in the galaxy.

"Barton!" Lark Versalles called after him. Kinsolving

forced himself to keep running and not look back. His resolve might have faded if he caught sight of Lark.

He plunged into the forest and found it denser than it looked from the mansion. Kinsolving slowed, then stopped. He cocked his head to one side and listened intently. After several seconds, he heard movement to his left. He brought up the laserifle and waited.

A small robot shot through the limbs, rustling the leaves as it went. Kinsolving jerked on the laserifle trigger and set fire to both leaves and the robot. It spun in a circle and crashed, causing a new fire. Kinsolving did not try to put it out. He bent double and hurried deeper into the forest, seeking out the man who had sent the robot killer.

In spite of his care, Kinsolving crashed into Denho. The pair recoiled and backed off, facing each other. Kinsolving had the upper hand; the laserifle pointed squarely at Denho's bulky midriff.

"Who are you?" the Terra Recreations vice president demanded. "You're not some simpleton worker, are you?"

"I want Cameron."

"Cameron? Is that the son of a bitch I'm chasing?"

"He has the block circuit with the data on incubating the plague virus. He must not get it off-planet," Kinsolving said.

"You're the one." Denho frowned, his forehead wrinkling all the way to the top of his skull. "The home office had warned me about you. We circulated an alert after the Lorr gave us a photo. You used to work for IM?"

"I can't let anyone involved with the Plan have the memory block Cameron's carrying."

"But, man, they're trying to stifle us!" protested Denho. "The Bizzies cut off our trade, they restrict our exploration, they treat us as inferior beings!"

Kinsolving wondered which of those reasons bothered Denho enough that he would slaughter trillions. He guessed that it was pride, of being considered less than intelligent. Ego drove men like Denho.

"But you don't believe that," Denho went on. "You believe the space dust they teach in the universities on Earth. We'll never *win* the Bizzies' respect. But we can *take* it."

Tiredness, an unwillingness to kill wantonly, misdirection—Kinsolving did not know which betrayed him. Denho had lulled him. The bulky man had reached inside his jacket and had withdrawn a small silver cylinder. From its tip sprang another of the plasma trackers.

"Shoot and we'll both be killed," Denho warned. He began backing off. "It will release enough energy to fry everything within ten meters."

"If I don't, you'll get away."

"You want Cameron dead. I'll kill him for you."

"And release the plague on a thousand worlds!"

Denho's ugly laughter sparked Kinsolving's resolve. His finger lightly flicked the laserifle's trigger, discharging only a tiny amount of energy. The speck of plasma homed in on the ionization trail—but Kinsolving had kept moving. He smashed into a tree trunk, spun around and dived behind a fallen limb. The explosion seared his already wounded back, but he survived.

Kinsolving poked his head up and saw that Denho had taken cover in time to avoid the plasma tracker's detonation. This time he showed no mercy. He leveled the laser and fired.

Denho was outlined in actinic glow—but he did not die. Through the shimmering curtain of energy Kinsolving saw Denho working at controls inside his jacket. He wore a protective field that captured the full energy of the laser, stored it and dissipated the potent charge gradually.

Kinsolving fired again, then attacked, head low and laserifle swinging like a club. He put all his strength into the blow and landed the laserifle barrel on the side of Denho's knee. Kinsolving felt a yielding and heard a loud snapping sound. An instant later Denho screamed in agony and toppled to the ground.

He clutched his injured leg. This gave Kinsolving the chance he needed.

Again Kinsolving swung the heavy laserifle's barrel. It crushed the side of Denho's skull. Blood and torn flesh clung to the laser weapon's barrel. Kinsolving staggered back and leaned against a tree. He had killed before, but he could never make a living out of it. Each death diminished him, turned him inside out and made him sick to his stomach.

"Very well done, Supervisor Kinsolving," came Cameron's mocking voice. "You exceed my projections on

your ability every time. I must reconsider the programming
on your personality parameters. Underestimating an opponent is dangerous."

"Damn you, Cameron. Where are you?" Kinsolving
swung the laserifle around and centered it on the spot
where he thought Cameron's voice emanated. He fired.
The small *pop!* told of a relay robot's death—but not Cameron's.

"A pity you had to do that. I have only a few of that
model of remote left." A deriding laugh infuriated Kinsolving. Then he forced himself to be calm. Cameron
goaded him into mistakes. "Yes," Cameron went on, "you
have shown great resourcefulness. A pity you do not believe in the goals of the Plan."

Kinsolving began stalking, listening for movement in
the forest that might betray Cameron's position.

"You have given me great sport. For that, I must commend you. I had considered killing Jessarette myself. Such
a boorish person. But no, I told myself, enjoy the spectacle
of Jessarette and Kinsolving stalking each other."

"He killed Vandy Azmotega. You're as responsible for
her death as if you strangled her with your own hands."

"Do I detect more than simple anguish over the death of
a fellow human? Can it be love you feel for her?"

Kinsolving moved away from the sound of Cameron's
voice, then began to circle. He pushed through a curtain of
vines and saw the purple and gray of the man's jacket. The
laserifle blast had destroyed the last of Cameron's relay
robots. The man himself spoke, trying to dupe Kinsolving
into thinking it was still being relayed.

But Kinsolving hesitated. He could not see Cameron's
face clearly. This might be another ruse, a more elaborate
trap set by the cunning robot master.

"I enjoyed watching as you were moved about as if you
were one of my mechanical friends," Cameron said. "Jessarette, Denho, both were annoyances. You performed
well, supervisor. Now it is time for you to die."

The way the gaudy jacket moved showed a real human
inside. Kinsolving thrust his laserifle through the vines and
aimed, the sighting beam squarely on the middle of the
jacket.

Before his finger tightened and sent a beam of coherent

light death into Cameron's back, Kinsolving heard a rustling sound to his right. He chanced a quick look.

Standing in the brush, a gray-complected Lorr raised a peculiar looking pistol and aimed it at him. Kinsolving let out a yell, pulled the trigger of his own rifle and saw the sighting beam jerk off target. Cameron screamed at the nearness of the deadly beam—but he continued screaming in pain. Kinsolving had not killed him.

A powerful fist crashed into Kinsolving's body, sending him reeling. He landed and shook his head to clear it. No one had been close enough to strike him. He realized, through the haze of pain masking his body, that the Lorr had fired his weapon.

"Halt, human one," came the Lorr's command. "You are the fugitive Barton Kinsolving. I arrest you for—"

The alien's words were drowned out when Kinsolving swung his rifle around and fired. Dry leaves ignited. A curtain of flame shot upward. Kinsolving marvelled at his luck. He had been aiming at the Lorr, not the ground. This worked even better for his purposes. He had no desire to kill the alien, but he wasn't going to be arrested.

Not while Cameron still lived. Not while others of his kind worked for the Stellar Death Plan.

Using the barrier of flames and the resulting black smoke as a shield, Kinsolving rolled to his hands and knees and painfully got to his feet. Not a muscle in his body failed to protest. His back had been burned. His bones hurt from the impact of the Lorr force weapon. But determination carried him onward.

He had almost killed Cameron. Almost. The next time would be his triumph!

Kinsolving stumbled through the vines and into the small clearing where Cameron had been. Kinsolving found tracks in soft dirt leading to the left. Bits of charred cloth marked the path better than the footprints. Behind him he heard the Lorr calling out in his own language, possibly summoning others.

Kinsolving cursed the Lorr police and their efficiency. They had not wasted an instant at the shuttle port. He only hoped that Lark had been successful in convincing someone of importance in the Lorr force that the viral plague posed immense danger to their worlds.

His finger tightened on the trigger when he saw a pair of small robots wiggling along the ground. He vaporized both of them.

"You're running out of machines to protect you, Cameron," he shouted. "I'm going to kill you. You'll never be able to spread that virus on other worlds. The secret will die with you."

Kinsolving lasered through a low shrub and stumbled into the bramble beyond. He ignored the stinging cuts he sustained on his lower legs. Cameron stood stock-still and the aiming beam pointed directly at his chest.

"You've ruined my jacket," the assassin said in an aggrieved voice. "I had it imported from Earth. It was very expensive. All natural fabrics and superbly tailored."

Kinsolving pulled the trigger. The laserifle hummed but the coherent bolt from its muzzle did not slay Cameron. The charge had drained through Kinsolving's repeated usage. The heat from the beam charred the front of the jacket and caused Cameron more pain—but it did not kill.

Kinsolving went berserk. He charged, swinging his laser like a club. Even with the adrenaline-powered attack, he was no match for Cameron. The trained killer stood silently, waiting, judging, then acting with blinding speed.

He batted away the laserifle barrel, stepped inside the circle of Kinsolving's arm and easily tossed him to the ground. Kinsolving landed with enough force to knock the wind from his lungs.

"So impetuous. You ought to know my training extends to fields other than robotics." Cameron reached down and grabbed Kinsolving's collar to pull him up.

"You will cease your conflict," came the curt command. A dozen Lorr, all with leveled weapons, moved to enforce that order.

A flash of disdain crossed Cameron's face. He said, "You lose, no matter what happens, Supervisor. I would have killed you. The Bizzies will lock you away on their prison world for the rest of your miserable life."

"Arrest him," shouted Kinsolving. "He's got the data on the plague that killed all the aliens on this world. It's in the computer block in his pocket."

"Wait," Cameron protested, hands raised. "He is a dangerous criminal. He killed one of your race."

"He is Barton Kinsolving, wanted for murder," agreed a Lorr policeman. "But we will also question you."

Cameron shot Kinsolving a look as hot as any laser beam. But Kinsolving felt no triumph. He had stopped Cameron and the data concerning the plague from returning to Gamma Tertius 4, but he had sacrificed himself in the process.

In winning, he had lost.

CHAPTER NINETEEN

BARTON KINSOLVING went cold inside when he saw the expression on Cameron's face. The sly grin made him wonder what vital point he had overlooked.

"In his pocket," Kinsolving said desperately. "A computer memory. It's got the data on the plague."

"You are a fugitive." The Lorr policeman stood impassively, his expression too alien for easy interpretation. Kinsolving saw, though, that he wasn't swaying the tall, limber-jointed alien.

"He's the murderer!" shouted Kinsolving. "He's responsible for the aliens dying on Paradise."

"Demented," Cameron said easily. "He ambushed me when I inspected property my company is considering for purchase."

"You can't let him go!"

"Both human ones," ordered the Lorr leader. The alien turned ninety degrees, his universal-jointed knee allowing the startling movement. He picked up his other foot, let his torso swivel to his intended direction of travel and stalked off.

Kinsolving and Cameron were both prodded along, but Cameron still showed no sign of uneasiness.

"They'll read the circuit and know," said Kinsolving. "You won't walk away, Cameron. They've got you."

"I won't be held. There is no formal charge lodged against me. Not on Paradise, not on any Bizarre world. You, though, are a desperate criminal fleeing your punishment. I did well informing the Lorr of your presence here."

"How did you know? Jessarette?"

"He showed me the photo taken aboard Almost Paradise. A clumsy man, Davi Jessarette," said Cameron. "A pity you had to kill him, too."

"You made sure I would. You said so!" Kinsolving tried to hold his anger in check. He knew Cameron was only goading him for the benefit of the Lorr. Kinsolving wondered which of the guards surrounding him carried a recorder taking down every word uttered. It could be any of them—or all.

He tried to determine logically what his best action might be. Cameron had found out about his presence on Paradise through Jessarette. He had alerted the Lorr. Had he done so anonymously? If he had put his name and legal likeness to the message summoning them, Kinsolving had no chance. The Lorr would think Cameron a fool for turning in one of his own kind, but publicly they would thank him.

And they would set the real killer free.

But Kinsolving doubted Cameron had signed the message personally. If any signature had been attached, it would be Jessarette's in his capacity as security officer for TR. The Lorr would be more prone to act on official notification.

"There, human things," said the Lorr officer. He shoved them into the flatbed of a cargo loader similar to the one Kinsolving had used earlier. "You will make no attempt to escape from my authority. Such crime will be instantly punished."

Kinsolving saw that the other Lorr watched attentively. He wondered what the price for failure would be if they let him escape again. Considering the size of the hunt they had already staged to find him, he thought it would be severe.

"I'll be glad to return to Gamma Tertius 4," said Cameron, lounging back. He favored his injured side where Kinsolving's laserifle bolt had burned him. Kinsolving had to sit upright, not even allowing his back to rest against the side of the bouncing loader. The pain that he had ignored for so long now welled up and threatened to overwhelm his senses. He had run too far, too fast, and been injured too many times.

All he wanted was to rest. But he dared not do that until he was sure that Cameron could not get the information back to Hamilton Fremont or any of the others on GT4.

"What do you get out of this?" Kinsolving asked. "A directorship?"

"Possibly," Cameron said, making a negligent gesture with his hand. "Such is of minor importance, compared to serving the Plan." He grinned. "There is so much activity concerning the Plan that one can overlook another important point. I am actually quite good at business matters. Intersellar Materials would profit from having me helping guide the entire corporation. After all, without the money-making capacity of the largest companies, the Plan would fall apart for lack of funding."

"Who is involved?" asked Kinsolving, intrigued in spite of himself. "I know IM's part. And Terra Recreations financed Suarez. What other companies?"

Cameron studied him, pale, cold eyes boring into Kinsolving's soul. "I rather think that is privileged information. I find it inconceivable that you will again escape the Lorr prison world. How you did that the first time I can only guess, but a finite risk exists that you might repeat this feat. It would be foolish of me to divulge more of the Plan to you."

"It's also crueler to let me imagine who is involved and what can happen."

"You have a good mind, Kinsolving. A pity you chose to betray your own kind in favor of . . . them."

Kinsolving smiled wickedly. "I'm not with them. Not in the way you think. I'm just trying to stay alive and do what's right. And you've made my life much easier."

"Oh?" Cameron raised a sandy eyebrow. "How have I done this?"

"The Lorr are cleverer at electronic spying than you are. Do you believe they'd stick us back here and not have surveillance? Everything you said about the Death Plan has been overheard. They know your part—and IM's."

"And," said Cameron, smiling in a way that chilled Kinsolving's enthusiasm, "you believe I have confessed and that you are going to be absolved of all crimes?"

The robotics genius shifted his weight slightly to one side and lifted his arm. A needle-thin one-centimeter-long robot clung to the fabric. Kinsolving saw a single red indicator light blinking on the machine like a baleful eye.

"What is it?"

"No," Cameron said, anticipating the man's question. "It isn't a jamming device. Rather, it is more sophisticated —and more subtle. The Lorr hear us speaking. The words, however, are supplied by my device. They might listen to their recording and, if they do, they will discover an innocuous little talk between us. I believe I programmed this one to substitute bantering dialog about sports. The Lorr would find it intensely boring, I am sure."

"Our voices wouldn't match. Voice ident would—"

"I'm sorry to crush your hopes. Voice identification *would* match. The robot records your words and then places them into my programmed patterns. A human expert could detect the differences. If they bothered to match our lips with our words, even the Lorr would see the difference."

"But they won't," Kinsolving said bitterly. The aliens did not expect confessions; they know who was guilty. Their courts had already decided. They would monitor only for disturbance or attempted escape.

"No," Cameron said softly, "they won't."

The cargo loader came to a smooth halt. The Lorr motioned for Kinsolving and Cameron to exit. Kinsolving frowned when he saw the building at the edge of the shuttle port. Paradise had no prison. Few criminals came here to ply their trade and with the constant surveillance, even the highest echelons of thieves would find the pickings difficult and sparse. But if Paradise had no formal prison, this building came close to providing an informal one. No windows had been cut into the thick plastic walls. Inside, Kinsolving saw little to give him hope. The original purpose for the small cubicles had long since been obscured by the addition of heavy mechanical locking bolts on the doors.

Kinsolving's only pleasure was fleeting. Cameron's face showed sudden concern. Anything electronic he could circumvent. Purely mechanical locks would pose a larger problem for him. But Kinsolving saw Cameron relax. The assassin had little reason to believe the Lorr would hold him.

"By the way," Cameron said as a Lorr guard shoved Kinsolving down the long, featureless corridor, "he murdered a Terra Recreations vice president, too. I'm sure you will find physical evidence near where you arrested him."

"Silence, human one," snapped the Lorr officer. "All materials have been impounded. We care nothing for violation of your local laws. However, in the spirit of cooperation and friendship between our cultures, this evidence will be given to human security personnel when we no longer require it."

"Just trying to help," said Cameron.

"The computer memory!" shouted Kinsolving as the Lorr guard shoved him into a tiny room. "Get it from Cameron. Read it!"

Kinsolving threw out his hands to keep himself from smashing facefirst into the wall. He winced in pain and turned. The room had been stripped of all furniture. The high ceiling contained a glow panel to provide light but Kinsolving couldn't jump high enough to touch it. The door closed firmly, and its heavy locking bars slid into place. The walls muffled the impact as he pounded on them. Even his laserifle might take several blasts to cut through plastic this thick. The impact laser might stand a better chance. But he didn't have it, either.

He had nothing but time. Kinsolving sank down to the floor and drew up his knees to his chest, arms circling his legs. He rested his head on his knees and tried to think.

Escape did not appear possible, but he could not resign himself to returning to the prison world. Better to die than be exiled to that brutal world for the remainder of his life. Dying presented moral problems, though, that had nothing to do with suicide.

If he died who would oppose the Stellar Death Plan? His death would be easy; untold worlds filled with living, breathing, thinking beings would also die. Kinsolving found this so repugnant that he knew he could not simply give up. He would continue fighting until the Plan was only a bad memory.

He looked up when the bolts securing the door pulled back. The Lorr officer and two others entered. In the corridor he saw three more aliens. He had no chance to overpower them and run.

"You, Barton Kinsolving. You will answer questions. How did you escape our prison world?"

"What about Cameron? Did you read out the computer memory block he had? It details how the plague virus was engineered. He intends to release the plague on thousands of your worlds."

"Mrs. Cameron has been cleared of charges in aiding

and abetting you. Evidence shows that he was another of your victims."

"He planned it all. He had Jessarette try to kill me. He set Denho against me."

"Mr. Cameron will be released."

"The computer block!" Kinsolving shouted. "At least study it. You've got nothing to lose and everything to gain."

Kinsolving dared to hope when he saw the expression on the Lorr's face. He had dealt with them often enough on Deepdig to know something of their thought processes. He had touched on a point the alien understood.

"The matter will be pursued further," the Lorr said. "How did you escape our prison world?"

"I did not kill your agent-captain on Deepdig," Kinsolving said, ignoring the Lorr's pointed question. "Cameron did. Check it. He was on-planet at the same time. He had been sent for that purpose by our superiors on Gamma Tertius 4."

"This is a matter beyond my jurisdiction. The court has decided your guilt. How did you escape the prison world?"

"You wouldn't commute the sentence if I told you?"

"Commute?" The officer turned and exchanged quick words in his own language with another Lorr. "I do not understand this word. How can a prison term be transported?"

"Never mind," said Kinsolving. The Lorr did not have the concept of leniency in their culture. He doubted that, even if they had, it would apply to a "human one."

The officer spoke rapidly with the others in the cell, then said to Kinsolving, "You will be taken away immediately upon clearance from this world. There is some difficulty in obtaining proper authorization due to your savagery."

"What?"

"It is believed that you had a part in the deaths of the planetary supervisor and the official in charge of this world. Further, evidence shows your involvement with the death of the security officer assigned by Terra Recreations to this world. Your crime wave has made our job more difficult."

"I . . ." Kinsolving bit off the words. He *had* killed Jessarette and Denho. Why deny killing Vandy and Suarez?

Two deaths, more or less, meant nothing to the Lorr. They had their fugitive and were content.

Spinning on their curiously jointed knees, they left the cubicle. The locking bars dropped back into place, turning this plastic room into a cell as secure as their prison world.

Kinsolving dropped his head once more to his knees, trying to think of some way out. If they searched Cameron, part of the Plan might be thwarted. And Fremont and Villalobos and the others on GT4 would not be pleased if Cameron lost the blueprint for manufacturing the bioweapon. This might place a strain on the cooperation between IM and TR. Anything that slowed the work of the Stellar Death Plan had to be good.

None of this helped Kinsolving. He dared not rely on Lark Versalles. She might not even know where the Lorr had taken him. Still, his thoughts kept turning to her. The *von Neumann* still hung in orbit. With luck, it had been repaired and was ready for departure.

Kinsolving caught his breath and held it. If the technicians had searched the cargo hold and found Rani duLong's body, it would only add to the charges against him. He hoped that Lark would have the sense to blame it all on him. An additional murder charge meant nothing to him.

The starship would be ready for flight. Kinsolving worked backward. Getting to Almost Paradise meant stowing away on the shuttle. Or perhaps not. Since Vandy's death, Paradise had to be in confusion. The Lorr had the evidence against him for killing Denho and Jessarette. The alien police officer might not have turned it over to what remained of the planetary security force.

So. He could shift away from this system if he got to the space station. He could get to Almost Paradise on the shuttle.

All Barton Kinsolving needed was a way to escape his cell.

"What would Cameron do?" he asked himself. "He's the master at this. Call down a robot and have it blast through the door?" Kinsolving shook his head at this fantasy. Even Cameron had seemed upset at the idea of being locked in a cubicle.

Something about Cameron chewed at the edges of Kinsolving's mind. Cameron had meticulously planned everything that had happened on Paradise. All the murders had been laid on Kinsolving's shoulders. The robot master knew Kinsolving would be returned to the Lorr prison world for the rest of his life.

"He wouldn't let a mere Bizzie take care of that," Kinsolving said aloud. "Cameron thinks they are incompetent. He holds them in deep contempt."

Even more telling was Cameron's ego. He would want the pleasure of killing Kinsolving himself for all the trouble he had been caused. Kinsolving had destroyed his part of the Plan on Zeta Orgo—and had injured him.

"Cameron wants me dead—and he would do it himself." Kinsolving tried different possibilities and always returned to this simple statement of Cameron's intentions.

"But how? A robot?" He looked around and saw no way for a robot to burrow in easily. And Cameron could not have known where the Lorr established their temporary headquarters. They had landed while he and Denho were fighting in the mansion and the woods beyond.

"He doesn't dare risk missing me when the Lorr load me into their ship. His robots are vulnerable to alien detection." Kinsolving remembered how the arachnoid policeman on Zeta Orgo 4 had easily destroyed Cameron's aerial assassins. Cameron never made the same mistake twice.

"He wants me dead. But how?"

Kinsolving mentally ran through every moment since confronting Cameron in the forest. He had tried to fire the laserifle; it had been almost drained; he had changed; Cameron easily threw him to the ground; Cameron lifted him by the collar and grinned. In triumph over—what?

Kinsolving reached back and ran his fingers along his collar. A tiny bead, cool and hard and small, sent a tingle all the way up his arm. Kinsolving skinned out of his tattered shirt and stared at the small device.

"Definitely Cameron's manufacture," he said softly. The device had no motile capability; he found no laser muzzle. "A bomb. What else can it be? Cameron has no need to spy on me. He wants me dead!"

Kinsolving bent closer and stared at the grain-of-rice-sized device. It could not hold much explosive, but at the back of his neck, it needed little to kill.

The tiny bomb shivered slightly. If Kinsolving had not been looking at it intently he would never have noticed.

He spun around and shoved the bomb and his shirt against the outer wall. He had been right. Cameron had sent the arming signal.

The bomb exploded with enough force to blow him backward across the cubicle.

But Kinsolving shouted in triumph. The bomb had blown a small hole through the thick outer wall of the cubicle. And the plastic had begun to burn with an ever-increasing ferocity. In seconds, a hole large enough for him to get through had been burned.

Barton Kinsolving held up the pieces of his shirt to shield his face from the heat, ran forward, tumbled through the wall and onto the tarmac. He had escaped!

CHAPTER TWENTY

BARTON KINSOLVING put his hands under his arms in an attempt to keep the oxygen off the burns. He looked over his shoulder and saw the ever-widening hole being burned in the plastic building wall. Whatever explosive Cameron had put into the small bomb had an incendiary effect not easily quenched.

Kinsolving ran on, almost stumbling, wanting to get out of sight. The Lorr would find out about his escape too soon. His muddled brain worked over the plan he had formulated.

"The shuttle," he muttered. "Up to the space station. To the yacht. Then shift to wherever the navigation computer locks onto first."

Weakness came over him in a debilitating wave. He stumbled and fell, rolled and came to his knees. Kinsolving looked up with bleary eyes and saw only a solid body. His eyes rose. For an instant he did not recognize her.

"The cosmetic dyes. You've reactivated them," he said to Lark.

"Barton!"

He fell forward, his pain too great to bear any longer.

When he awoke, he heard heavy equipment in the distance. One eye popped open and he cautiously studied his surroundings. Kinsolving feared that the Lorr had again captured him. But this did not seem a likely place to hold a dangerous escapee.

"Lark?"

"Here, Bart, darling," she said. The blonde slipped down beside the pneumatic-cushioned bed. She took his hand and held it gently. "I brought you back to the place Sheeda and I had stayed."

"The noises?"

Lark smiled wanly. "The robots have started renovating it for the next guests."

Kinsolving stretched. Little pain tore at his senses. Lark answered his unspoken question. "The automedic worked on you again. I had to destroy it because it wanted to put you into a life-coma. It said your wounds were very dangerous."

"I got away from Lorr," he said. "But I don't know whether I convinced them that Cameron had the computer memory block."

"I . . . Barton," she said almost contritely, "I didn't tell the Lorr about the plague."

"Why not?" Kinsolving knew he should be shocked or surprised or show some emotion. All that had drained from him. He floated softly, warm and content and beyond reaction.

"I didn't know how to do it. I had so much else to do. Sheeda." Lark swallowed hard. "Her remains are on the way back to Onar."

"I'm sorry," he said, meaning it.

"What would I say to the Lorr? Here, I happened to find a way of killing off your entire race?"

"Tell the Lorr that you stole it from Cameron." Kinsolving lay back, trying to drift off into unconsciousness and failing. "I've got to lift off-planet soon. We have to shift away from Paradise. There's nothing more for us to do here."

"Us, Bart?"

He turned and peered at her. Kinsolving knew how selfish it was of him to involve Lark. Her entire world revolved around parties, flitting from planet to planet and experiencing the life that the superrich enjoyed. Paradise was her sort of world. For him it carried more than a hint of decadence.

"I want to get Rani's body back to her brother. That's bothered me more and more. He deserves to know what happened to her."

Kinsolving closed his eyes and experienced a flash of guilt. How he misjudged her. Outwardly Lark was nothing more than a hedonistic rich kid. Now and again he saw traces of a real person beneath the surface.

"Get me up to Almost Paradise and I can get away. You can return to Earth with Rani's body. I don't think they've found it in the cargo hold. We would have been detained a long time ago if they had."

"I'll give the block circuit to the Lorr," she said, "but I can't promise any more." She dropped down, lying partially on him, and buried her face in his shoulder. He felt her shaking, and hot, wet tears soaked into his shirt. "I'm sorry, Barton. None of this is the way I want it. I get so confused. Why did Sheeda have to die? And Rani? And all the others?"

He said nothing. If it had not been for the Plan and trained killers such as Cameron and Jessarette, Lark's friends would still be alive.

Lark pushed away suddenly, tears making odd markings on her cheeks above the ever-changing flow of cosmetic dyes. The somber colors of the dyes told him that she was depressed.

"I'll do it now. You try to get aboard the same shuttle. We can create a diversion and the Lorr won't notice."

Kinsolving did not press the point. Such a scheme sounded too implausible to work, yet he had escaped from even worse situations. He heaved himself to a sitting position, let the dizziness pass, then stood. On legs that wobbled only slightly, he ordered fresh clothing from a robot servant, dressed, then he followed Lark from the room. The cab they took to the shuttle port was almost a relief. He had walked too much, with too many injuries, on Paradise.

"The Lorr," he said, pointing their guard positions out to Lark.

"Get down. When I go to them, slip into the departure room. There won't be much chance for you to get into the shuttle, so move fast."

He nodded. Lark stared at him, her eyes so blue that he felt a lump form in his throat. She bent and kissed him lightly, pressed one of her credit identicards into his hand, then jumped from the cab.

He started to call her back, to tell her to go directly to the departure areas and forget this, but it was too late. She walked briskly to the nearest Lorr and began talking animatedly with the alien.

Kinsolving slid from the cab and, bent low, hurried into

the departure lobby. The Lorr guarded the outside only; none were inside.

Still, Kinsolving dived for cover when he saw Cameron talking with a tall, well-built man in a dark blue business suit. From under the chair, Kinsolving peered up at the pair. He almost shouted when he saw Cameron reach into his pocket and pull out the computer block circuit and hand it to the man. It vanished into an inner pocket with the speed of light.

The pair went on talking, only a few words drifting to Kinsolving.

". . . go somewhere else before returning to GT4," Cameron said.

The other man nodded.

Both turned and faced the door when three Lorr entered. Kinsolving recognized the alien in the lead as the officer in charge.

"You, human one," the Lorr said, pointing at Cameron. "You will accompany us. There are serious charges filed against you."

"What charges can there be, sir?" asked Cameron. "This is a human-controlled resort, not a Lorr world. What crimes against the Lorr can I possibly commit?"

"We have examined the primitive computer memory circuits. The bioweapon released on this world that killed several of our citizens is detailed. You will endure questioning."

"Endure, yes," Cameron said, sighing. "I have no computer memory block and am quite innocent of these charges. I can prove it."

"There is a witness. She, too, is being detained."

Kinsolving heard this and stifled a curse. He had worried that Lark would be held as a witness, but there seemed to be no other way to stop Cameron other than direct confrontation.

And the Lorr ignored the man who had received the computer memory block from Cameron. They escorted Cameron away. The assassin never looked back or gave any hint that he had ever seen the courier before.

"Board for Almost Paradise," came the announcement.

Kinsolving scuttled from under the chair and ran to the

memory circuit. And there would be time for him to determine whether Ala Markken had betrayed him intentionally.

Barton Kinsolving went to find an acceleration couch. This journey might prove a long one.

MORE SCIENCE FICTION TITLES
AVAILABLE FROM
NEW ENGLISH LIBRARY PAPERBACKS

ROBERT E. VARDEMAN

☐	39001 2	The Keys to Paradise	£4.99
☐	41351 9	The Jade Demons Quartet	£4.95
☐	42854 0	Weapons of Chaos	£4.50

R. VARDEMAN & V. MILAN

☐	05661 9	The War of Powers 1	£4.99
☐	05788 7	The War of Powers 2: Istu Awakened	£3.99

BRIAN STABLEFORD

☐	50103 5	Invaders from the Centre	£2.99
☐	50612 6	Journey to the Centre	£2.99
☐	51107 3	The Centre Cannot Hold	£3.99